D1246707

LOOKING FOR JANE

LOOKING
FOR
JANE

HEATHER
MARSHALL

ATRIA BOOKS

New York London Toronto Sydney New Delhi

An Imprint of Simon & Schuster, Inc.
1230 Avenue of the Americas
New York, NY 10020

First Atria Books hardcover edition February 2023

ATRIA B O O K S and colophon are trademarks of Simon & Schuster, Inc.

For information about special discounts for bulk purchases, please contact Simon & Schuster Special Sales at 1-866-506-1949 or business@simonandschuster.com.

The Simon & Schuster Speakers Bureau can bring authors to your live event. For more information or to book an event, contact the Simon & Schuster Speakers Bureau at 1-866-248-3049 or visit our website at www.simonspeakers.com.

Manufactured in the United States of America

1   3   5   7   9   10   8   6   4   2

Library of Congress Cataloging-in-Publication Data
Names: Marshall, Heather (Heather J.), author.
Title: Looking for Jane / Heather Marshall.
Description: First Atria Books hardcover edition. | New York : Atria Books, 2023.
Identifiers: LCCN 2022040615 (print) | LCCN 2022040616 (ebook) |
ISBN 9781668013687 (hardcover) | ISBN 9781668015322 (trade paperback) |
ISBN 9781668013694 (ebook)
Subjects: LCGFT: Novels.
Classification: LCC PR9199.4.M3548 L66 2023 (print) | LCC PR9199.4.M3548
(ebook) | DDC 813/.6—dc23/eng/20220912
LC record available at https://lccn.loc.gov/2022040615
LC ebook record available at https://lccn.loc.gov/2022040616

ISBN 978-1-6680-1368-7
ISBN 978-1-6680-1369-4 (ebook)

For R
A most wanted child to a most willing mother.

LOOKING FOR
JANE

2010

· · · · · · · · · ·

I t was a perfectly ordinary day when a truly extraordinary letter was
delivered to the wrong mailbox.

The boxes were identical, positioned side by side and made of the
same thin, cheap metal, now slightly rusted near the hinges. They were
drilled into the brown brick wall beside the door to the antiques shop;
the door whose bells jingled delightfully—or irritatingly, depending on
whom you asked—every time a patron entered or exited.

The mailbox for Thompson's Antiques & Used Books was on the left
and displayed the number one in a peeling gold sticker. The mailbox for
the apartment above the shop was on the right with a matching label
that bore the number two. There was hardly any difference, really, and
yet it made a great deal of difference to Nancy Mitchell, who lived in the
apartment upstairs and didn't know about the letter she hadn't received.

The address line didn't specify which unit number the letter was destined for at the old building on College Street, and so the envelope was
dropped unceremoniously into the box for the antiques shop while the
mail carrier continued on his hurried route without a second thought.

The letter held its breath for three hours—squashed between a postcard from the store manager's son, who was currently traveling in France, and that Friday's junk mail—until the proprietor brought it inside on the way in from a cigarette break. She tossed the entire pile of mail into the in-tray, where it would later be sorted—and so critically misplaced—by a careless employee.

Its contents wouldn't be discovered for another seven years. And that letter would change three women's lives forever.

PART I

CHAPTER 1

Angela

. . . .

TORONTO | JANUARY 2017

Angela Creighton is late for work.

She was up late the night before, and this morning she wakes with a poorly timed migraine. Careful not to disturb her wife's Sunday morning lie-in, she tiptoes to the kitchen, where she washes down a painkiller with a glass of pulpy orange juice, toasts a bagel, and slathers it with too much garlic cream cheese. Clamping her breakfast between her teeth like a retriever, she tugs on a hat and cinches the waist tie on her plaid coat, then quietly closes the apartment door and hurries down the stairs of the walk-up.

Out on the sidewalk, Angela rushes to the bus stop as she munches the bagel while fishing her sunglasses out of her purse. Normally she would enjoy it, since sunny days in the winter are few and far between. But the light is making her wince and her head is throbbing like a bullet wound behind her eyes.

She was over at her friend Jenn's last night for their monthly book club, which had, as so many book clubs are wont to do, descended into a wine club over the past six months. Now they drink too much cheap pinot grigio, inhale charcuterie and cheese with a desperation that suggests it might be their last meal on death row, and sometimes talk about books they've read.

Angela hadn't taken part in any wine-drinking pursuits for the past several months, but she let herself go last night. It was the sole, pathetic shred of silver lining from the miscarriage, and she capitalized on it in spectacular form. She and Tina will be setting out on another round of fertility treatments once her body heals enough to try again, so she figured she may as well enjoy the booze in the meantime. It's her second miscarriage in a year, and the stakes are starting to feel higher every time an insemination treatment or a pregnancy fails. A steady flow of alcohol helps the hurdles appear a little lower, if only for a short while.

The bus trundles up to the curb and Angela boards, drops a token into the metal slot, and finds an empty seat near the rear door. The shop she manages—Thompson's Antiques & Used Books—is less than ten blocks west, and she stumbles off the bus onto the slushy curb a few stops later.

The entrance to the shop is just inches from the edge of the sidewalk on bustling College Street, and Angela presses herself against the door to stay out of the way of the passing pedestrians as she fumbles with her keys. Throwing her hip a little against the old warped wood, she bursts her way inside and shuts the door behind her.

Angela likes it in here. It's a peculiar hybrid of a shop, home to plenty of used books that cycle through its doors on a regular basis, and a motley collection of antiques that never seem to sell. It smells like furniture polish, coffee, and that dusty scent of old books that's both rotten and enormously appealing. It isn't a big space, only the size of a modest apartment. There's a small storeroom behind the cash desk that houses several dusty, neglected boxes and a cheap drip coffeemaker Angela brought in during her first week on the job.

She feels her mood lift a fraction at the now-familiar smell of the place. She's always been a book lover, and she and Tina share an eclectic taste in decor, so the whimsy of the antiques shop suits her just fine. There's always a bit of buried treasure to be discovered in here.

Angela flicks the light switches, walks to the old writing desk they use as a sales counter, and slides her purse underneath with her foot. She turns on the computer till—by far the most advanced piece of technology in the shop—then retreats to the storeroom to put on a pot of mercilessly potent dark roast. When she was pregnant, all she drank was decaf, determined that the placebo effect of coffee could still be achieved by brewing it at double strength. But today, with a sharp jab of bitterness to her heart, she puts on a large pot of regular brew.

Chipped mug of coffee in hand, Angela mentally shakes herself and sets about the usual tasks of sorting new inventory and following up on order holds. For the life of her, she can't imagine why the store has stayed in business this long, especially with real estate prices being what they are in this city. The small apartment over the shop has been rented out as additional unnecessary income since the property was first purchased by Angela's aunt Jo (who married Old Money and really has no need for employment). Although she could easily sell the place for a fortune in a matter of days, Angela suspects her aunt has kept the shop running simply for something to talk to her immaculately groomed friends about during their weekly manicures.

Prior to starting at Thompson's, Angela had hopped around in retail, most recently working for an uptight manager at an overpriced shoe store. Although she couldn't prove it, Angela suspects she was "laid off for the season due to a decrease in sales" when her boss found out about the pregnancy several weeks too early. He was a fifty-something conservative and borderline homophobe, almost certainly of the school who believed maternity leave was nothing but a corporate inconvenience. Angela had confided the news of her pregnancy to a coworker after she ran out of excuses for her frequent trips to the staff washroom to throw up, and she's sure the coworker blabbed.

So when she found herself out of work, smack in the middle of her thirties after undergoing budget-draining fertility treatments, she plumbed all her networks looking for a new job—*any* job—that would allow her and Tina to pay their rent and still build a nest egg for their new addition. At their last family Thanksgiving, Aunt Jo, with a wave of her magnificently bejeweled hand, offered Angela a managerial role at the shop so that she herself could "finally start phasing into retirement." Though her experience with antiques was negligible at best, Angela was in no position to decline, and she knew Aunt Jo wouldn't ever fire her own niece for becoming pregnant. Jo handed her the keys three days later.

On Sundays, Angela's the sole staff member, but it's usually a sleepy day anyway, particularly in the fall and winter months when tourism slows to a glacial crawl. After the new inventory is sorted, she moves on to the task of processing the unclaimed holds. This is one of the most frustrating chores on Angela's list. Eight times out of ten, the furniture is reserved by an eager out-of-town "antique hunter" (usually self-proclaimed and newly minted) who journeyed into the city with rich friends on a shopping excursion. They shiver with glee at a prospective purchase, then demand a hold be placed so they can come back with a truck of appropriate size with which to haul away the object of that Saturday's treasure hunt. And almost every time, the shopper then dodges Angela's phone calls long enough that she releases the hold, and the would-be buyer is spared the shame of admitting the sale was a passing fancy. This process means that Angela spends a good portion of her Sunday mornings tearing pink hold stickers off the items and leaving them in their cozy corners of the shop, where they can await the next near-purchase tease, like aging orphans.

First on the list is a small three-drawer dresser. Angela knows exactly which one it is, and wanders to the very back of the shop. Approaching it, she notices the bright pink slip of paper that indicates a hold stick-tacked to the front of the top drawer. She yanks the slip of paper off, causing the dresser to lurch and the drawer to slide out a notch.

"Ah shit. Ouch!"

Coffee splashes over her hand. She licks it off, then peers through the crack, glimpsing a curious spot of white inside the darkness of the drawer. She casts her eyes around for a safe place to set her mug. She uses the pink hold slip in lieu of a coaster and places her coffee on a nearby bookshelf, then pulls open the drawer.

Just then, the bells above the door jingle, welcoming the first customer of the day. With a knot of intrigue in her stomach, Angela shuts the drawer and navigates her way back to the front, carefully stepping over and around piles of haphazardly stacked books.

"Hello!" she calls.

"Hi, there," says a teenage girl with mousy brown hair and hunched shoulders.

"Is there anything I can help you with?" Angela asks, pulling her scarf closer around her shoulders. A wintry draft has swept in with the girl, which irritates Angela, somewhat unfairly, she knows. She wants to get back to the drawer.

"Not really. I'm just browsing, but thanks."

"Certainly," Angela replies. "Let me know if you need anything."

The girl smiles vaguely and turns to inspect the nearest bookshelf. It's the politest possible snub, but Angela takes it as a welcome dismissal. She returns to the dresser and opens the top drawer again.

Reaching in, she removes a heavy marble box and places it gently on the weathered floorboards. It was the white stone that caught her attention. Nearly all the antiques in the shop are made of some variety of wood. The rest is mostly brass and silver: tarnished picture frames with intricate Victorian scrolling, hand mirrors that call to mind Regency-era puffy hairstyles capped with lace bonnets, and collectible teaspoons with faded crests and intricate familial coats of arms.

Angela hasn't seen anything made of marble since she began working at Thompson's, and this is a beautiful ivory stone shot with sparkling gray ripples that some antique hunter may actually want to buy. Abandoning her lukewarm coffee, Angela carries the box to the front desk. She glances up to check the browsing status of her single patron, then perches on the bar-height stool and flips open the gold clasp of the box.

Inside is a stack of what appears to just be yellowed paper, but as she removes one of the pages, she notices the elegant cursive handwriting on the front of the top envelope.

Letters. A stack of them. Angela lifts them out one by one, counting—five letters. All old, by the look of them. *Not surprising*, she thinks, given that this is an antiques shop. That, and the fact that no one really sends letters much anymore. That aging, once-bustling pursuit is now undertaken solely by stubborn, overperfumed elderly ladies.

She holds one of the letters up to the light flooding in from the storefront windows. Unlike its fellows, which are naked of their former envelopes and appear to be mostly bank statements, this one is still sealed, the edge along the flap slightly bubbled, as though the glue had been wet with too much moisture. The stamp looks modern. The slanting cursive writing in the top left-hand corner of the envelope lists the return addressee as one Mrs. Frances Mitchell. It's addressed to Ms. Nancy Mitchell, and something stirs behind Angela's navel as she reads the address of the antiques shop.

The writing looks shaky, though Angela can tell it had, in decades long past, been beautiful, graceful penmanship.

BANG!

Her heart shoots into her throat. She looks over to see the mousy-haired girl muttering an apology as she bends to scoop up a large book. Angela manages a small smile, her pulse still pounding, but the girl waves goodbye with a mumbled, "Thank you," and the bells above the door jingle as she exits the shop, ushering in another gust of cold air.

Relieved to be alone again, Angela runs her fingers over the edge of the envelope seal, weighing her intrigue. The date stamped in red ink across the top of the envelope says the letter was posted in 2010. And yet it remained unopened. Who had it been intended for? Did the letter simply go astray from its destination? But no, the shop's address is indeed scrawled across the front, along with the mysterious name of Nancy Mitchell.

It was destined for *this* address.

Angela knows it's technically a crime to open another person's mail, but her curiosity has bested her moral code. She plucks the brass letter opener from the heavily ink-speckled Mason jar they use as a pen cup, slides the tip underneath the corner of the envelope flap, and, with a satisfying tear, slits it open. She pulls the letter out and unfolds it with the tips of her fingernails, as though avoiding the traces of incriminating fingerprints. The paper is heavy and lightly textured. Expensive. Purchased by someone who wrote a lot of letters and took the time to make sure they carried weight.

Intrigued, Angela begins to read, eyes darting back and forth across the page underneath her dark bangs:

Dear Nancy,

It is my intent that this letter reaches you after I am gone. I instructed my lawyer Mr. Klein to post this upon my passing. I am sorry for this, and I have my reasons, but I wanted to ensure you were made aware of certain facts pertaining to your own history.

Nancy, I have loved you as much as a mother can love her daughter. I have done the best I know how, been the best mother I could. Although, my dear, I am human, and therefore imperfect.

There is no way to tell you this other than to simply write the words: your father and I are not your biological parents. We adopted you as a baby.

We tried for years, prayed hard and daily for God to send us a child, but it was not to be. And so we sought out a baby girl to adopt, and were referred by our family doctor to St. Agnes's Home for Unwed Mothers here in Toronto.

You were born on the day you know to be your birthday: April 25th, 1961. We were told your birth mother and father were a young couple, only teenagers, who were unmarried and had lost their way. They had no money, and could not afford to raise you. They said your mother gave you up willingly for adoption, with a heavy heart and a hope that we could provide you with a brighter future than she could, young and poor as she was. Her story broke our hearts, but we thanked God for her selflessness and for bringing us this most precious gift. Our celebration was her grief.

We raised you and loved you as our own. The priest and warden at St. Agnes's counseled us not to tell you, to simply move on as though you were our own child from God, that it would be easier for you that way. We took their advice. We believed they knew best. But not a day has gone by that I have not questioned that decision.

When we brought you home, I found a pair of yellow booties tucked deep inside the blanket they had wrapped you in. I assumed your birth mother had sent them as a gift of goodwill, but I couldn't bear to use them, so I locked them in a safe drawer. I was afraid if I told you about her, that you would see me differently, and I couldn't help but imagine her out there somewhere missing you terribly. I tried to rid myself of my guilt by lighting a candle at church and praying for her every year on your birthday.

But here, my darling . . . here is where I must beg you, with every ounce of my heart and soul, for your forgiveness.

Not long after your wedding, your father and I discovered that you were not given up for adoption willingly and with a full heart, as we had been told. We were lied to, Nancy. And we, in turn, have lied to you.

There was a story on the news about some girls who had sought refuge at St. Agnes's, but were forced to give up their children by threat or worse. The Home was shut down not long after you were born. The people who ran it seemed to us to be good people. We wanted a child so desperately, and we believed them. We had no reason not to. We did not know. After the news story, I revisited the drawer and found the enclosed note stuffed deep inside the toe of one of the boots. You can read it for yourself, my dear.

Your father did not want to tell you, even then. And then he was gone, and still I didn't tell you. I have no excuse for myself other than cowardice. I am so sorry, Nancy. If I have learned anything from this, it is not to keep secrets. They fester like wounds, and take even longer to heal once the damage sets in. It's permanent, and crippling, and I want more for you than that.

Your mother's name was Margaret Roberts. She was much younger than me when she gave birth to you, so she may still be alive. I would encourage you to seek her out, to find solace in my death by reuniting with your Other Mother, as I have called her in my mind all along. I want you to move forward, and I hope you will not hold resentment for your father or me.

I have loved you with the deepest love in my heart, my darling. And so I know how hard it may have been for your Other Mother, for Margaret. Since I read her note, I have prayed every day for her forgiveness. I have taken care of her child, my child—our child—with tenderness. But I suppose God will settle our accounts as He sees fit. It is in His hands now.

Please forgive me, dear. I pray we will meet again one day, a long time from now.

Mum

Angela places the letter down on the writing desk and reaches for a box of tissues to dab the tears that have sprung to her eyes.

"Jesus Christ."

She thinks of her own family, of the mother she knows as Mom, and the woman who gave birth to her, Sheila, whom she finally met five years ago. To have lived her entire life not knowing she was adopted is a foreign, devastating concept. Her heart bleeds for all three of these women: the daughter Nancy; her mother Frances, who carried the weight of this secret for so long only to have the confession go astray;

and Margaret Roberts, scribbling in a hidden note that she was forced to give her baby up for adoption . . .

The note.

"Where is it?" Angela asks the empty store. She checks the desk, then leans down to scan the floor. When she shakes the envelope, a small piece of paper flutters onto the desk like confetti. It's yellowed, and a bit wrinkled. One of its edges is singed, as though it were nearly burned at some point.

Angela reads the brief handwritten missive. It's only two lines long, but she lingers on the last five words, her vision blurring.

She rereads the note several times before setting it on top of the letter. She needs advice. She reaches for her phone, cradling it in her hand as she considers whom to call first. After a quick scroll, she clicks on the name and puts the phone to her ear, wipes away a lingering tear from her cheek.

"Mom? Hi, it's me. Do you have a minute to talk?"

CHAPTER 2

Evelyn

. . . .

TORONTO | OCTOBER 1960

When Evelyn Taylor arrives at St. Agnes's Home for Unwed Mothers, her first thought is that she'll be lucky to make it out alive.

It looks like an abandoned castle whose residents have long since packed up any joy they once possessed and handed over the keys to the rats and creeping ivy. It might have been a beautiful manor once, with the curving peaked facade of the top-floor windows and deep brown brick exterior surrounded by lush trees. But as Evelyn's father pulls the car over to the side of the street in front of the house, her gaze flickers up and she glimpses a pair of pale eyes staring back at her out of one of the upper-floor windows. Two hands emerge from behind the curtains and pull the girl away. Evelyn blinks, and the figures are gone. She wonders briefly if she imagined them. The aura of the place is forbidding, and a cold sense of dread plunges down deep into Evelyn's gut before she's even opened the car door.

Her father remains in his seat, staring resolutely at a space in the middle distance, somewhere on the hood of his car. She wonders what's going through his mind. He clears his throat.

"Well, goodbye, then," he says, not meeting her eyes.

Evelyn reaches for the door handle. Once she's upright on the sidewalk, she opens the back door of the car and tugs out her traveling case. Her father doesn't offer to help. He hasn't even turned off the ignition.

After Evelyn shuts the door, there is a brief pause before she hears the gearshift lock into place, and the car pulls away from the curb. She watches the shiny, clean bumper of the sedan retreat around the corner, the back of her father's head visible over the top of the beige seat.

As she stands outside the home in her low-heeled buckled shoes, she's unable to move, her mind dully processing her new reality. Her mother made a phone call, Father Richard visited the house for tea, and the decision to send her to St. Agnes's was reached by the time the priest requested his second cup of orange pekoe.

On the one hand, she's grateful to be out from under her mother's dark glances, to have a little room to breathe while she waits out this pregnancy. But on the other, she's heartbroken and appalled that she must be here at all, and afraid of what awaits her behind that heavy wooden door with the large brass knocker. No one told her what to expect. She feels as though she's been swept up by a tornado like Dorothy in *The Wizard of Oz* and dropped miles away from her home in a strange place. Everything seems upside down. Distorted and wrong.

She can feel the pressure of the neighbors' eyes on the back of her neck, imagines their nosy pink faces pressed against the glass of their sitting room windows, peering out at the new resident with her disgrace on full display.

She knows she isn't the first, and won't be the last. Perhaps by now the neighbors don't care much anymore. Maybe the spectacle of the pregnant girls wore off years ago, long before Evelyn unfolded herself from her father's car onto this well-worn curb on Riverdale Avenue. She briefly considers making a run for it, but then turns, with an air of tense resignation, toward the steps up to the front door.

Evelyn takes hold of the heavy knocker, slams it down onto the polished wood three times before letting it fall with a dull thud and a squeak of its hinge. She waits. The wind rustles the brown leaves in the trees beside the front porch. The air is dense and electrified from the coming autumn storm, and the dark rolling clouds are just visible above the peaks and chimneys of the old row houses.

She can hear muffled sounds from inside the house, then a door shutting and a woman calling. Another responds, her voice deeper than the first. Footsteps draw nearer to the other side of the door and Evelyn's stomach clenches. She sets her shoulders and tilts her chin up as she hears the lock slide back.

The first thing she sees is the woman's eyes underneath the habit that covers most of her forehead. They're as gray and cold as the stormy sky to the west, and look even less welcoming. The nun opens the door fully and stands with her arms akimbo. A tea towel is looped through a belt at her waist beside her rosary beads and what Evelyn nervously suspects may be a whip. A crucifix gleams on her chest.

"You'll be Evelyn Taylor." Not a question. "Well, then, come on in and let's get a look at you."

She moves back from the door and Evelyn steps over the threshold. The nun's cold eyes make her instinctively place a hand on her belly, a gesture she instantly regrets.

"Don't go holding yourself like some poor lost lamb. You got yourself and that baby into this fix." She nods at Evelyn's still-flat belly. "And no one here has the time or inclination to feel sorry for you."

Evelyn drops her hand.

"Come into the sitting room, then. My name is Sister Mary Teresa. I'm the warden of St. Agnes's."

The nun marches through a doorway off the front hall and Evelyn follows like an obedient puppy. As she passes through the rounded archway, she notes the beautiful stained glass in the transom above and the crucifix nailed to the wall beside it. The sitting room is simple, papered over in a yellow floral print. It's only late afternoon, but the lamps are all lit. A set of heavy brown drapes is pulled shut over the big front window and Evelyn has to fight her instinct to flee back to the front door and escape into the fresh air.

"Sit, please," Sister Teresa says, indicating a faded and worn Queen Anne wing chair across from the rigid-backed Chesterfield sofa.

Something in her tone causes Evelyn to interpret it as an instruction more than an invitation. She perches on the edge of the chair and starts to lean back.

"Posture, Miss Taylor. Posture is paramount to a young lady's physical presentation, particularly if she is pregnant."

Evelyn sits up again, sighing out her discomfort. *What would this professional virgin know about being pregnant?*

"So," Sister Teresa says, a crisp cut into the proceedings. "How did you get yourself pregnant?"

Apparently even less than I thought . . . "I didn't get myself pregnant," Evelyn begins. "You can't get yourself preg—"

"Excuse me, Miss Taylor. You should know straightaway that we do not tolerate insolence in this household."

Evelyn nods. "My apologies, Sister Teresa."

"Thank you. Now, how did you become pregnant?"

Sister Teresa settles a clipboard on her lap and eyes Evelyn over the top of her wire-rimmed glasses, pencil poised eagerly midair. In the pause that follows Sister Teresa's question, Evelyn notices that the house is silent. She would have expected noise, laughter or chitchat, the banging of pots and pans in the kitchen.

"Miss Taylor?"

Evelyn thinks back on her nights with Leo, and her throat constricts. She can feel his weight on top of her, pressing himself into her as he whispered that he loved her, that this was all okay because they were going to be married soon. She never thought she could get pregnant so easily.

"There was no rubber," she manages to mutter, her face flaming.

Sister Teresa scribbles this down. "And did you know the father?"

"Yes."

She makes a tick on her sheet. "How long had you known him? How many dates had you been on? Were you going steady?"

"He was my fiancé. We were engaged to be married."

"Was this your first time having intercourse?" Sister Teresa asks.

Evelyn swallows the memory. "Yes."

"You say you 'were' engaged to be married? Does the putative father have any interest in this child?"

"I'm sorry, the what?"

"The putative father," Sister Teresa replies, looking up from her clipboard. "The alleged father."

The nun may as well have reached over the coffee table and slapped Evelyn across the face.

"He's not alleged. There's no question whatsoever."

"It's what we call all the fathers."

"He *is* the father. We were in love, we were going to be married, like I said."

"What happened to him?"

Evelyn hesitates. "He died. He ... he had a heart attack, and he died." The words taste like vinegar.

Sister Teresa's mouth pinches into a frown. "I am sorry to hear that. Although I'm sure you have been told that intercourse while engaged is still intercourse outside of marriage, Miss Taylor."

Evelyn blinks back hot tears. The nun returns to her clipboard.

"Now, then. A few more questions before I show you to your dormitory. Are your parents both living? I believe it was your mother who called to make the arrangement for you to stay with us."

"Yes, they're living."

Another tick. "Siblings?"

"One brother."

"Is he married? Younger? Older?"

"Older and married."

"Do you have any friends?"

"Well, yes, I suppose. A couple of girls from my school days."

"And none of your friends know of your condition?"

"No."

"Does your brother?"

"Yes, he does. His wife does, too. And I was thinking maybe—"

"All right, then." Sister Teresa returns her gaze to Evelyn. "Given your situation, we would expect that you prepare to give the child up for adoption. We have a list of several couples who are hoping to adopt in the next few months. Lovely married couples. Devout to the faith, well-off, established. Honorable." She lingers over the last word. "You will relinquish the baby at the end of your term." She makes one last tick on her clipboard.

Stunned, Evelyn remains silent, her mind racing as the panic starts to rise in her chest, threatening to overwhelm her. She can't breathe properly. Why aren't any of the windows open?

"Is that, I mean, is it required that I give the baby up? I didn't discuss it with my parents before I came here. There was no plan of any kind."

Sister Teresa's cold eyes peer at her over the top of her glasses. "Plan? The *plan*, Miss Taylor, is for you to wait out your pregnancy and give birth in a discreet, controlled environment so that you may return to your family with your reputation mostly intact. The benefit to you should be obvious. The benefit to us is that we in turn have the opportunity to place healthy babies with deserving couples wishing to adopt."

"But this baby, my baby . . . it was conceived in love. Surely that must mean something. I was going to marry the father. I loved him." Evelyn's voice cracks. "I lost him. Must I lose his baby, too?"

"The house rules are thus," Sister Teresa continues at a gallop, as though Evelyn hasn't just borne her heart to the woman. She plows through the policies in a well-practiced monologue. "You will use only your first name within these walls. *Only* your first name. I cannot stress this enough. Our girls and their families value discretion while the girl is housed here. As you are no doubt aware, most families feel a great deal of shame about their daughters' predicament, and we promise as much privacy as possible. Mind your own business, and do not ask questions. You will not discuss your home life, family, friends, past experiences, or other details with your roommates or any of the other inmates. Each of you is here for a reason. Keep it to yourself.

"You will not leave the house without express permission, nor will you go near the windows or open the curtains. We do not have a telephone on the premises. You may write letters to your loved ones, but not the putative father, though in your case, of course, that rule is moot. We will review all incoming and outgoing correspondence for the sake of your own privacy and safety. You will do as you are told by any of the sisters on our staff, or by Father Leclerc, your new priest. You will attend his mass here in the sitting room every Sunday morning. You will also attend various lessons to provide you with the set of skills you will require to be a good wife and housekeeper once you have reformed yourself. They include cooking, sewing, cleaning, knitting, and of course religious study. After you have given birth, you will move into the postpartum dormitory. Once our physician has agreed you are fit to return to work, you will continue to work off your debt for a three-month period until you are released back into the care of your parents. That is standard practice in every home of this kind."

Three months?

Evelyn clenches her fists in her lap as Sister Teresa finishes her pronouncement and stands up.

"Come along, then, Miss Taylor. Or Evelyn, I should say. That's the last time you'll be using your surname for a while. Supper is nearly ready, and we run a tight schedule. Pick up your case and I will show you to your dormitory. You'll be sharing with two other girls for now: Louise and Anne. Your third roommate, Margaret, is due to arrive tomorrow."

Evelyn forces herself up from the chair.

"Yes, Sister Teresa," the nun prompts her.

Evelyn drops her gaze to the handle of her traveling case. "Yes, Sister Teresa."

CHAPTER 3

Nancy

· · · · · · · · · ·

TORONTO | SUMMER 1979

Nancy Mitchell pulls on her red rubber boots and navy rain jacket in the front hall of her parents' house as butterflies flutter in her stomach. She doesn't like lying to her mother, but she has to extract herself from their argument in time to meet her cousin Clara.

"We're already late for Susan's birthday party, Mum," Nancy says. "I have to go."

Her mother exhales irritably. "I don't think it's appropriate for two young girls to be out at parties in the dead of night unescorted."

Nancy tries to shake off her mother's admonitions. Frances Mitchell was born and raised in England until her parents moved her and her sisters to Canada when she was only fourteen. But she's clung to the cultural values of decorum and propriety her entire life. They ground her. They make life stable and predictable. A set of rules to live by.

"We're not girls, Mum, we're old enough to vote now, remember?"

"Well, where is this party, anyway? You haven't said."

"Oh, leave her be, Frances," Nancy's grandmama croaks from the rigid-backed chair beside the living room window.

"Well, I worry," Frances says.

"Yes, but all of motherhood is just chronic low-level fear at the best of times, dear. You know this. And besides, a woman is entitled to a few secrets, after all, now, isn't she?"

Frances shoots her mother a withering look and storms off into the kitchen. A few seconds later, the smell of Comet cleaner fills the air. Every time she and her daughter have an argument, Frances vents her frustration by donning a set of rubber gloves and scrubbing her kitchen to within an inch of its Formica-topped life.

Tonight's argument was—once again—triggered by Nancy's need for independence. The fact that she's decided to move out of her parents' home to attend university in the same city has caused Frances to cling to her with even more vehemence than normal, and Nancy doesn't have the patience for it anymore.

She plants a kiss on her grandmother's papery cheek. "Thanks, Grandmama. I hope you're feeling better. I'll see you in the morning."

Flipping the oversized hood on her rain jacket, Nancy shuts the door behind her with more force than she intended and ventures out into the rainy night. She knows she did nothing to help avoid tonight's argument, but she's been on edge all day in anticipation of her appointment tonight with Clara.

Unlike her mother, Nancy isn't one to shy away from bending the rules—or, if the occasion calls for it, outright breaking them—but sneaking out to see an illegal abortionist isn't exactly within her comfort zone.

She agreed to it without really thinking, but her misgivings have increased since she first said yes a week ago. Clara called last Wednesday night and begged Nancy—choking on her words with sobs that became more and more fractured as her panic rose—to come with her as she gets an abortion. She had heard about a man who would do it for eight hundred dollars, she said, and no one ever needs to know.

"Does Anthony know?" Nancy asked her. Clara's boyfriend Anthony has a temper like napalm; it sticks to anything he throws it at and burns everything in his path.

"No, of course not. He wouldn't let me. You know that."

That's exactly the answer Nancy expected. She sighed and dropped her voice. "Are you *sure* about this, Clara?"

"Yes!" Clara wailed. "Mom and Dad'll kill me. This isn't a choice. There's no other option, Nancy."

"But, I mean, is this guy legitimate? You hear horror stories, you know? What if he's some quack?"

"I don't think so. The friend of a girl I work with at the diner used this guy, and everything was fine. That's who told me about him. He's out in the East End."

"Is there . . ." Nancy hated herself a little for asking it. "Is there anyone else who can go with you?" She held her breath for the answer, curling the phone cord around her index finger.

"No," Clara said. "I need you. I need a girl with me, and you've always been the closest thing I have to a sister." An overstatement. "I can't do this by myself. *Please* help me."

And so Nancy waits underneath the misty glow of a streetlamp outside Ossington Station at nine o'clock on this rainy Friday night in August. She can't see much through the downpour, but as a small silhouette emerges in the darkness, she suspects—given the hunched shoulders and harried pace—that it's Clara. Nancy raises a hand and the figure hurries toward her. Her eyes are wide, the gray-blue standing out against her pale face. She throws her wet arms around Nancy's neck, and Nancy can feel her shaking.

"Try to stay calm, Clara," Nancy says, pulling away. "It'll be over soon."

The girls enter the subway station, drop their tokens into the metal box. They land with a *clink*, one after the other, on top of the hundreds of other tokens from that day's commuters. Normally it's a sound Nancy quite likes. It's the sound of *going places*. Of visiting friends or adventurous Saturday afternoon excursions to the St. Lawrence Market. She loves just walking around the city, popping into shops, galleries, or cafés whenever the mood strikes her, discovering new and peculiar oddities and hidden gems within the boundaries of the city she loves so much. But tonight, the sound seems to echo off the walls of the quiet subway station with eerie magnitude.

They hurry down the stairs to the train platform, breathing in the smell of the subway: somehow damp and dusty at the same time, with pungent undercurrents of rotting garbage and urine. Their fellow travelers are all staring down the dark tunnel in impatient anticipation for the distant light of the train and the rush of wind that precedes its arrival. When Nancy and Clara finally board, they take two seats right across from the doors.

She notices Clara is staring resolutely at the empty seat across from her, her face white above the small gold cross hanging around her neck. Nancy's never known anyone who got an abortion. Or at least, she thinks with a jolt, no one that she knows of. She isn't entirely sure what to expect, and that makes her nerves tingle. She's the type of person who's most comfortable when she has all the information, for better or worse. But tonight it feels like she and Clara are groping blindly with only the vaguest sense of direction.

After several stops, Clara glances up at the map on the wall above the doors, stands, and clears her throat. The sound is small, like a little girl's. Nancy rises from her seat as the car lurches to a halt.

On the street outside the station, Clara pulls a crumpled piece of paper out of her pocket and squints at it in the light from the streetlamp overhead.

"This way, I think," she mutters.

They turn right toward a side street that takes them deeper into a shabby neighborhood. The farther they wander into the deserted streets, the more nervous Nancy becomes. The unfamiliar houses are packed in tightly and seem to bear down on them. After ten minutes' walk and two backtracks, they arrive at the address. It's a triplex building with peeling paint and sagging eaves. A rusted screen door hangs drunkenly off its hinges. The lights are on in the unit on the top floor, but the main floor is dark. They can just see a peek of yellow light through a gap in the basement curtains.

"He said side door," Clara says, but she doesn't move. She looks confused, as though she isn't quite sure why they're standing in the middle of this strange street in the pouring rain.

Nancy licks her dry lips. "Clara? Are we … do you still want to do this?"

An overwhelming part of her hopes her cousin will say no, she's changed her mind, let's go on home and we'll figure it out somehow. But instead she nods. "Yes."

Nancy swallows the sour lump in her throat and follows Clara down the lane between the houses. It's pitch-black and the pavement shimmers with rain.

Clara knocks on the back door. A light flickers to life through the glass above and they hear a series of locks being turned, then a man appears in the crack of the door. He has a rough, reddish brown beard and round glasses perched on a slightly sweaty face. He takes in Clara and then looks behind her at Nancy.

"Which one of you called me?" he asks.

"Me," Clara answers.

"Do you have the eight hundred?"

"Yes."

"Let me see it, girl."

Clara unzips her coat and withdraws a wad of twenty-dollar bills from the inner pocket. Nancy's jaw clenches. She knows Clara's been saving her tips from the diner to pay for school. She'll have to work double shifts now to make up for this.

"Okay, then," the man says. "Come on in. Be quick about it."

He opens the door wide and Clara steps over the threshold. Nancy hesitates a moment before following. She regrets this decision like hell, but there's no point abandoning Clara now that they've come this far, and as the elder of the two girls, she feels responsible for her cousin. The man leads them down a narrow, bare staircase to the basement apartment. The damp and cold increase with each step. When they reach a small bedroom at the back of the unit, Nancy's stomach flips at the sight before her.

In the center of the room is what appears to be an old wooden dining table covered in a sheet with a small flat pillow at one end. The sheet is black. Nancy realizes with a lurch that it's likely because it's stained with blood from all the women who have lain on that table before. It reminds her of the black draping at a funeral.

There's a small stool at the bottom of the table beside a metal cart that looks like it was found in the garbage bin behind a hospital. It's vaguely medical, but rusted and missing a wheel. In the corner, there's another small table with a large bottle of rubbing alcohol, a garbage bin, some silver instruments, towels, and a radio that seems conspicuously out of place. It's the instruments that draw Clara's eye, and her head starts to shake.

The man closes the door behind them. "All right, then, take off your pants and underwear and get up on the table."

Nancy jumps at the click of the lock and feels her heart rate accelerate into overdrive. The man still hasn't told them his name. "Clara . . ." she says.

"Okay," Clara whispers, and does as she's told. Nancy's instinct is to face the wall in an attempt to give Clara some privacy, but there's no point. The room is small and there's no blanket or anything to cover Clara. There will be no dignity in this experience, and by the set of

Clara's jaw, Nancy can tell she's too determined to not be pregnant to bother with something as insignificant as her dignity.

"Drink this." The man hands Clara a bottle. It doesn't have a label, but Nancy hopes it's alcohol to numb the pain. Clara drinks three large gulps and splutters in disgust. Some of it drips down her chin, and Nancy steps over to her to wipe it away. It smells strange.

"It's my own little cocktail," the man says with a half grin. "Good for the nerves at a time like this. The ladies seem to like it, anyway."

Clara closes her eyes, but tears pour out the corners, falling back into her blond hair. Her bottom lip is trembling. Fear skitters down Nancy's spine. She can't imagine how Clara must feel. Nancy takes her hand, squeezes it tight, but Clara doesn't return the pressure.

At the table in the corner of the room, the man pours rubbing alcohol on the tools—knives, scalpels, some kind of long stick, and other instruments—then he settles himself down on the stool at the bottom of the table and places the items on the tray beside him. He pulls on a pair of blue surgical gloves, snapping each of the cuffs into place. It hits Nancy now—what's about to happen to Clara's body, the things she might see and hear and smell.

"I'm right here, okay?" Nancy murmurs into Clara's ear, brushing her damp hair back off her forehead. Clara's half-conscious now with whatever this guy gave her to drink.

"Tell her to bite down on this," the man says to Nancy, passing her an old belt. She has to force down the vomit that surges up her throat. There are dozens of teeth marks all along the edges of the brown leather.

"Jesus Christ," Nancy mutters.

"He's not gonna help you in here, honey."

Nancy ignores the man. "Clara, bite down on this. Come on." She feeds the belt between Clara's teeth with difficulty, but Clara finally bites it. "I've got you. You're going to be okay."

The man picks up one of the instruments and peers between Clara's legs. Nancy can hear the clicking of the tools. The chemical stench of the rubbing alcohol is burning her nostrils. He clears his throat, then switches on the radio and turns it up full-blast.

Nancy jumps again, her nerves already frayed like a cut rope. "What the hell?" she bellows over the music.

"Trust me!" he calls across Clara's bare legs. "This isn't my first rodeo, baby!"

It takes less than a minute for Nancy to understand why he's blasting the radio. Clara's eyes snap open and a scream issues from her mouth that could wake the dead. Her once-loose grip tightens on Nancy's hand.

"Hold her down!" the man shouts at Nancy. "She can't move!"

Sickened with herself and the man in equal measure, Nancy presses down on Clara's chest with her free hand as "Sweet and Innocent" by Donny Osmond blares through the tinny speakers.

Out on the street, all the neighbors hear are the cheery upbeat notes, the saccharine lyrics of the teenage crooner. The song Nancy will associate with this night for the rest of her life. The song that will make her want to smash her car radio with a hammer and flee from a friend's party two hours early.

Clara's screams continue as tears drip down her temples, soaking the black pillowcase beneath her blond hair as Donny belts out his ballad to a girl who was just too young.

. . . .

The subway doors slide shut and the train starts to move, transporting the girls back downtown the way they came, away from the horror of that dank basement. A sob bursts from Clara's mouth, followed by the tiniest whimper.

"Oh, Clara," Nancy says. "It's over now. It's going to be okay."

"Thank you, Nancy."

Clara rests her head against Nancy's shoulder, and Nancy awkwardly extracts her arm from between them and pulls Clara into a half hug. They stay like that for several stops, swaying with the rhythmic motion of the train. It's nearly midnight now, and their subway car is mercifully empty.

When they're two stops away from Ossington, Nancy gently nudges Clara. "We're nearly there."

Clara doesn't respond. Her head is heavy against Nancy.

"The next station is Ossington. Ossington Station," the monotone voice announces through the speakers.

"Clara," Nancy says again. "Come on, stand up."

No response.

"Clara?"

Nancy dips her head to get a better view of Clara's face.

It's deathly pale, and her lips are blue.

"Clara!" Nancy shakes her cousin's shoulders, her own heart hammering in her throat. Clara's eyes open a fraction, and she moans a word Nancy can't make out. "Come on, get up, we need to get you home *now*."

"Arriving at Ossington. Ossington Station."

The train begins to slow. Nancy reaches underneath Clara's small arms and lifts her up. She's so tiny, it isn't that difficult, but as she hauls Clara to her feet, Nancy gets a full view of the subway seat beneath her. Underneath her rain jacket, Nancy breaks out in a cold sweat.

The seat is so soaked in blood that the fabric is shining.

"Oh shit! Oh Jesus. *Fuck!*"

Clara's head lolls on her neck like a child's doll. When the subway doors slide open, Nancy half drags her off the train onto the empty platform. The whistle sounds and the train pulls away from the station, whipping Nancy's hair back as it picks up speed. Clara moans again.

"Clara!" Nancy gasps. "Clara, I need you to help me get you up the stairs. I need you to walk. *Please!*"

Clara blinks at her through heavy eyes, and mouths something Nancy can't hear. But she does lift her legs, slow and weak, enough to help Nancy get her to the top of the stairs. The station is empty. There isn't even anyone on duty in the tollbooth.

Nancy backs into the crash doors out onto the street, still dragging Clara with her like a medic hauling a body off a battlefield. It's stopped raining, and the air is heavy with humidity and the smell of mud. She heads for the traffic lights on Bloor Street one block down.

After what seems an eternity, Nancy spots an approaching cab.

"Taxi!" she screams, throwing her hand in the air. It pulls over to stop in front of her. Propping Clara up with one arm, Nancy struggles to open the door with the other. She nearly dumps Clara into the car, then throws herself in after her.

"We need the nearest hospital," Nancy snaps at the driver.

"You want St. Joe's? Probably closest." He meets her eyes in the rear-view mirror. "Hey, she don't look so good, she better not be—"

"Just drive!" Nancy shouts at him.

He shakes his head and speeds away from the curb without signaling.

In the back seat, Nancy gives Clara another small shake, smacks her cheek as forcefully as she dares without hurting her. "Clara, stay with me. Just stay with me. Stay with me."

. . . .

Nancy has never sat in a hospital waiting room alone before. She's waited with her mother during her Grandmama's many illnesses in recent years, but sitting in a waiting room with your parent is entirely different. There's someone older and wiser to be the point of contact for the doctor, someone to get you a cup of tea and tell you it's going to be okay. Tapping her rain boot on the tile floor and biting her nails nearly to the quick, Nancy suddenly feels far more adult than she ever has before. She's responsible for someone here. *She's* the point of contact.

Nancy arrived at the emergency room with Clara half-conscious and hanging off her shoulder as blood dripped onto the white tile floor beneath their feet. Nancy kept her mouth shut as much as possible with the triage nurse. Her mother—a woman with an impeccable sense of etiquette which she carried with her like a piece of heavy luggage when she immigrated to Canada—has always taught Nancy to mind her own business, reciting her favorite idiom ad nauseam: "Just keep yourself to yourself." Why Nancy arrived at the hospital doors with Clara half-conscious and bleeding isn't anyone's damn business. Their job is to treat their patient. But on the other hand, this isn't some innocent heart attack or unlucky car accident. Clara's injuries are the result of something illegal. As she thinks about the possible implications, Nancy's heart hammers somewhere in the region of her tonsils.

She looks down now and notes the bloodstains on the calves of her jeans. She'll have to wash them in the bathtub tonight before her parents see them. She hopes her mother won't be waiting up for her. A moment later, her stomach flutters as the doctor bursts through the swinging doors. He's tall, with a dark buzz cut and a face like a thunderstorm.

"You! Girl!" he barks in Nancy's direction. Half a dozen other people in the waiting room look up in mild alarm.

"Y-yes?" Nancy says.

"Come with me." He beckons with an imperious hand, and she follows him back through the swinging doors into the bowels of the emergency room, the place you only go to if someone you love is really in trouble. Apparently, Clara is.

"You need to start talking about what happened to your friend," the doctor demands. "You barely said a word when the triage nurse asked you what was wrong. You just said she's bleeding a lot, which she is. She's hemorrhaging, actually. It's really bad." He crosses his arms. "Start talking."

Nancy's tempted to, she really is. Clara is in serious condition, but that's nothing compared to the trouble they're going to be in if she confesses that Clara underwent an illegal back-alley abortion.

"Is she . . . is she going to make it?" Nancy parries the doctor's question with one of her own.

"I think so, yes. But barely. We need to know exactly what's going on so we can treat her fully. She's unconscious now and can't tell us anything. We're transfusing her. She lost a lot of blood. A *lot* of blood."

"So, she's going to survive."

He shakes his head, and for a moment Nancy fears the worst. A rush of cold hits her veins before she realizes he's judging their behavior, not Clara's fate. "Yes. She will."

"Okay. Thank you." *Thank God.*

"But you want to know what I think?" He steps closer to Nancy. He smells like rubbing alcohol and pine aftershave. "I think she had a little problem and the two of you decided you'd take care of it yourselves. Is that what happened?"

Nancy freezes, fighting the shiver she can feel rising in her body. "No."

"No?"

"No. I don't know what you're talking about."

"I've been around a long time," the doctor says, "and you know what? When we get girls in here hemorrhaging, it's because they attempted an abortion and perforated an organ. This kind of shit not only kills babies, it kills women, too. That's why it's illegal."

Nancy can feel the anger coming off his body. "We didn't attempt any abortion."

Half true.

"Well, I happen to think you did."

He stares her down, and they end up in a stalemate. She's not going to say any more, and he knows it.

"This is the end of my shift, but you better be prepared to answer some questions for the doctor that's relieving me. Because I can tell you one thing: If she suspects the same thing I do, she's going to be calling the police before she even thinks about discharging your friend. You can go ahead and lie to *them* and see how far that gets you." He points to a small observation room to Nancy's left. "Sit," he orders. "And wait for my colleague to come talk to you."

Nancy doesn't even think about arguing. She steps into the room, settles herself down on the chair, and waits. The pure white panic she felt when she saw all the blood on the subway seat dissipated somewhat once they took Clara into the emergency room, but it's rising again now. She's tapping her foot incessantly.

She looks up at the wall of the exam room. The clock says it's nearly one in the morning. No wonder her eyes are itching. Nancy watches the hands move as the minutes tick by, knowing she'll arrive home horrendously past her curfew and will have to face the consequences later.

The ward is quiet. All she can hear is the sound of a few doctors and nurses calling to each other, the occasional collegial laugh, the beeping of machines in the distance. Nancy leans back in the plastic chair and closes her eyes.

Twenty minutes later, a doctor appears at the door, her face grave. She looks about fifty, with a high forehead and graying brown hair pulled back into a low bun.

"Hi, there, Miss . . . ?"

"Nancy. My name's Nancy."

"Okay. Nancy. I'm Dr. Gladstone."

"Um, hi," Nancy says, standing. "How's Clara? The other doctor said . . ." She trails off.

Dr. Gladstone glances over her shoulder, then steps over the threshold of the room and closes the door behind her. Nancy takes a step back, unsure what's happening.

"We're pretty sure we know what happened here," Dr. Gladstone says. "My colleague suspects certain things. Certain illegal things."

"I don't know what you're talking about," Nancy says. She doesn't plan on answering any of this doctor's questions, either.

"Your friend is lucky to be alive." Dr. Gladstone pauses, lowers her voice. "Listen to me carefully, Nancy. I don't actually want you to say anything specific. But if I'm on the right track, I need you to give me some indication that that's the case so that I can provide the right treatment for your friend. Can you do that for me? There's no reason for me to call the police. I know my colleague threatened that, but that's not how I operate. I need you to trust me."

A long moment stretches out in the tiny space between them, then Nancy nods and scratches her nose.

"Okay, thank you. That's all I need to know. I'll record this as a spontaneous abortion. A miscarriage," she adds in response to Nancy's blank look. "I'll have a look at her uterus and make sure all the tissue has been removed so she doesn't get an infection."

Nancy lets her breath out slowly. "Thank you," she says, and means it.

"But I need to tell you something," Dr. Gladstone says quietly. Nancy leans in to hear her. "If you, or a friend, or any other girl close to you ends up pregnant when they don't want to be, you need to call around to doctors' offices and ask for *Jane*."

Nancy's brow knits. "Jane?"

"Jane. Call around, keep asking for Jane, and eventually you'll get what you need."

"But I don't under—"

"Just tell them you're looking for Jane."

Dr. Gladstone turns on her heel and opens the door, then heads into the brightness of the emergency room corridor. Her white cloak whips out of sight, leaving Nancy alone in the exam room.

CHAPTER 4

Evelyn

· · · · · · · · · ·

LATE FALL, 1960

E velyn wakes suddenly as a high-pitched moan floats into the room
from the dormitory across the hall.

It's the early hours of the morning. That time just before dawn
when the light is blue-gray and everything is silent, the world is waiting
for the curtain to rise, and the night dwellers—the nocturnal animals,
criminals, and thieves—are slinking back to the darkness of their dens
before the sun breaks on the horizon.

Evelyn was dreaming of her own bed. The bed at her parents' home,
with its knotted pine posts and headboard, comfortable mattress, and
goose-down pillows. The soft flannel sheets her mother used during the
winter for added warmth. The walls of her bedroom covered in textured
wallpaper and the thick pink rug under her feet when she swung them
out of her bed in the morning. Not like this place, St. Agnes's, where
the scratchy carpet slippers have no padding in the soles and are too
tight for her frozen feet.

Evelyn lies on her side in bed, struggles to pull the thin sheets and
blankets over her body to seal out the chill, but no matter how hard

she tries, her feet, shoulders, or elbows are still exposed to the cold air of the dormitory she shares with three other girls. All "fallen" women, all young. All waiting in a polite queue, allegedly to be redeemed.

In the bed next to hers, Margaret shifts. Her roommate hasn't been sleeping lately. Although the house rules forbid it, Evelyn and Margaret have become fast friends over the past few weeks.

She arrived the day after Evelyn, appeared in the doorway as Evelyn unpacked her suitcase into the tiny dresser at the foot of her bed.

"Call me Maggie," she said, when Evelyn introduced herself. "How long have you been here, Evelyn?"

"Oh, just since last night. Did Sister Teresa do your intake?"

"Yes. These rules are mad. And I suppose this is the prison uniform, is it?" Maggie asked, holding up a drab gray shift dress.

All the "inmates," as Sister Teresa calls them, were given the same day dresses and nightgowns. The term reflects the grim, punitively militaristic environment the nun has curated within the home. The staff keep the girls busy with cooking and cleaning, shining shoes, and scrubbing the laundry they take in from the neighborhood to subsidize the home's upkeep. They have scheduled outdoor time in the back garden only at predetermined hours of the day, and under strict supervision. The home is intended to be a place of anonymity. The girls aren't allowed to talk about much with each other. No one uses their last name. No one is supposed to talk about how they got pregnant. But the one thing all the girls whisper about, obsess over, is everyone else's due date. It's the first thing each new girl gets asked.

Maggie is due two weeks after Evelyn, so they're on this ride together. Evelyn takes each turn just slightly before Maggie does, twitching the wheel and leading the way for them both. The girls don't have their own mothers or older sisters to provide guidance during their pregnancies, and the nuns certainly can't—or won't—offer any. The physician who comes in to see the girls never answers any of their questions. Ignoring his patient, he talks to Sister Teresa as though the pregnancy is a rather uninteresting science experiment he's reporting on, like phases of mold growth. And so, with this dearth of information, the girls turn to one another for support, though never under the watchful gaze of Sister Teresa, or the Watchdog, as they call her. Because, after all, St. Agnes's is a place where everything is kept hidden.

Another moan rings out from down the hall and Maggie opens her eyes. Her thin arm rests protectively over the curve of her tiny belly. She's only just beginning to show. "Do you hear that?" she whispers.

Evelyn nods. "It woke me up. I think it's Emma."

"She told me last week while we were in the kitchen that she wanted to change her mind about the adoption, but ..." Maggie trails off. Evelyn shakes her head. They both know that changing one's mind isn't an option at St. Agnes's. "She's been crying a lot in the mornings. I don't think she has anyone in her dormitory, you know, like this." Maggie offers Evelyn a weak smile.

They hold each other's gaze for a while in silent conversation. Eventually Emma's sobs subside, the echoes sinking into the faded wallpaper of the hallway. These walls have absorbed many years' worth of anguished cries. Whispered pleas and prayers.

Evelyn shivers so violently that her teeth start to chatter. "It's so cold. It feels like winter already."

"I know. Come here." Maggie gestures for Evelyn to join her in bed, scoots herself over as far as she possibly can on the narrow mattress. Four inches, if that.

Evelyn throws her own pathetic blanket over her friend before lowering herself onto Maggie's bed. Maggie stifles her laughter while Evelyn tries to settle in. After a minute of struggling, they find a comfortable position and Maggie burrows her head into the crook of Evelyn's neck.

"I asked Sister Agatha last week to see if she could scrounge up some extra blankets somewhere. She said she'd try, but the dormitories are full right now, so there isn't much of anything to spare," Maggie says with a sigh.

The home is staffed by three nuns who live on the premises along with Sister Teresa and Father Leclerc. They go about their business and carry out Sister Teresa's bidding with a quiet resolve. Only Sister Mary Agatha is patient with the girls in a way the other staff aren't. She's diminutive in stature, plain and pale, and reminds Evelyn of a house mouse. She's also genuinely kind, a welcome counterbalance to Sister Teresa's snide aggression. She's the only member of the staff who calls the girls "miss," and she's sweet with the babies. Evelyn thinks it's a bit of a shame Sister Agatha decided to take the veil. She might have made a wonderful nanny.

"Hey, what's your last name, Evelyn?" Maggie whispers now from beneath Evelyn's chin, interrupting her thoughts.

"Taylor," Evelyn says, and the contraband confession triggers a lurch of excitement in her chest. "What's yours?"

"Roberts. It's nice to meet you, Miss Taylor."

Evelyn smiles. "It's nice to meet you, too, Miss Roberts."

Silence for a while as they both warm up.

"What do you want to do when you get out of here?" Maggie asks.

After is something Evelyn's been thinking about a lot lately. She hesitates, unsure how her friend will react to her answer.

"I, um . . . I've been thinking about going to university. Maybe medical school."

Maggie gasps, and Evelyn worries their roommates will wake up, but they don't. "Really? That's a big idea. What makes you want to do that?"

Evelyn chews the inside of her cheek. "It's something I've thought about for a long time. The boys in our families are always told they can do or be anything they please, right? But us girls are just meant to get married or be teacher-spinsters for the rest of our lives." She feels Maggie's body quake with laughter. "It's true!"

"I know it is," her friend says. "My mother's the same way."

"Since I won't be getting married anymore, I just thought . . . if I have the chance now, I might want more than that."

"What kind of doctor would you want to be? There are all kinds, aren't there?"

"M-hm. I've thought about maybe being a doctor that deals with bones."

"Bones?"

"I don't know." Evelyn shrugs, considering how best to articulate what the possibility means to her. "I guess I'd like to be able to put broken things back together. Or maybe I could work on patients' hearts, you know. Try to help save people like my poor Leo."

Maggie looks up at Evelyn. "You should do it. Really you should."

Evelyn smiles. "Maybe I will, Miss Roberts." She pecks Maggie's forehead with a kiss. "Maybe I just will."

"Dr. Evelyn Taylor," Maggie says slowly. "It has a nice ring to it, don't you think?"

Maggie drifts off, but Evelyn's mind is too occupied to sleep now. It won't be long before their day begins. Just as the one before, they'll attend prayer in the parlor room, then eat breakfast in the dining room. One-third of the girls cook breakfast for the whole household each morning, assisted by a couple of the nuns. After breakfast will be knitting, sewing, and other dull tasks, then lunch, prepared by another third of the girls. Their afternoons are dedicated to cleaning and chores. Dinner is cooked by the remaining third of the inmates. After dinner there's time for Bible study or other reading from the miserable collection of books on the parlor shelf before bed at ten o'clock sharp. Every moment of every day is scheduled down to the minute.

Evelyn casts her brown eyes up at the white ceiling with its dark rings of water stains, then around the room at the other girls, who are still sleeping. At the end of each bed is a small dresser for their things, but no mirror or other vanities. Those are not permitted in their dormitories or the communal bathroom. Sister Teresa tells them they should be focusing their energy and attentions inward—on growing their babies—and outward—praying on the misdeeds that landed them each in this lamentable predicament. Though she knows how each girl became pregnant from their intake meeting, the Watchdog still treats them as though they have all chosen to sin, that they are the seductive mistresses of their own misfortunes and should consider themselves lucky the Church has allowed them houseroom during their pregnancies.

And despite the rule against it, most of the girls do talk to one another about how they got pregnant. After all, there isn't much else to talk about.

Fifteen-year-old Louise in the bed across from Evelyn became pregnant by her brother's friend, who was seven years her senior and full of pretty promises that evaporated the moment she said the word "pregnant." And Anne, asleep over by the window, resorted to selling her own body out of financial desperation when her husband abandoned her and deserted to British Columbia with his secretary.

A couple of weeks ago, Maggie confided in Evelyn that she herself had suggested to her parents that she go visit her aunt in Scotland for the duration of her pregnancy, and give the baby up for adoption there. She told Evelyn she had figured it might be easier to put a continent between her and any temptation to find the child later on, but her mother had declined without explanation. Maggie didn't tell Evelyn exactly how her pregnancy came to be, but Evelyn has her suspicions.

Evelyn hasn't talked about her own pregnancy to anyone but Maggie. She told her the truth: that she wasn't even aware she was pregnant when Leo had the heart attack. *A ticking time bomb*, the doctors had said in hushed tones as Evelyn crumpled into the wooden chair in the hospital waiting room. Just a defect lying in wait. *Bad luck*, they muttered.

Evelyn buried her fiancé in a state of numb grief, tossed a bouquet of white roses onto his lowered coffin instead of carrying them with her down the aisle at their wedding. She hadn't even considered what might be next for her when she realized she'd missed her period that month. She was still wearing her black mourning dress, floating on a wave of heartache that led her straight to St. Agnes's front door with no resistance.

She should have protested, refused, she thinks now. But then, where would that have left her? Living on the street with a baby? Good girls aren't supposed to get pregnant out of wedlock, but if you do, you "do the right thing for everyone"—a phrase she heard her mother recite at least a dozen times—and you give up your baby. It's as simple as that.

But it certainly doesn't feel like the right thing for Evelyn; this baby is all she has left of Leo. She wishes she could keep it, but her parents won't allow it. They made that much clear to her when they arranged for her to come to St. Agnes's in the first place. At no point did anyone ever ask Evelyn what *she* wanted. This baby is growing inside her, but she has no say in its fate. Is she even allowed to call herself a mother?

The single tear that has been quivering at the corner of her eye falls hot against her cold cheek and is quickly absorbed into the thin pillow. Evelyn takes a deep breath and lets it out slowly, trying to expel the dark thoughts into the cold air of the dormitory, but they hover over her and Maggie, entwined together on the narrow bed. She can't escape them. They're part of the punishment, the penance the girls pay in this secluded cell in a forgotten corner of the city. There are no dreams here, there is no light. The darkness will linger. For some, only months. For others, years. And others still will never see the light again.

These girls are fallen. And they will all pay for their redemption.

CHAPTER 5

Angela

. . . .

JANUARY 2017

S tanding at the door of her apartment, Angela catches a whiff of garlic and onions, the scent dancing with the muted sounds of soft jazz. Tina has already started on dinner. As usual, minced garlic gets tossed into a frying pan before they've even decided what they'll be having, and Angela knows Tina will have a glass of wine waiting for her on the side table in the living room. Smiling, Angela turns her key in the lock and pushes open the door.

Their apartment is a good size for downtown Toronto: one master and two other tiny bedrooms, a larger open space that doubles as living room and dining room, a galley kitchen, and a windowless bathroom. Their only storage is the entryway closet, the telephone-booth-sized bedroom closets, and whatever they can manage to shove underneath the beds and the bathroom sink. Tina has lived here for twelve years, and Angela for six, so they've had plenty of time to make it their own. Their walls are painted in bright, bold colors—teals, reds, yellows, and greens—a haven to hibernate in during the bleak winter months when everything from the streetscape to clothing to the cloudy sky above is shrouded in a hopeless shade of gray. Multicolored rugs soften their footfalls on the creaky parquet floor, and cast-iron candle sconces warm the rooms with a soft glow.

Angela shuts the door behind her now, tosses her keys into the blown-glass bowl on the spindly wooden entryway table, and hangs her coat up in the closet. Swapping her slushy winter boots for slippers, she hangs her purse on a hook, fishes the envelope from its depths, then shuffles down the hall and into the living room.

"Hey-hey!" Tina calls. Steam is emanating from the kitchen doorway, and her face appears in the pass-through window out into the living room, pink with heat. "I'm making fresh pasta. Your wine's on the table."

Angela plants a kiss on her wife's lips through the window. "I knew I married you for a reason."

Tina smiles. "My pasta?"

"M-hm."

"Well, I'm glad my good looks, charm, and exhaustive education haven't gone to waste in attracting a mate."

Angela laughs and kisses her again.

"Go sit, I just need to get the sauce simmering."

"Thanks, T."

"What's that?" Tina nods at the envelope clutched in Angela's hand.

"Something I want to talk to you about, actually. I'll wait till you come out."

"Everything okay?" Tina's brow instantly crinkles underneath her short blond hair.

Angela nods. "Nothing to do with me. Don't worry. I just want your advice on something."

"Oh, okay. Good." Her wife's face muscles relax. They've both been on edge since the miscarriage. They've spent eighteen months and tens of thousands of dollars only to watch their dream of a family repeatedly slip through their fingers. Neither of them can handle any more bad news at the moment.

"I'll be out in a sec." Tina disappears back into a cloud of steam.

Angela wanders over to the couch and flops down in her spot at the end of the three-seater. Their black cat, Grizzly, slinks around the corner of the coffee table. He's the size of a large raccoon, but nimbly hops up into her lap.

"Hey, Grizz." Angela strokes his glossy fur in an absent sort of way as the sounds of Ella Fitzgerald and Louis Armstrong harmonizing waft from the record player on the sideboard.

She picks up the envelope and slips the edge of it back and forth through her fingers, thinking. On the bus back from work she started having misgivings about opening the envelope and removing it from the shop. Which is silly, of course. It didn't *belong* to the shop to begin with. And no, perhaps she shouldn't have opened it, but it had been posted so long ago, and was clearly forgotten. Was she not doing the intended addressee, Nancy Mitchell, a service by opening it? If she hadn't, it might never have been discovered at all, and this woman would never know that she was adopted. Angela sets the envelope down on the couch cushion beside her and picks up her wineglass with the other. She takes a sip and grimaces. It's the fake wine she's been drinking out of desperation since they first started their fertility journey. Her wife emerges from the kitchen, holding a glass of her own.

"I figured after last night, you might want to revert to the fake stuff," Tina says, indicating Angela's glass.

"Yeah, you're probably right."

"How is it, anyway? Is it basically just grape juice?"

Angela stares into the red depths, considering. "It's more like wine than grape juice, but more like vinegar than wine."

Tina chuckles and settles herself down on the other end of the couch. Both women turn their bodies inward to face each other, knees tented in front of them, the toes of their matching slippers touching.

"How was your day?" Angela asks, stalling.

Tina takes a sip of her real merlot. Angela catches a whiff of it and her stomach churns. "Fine. Uneventful. Did some cleaning, got groceries. Prepped for lectures tomorrow. How was the store? Usual sleepy Sunday?"

Angela looks down into her glass, swills it in her hand like a gold prospector, hoping the right words will float to the surface. "Not quite."

"Do tell."

Angela isn't sure how to begin, so she opts for fessing up. "I found a piece of mail that must have gone astray at some point, was never delivered to the person it was addressed to. The weird thing is, it was addressed to the shop. Well," she corrects herself, "the *address* of the shop. But it was meant for someone named Nancy Mitchell."

"Is that it?" Tina asks, pointing down at the envelope between them. "You opened it?"

"Yeah. I know. I feel weird about it. But the postmark said it was mailed in 2010 and it was buried in a box inside a drawer that no one's opened for years. Aunt Jo never bothered to organize that place. It was never going to be found."

"So what's in it?"

Angela gives her wife a meaningful look over the top of her knees. "It's a huge letter. It's not long, but I mean the contents. It's . . . heart-breaking."

"What's in it?" Tina asks again.

Angela removes the letter and the accompanying note from the envelope. She passes them to Tina, then reaches for her wineglass, taking another sip as Ella and Louis begin the chorus of "Our Love Is Here to Stay." A few seconds later, Angela hears the hiss of water on the stovetop.

"Can you—"

"I'll put the pasta in," Angela says at the same moment. Tina smiles, and Angela walks into the kitchen. When she returns a minute later, Tina has finished reading.

"That's some letter."

"I know. And this woman, Nancy, her birth mother was at one of those maternity homes they had after the war, for unmarried mothers, you know? Religious organizations like the Catholic Church and Salvation Army ran them. I did a quick search today; it's a part of our history I didn't really know about, and it's bleak as hell."

"Poor girl."

"Yeah."

Tina pauses. "So, what now?"

"That's what I want to talk to you about. It seems the adoptive mother's last wish was that this Nancy person go find her birth mother. I feel like I need to find Nancy and give her the letter and the note. She needs to know. I did the math, and the birth mother is probably still alive."

Tina is quiet for a moment. Angela has trouble with silences; she always feels a need to fill the empty space.

"I called my mom right after I opened it. I was actually quite upset."

"I can imagine. Must have hit a bit close to home for you."

Angela nods. "Exactly. It did. Mom thinks if the birth mother really wanted Nancy to have the information, then I should try to find her. She knows how much I needed to find Sheila, how that affected me growing up. And it worked out well, right?"

Tina lets out a sigh. "That may be true, but honestly, Ange, I don't think you should do anything about it."

Angela freezes. "What?"

"It's such a *huge* confession, like you said."

"I know! That's why I think I need to find Nancy."

"But what good will it do? What if she doesn't want this information? It would upend her life. This is an enormous shock."

Angela sets her glass down again and pulls her knees back toward her chest, clutching the letter against her body. She feels somehow betrayed by Tina's reaction, though she doesn't quite know why. A lump forms in her throat. "But why shouldn't she know? Do you have any idea what it's like to be adopted and not know your birth mother?"

Tina touches her arm gently. "Of course I don't, hun. I wouldn't ever pretend to understand how that feels. But this Nancy person doesn't know what she doesn't know, right? And I just don't think it's your place to decide whether or not she has this information. It was her mother's place to tell her, but the letter never got delivered. I won't say maybe it was never *meant* to be delivered, but . . ." She shrugs. "Maybe it's just as well that Nancy never received it. Her mother died with peace of mind, thinking her daughter would receive her confession and go find her birth mother. But because it wasn't delivered, Nancy's life wasn't turned upside down with the knowledge."

"What are you saying?"

"I'm just saying maybe it's better this way. Maybe you should just leave well enough alone. If you go looking for Nancy, you could end up in the middle of something really messy."

Angela feels a surge of defensiveness. Tina is a women's studies professor at the university, still getting traction in her career. She's the rational sort who makes decisions based on evidence and fact and isn't as tuned in to her emotional side as Angela is. It's part of what makes them a good match, the way they counterbalance each other, but it means they sometimes butt heads.

"I felt like . . ." Angela takes a sip of her fake wine, now wishing it were alcohol. "I love my mom *so* much, but before I finally met Sheila, I felt like a piece of me was missing. Like there was this hole in my identity that nothing could fill but her. I felt like an incomplete puzzle, but I didn't even know what the missing piece looked like, you know? And after I found Sheila—"

A buzzer goes off in the kitchen.

"I'm so sorry, sweetheart, but the pasta's ready." Tina squeezes Angela's knee as she pushes herself up from the couch.

"Seriously, T?"

"If it overcooks, it'll be total shit. Just give me a sec." Tina rushes into the kitchen. There's more clanking of pots, then the gush of water as the pasta is drained. "Come on and eat," she calls.

Angela nudges Grizzly off her lap and counts to ten to calm herself down. She wanders into the dining room and refills her glass. Tina appears moments later with two steaming plates full of tender homemade tagliatelle and marinara sauce.

"Cheers," Tina says.

Angela clinks her glass with an ill grace, still mulling over her wife's reluctance. But how could she possibly understand? There's silence for a few minutes as they each dig hungrily into their dinner and Angela lets her thoughts marinate.

"The thing is," she says, "I have a different perspective on this than I would have had before."

Tina sets her fork down. "The pregnancies?" Her face seems to sag a bit as she says it.

Angela takes a sip of her drink to try to ward off the tears that are prickling. "I feel like a mother already, T. Regardless of . . . everything. And I just can't fathom Nancy not having this information when her birth mother and her adoptive mother both wanted her to know where she came from."

Tina holds Angela's eyes across the candles in the center of the table. The record plays quietly in the background.

"And this Margaret, the birth mother," Angela continues, "I know it's not the same thing, but she had a child forcibly taken away from her. Just imagine that for a second. You and I both know what it feels like to lose the *possibility* of a child. How exhausting it's been to chase motherhood. Sheila gave me up willingly, for reasons that made a lot of sense for her. But to be forced to give up your child, it's just . . ." Angela searches for a sufficient word, then shakes her head. "Unspeakably cruel, I guess. I can't not act on this."

Angela keeps eating out of respect for Tina's efforts with the meal, though her appetite has evaporated. She can sense the heat of Tina's gaze on her forehead.

"Okay. I get it," Tina says gently. "Do what you want to do, love. I just wanted to play devil's advocate, you know? I just think there's another side to this that you may not be fully considering because you're a bit . . . biased, I guess is the word for it. Clouded. Not everyone would choose the same thing you did. Not every adopted child wants to find their birth parents. And those who do, don't always find what they hoped to. They're not all like Sheila, you know? That's all I'm saying." Tina pushes her chair back with a scrape and steps over to Angela to plant a kiss on the top of her head. "Really, do what you want, Ange. I love you and I'll support you whatever you decide, okay?"

Angela sighs, avoiding Tina's eyes. She nods.

Tina squeezes her shoulder and collects Angela's plate and cutlery, stacking it on top of her own. "I'm gonna go get on the bike, if you don't mind. Work off some of this pasta."

"Sure."

There's a prickly tension between them now.

"What are you gonna do?"

"Oh." Angela hesitates. "Probably just finish this so-called wine and relax a bit. Maybe read a book."

"Okay. Love you."

"Love you, too."

Tina drifts off in the direction of the kitchen while Angela retrieves her phone from her purse. She flops back down on the couch, opens Facebook, and scrolls through the inane chatter and disconcertingly targeted ads in her news feed, pausing to like an occasional post. She isn't on social media much anymore. The never-ending stream of pregnancy announcements and baby photos just triggers rage in her. She knows it's unfair to feel that way, and that she should be happy for her friends' growing families, but sometimes—like now—the generosity of spirit she would like to feel gets weighed down by bitter jealousy.

When she hears the spare bedroom door shut, followed by the muffled *beep-beep-beep* of Tina turning on the stationary bicycle, Angela wanders down the hall, past the closed door where Tina has started her spin session, and turns the handle on the third bedroom door.

It's dark and cool in here. A faint whiff of paint still lingers in the air, weaving with the woody smell of new furniture. She only comes in here once in a while, usually when Tina isn't home, or when she's in the shower. Angela saw the look in Tina's eyes once when she caught her sitting in the rocker, clutching a teddy bear to her chest, imagining it were a baby.

Angela walks over to the dresser and switches on the small table lamp, setting her glass down beside it. The bulb casts a golden glow over the whole nursery as she sits down on the unworn cushion of the rocking chair. She glances over at the white slats of the crib to her left, the blankets folded neatly over the side of it in a rainbow of pastel colors. A mobile hangs from the ceiling, felt pieces in the shapes of elephants and giraffes are suspended in midair. The changing table beside the crib is well stocked with unopened diaper cream and brand-new flannel receiving blankets. They set up the nursery last year, back when they were temporarily overjoyed at the seeming success of their first round of fertility treatments. But now the room just feels fake and cold, a stage for a play that Angela fears will never be produced.

She heaves a deep breath, listens to the whirring of the bicycle in the room next door, the faint beats of up-tempo hip-hop music that clash with the serenity of the nursery. She looks up at the row of stuffed animals perched on the floating shelf on the wall across from her and wonders whether Margaret Roberts ever bought anything for her baby. Based on what she read in her web search today about the maternity homes, she doubts it. And then to have that child taken away from her, against her will . . .

Angela sees Tina's side of things, but she isn't sure doing nothing is truly an option now. She knows herself, and she knows this will eat at her. In Angela's experience, people regret the things they didn't do far more than the mistakes they actually made. It's *in*action that causes you to lie awake into the early hours of the morning, second-guessing your own judgment. It's the what-ifs and should-haves that crouch down deep in that buried chamber of your soul. They latch on tighter; their teeth are sharper.

With a sense of self-righteous recklessness, Angela reopens the Facebook app on her phone and types the name *Nancy Mitchell* into the search box. Several profiles pop up on her screen. She filters for the greater Toronto area, though Nancy could be living in Australia by now, for all she knows. But it's a place to start. She scrolls through the profiles, clicking on each one who looks vaguely the right age. She sees snapshots of the women's lives, some with open profiles and others with higher privacy settings. Photos taken on family vacations, the women's arms wrapped around the shoulders of sullen teenagers who grudgingly agreed to pose with their mother. Posts about hobbies, gardening, and crafting. Political opinions. Senses of humor. As the personalities and histories of the women take shape, Angela's fingers grow cold with nerves. Is she doing the right thing? There's a living, breathing woman on the other end of each profile whose life could be ruined with this bombshell now in Angela's possession.

She finds five Nancy Mitchells who fit the specs of her search. She types out a message to the first of them, then copies it and sends it to the others.

Hi, I work at a store called Thompson's Antiques & Used Books in downtown Toronto. I recently found a letter addressed to a Nancy Mitchell, and I wondered if you have ever had any connection to the store. If so, this letter might have been intended for you. Let me know. Thanks!

She sets her phone down on her knees and takes a deep breath, followed by what habit tells her will be a grounding swig of wine, though the non-alcoholic imitation does nothing to calm her nerves.

Two responses come back almost instantly, and Angela's heart leaps up into her throat. The first is a terse, *Not me.* The other is a more compassionate and polite decline, wishing her luck in finding the intended Nancy Mitchell. She feels both disappointed and immensely relieved, but still she waits another few minutes. When no other messages arrive in her in-box, she sets her phone down on the side table. Without noticing what she's doing, her other hand comes to rest on her own belly button.

"Oh, Margaret," she whispers to the young girl, a shadowy ghost in her mind's eye. "Did you ever find your baby girl?"

CHAPTER 6

Evelyn

· · · · · · · · · ·

WINTER 1960-1961

T he worst part of Christmas is the fact that the girls of St. Agnes's are spending the month of December clutching embossed red hymnals in their young, ringless hands while reluctantly belting out odes to a virgin and her baby.

On a snowy Sunday morning during the second week of Advent, Evelyn and Maggie sit side by side, their eyes on Father Leclerc at the front of the room, halfheartedly mouthing the words to "Hark! The Herald Angels Sing." Evelyn wonders how much conscious thought went into planning the carol sings and Advent Sunday hymns, and whether it had occurred to Father Leclerc at any point in the proceedings that singing about Mary and the Christ child might be reinforcing a sense of romantic longing in a group of girls who are meant to be giving up their own babies in a matter of weeks. The home's resident priest is a pale, doughy man with a voice like cold oatmeal. He shares their table to lead the saying of grace at mealtimes, serves Communion, conducts Bible study on Sundays, and offers confessionals for those who desire it, though Evelyn can't imagine why any of the girls would want to spend ten minutes alone with the man, expounding on their sins.

They finish the hymn and are permitted to sit down again. For the girls whose bellies are in full bloom now, the relief makes itself known in a chorus of sighs and grunts. Father Leclerc surveys them with the air of a man about to dig into a hearty meal, then begins his sermon.

"Everything that has happened to you in your life, everything that has happened at this home, and your time leading up to it, is God's will," he says with a smile. "Remember that, girls. Like Mary, your bodies are undertaking God's work . . ."

"Maybe *we* should have claimed our pregnancies were immaculate conception," one of the girls, Etheline, mutters under her breath from the row in front of Maggie and Evelyn. Her words are met with appreciative tittering from the others, but Evelyn looks around to check whether Sister Teresa might have overheard behind her. The Watchdog glares back at her through her thick glasses, fingers the whip in her belt loop, and gestures for Evelyn to face the front. She doesn't need telling twice.

"You are fulfilling the needs and desires of women who are not able to bear children," Father Leclerc continues, "which is also God's will. He always has His reasons for the trials that befall each and every one of us, and it is not for us to try to understand them."

Maggie shifts in her seat, clears her throat loudly. Evelyn glances over at her and sees that her neck and face are flushed red.

"Are you all right?" she whispers to her friend.

Maggie's jaw clenches, but she nods. "Shh."

Father Leclerc holds his Bible close to his chest, hugging it as one would a child. "When you feel saddened or hard done by or punished, remember that God alone chose for you to bear these children for the good women who cannot conceive their own. You must always accept God's will, fully and truly and without question. Remember that you can, clearly, conceive and bear children. At a later time in your lives, once you are married in the eyes of God, you can conceive again and bear *legitimate* children for your husbands."

Evelyn considers the priest's words as she runs her hand along her belly and feels a responsive kick from her baby—her baby who would be deemed a bastard by the Church, if she were able to keep it. She was so close to having been married in the eyes of God. Just a few more months, and her baby would have been legitimate, even if Leo had still died. If they had only been married, she would have been pitied as a mourning pregnant widow, would she not? Surely she would have been taken care of by her parents, instead of being hidden away in the dark halls and stuffy rooms of St. Agnes's. They would have welcomed a grandchild, and Evelyn would have been allowed to hang on to all that remained of her sweet Leo.

Father Leclerc's voice floats back to her as she fights the urge to weep. "What is one child given away, if you can go on to have more? You will see this child again in heaven. And in the meantime, he will make another good family so very happy, and that family can provide more than you ever could. Your baby could have the best life possible." After this pronouncement, his eyes search those of his young congregation again. "And you wouldn't want to cheat your baby out of the best, would you?"

. . . .

On a Thursday afternoon in early March, Evelyn pauses from her sweeping. She straightens up and leans her weight on the broom handle, trying to relax her back muscles. Her belly is big enough that it's weighing her down and causing strain. With only a few weeks left in her pregnancy, she's tired all the time now, and her hips ache constantly. After a moment's rest, she returns to her task.

She's just finishing with the dormitories when Sister Mary Helen approaches her. She's a heavy, stout young woman with dark brows and a brisk but pleasant enough demeanor.

"Could you sweep the offices downstairs as well, Evelyn?" she asks, shifting a teetering stack of linens from one arm to the other. "Lucille was supposed to, but she's come down with a terrible headache."

"Yes, okay," Evelyn says, sighing. Lucille has a notable talent for coming down with all manner of ailments when she's keen to avoid work.

"Thank you," Sister Helen says. "Once you're done, feel free to do what you like before dinner."

"Thank you, Sister."

Sister Mary Helen scurries down the staircase with the linens, muttering to no one in particular. Evelyn takes a moment to steady herself on the broom again before she follows the nun down the creaky stairs to the main floor. She hates going downstairs, since it means she'll have to heave herself all the way back up again.

On the first floor, she starts sweeping at the end of the long hallway that runs beside the kitchen wall, then makes her way toward Father Leclerc and Sister Teresa's offices near the storage closet. With a grunt, she kneels to coax the grit into the dustpan, catching a snippet of conversation through the open door of the Watchdog's office.

". . . adjust the pricing, Father. There is greater demand since last year."

"But this system is not intended to gouge the pocketbooks of good families, Sister."

Evelyn stops her sweeping and cranes her ear toward the office.

"Not gouging, Father, no. We would never do that, of course. All I am saying is that I think it would be prudent to . . . reflect the current market in our pricing scheme. Other homes are doing the same. They are charging what the market will bear. Babies are beginning to be purchased from overseas, and families will pay double for a white, Christian-born, local child. This home is a source of income for our parish and I believe we owe it to ourselves—and our parishioners—to ensure we are generating the highest possible return on our investment."

Evelyn's breath catches, solidifying in her lungs like cement. After a moment, Father Leclerc sighs, and Evelyn can picture him tapping his left foot, as he does during his sermons.

"I would be comfortable with a fifteen percent increase over last year, but no more. Let us see what the response is. This will not be retroactive to the families currently on the reservation list, correct?"

"No," Sister Teresa replies. "An increase going forward."

"All right, Sister. Well, dinner will be served soon, I imagine. I best go prepare for grace. I'll leave you to it."

"Thank you, Father."

The sound of wooden chair legs scraping against the floor shocks Evelyn into movement. Stunned, she struggles to her feet and shuffles as fast as she can back down the hallway, stashing the broom and dustpan in the hall closet near the kitchen. Her lungs fight to get a full breath as she rounds the banister at the bottom of the staircase and climbs as fast as she can to the second floor. Turning the corner at the landing, she nearly collides with Sister Agatha.

"Miss Evelyn! Oh, you gave me such a fright. What—?"

Evelyn pushes past the nun and rushes to her dormitory at the end of the hall. Maggie is on her bed and looks up from her novel in alarm.

"Evelyn? What's wrong?"

Evelyn's face crumples. Maggie holds her arms out and Evelyn falls into them as she cries into her shoulder.

Agatha appears at the door and gently closes it against the noise wafting up from downstairs as the girls begin to convene for dinner. "What happened?" she asks, her brows knitted in concern.

Maggie just shakes her head and rubs Evelyn's back. A minute later, Evelyn is cried out, and she sits up and turns to Agatha. "Did you know?" she demands.

Agatha frowns. "Did I know what?"

"That they're selling them? *Selling the babies*. Like puppies from a kennel!"

Agatha's hand whips up to her mouth in shock.

"What?" Maggie cries.

"Yes! I was just—" Evelyn pushes herself up off the bed, away from Maggie, and starts to pace the room. "I was just downstairs sweeping, and the Watch"—she corrects herself,—"Sister Teresa was in her office with Father Leclerc, and I overheard them talking about pricing schemes and the market and increasing the price of this year's . . ." Her throat is squeezing shut against the words. "Babies."

"Selling them?" Agatha asks, her face aghast.

"Yes!" Evelyn says, holding Agatha's gaze. She realizes the nun isn't much older than she is. She had always seemed older somehow. Drained, Evelyn hacks a heavy, mucus-filled cough, then slumps back on the bed.

"I swear I did not know," Agatha says. Her eyes are wide, darting back and forth between Evelyn and Maggie, who sit in stunned silence. When she speaks again, her voice is thick with emotion. "But I confess I don't know what to do with this information."

"How can we stay here?" Evelyn says to Maggie, then turns to Agatha. "How can *you* stay here? How can you continue to . . ." She can't find the words. "Adopting the babies is one thing, but *selling* them?"

Sister Agatha's chest rises and falls with a deep breath. "I will pray on it. I hope God will guide me. Perhaps He had Sister Teresa assign me the upstairs cleaning tonight for a reason. So that I could run into you and know this."

Maggie scoffs.

"I'm not sure I believe in that," Evelyn says.

"You don't have to."

"We need to get out of here, Sister Agatha. I can't let them sell my baby. *Leo's* baby. Oh my God. Maggie? What do we do?"

Maggie's eyes are heavy. "Evelyn, what do you mean, 'get out of here'? We have nowhere else to go."

. . . .

After speaking with Agatha, Evelyn goes to bed early and without dinner. With a twinge of guilt, she ignores Maggie's concerned inquiries, muttering that she's feeling nauseous and doesn't want to be disturbed. The truth is that she needs time and space to think, two things that are in short supply inside the home.

She desperately wants to confront Sister Teresa about the massive deception she's orchestrating against all the girls, but she doesn't even know where to begin. Her heart breaks for the other girls, for Maggie, but the selfish part of her is fixated on her own baby. What would Leo think of her, if she didn't at least try to prevent their child from being sold to some strange family?

By the time Evelyn has come to her decision, the other girls have finished dinner. She feigns sleep, holding her round belly as her baby rolls and pushes against her hands from inside. Legitimate or not, she knows this baby is a miracle. She lies awake long after her roommates are all in their beds. Maggie often has bad dreams and wakes up in a hot sweat, but the absence of whimpers in the bed beside Evelyn tells her that her friend is chasing sleep tonight, too.

The following day, Evelyn wanders down the hallway that is now filled with nothing but the damp smell of winter slush and the memory of the terrible conversation between the Watchdog and Father Leclerc.

"You may enter," Sister Teresa calls in response to Evelyn's polite knock.

Evelyn takes a deep breath, hitches a stiff smile onto her face, and turns the handle. She has only been in here once, shortly after the new year for her half-term health care update, which lasted less than five minutes. Now Sister Teresa is seated at her desk, surrounded by stacks of paper and a pile of addressed envelopes that catch Evelyn's eye; she recognizes her brother's address in her own handwriting on the top of the pile.

"Yes, Evelyn. What do you want?" The Watchdog's round face is tucked tightly beneath the fabric of her habit. The wire-rimmed glasses perch on top of a button nose, magnifying the coldness of the gray eyes behind them.

"Yes," Evelyn says, noting that the nun does not invite her to sit. She intends for this to be a short meeting.

"Yes, *Sister Teresa.*"

"Yes, Sister Teresa."

"What do you wish to speak to me about? Make it quick, Evelyn. I am rather busy at the moment and, if I am not mistaken, I believe you should be in the kitchen right now."

Evelyn clears her throat and rests her hands on her large belly. "It's about my baby, Sister. I'm *not* reconsidering an adoption, but I—I was rather hoping my brother and his wife might be willing to take it."

"Mmm. I see." Sister Teresa sets her pencil down and surveys Evelyn, who stands straighter, squaring her shoulders and trying to look more mature, like a woman who can make her own decisions. But the nun's gaze nails her to the office wall like a pin in a butterfly specimen and she feels even smaller than before.

"Do you know, Evelyn, that while you are staying here with us, you are housed, fed, and clothed, completely free of charge?"

Evelyn wants to shift her weight but keeps her feet firmly in place. "Yes, Sister Teresa."

"We do not charge a housing fee here because the work we do is philanthropic, driven solely by our faith and our love for God. Our mission is to reform our girls and show them a path, light the way with the love of our Lord and Savior. In return, we expect obedience, humility, adherence to the rules of our faith and this establishment, and that you work for your keep. That is all we demand in return. If you want to give your baby to your brother, then he and his wife can house you, feed you, clothe you, reform you, and provide corrective nourishment for your wayward soul. If they are, as you suggest, so interested in the prospect of adopting your child, I would assume this option was offered to them prior to your mother making the arrangement for you to stay with us?"

Evelyn's mouth has gone dry. "I don't know. I wasn't—No one asked me."

"You will relinquish your baby at the end of your term. That is all."

"But I've written to my brother already." Evelyn finds her voice again, gestures at the envelope on the warden's desk. "I truly believe he might say yes!" Her hopeful eyes search the Watchdog's face for some trace of compassion or understanding, some long-forgotten depth of feeling.

But the nun's mouth twists into a sneer of a smile, revealing a straight line of pure white teeth. "Well, then. Let's just wait and see if he responds, shall we?"

. . . .

That evening, Evelyn and Maggie spend their pre-bedtime hour down in the parlor near the fireplace, huddled up against the late winter's chill with three other girls and a pot of weak tea.

Despite the circumstances, the atmosphere of the room is quite pleasant. The fire crackles away in the grate, releasing the wintry scent of cedar and smoke into the air as the shadows from the golden flames dance across the worn rug. The other girls chat away on the couch, their teacups balanced on their bellies, their knitting forgotten, while Evelyn and Maggie engage in a heavy conversation in the wing chairs in the corner of the room. It's the first opportunity they've had to discuss yesterday's revelation in relative privacy.

"How is this allowed?" Evelyn hisses at Maggie. "It must be illegal! Don't the adoptive parents know that?"

Maggie shakes her head. "I don't know."

"Surely Sister Agatha could do something if she tried—"

"I truly don't think she can," Maggie says, momentarily taking her eyes off the pair of yellow booties she's been knitting. "What would become of her? This is her life. She doesn't know anything else. She was appalled, she knows it's wrong, but . . ."

Evelyn shifts; she can't get comfortable in any position lately. "I spent my spare time before dinner writing another letter to my parents and my brother. I told them they're selling the babies, and that they need to come get me. I think you should do the same, Maggie."

Maggie stares at the booties in her hands, but her needles have stopped clicking. "Evelyn, they read all of our mail, remember? The Watchdog is going to see that. She must have already seen the one you sent your brother. You said it was on her desk when you went in there?"

Evelyn nods.

"Then how do we even know they're posting our letters at all? I've written to my family, too, and they never write back. And besides, my parents won't believe me. They never believe me. That's how I ended up in here to begin with." Maggie looks up at her now and swallows a knot that goes down like dry toast. "They didn't believe their friend would . . . you know. Do such a thing." Her face turns a blotchy red.

"Oh, Maggie," Evelyn says. This is exactly what she suspected all along. But her friend waves a hand.

"I don't really want to talk about it. I'm sorry. I just can't. I'll tell you one day, I promise."

Evelyn nods, though she feels a rush of rage on Maggie's behalf. "That's okay."

Maggie returns to her knitting. "Blast," she curses under her breath. "Dropped a stitch."

Evelyn looks across the room at the three other girls, chatting by the fireplace. She knows Bridget, the redheaded one in the middle of the couch, actually *wants* to be here. She became pregnant by her boyfriend and requested to come wait out her term at the home so as not to develop a *reputation* at school. Friends think she's gone to an aunt's to help cook and clean while her aunt copes with cancer. But Evelyn wonders what kind of secrets the other two might be hiding. People are good at keeping secrets. That's why all these girls are at St. Agnes's in the first place.

"Hello, girls." Sister Agatha appears in the archway, a large brown teapot in hand. "I thought you could use a little warm-up."

Maggie beams up at the nun, her eyes shining. "Thank you, Sister Agatha, you're very kind." She gives Evelyn a pointed look.

"Thank you, Sister Agatha," Evelyn chimes in. She still doesn't trust the nun entirely.

"Oh, it's no bother. Lights out in a half hour, though, eh?"

"We will," Maggie assures her.

Agatha picks up the old tepid teapot and drifts off back down the hallway to the kitchen. There's a long pause as both Evelyn and Maggie mull over their own thoughts.

"I feel like we need to get out," Evelyn says quietly.

Maggie looks up from her yarn. "You already said that. What do you mean, 'get out'?"

"I mean *get out.* Escape."

"The doors are dead-bolted, haven't you noticed? They've designed this place so there's nowhere to hide."

Evelyn eyes her friend. "You were looking?"

Maggie flushes. "Back around Christmas, after Father Leclerc's sermon that made me so angry. I had a look at the doors in the kitchen and the front hall. They have the usual locks, but also dead bolts. So who has the keys? I bet you only the Watchdog, on that ring on her belt. God help us if there's ever a fire."

"Be that as it may, I've been trying to think of a plan." Evelyn drops her voice so low that Maggie has to move her chair closer until the arm is touching Evelyn's. She notices Bridget glance over at them.

"Evelyn, I don't have anywhere to go, even if we did escape," Maggie says, her shoulders slumping.

Evelyn hesitates. "What if you came with me? To my parents' house, I mean, or my brother's?"

Maggie shakes her head, looks up at the clock on the mantel. It's nearly time for bed. She pushes herself up, belly-first, from the chair. "Would you just drop it, Evelyn?" she hisses. "What you're suggesting is a fantasy. This—here—" She gestures around the room, though her eyes are locked on Evelyn's in the firelight. "This is my reality. I have nowhere to go. Period. We're weeks away from delivering. There is no solution here. We just have to deal with it and hope to God we might be able to find our babies after we leave."

"Maggie—" Evelyn begins, mortified at having upset her friend so.

Maggie snatches up the yellow booties. "Please just stop talking about it, okay? Make your own plans, do what you want, to find a way out. But I can't ride along on the coattails of this delusion of yours, Evelyn. I'm sorry. Good night."

And she waddles from the room, leaving Evelyn alone.

CHAPTER 7

Nancy

. . . .

SPRING 1980

"Did I ever tell you about the cloak I made your mother for her wedding day?" Grandmama asks Nancy.

From her perch on a hard chair beside her grandmother's bed at the nursing home, Nancy smiles. "No, I don't think you have."

She has, on a number of occasions, but Nancy plays along.

Her grandmama's health has been declining for years. Back in the fall, after a serious incident involving a set of lace curtains that caught fire and nearly burned the house down—and much passive-aggressive posturing—Grandmama and Nancy's mum agreed that a nursing home was the best place for her to live out her remaining years. Alternating between a very English stiff upper lip and a trembling lower one, Grandmama moved into St. Sebastian's Home for the Aged. Nancy visits her every Tuesday night for a cup of tea and a chat, which almost always involves examinations of The Past.

Grandmama refers to it that way, too, the capitalization clear in her reverent tone and the way she waves her withered hand through the air as though casting a spell when she says it.

The Past, my dear.

All the many memories, the regrets and triumphs, joys and sorrows, incidents and mundanities that are stitched together by the threads of time and bound into the great tapestry of one's life. The Past, depicted one square of fabric at a time. The squares that Grandmama likes to take out and examine whenever Nancy visits her.

Nancy often thinks Grandmama wants to review The Past with her more than anyone else because her granddaughter is an impartial judge. Whenever Grandmama presses her for an analytical eye, Nancy always stays neutral. What would it accomplish to criticize her grandmother's decisions at this point in the old woman's life? It's not as though she can change them, and calling attention to glaring inconsistencies or times when her grandmother was unnecessarily harsh or unfair serves no purpose other than to distress a dying octogenarian.

"It was a freezing cold winter day when your parents got married," Grandmama says now. "An evening ceremony, you know. In January. I told your mother a June wedding was more fitting, like her sisters had, but she wouldn't agree, of course."

Nancy's mother and Grandmama butted heads about almost everything. Evidently, obstinacy is a proud family tradition.

"It was so soon after your father proposed at Christmastime, but I suspect she wanted to get going on having a baby. Didn't want to wait any longer. And we all know how that turned out," she adds, reaching a papery hand over to pat Nancy's knee. "At any rate, I told her that if she simply *insisted* upon winter nuptials, she must at least allow me to make her a cloak to wear over her dress.

"White silk on the outside, it was, with a big hood, and I sewed a beautiful emerald velvet lining into it. When they came out of the church and stood on the front steps, the snow had just started falling. It was quite a sight, I must admit. Nothing compared to the sun and blooms of a June wedding, but still lovely in its own way."

"It does sound lovely, Grandmama," Nancy says. "I've seen photos, but she isn't wearing the cloak. I think they were taken inside the church."

"Your parents had the reception back at our house, your Grandpapa and I," Grandmama continues. Nancy isn't even sure she heard her reply. "A simple affair, but that's what people did in those days. They didn't have a house of their own yet. They were about to move into that little one out in the Danforth—tiny thing it was, too."

Nancy half listens as her thoughts start to wander to the schoolwork waiting for her at home. An essay on the Vietnam War.

"It took another few years before they were able to afford that nice place in the Annex. I think that was right around the time they got you."

Nancy's mind is pulled back to the present. "*Got* me?" she asks. "You mean *had* me?"

As Grandmama has gotten closer to The End (also capitalized), she's displayed less and less restraint while sorting through The Past. Lately, she hasn't been careful with the delicate memories, and has let several fall and shatter at her own feet before muttering, "Never mind, dear, I didn't mean that," as she does now.

This time, though, Nancy is undeterred. "No, Grandmama, what do you mean by that? What do you mean 'got me'?"

"Oh, Nancy," Grandmama says, brushing away the incriminating words still lingering in the air between them. "I meant when they had you, of course. I misspoke. I'm tired, my dear. I think it's best that you head home now. I'll see you again next week. Come give us a kiss, now, and be on your way."

But as Nancy descends the creaking staircase of the old manor house, a deeply uncomfortable suspicion begins to stir within her being. Because these disjointed pieces all add up to something. Questions to her mother that went unanswered as a child. The fact that she doesn't really look like either of her parents—a reality her mother has continually written off with an airy wave of her hand as she chuckles. "Genes do sometimes skip a generation. More tea, dear?"

It's just a series of gut feelings Nancy can't seem to connect with anything stronger than the weakest thread.

Until now, the idea was just an undefined, shapeless shadow in a dark corner of Nancy's brain. But her grandmama's comments echo in her mind as she boards the subway car that takes her back to her apartment. The thoughts continue to whir when she arrives home and shuts her bedroom door behind her.

It's as though something dark has latched onto her heart. She already knew it was there, though she couldn't sense its edges yet. But when she crawls into bed still fully clothed, Nancy can finally feel the prickly outline of the shadow, a truth she had previously been determined to ignore.

· · · · · · · · · ·

Three days later, Nancy finds herself standing on the front porch of her parents' house, staring at the familiar silver door knocker, a large M wrapped in twists of ivy. She considers the name for a brief moment, contemplates her own identity with it.

Of course you're a Mitchell, she tells herself. *This is ridiculous. You should just turn around and go home.*

But a persistent voice in Nancy's mind argues back.

Then why can't you let this go? Why haven't you just dismissed it as the ramblings of an old woman whose mind is on the decline?

And the truth is, she's already starting to regret this plan. When she learned that her parents would be going out to dinner tonight with their friends the Morgensterns, she invited herself over for afternoon tea, telling her mother she needed a quiet place to study for the evening.

"I'm just going to do some homework here, Mum, if you don't mind," she'd said on the phone. "It gets too loud here at the apartment, and I really need to get down to work on this final English paper." She crossed her legs at the ankle then, to keep her feet from jiggling with nerves. "Besides, your couch is way more comfortable than mine."

Her mother sighed. "Well, you didn't have to move out, you know."

"I know, Mum."

Except her apartment isn't that noisy; her two roommates are generally reasonable. She's here to search her parents' room for information. She doesn't know what she's looking for, exactly. Just some form of confirmation that what Grandmama told her might be true.

Or hopefully not.

Screwing up her nerve, Nancy is just about to reach into her purse for her key when her mother opens the front door.

"Nancy, dear, whatever are you doing lurking out here on the porch? You'll catch your death. It's freezing out."

"It's ten degrees, Mum," Nancy says, stepping over the threshold and shutting the door behind her. "And besides, that's not how viruses work."

Frances clicks her tongue at her daughter with an exaggerated eye roll. "Yes, yes, you're very clever."

"Good to see you, Mum," Nancy says, planting a kiss on her heavily powdered cheek. Her mother air-kisses her back through salmon-pink lipstick.

Nancy hangs her coat and purse on a hook in the wall, kicks off her hiking boots, then sets them neatly on the boot tray as her mother watches with a critical eye. Frances reaches down and picks up a speck of mud that shook loose from the sole of Nancy's boot, opens the front door, and tosses it out onto the porch. Nancy smiles tightly.

"Is the tea on already?" she asks, knowing it will be. "Can I lend a hand?"

"No, no, dear, come on in and sit down. I hate it when you act like a guest."

"Sorry, Mum."

"Oh, never mind," Frances says. "Your father says you need your independence and all that. I've just never quite *adjusted*. You know that."

Nancy nods and flops down on the couch. "I know. I'm sorry it's hard for you."

Frances pats a curl on top of her head. "Yes, well, time for tea, then." She bustles off to the kitchen and returns a minute later with a platter of Peak Freans cookies and over-milked orange pekoe.

"Is Dad here?" Nancy asks, leaning forward to take a raspberry cream cookie.

"He's just upstairs finishing getting ready. He'll be down." Frances settles herself on a large wing chair and pours tea for them both. "I have something for you, just there." She indicates a shopping bag from the Bay that Nancy hadn't noticed. "Open it!"

"Aw, Mum, you didn't have to do that." Nancy's insides squirm with guilt.

"Yes, I did. I saw it and thought it was gorgeous, just your colors!"

Nancy pulls the bag toward her. Reaching in, she lifts out a dress. It's blue and pink floral with puffy sleeves, something Nancy wouldn't be caught dead in.

"I was just thinking you'll want something nice for dates and things. You'll never impress Mr. Right with all that denim you wear. And those big sweaters do nothing for your figure, dear."

Nancy takes a deep breath and lowers the dress back into the bag. "Thanks, Mum, it's lovely."

Frances smiles over the rim of the Royal Doulton. "I'm glad you like it. And on the subject of dresses, I have some rather big news. Clara and Anthony are engaged to be married!"

"Oh my gosh, wow!" Nancy feigns surprise. Clara had called her a week ago to deliver the news, which Nancy felt was less than cause for celebration. For one thing, Nancy thought Clara could do a whole lot better than her mercurial, vituperative boyfriend Anthony. And for another, she knew this news would spark a renewed determination in Frances to see Nancy married off at the earliest opportunity. Nancy just hadn't predicted that determination would arrive in the form of a puffy-sleeved floral dress.

"Lois called me yesterday to relay the news," her mother continues. "It sounds like Clara's decided not to go to school and to get married instead." Her gaze lingers on her daughter.

"Mum," Nancy says, "you can do both nowadays, you know. Marriage doesn't have to preclude school, and vice versa."

"There'll be an announcement in this weekend's paper," Frances says, ignoring Nancy's comment. "So I imagine we'll all be off to a wedding not long from now. I thought maybe you could wear that new dress, too. I'm sure there will be lots of eligible young men there to catch your eye."

She winks at Nancy, who forces down a sip of tea. As much as she likes Clara, she's already considering how she can weasel out of having to attend the wedding. A poorly timed exam might do the trick. And besides, she's had trouble seeing Clara at family events ever since That Night. The sight of her cousin just brings back a host of memories she's tried very hard to forget.

Blond hair splayed out on a black pillowcase.

Blood on her jeans in a cold hospital waiting room.

A mysterious woman named Jane.

She and Clara haven't ever spoken about it. What was there to talk about, really? It's a secret between the two of them, no one else's business. If Nancy were in Clara's shoes, she would probably never want to talk about it again, either.

Just keep yourself to yourself.

"Are you quite all right, dear?" Frances's voice filters through the images running through Nancy's mind.

"Of course. Yeah. Very exciting for them."

Nancy drinks her tea in silence and allows Frances to wax critical about the style of wedding Clara might have, taking into account her sister Lois's dreadful taste in color palettes. Mercifully, Nancy's dad emerges from upstairs a few minutes later.

"Hey, there, Beetle," he says, pulling Nancy into a tight hug. "Good to see you. I overheard your mother pushing her marriage agenda on you. Thought you might need a rescue."

"Bill!" Frances cries. "I was not—"

"Yes, you were, dear."

Nancy chuckles, but softens at the hurt look on her mother's face. "It's okay, Mum. Thanks for the dress. You guys should, uh, get going."

She swallows on a tight throat, considers whether to abandon this reconnaissance mission, which in all likelihood will turn up nothing at all.

"We should," Frances agrees. "I just need to go freshen my lips. Be back in a wink. Oh, and Nancy," she adds. "When you leave, be sure to check the freezer. I've set aside some shepherd's pie leftovers for you to take back to the apartment."

"Jesus H, Frances, the girl knows how to feed herself," Nancy's dad says.

"I know she can feed herself!" Frances says, stung. "A mother just has an inherent need to feed the child she loves. You two need to cut me a little slack, you know. I'm trying."

Waiting in the hallway, Nancy does her best to shake off the dark shadow that's settled around her shoulders. Five minutes later, she hugs both her parents and waves from the front porch as they pull out of the driveway. Her mother waves back out of the open car window, chubby hands stuffed into those silly out-of-date gloves that only English royalty wear anymore.

"It's a mark of refinement for a lady to wear gloves to a fancy affair," her mother always says, but Nancy knows Frances wears the gloves because they cover her perpetually bitten-down nails and ragged red cuticles, and the thick scar on the back of her left hand, a souvenir from a kitchen accident that occurred long before Nancy was born.

And it's not just the gloves. There's a decorative bowl on the dining room table that no one is allowed to move or use. Its only purpose in life is to camouflage a large watermark from a long-ago carelessly placed glass. Frances has repapered the upstairs hallway seven times over the past ten years, anytime a piece gets nicked or torn or starts to fade. Furniture gets rearranged to cover stains and the wear from foot traffic on the carpet. Her mother's few early gray hairs are dyed at the hairdresser's on a biweekly basis. Nancy has never even seen her without makeup on. Her mother has hidden all manner of imperfections for as long as Nancy can remember.

She waits in the living room to make sure her parents don't return for anything; her mother almost always forgets to bring a shawl. The rest of the house is silent, but the huge old cherrywood grandfather clock ticks away as Nancy chews on her fingernails, staring blankly at the wings of the pink patterned armchair.

After fifteen minutes, Nancy is quite sure her parents aren't coming back anytime soon. She doesn't hesitate as she climbs the stairs and takes a right at the top of the landing instead of turning left toward her old bedroom. She doesn't know the creaks in the floor on this side of the hallway, and it's an unfamiliar feeling to turn the knob on her parents' bedroom door. It seems like an invasion of their privacy, a display of her lack of trust. Her heart hurts at the thought.

But it's true. I don't trust them. Not about this, anyway.

What had her grandmama said? *That was right around the time they got you.* The words reverberate as Nancy wrestles down the anxiety that flickers in her chest. She pushes the door open and steps into the darkness of the large master bedroom. The air is still and smells strongly of her mother's hair spray and perfume—a French jasmine blend Nancy's father gives her every Christmas, even though he doesn't like the scent. She would have spritzed herself in it before she pulled on those white lace gloves and set her hair for the fourth time.

Nancy's fingers fumble on the wall just inside the door until she finds the light switch and flicks it on. She strides across the rug toward her mother's dresser. If her parents are hiding something, she has a feeling that it will be in The Drawer.

The Drawer is a family reference of sorts, her mother's hiding place for special birthday gifts, important documents like her parents' marriage certificate, her father's checkbook, and her mother's two expensive pieces of jewelry: her engagement ring, too tight to be worn now, and a pearl necklace Grandmama gave her on her fortieth birthday. Nancy looks over her shoulder again, ears straining for the sound of a car door opening, a key in the lock, her father's deep booming voice echoing up the stairs. But there's nothing and no one to stop her.

She half wishes there were.

Nancy licks her dry lips and pulls The Drawer open with some difficulty. It isn't often used and the mechanism doesn't slide smoothly. She's only opened this drawer once—back when she was a child and at her mother's request—to retrieve the pearls. Her parents were off to "the fanciest damn wedding we've ever had to attend," as her father put it. Nancy recalls that moment now as she looks down at the navy velvet box that holds the necklace.

There's an assortment of other items: important-looking envelopes, a few sets of lace gloves, and the purple box Nancy assumes must contain the sapphire engagement ring that, with a strange twinge in her gut, she realizes will one day be hers. She takes note of the placement of the items and tries to commit it to memory so she can return everything to its proper place once she's finished. Then, heart banging in her throat, Nancy lifts out the jewelry boxes and gloves, and inspects the envelopes one by one, careful not to tear any of the unsealed flaps. But it's just the documents she already assumed were in there: wills and house deeds and other boring adult paperwork. She stacks them in a neat pile on the dresser, then checks the back of The Drawer. As she pushes aside her own ivory lace christening gown, her hand brushes soft leather. Nancy wiggles her fingers into the tight space and nudges the little case forward. With a leap in her stomach, she sets it on the carpet and kneels beside it.

She stares at the box for a moment. It's unfamiliar, a small brown leather case with a little handle, not in keeping with her mother's delicate, feminine taste, and she wonders if it's her father's. Tilting it up, Nancy sees the metal dials along the mouth of the box, not unlike the combination lock on a man's briefcase. She tries to depress the latch, but the lock won't open.

"Shoot."

This must *be it*, Nancy thinks. Her parents don't even have a lock on their own bedroom door. Generally speaking, they don't have anything to hide. Or at least, that's what Nancy had thought all her life, right up until this moment.

Nancy examines the box again. There are six brass dials, each with the numbers 0 through 9. Six digits. She sits back on her heels and chews her lip. What could possibly be so secret that her parents went to the trouble to lock it up and tuck it away from her, their only child? This box has something to do with her, she knows it. But what could it be?

Her school report cards aren't important enough to be under lock and key. Old love letters from an ex, maybe? She can't imagine either of her parents ever exchanging romantic letters with a lover, let alone keeping them after the flame was out. Is it her birth certificate, the one her mother says got lost and needs to be replaced?

Her birth certificate.

Her birthday?

Nancy holds her breath and spins the first dial to 0. She exhales and enters the remaining digits: 4—2—5—6—1. She jams her finger against the spring lock.

It doesn't budge.

"Seriously?" she mutters. She was sure her birthday would work. Her mother isn't very creative. Nancy's legs are getting pins and needles from kneeling. She tries to stand, but stumbles and throws her arm out, catching the edge of the chest of drawers for support.

"Bloody foot."

Bracing herself against the chest with one hand, Nancy reaches down and massages her toes, wincing against the discomfort. Then she smiles to herself. She may well be her mother's daughter; the English slang has certainly rubbed off.

There is one beat of shivering time, just one tick of the clock on the wall before the thought slides into place in her mind. Nancy throws herself back down onto the carpet next to the box. Her foot is painful, but she hardly notices.

Her breath is suspended as she spins the first four dials again, entering her birth date first, then the month, the way the English do.

2—5—0—4—6—1 . . .

CHAPTER 8

Evelyn

. . . .

SPRING 1961

"Well, then," Sister Teresa barks, "it's time for you to go to the hospital. Stay here and get your birth bag from underneath the bed. We will call you a taxi."

Evelyn holds her belly as a wave of panic washes over her aching body. "A taxi? Does—does someone come with me? What do I do?"

Without answering, the Watchdog sweeps from the room, her habit whispering along the floorboards. Evelyn takes shallow breaths, squirming to get comfortable on her hard mattress. She looks at Maggie, sitting up in bed with her legs crossed, her huge belly resting in her lap like a heavy sack, arms wrapped around it. Louise and Anne peer over at her from their beds, their eyes reflecting Evelyn's fear in the golden light of their bedside lamps.

"Are you okay?" Maggie asks.

Evelyn shrugs and lets out a ragged laugh. "I don't know, Maggie. I don't know."

She woke up to the pain a few minutes ago with only a faint presumption that she was probably in labor. It's only now, as the cramps have begun deep in her pelvis and hips ("contractions," Sister Teresa called them a moment ago), that Evelyn realizes how entirely unprepared she is for this. Throughout the months she's been at the home, Sister Teresa, the nuns, and Father Leclerc have only ever focused on what should happen *after*.

After you get out of here, you can move on with your life.

After you give birth, you'll go find a nice boy and get married, do this properly next time.

After, you can pretend like this whole big mess never happened.

After.

The ordeal of childbirth was never discussed. The *during*. The thing itself. The girls have all come here to give birth, yet that's the one thing no one has prepared them for.

"What happens now?" Evelyn asks aloud, alarm rising in her voice. "What's it like?"

But no one answers. Maggie just cradles her belly, Anne stares up at the water-stained ceiling, and Louise closes her eyes tightly as though trying hard to imagine she's somewhere else. The only girls who can answer are the ones who are already gone. The ones who stay on to pay off their keep are kept in separate postpartum quarters, assigned different tasks.

Despite Evelyn's surge of determination that she and Maggie needed to find a way to escape the home, she wasn't able to come up with a feasible plan for such a rebellion. They weren't wanted at their family homes, and there was nowhere else two pregnant girls could go. They'd end up begging on the street. Maggie was right. The maternity home was their only option.

With a crushing realization, Evelyn finally accepts in this moment that the home, this system, is just one big well-oiled machine. Every cog is carefully designed for a specific purpose: selling children to desperate couples. The girls don't actually matter. It's nothing but a baby factory disguised as a reform mission, and it's Evelyn's turn to churn out the next product.

Bile rises in her throat at the thought, and Evelyn releases the sob she's been fighting against. Maggie rises from her bed and steps across to Evelyn's, pulling her into as tight a hug as she can with their bellies bumping between them.

"I'll miss you, Evelyn," Maggie whispers. "Good luck."

"Excuse me!" The Watchdog is back at the door, snapping her reprimand. "Have you forgotten yourselves? No physical contact between inmates!"

Evelyn glares at the Watchdog over Maggie's shoulder, and feels a rush of pure hatred for the woman. The girls pull apart. Maggie nods encouragingly and offers Evelyn a smile that doesn't quite meet her eyes. Evelyn picks up the traveling case she prepared last week, wipes her eyes with the back of her hand, and follows the nun out the door.

. . . .

The taxi pulls up outside the hospital. Evelyn rubs one hand along her belly and clenches the handle of her traveling case with the other. Her knuckles stand out stark white with the effort it takes for her to cling to these last few hours, the shred of precious time before everything changes. For now, her baby is still her baby, and the impossible gravity of saying a final goodbye to her child hasn't yet weighed her down, cracked her like splintering wood.

"Here we are, miss," the driver says, looking over his shoulder at her. His voice has a little purr on the r's, a Scottish lilt.

Evelyn nods once and reaches for the door handle.

"No, no, sweetheart, ye stay put. Let me get the door for ye."

The driver darts around the car, head bent against the cold spring rain that pours down and beads on the windows. The yellow and red lights on the outside of the hospital glitter through the raindrops like Christmas. The door opens beside her and the driver reaches in.

"I'll take yer case, miss," he says.

He transfers it into his other hand, then holds out his forearm to steady her as she gets out of the car. She managed to compose herself throughout the contractions in the back of the taxi, clenching her teeth against the pain, but this gesture from a stranger brings the tears back to her eyes. She stands on the slick sidewalk and he hands her the case with a small smile.

She offers him the bills. "I'm sorry. I can't tip you. This is all they gave me."

"S'okay, miss!" he says, taking the money. He doesn't even count it, just stuffs it into his pocket. "You take care of yerself, now, and God bless ye and that babe."

The rain is soaking her face. "Thank you, sir."

And without thinking about what she's doing, Evelyn takes a step forward and wraps her arms around the man. His body stiffens in a moment of hesitation before he responds in kind, patting her head with a paternal hand, and Evelyn feels more connected to the world and to her own body than she has in months. She closes her eyes and breathes in the unfamiliar smell of the man.

"Thank you," Evelyn mutters again in his ear. The rain drips off his hat, landing with a tickle on her nose.

"Least I can do, miss," he answers, then releases her. "I've got a daughter about yer age. I wouldn' wan' her comin' here all alone like this." Their eyes meet again briefly before he jogs back around the front of the car and hops into his seat, shutting the door with a dull thud.

The taxi pulls away from the curb as another contraction grips her and she nearly doubles over on the sidewalk. Resigning herself to it, she stumbles to the doors of the hospital. Her globe of a belly precedes her, announcing the title of her shame as her traveling case smacks against her damp thigh.

Two young women in the lobby stare at her through the glass door, their mouths moving. Neither of them comes to help as Evelyn struggles with the door. She keeps her head down, avoiding their eyes.

It's not that she's too young, she knows. Plenty of girls her age have babies. It's that—like the taxi driver said—she's alone. She's come to the hospital to give birth with no chaperone or companion at all. No husband, no mother. The conclusion is drawn long before Evelyn has even reached the reception desk.

"Um, excuse me," Evelyn says to the nurse. She has bright red hair and gray eyes, lips stained around a pinched mouth that loves to gossip. "I, um, I need to . . ." Her voice drops. "I'm here to have a baby."

"St. Agnes?" the nurse asks loudly. Her voice echoes into the white space.

"Yes, how did you—?"

The nurse stands and indicates that Evelyn should follow her. "This way, come on."

Evelyn's wet shoes squeak on the tile floor as she trails the nurse down the hallway like a waddling duckling. She can feel her face burning hotter with each person she passes, and breathes a sigh of relief when they finally step into the elevator and the doors close, offering a moment of privacy and dignity, however brief. The nurse presses the number 4 and the elevator lurches upward.

"The matron from St. Agnes's called and told us to expect you," the nurse finally says.

Evelyn nods and looks up at the floor indicator.

"You're not the first," the nurse continues. "And you certainly won't be the last. Just don't think too much about it. It'll be over soon."

The doors open. Evelyn blinks away the tears that have sprung to her eyes again and tries to keep up with the nurse's quick pace. They make a right turn, then reach a set of doors with a sign declaring the hallway beyond it the maternity ward. To the left is a waiting area full of chairs. There are two men sitting in them, bleary-eyed under a cloud of thick cigarette smoke. One of them is sleeping, slumped over in his chair. The other has his ankle crossed over the opposite knee, cigarette in one hand, flipping through a newspaper laid out in his lap. Like he's sitting in the park on a Sunday afternoon with not a care in the world.

The nurse pushes through the doors and Evelyn follows.

"That man back there," the nurse says, not making eye contact with Evelyn. "Wife is in labor bringing their sixth baby into the world. Told me she only ever wanted three. Poor thing."

They pass a couple of rooms, and Evelyn catches glimpses of pink bedspreads, yellow curtains, and bouquets of flowers propped up in vases. The nurse leads her down to the last room at the end of the long hallway, and Evelyn's breath hitches. The tiny room has a sad, institutional air about it. Lank beige drapes hang over the single window, a thin wool blanket covers the narrow bed, and the floor space is limited even further by dozens of brown cardboard boxes stacked four feet high along two of the walls.

"It's a bit of a squeeze in here, I'm afraid. It doubles as a storeroom for the ward." The nurse pulls a hospital gown out of a small metal dresser beside the bed, thrusts it into Evelyn's free hand. "Get changed into that. Settle yourself down in bed and the doctor will come see you when he does his rounds later on."

Evelyn nods, takes the gown.

"There's a bathroom across the hall if you need to pee." The nurse pauses, a flicker of compassion in her heavily lined eyes. "What did you say your name was?"

Evelyn clears her pinched throat. "Evelyn."

"Evelyn what?"

She's been denied her own last name for so long now. The question stirs something inside her, a thirst for something true. "Taylor. Evelyn Taylor."

"All right, Evelyn Taylor, I'll let the doctor know and we'll start you a chart." She turns to leave.

"What happens?" The words burst from Evelyn's mouth before she can stop them.

The nurse lets out a sigh. "They don't tell you girls much, do they?"

Evelyn shakes her head. "No. Nothing."

The nurse shrugs a shoulder. "It's not really for me to say, but it's painful. Be prepared for that. And it could be a long night. You girls are usually here for a few days if nothing goes wrong, then you're discharged back to the home."

"What do you mean, 'if nothing goes wrong'?"

"If there are no complications with the birth or the baby. If you start to heal up okay, if there's no infections."

Evelyn's face burns with embarrassment at her own ignorance, but she's desperate to know what's coming in the home stretch, the final stage of her ordeal. "What do you mean, 'heal up'?"

The nurse's eyes flit to the clock on the wall. Someone's being paged over the speakers. She meets Evelyn's eyes. "Honey, having a baby rips you up. All between your legs will be sore. You'll probably have stitches. And if we have to do a cesarean, you'll have a big incision."

Evelyn can't keep up. "What's a—what you just said?"

"A cesarean section, a C-section. It's when the doctor has to cut you open to get the baby out. But he'll try not to do that, don't worry."

Evelyn's panic tightens in her chest. "What do you mean, 'cut—'"

"I'm sorry, but I don't have time for this. I have to get back to the desk. Get your gown on and get into bed. Good luck."

She turns and leaves Evelyn alone in the room. Evelyn lays her traveling case down beside the narrow bed and peels off her wet stockings with difficulty, leaning over her enormous belly as the contractions squeeze and pulsate. She cries out once, but bites down on her bottom lip, pinching her eyes shut against the pain. A minute later when it finally subsides, Evelyn opens her eyes, breathes in deeply, then lets it out in a long exhale. As the nurse said, this could be a long night.

Down the corridor, a woman lets out a cry. She hears a man's stern voice responding, then the ticking of the clock on the wall. It counts down the seconds for her—the time she has left before her baby is born, before she might be cut open by this faceless butcher-doctor.

Evelyn blinks back fresh tears and wrestles her body out of the rest of her clothes, folds them neatly, and sets them down on top of the small dresser. They're still damp, and she wonders if someone will offer to hang them up to dry. She heaves herself into the bed and pulls the beige wool blanket up over her belly and breasts. She glances to her left. She's become so used to Maggie's presence in the bed right next to hers. She wishes they could go through this together, as they have every other stage of their pregnancies.

The clock ticks away another few minutes of silence before another contraction begins. Evelyn throws her arm out to the side, reaching instinctively for a hand to hold. She needs someone to help her through this, to brush her hair off her sweaty face, whisper that it's going to be okay, that she's brave and doing great. That her baby will be in her arms soon, a beautiful baby girl with eyes like a summer morning. But her hand closes on thin air, and in that moment she's positive she has never in her life felt this utterly, profoundly alone.

· · · · · · · · · ·

Three hours and several painful contractions later, the doctor comes to her room. He introduces himself as Dr. Pritchard, then, without telling her what he's doing, lifts the sheets and blankets and starts feeling around between her legs, pushes his fingers up inside. Evelyn gasps; she wants to weep with humiliation. He declares her only eight centimeters dilated, whatever that means, and tells her he'll come back later. Evelyn stumbles out of bed, fills a glass of water, and flops right back down, exhausted.

She labors alone all night, listening to the crooning of the maternity ward nurses as they comfort the other women. She strains her ears, trying to catch any snippet of their conversation that might tell her what to expect as the contractions become more and more frequent. She wonders, while writhing on her hands and knees at one particularly low point in the night, whether she might be dead. What if no one is coming to check on her because she's a ghost? Maybe she's already given birth and died in the attempt and her poor lost soul is stuck in this hospital storeroom, laboring for eternity.

But when the contractions are nearly constant and Evelyn starts to feel an intense pressure between her legs, her only instinct is to start screaming for help, and—finally—it comes. Dr. Pritchard breezes into the room with one of the maternity nurses, and she pushes and cries through the searing pain until her baby enters the world in a bloody, slimy burst.

Evelyn hadn't been prepared for any of it, but the sound of her baby's first cry feels like Christmas morning. Like her heart has been split into two and is now part of this tiny person in the doctor's hands. The doctor actually smiles at Evelyn over the top of the sheet.

"A baby girl. You're going to make some nice couple very happy, Evelyn."

Evelyn can barely register what he said, because here is her daughter. Purple and pruned, her face scrunched up tight in protest of the coldness of the room, spluttering as she takes her first breaths. But she's the most beautiful thing Evelyn has ever seen. She's shaking with relief and something more overwhelming and deeper than anything she's ever felt before.

The doctor cuts the cord and hands the baby to the nurse, who walks her over to a counter beside the sink, and Evelyn watches her back as

Dr. Pritchard snaps off his bloody gloves and hands her a clipboard and pen, pointing to a line at the bottom, marked with a red *X*. He tells her she has to sign it before she's allowed to hold the baby. Evelyn signs the sloppiest signature she's ever written. She isn't even looking at the clipboard; she can't take her eyes off the nurse.

"You sit tight now, and I'll be back to finish off with the afterbirth and then stitch you up," the doctor says, sweeping from the room.

Evelyn ignores him. She sees her baby's little arm flailing over the crook of the nurse's elbow until they're bound tightly in a swaddling cloth. She's crying, and it makes Evelyn's heart ache with the most bittersweet mix of elation and anguish. She struggles to sit upright and feels a throb between her legs as something warm and wet trickles out. She doesn't look down.

She reaches her arms out to the nurse, hands trembling. "Can I hold her? Please?"

"See if she'll suck," the nurse says, tugging Evelyn's gown down to expose a heavy breast.

Evelyn holds her baby close, watches as the little pink mouth noses around her nipple. After several more minutes and lots of tears, the baby latches on, and even as Leo's face flashes into her mind, Evelyn instantly knows she has never felt pure love until this moment. She clasps her baby as close as she can, strokes her wisps of brown hair, the impossibly soft skin on the back of her neck.

"Oh my God," she says with a shaky laugh. "She's so *real*."

The nurse nods. "I've got a little girl, too. It's sort of like looking at another version of yourself, isn't it?"

The nurse glances at Evelyn, who is so focused on her baby that she doesn't look up to see the depth of sadness in the nurse's eyes. If she did, she would see that the nurse's conscience weighs so heavily that some nights she has trouble sleeping.

"Well, I'll leave you to it, dear. Dr. Pritchard will be back in a few minutes." She quietly walks from the room and closes the door behind her, leaving Evelyn alone with her baby.

"Hello, sweet baby," Evelyn whispers into her daughter's ear. Like it's a secret, just between the two of them. She kisses the wet silky top of her head. "I've been waiting for you."

. . . .

They keep Evelyn and her daughter in the hospital for over a week; they want the baby to gain more weight before she's discharged. There's no one waiting for this bed in the forgotten corner of the maternity ward, and so they stay.

The kind maternity nurse brings her a proper housecoat from the ward closet to wear over her nightdress instead of the hospital gown, and on the second day, Evelyn shuffles down to the waiting room in her own worn-out slippers to scrounge up some outdated beauty magazines for a bit of entertainment. She has a novel, too, a smart copy of a mystery one of the other new mothers left behind. Her husband brought it in for her and she didn't want it. Evelyn can't help but wonder what this experience would be like if things had gone differently and she had Leo to bring her presents and flowers and well-wishes from their loved ones, massage her feet, lie to her and tell her she looks fresh and beautiful.

Not at all tired, my dear. Don't you worry.

Evelyn promises herself that she'll tell Maggie everything she can about the labor and birth process before her friend has to undergo the same experience. She'll be separated into the postpartum dormitory once she returns to St. Agnes's, but plans to whisper the details to her friend during Bible study or outdoor time. She'll sneak into Maggie's dormitory in the middle of the night if she has to. Anything to make sure Maggie has the information she needs to be prepared for not just the labor, but the overwhelming love she'll feel when her child is placed in her arms. It's that love that has made Evelyn happier than she has been in over a year. Maybe ever.

Her favorite thing to do is walk down to the nursery to visit her baby. Sometimes there are other mothers or fathers there, but often it's just her alone, pressing her forehead and hands against the glass, eager to get as close as she can to her daughter. Evelyn's hands itch when she isn't holding her, and she's even feeling phantom kicks in her belly. They're only bringing her to breastfeed once a day now. The doctor says formula is far better for her baby's health, but she misses the feeling of that little rosy mouth.

On her fifth day at the hospital, Evelyn wanders down to the incubators in the late afternoon with a Styrofoam cup of weak coffee in her hand. There are two men there today, a tall redhead in his twenties, not much older than Evelyn, and an older gentleman with some dignified gray flecking his black temples. Evelyn pads up behind them, keeping her eyes downcast. The sense of shame has worn off a little over the past few days, but she still worries the other parents will know where she's from, or notice there's never a man there with her, gazing at the babies like these proud fathers do.

"Which one's yours?" the older man asks the redhead.

"That one"—he points to a bundle wrapped in blue—"with the name card George. Named him after my father. Our first." He smiles, his hands in his trouser pockets.

"Atta boy." The older man claps him on the back like a hockey coach with his star player. "Congratulations."

"Thanks. And you?"

"Right there," the man indicates with a nod. "Gracie. Our sixth and hopefully last, but you never know. Sometimes there's just no stopping it, eh?" He nudges the young father, who chuckles.

Evelyn sidesteps down the hall to put some space between her and the men, but they don't even seem to notice her.

"Lots of spring babies," the man goes on, a farmer observing his reaped crop. "Never seen so many in here at once. I like looking at all the names. Interesting to think who they're gonna grow up to be. What kind of families they come from. Mostly good stock. You do see a few coloreds in here from time to time, though. Good smattering of Jews, too." The younger man's smile falters. "I've seen another one off in the corner like that before, too. Never any name tag like the others."

Evelyn realizes he's pointing at her daughter. Sister Teresa had told them it would be easier to say goodbye if they didn't name their babies. Besides, no one had asked her whether she even had a name picked out.

"And that one there's tiny. Doesn't look like it's thriving like the others are."

Evelyn is stung. How was she supposed to have given birth to a fat baby, with the rations they're fed at the home?

"I've wondered before if they're diseased or something," the man continues. "I asked one of the nurses about it once. I said, 'If there's something wrong with that one, I don't want it in with my kid and the other healthy ones!' But she said it's just where they put the whores' babies, you know. They get adopted anyway, so no sense putting a name on it that's only going to be changed."

The new father frowns, takes a step back from the glass. "Well, I should get back to my wife."

"All right, son. Congratulations again to you and the missus."

"Thank you." They clasp hands and the younger man turns and wanders back down the hallway.

Evelyn's mind is reeling and she feels like she's going to be sick. She ducks her face to hide her swelling red nose, tries to follow in the retreating father's wake, but the older man is too quick for her.

"Hello, there, sweetheart!" he bellows, and Evelyn gags on the stench of stale cigarettes. "Didn't see ya there. Come to visit your little one? Which one is it?"

She can't answer. Instead she turns and flees back down the hallway, crashing through the doors of the maternity ward, shuffling as fast as her stitches allow while the ties of her housecoat flap behind her. She doesn't stop until she reaches the end of the hallway and realizes there's nowhere left to run.

CHAPTER 9

Nancy

. . . .

SPRING 1980

2—5—0—4—6—1.
The leather case opens easily with this new combination of numbers. Nancy's stomach does a little flip. She carefully lifts the lid.

It's a set of pale yellow baby booties, hand-knitted, in perfect condition.

Nancy sits there, puzzled. Why would such an ordinary item need to be hidden away like this? Maybe they were her first pair of booties, she thinks. Maybe this box is just for safekeeping, and nothing more. Nancy turns them over in her hands, inspecting them, and feels something hard in one of the toes. She sticks her fingers in and fishes out the culprit—a tiny piece of paper, folded in on itself multiple times.

She unfolds it.

Jane—My name is Margaret Roberts, and I am your mother. I love you. I did not want to give you up. I will never stop searching for you. I hope you have a beautiful life. For the rest of my days, I will always love you.

Nancy's fingers are shaking so hard that she drops the note.

Shock crashes over her in cold waves. Her ears buzz in the stunning silence of the room and her eyes blur. She feels sick and numb and breathless. Her grandmama's comment wasn't a slip of the tongue. She's been in on the lie, too. Who else knows? How many of her loved ones have been keeping this secret from her?

Nancy snatches up the note, holds it and the booties in her cupped hands like a bomb, steadying her balance. She can sense them heating up, growing heavy. Maybe if she can just keep still enough, lock her gaze, and not even dare to breathe, she can tuck them back in the box and avoid the explosion.

How stupid she's been. How did she not realize how dangerous it was to open this box? To come looking for it in the first place and idiotically—*childishly*—set her world spinning on all its axes? She curses her own stubbornness.

Just keep yourself to yourself.

Trying to swallow the sharp dryness in her throat, Nancy lays the booties and note down as gently as she can on the carpet beside the open box, wincing as she pulls her hands away, still waiting for the detonation.

She wipes the tears from her eyes with the back of her hand and stumbles to her feet, lurching to the dresser to pluck a tissue from the box hidden underneath a shiny pink plastic cover. As she blows her nose, she studies the little pile of evidence on the floor. The box is opened wide, like a man's chest on an autopsy table. It's glowing in the yellow light flooding into the room from the big window at the end of the hall.

What do I do now? Nancy wonders. Gather up the box and wait downstairs for her parents to come home? Ambush them with a reality they thought was thoroughly hidden? She wants answers to the geyser of questions that just erupted in her mind. What lengths did her parents go to in order to adopt her? What reproductive hell had they been through? Or *had* they? Was her adoption a gesture of Christian philanthropy, and nothing more? Nancy's stomach turns into cold steel as it hits her now why her mother has always been so overbearing, so protective.

"Oh, we tried and tried, and then you came along," her mother had told her once. "Our little gift from God." Nancy cringes at the memory of what she now knows was a lie. Or a cleverly crafted truth. Looking at the small leather case, she can hardly believe it held a secret this enormous.

She doesn't know what to do with this information. She can't hold it in much longer, but she doesn't know where to put it. It's taking up every inch of emotional real estate she possesses. It threatens to choke her as it climbs its way up her throat, an insect she's swallowed whole. She's feeling everything all at once. She wants to scream at her parents—*her parents?*—rail against them for keeping her identity a secret for so long, with no indication they were ever planning on telling her.

She can hear children playing out on the street, riding their bicycles in the spring evening. She thinks about her own childhood, full of love and joy and homemade jam. Pretty dresses and teetering piles of gifts at Christmas. Bedtime stories and summer sleepover camps. The best childhood a girl could ask for, really. Her parents are still her parents. They raised her and love her. Has she actually missed out on anything?

Nancy picks up the note in one hand, the yellow booties in the other. She reads the note four more times, the one sentence searing itself on her heart like a brand.

My name is Margaret Roberts, and I am your mother.

Margaret Roberts.

She repeats it over and over in her head, sees the letters appear in her mind's eye like the leading lady's name on a movie screen. Only they're in Margaret's unfamiliar handwriting. Her mother's handwriting.

"Who are you?" she asks the walls.

And why did Margaret give Nancy up for adoption when she's claiming in this scribbled note that she wanted to keep her? Her stomach lurches on a new thought: Why hasn't she ever tried to find Nancy? If what she says in the note is true, and she never wanted to give her baby up . . . Nancy's heart falls at the thought. Maybe she changed her mind after she wrote the note. Maybe she didn't really want a baby after all.

But her parents *did* want her. They went out of their way to adopt her, didn't they? Haven't they shown Nancy how much she means to them, how much they love her? Do they deserve the pain of knowing their only child distrusted them so much that she snooped around their bedroom to uncover their lie? Maybe they never found this note, hidden in the booties. Or maybe they have and they've tried to contact her birth mother. Maybe they're just trying to protect her.

Maybe.

The sun starts to set. Nancy continues to sit frozen on her parents' bedroom carpet as the glowing orange light streams through the window.

The room has grown dark by the time she folds up the note and shoves it back down into the toe of the bootie. She places the booties gently back in the box and shuts it, rotates the dials to random numbers.

She walks back over to the open drawer, the contents carefully laid out on top of the dresser, reflecting their placement inside. Nancy lowers the leather box and slides it into its former place in the dusty back corner. She sighs deeply before replacing the other items and closing The Drawer. She leaves the room on legs that don't quite feel like they belong to her. She can smell her mother's perfume still. It follows her out of her parents' bedroom like an accusatory lover.

She pauses at the top of the stairs to listen to the ghosts.

Her mother calling her name from the sitting room, beckoning her down to walk the six blocks to mass on Sunday mornings. Her father's gruff but loving voice muttering, "Good night, Beetle," as he turned off the light and closed her bedroom door, leaving it open just a crack so the moonlight from the hallway window could creep into Nancy's room, soothing her fear of the dark. The creak of the floorboard right outside her bedroom, so inconvenient for sneaking in after curfew.

Nancy runs her hand along the banister, remembering how she screamed down at Frances from this very spot during their first blowout argument. It was about Nancy moving out to go to university.

"But it's only a few streetcar stops away!" Her mother protested. "You're not even married! Why do you want to leave us? What will people think?"

Nancy's father calmed her mother down eventually, reminding her that Nancy was an adult and would be leaving home sometime soon anyway. He understood Nancy's need for independence, for time away from her mother's constant supervision. He isn't a man of many words, and runs his household in the manner of a good-natured health inspector. But he loves Nancy deeply and she's always known he would do almost anything for her.

Nancy descends the stairs in a trance and wanders into the kitchen, flipping on some lights that flicker to life, illuminating the gleaming countertops. She fills up the kettle and busies herself with some Earl Grey leaves, spilling them when she misses the edge of the tea ball. She absently sweeps them off the counter into her hand and shakes them into the garbage bin beneath the sink. A minute later, the kettle's whistle makes her jump and she nearly burns her wrist in her haste to get it off the stove.

Tears are welling in her eyes now as she watches the brown tea bloom inside the porcelain cup. She shoves her hand into the box of Peak Freans on the counter and stuffs a whole raspberry cream cookie into her mouth, immediately hears her mother's admonishment in her head for demonstrating such appalling manners.

Her mother. Her mother is Margaret Roberts.

Nancy lets the tears slip down her face. The only sound comes from the grandfather clock in the hallway. It ticks in time with Nancy's thoughts as they fall into place, one after another.

"My name is Jane."

She says the words aloud to the empty kitchen. No one heard. No one will know.

When Nancy finishes her tea, she washes the cup and sets it in the drying rack. The kitchen now smells like the lemon dish soap her mother has always used, and it takes Nancy back to childhood Saturdays, watching Frances clean the floors while she helped with the dishes.

She can't confront her parents about this. At least not tonight. She needs to get back to her apartment, where ghosts don't lurk in every corner and she can think clearly, rationally about this.

As she heads for the front door, she holds her breath against the citrus scent. For the rest of Nancy's life, guilt and betrayal will smell like lemon dish soap.

CHAPTER 10

Evelyn

. . . .

SPRING 1961

E velyn's head snaps back as Sister Teresa wallops her across the face with a powerful open palm.

"With our Lord as my witness, if you do not quiet down this instant, you will lose your privilege to say goodbye to the baby. Calm yourself, Evelyn!"

Evelyn absorbs the nun's blow, gripping the arms of the chair she's sitting on in the Goodbye Room.

The Goodbye Room, as the girls have come to call it, is little more than a closet at the end of the hall up on the third floor. There isn't even a rug, just a bare wooden floor supporting the creaking weight of a pair of large oak rocking chairs, their worn blue cushions sagging sadly over the edges of their seats. It's the room they sequester each of the girls in for their last goodbye to their baby. A designated, separate room they'll never have to set foot in ever again, ostensibly so they won't have to be reminded of the pain of parting from their child. As if such visceral anguish could ever be contained within four paper-thin walls.

The pain leaks through all the tiniest cracks. It seeps up from between the worn floorboards like floodwater, muddy with silt and carrying the stench of regret.

They've moved the other girls out of the upstairs floors to their chores and into the parlor so they don't bear witness to Evelyn's tragedy, knowing that their own time will come just as surely, in only a matter of weeks. But this protocol isn't a sign of compassion for the girls.

It's riot control.

Through the shock and sting of the slap, Evelyn still registers Sister Teresa's language. Not *her* baby. Never her baby. *The* baby. The couple's baby. The product. A retort stabs at the back of Evelyn's throat, but her eyes flash down to the whip in the Watchdog's belt loop.

"Good. Now, here—sign this." Sister Teresa thrusts a piece of paper and pen at Evelyn.

"What is it?"

"It is a document swearing that you will never go looking for the baby. A standard contract."

"I already signed something at the hospital."

"Those were the adoption papers. This is to confirm that in choosing to relinquish the child, you are forfeiting all future contact."

Evelyn can feel the cold smoothness of the pen in her clammy hand. She feels hate rising like fire in her throat, but it scorches her tongue before she can spit in the Watchdog's face.

"I didn't choose this," she says.

"Oh yes, you did. Do not delude yourself. You must sign it, Evelyn, or you will not see the baby."

Evelyn smooths the piece of paper out on her lap. It's a typed document with her name on it. Her daughter is listed as Baby Taylor. Underneath that are the words *Father unknown.* A surge of grief for Leo, of anger that he has been so unceremoniously erased from his own child's identity, clutches her heart. Evelyn licks her lips, then holds her breath and, swearing a silent oath that she has no intention of adhering to this contract, signs her name on the line. The ink hasn't even dried before the Watchdog snatches it out of her hand and leaves the Goodbye Room, shutting the door behind her.

Evelyn hears Maggie's voice on the other side. The nun says something to her, and the door opens again. Maggie slips inside, her face pale underneath a sad smile.

"Hi," she says, taking a seat in the chair across from Evelyn.

"Thank you for being here, Maggie. I know it's not—it can't be easy for you to be here again." Evelyn's voice catches.

Maggie's chest rises and falls on a deep breath. The sunlight pouring in through the window illuminates her hair like a halo. "No. But I wish someone could have been with me."

Sister Teresa's house rule allows the girls to have another inmate with them for moral support in the Goodbye Room, but only if the other girl has already said goodbye to her own baby first. Maggie gave birth to her daughter before her due date, just days after Evelyn was discharged. The adoptive family came for Maggie's baby the same night she returned from the hospital. She was sent up to the Goodbye Room straightaway after dinner. Since Evelyn hadn't yet relinquished her own daughter to the adoptive parents—who were still, she was told, preparing their nursery—she wasn't allowed to be with Maggie. She never saw her friend's baby. Maggie was moved to the postpartum dormitory that day, but Evelyn sneaked down the hall and got into bed with her later that night, held her tightly, stroked her hair as she sobbed into Evelyn's chest.

"I'm sorry, Maggie," Evelyn says now, reaching out to squeeze her friend's hand.

Maggie returns the pressure with stony eyes. She's closed herself off the past few days, and she's visibly thinner. "It's okay. It was bad timing. All of this is just bad timing."

Evelyn nods, rolls her shoulders back. She has to get a handle on her emotions, like Maggie has, or her baby will be gone and she'll never get to say a proper goodbye.

If only her brother had responded to any of her letters. She could be bringing her baby home to him and his wife, to be raised as their child. Evelyn has dreamed of the iced lemon birthday cakes, paper hats, and gifts from the woman her daughter might have called auntie. Of the pretty dresses she would sew for the little girl. Helping her through her first heartbreak and toasting a glass of champagne at her wedding, all disguised as the love of an aunt so fond of her only niece. Hiding in plain sight.

If only.

If only she had something she could give to her daughter as a token, a reminder that her mother had lived and breathed, labored for her and birthed her, held her close and whispered, "I love you," in her ear.

"Here, I came prepared." As though reading Evelyn's mind, Maggie leans forward and hands her a piece of paper and a pen that she withdraws from the pocket of her linen skirt.

"I wrote my baby a note and shoved it into the toe of those booties I knitted. I stuffed them inside the swaddling blanket. I doubt she'll ever get to read it, but I didn't know what else to do. I just couldn't let her go without some piece of me." She pinches her lips.

Evelyn's heart is hammering. She glances at the door.

"I don't—I don't know what to say."

"Just tell her you love her. That's all she needs to know. That's what I wrote to my little girl." Maggie clears her throat. "That I would always love her."

Evelyn scribbles a few words, fighting back tears, but several fall, hitting the paper. She'll send along a piece of her broken heart with the little bundle that will, in mere hours, be held by another woman who handed over a bag of money in order to call herself a mother. Evelyn gags on the thought as she folds the paper into the tiniest square she can and stuffs it under her thigh as the door to the Goodbye Room clicks open.

It's Sister Agatha with the baby, and Evelyn is grateful. She can't bear to see her daughter in the arms of the Watchdog at a time like this. Agatha holds the baby with the same amount of care Evelyn does, gazing at her soft forehead, unwrinkled and perfect underneath a fuzz of silky hair. She's wrapped in a nicer blanket than usual. It's actually beautiful, a hand-knitted swaddling blanket in the palest pink, like a kitten's nose. Evelyn notes it grimly; the home must put up a front to the adoptive parents when they come to pick up their purchase.

"Hello, girls," Agatha says as she passes Evelyn the pink bundle. "Here you go, Miss Evelyn. It's only supposed to be five minutes, but I'll give you as long as I can." She whispers it. Like a secret, or her deepest fear.

Evelyn can't speak.

"Thank you, Sister Agatha," Maggie says, her own voice thick.

Agatha nods. She can't meet the girls' eyes, although they're only a foot apart. "I'm so sorry."

She leaves, shutting the door with a soft thud, and Evelyn gazes down into the face of her daughter for the last time.

"Sweet little one," she murmurs into the sleeping baby's ear. Her face is serene, and Evelyn realizes, in an explosion of panic, that she must commit every detail to memory: the curve of her little chin, the long lashes so dark they seem wet. Her high cheekbones and steeply curved nose. She swears she'll watch for that chin, those lashes, that nose in the face of every child, teenage girl, and young woman she passes on the street for the rest of her life. One day, she wants to look into the face of her daughter and say: *I know you. You're mine.*

Evelyn wishes her daughter were awake so that she could see her eyes, but she can't bear to disturb her when she's so peaceful. Instead,

Evelyn rests her little body gently against her own chest. She hasn't been allowed to breastfeed since the hospital, but she holds the baby against her anyway, hoping with vain desperation that her daughter will remember the thump of her mother's heartbeat, the smell of her breath, the feel of her skin at the base of her throat.

Something. Anything.

She takes a shaky breath, then lets it out as steadily as she can. She can hear the voices of the other girls downstairs in the kitchen, the jangling of pot lids as they prepare for lunch. Moving on with their day.

"She's beautiful, Evelyn," Maggie says.

Evelyn tears her eyes away from her baby to meet her friend's. "I'm sure yours was, too."

The tears finally fall from Maggie's chin into her lap. Sunlight pours in through the window. Everything is glowing.

Evelyn reaches under her thigh for the folded note. She gently unwraps half of the blanket and tucks the piece of paper into the bottom of the swaddling folds as tightly as she can. She wraps her daughter up again and manages a smile.

"Ten fingers, ten toes, two eyes, two ears, a mouth, and a nose," Evelyn says, reciting the little rhyme she made up during their stay in the hospital. She runs the tip of her index finger from the top of her baby's forehead, between her eyes, then down the bridge of her nose to the little button tip.

She brushes her hand across the top of her daughter's head, leans down, and breathes in her smell. The clock on the wall relentlessly ticks away the cruel minutes, reminding her that every second is precious right now.

Don't look away from her, it says.

Tick.

This is it.

Tock.

This is all you get.

Tick.

Pay attention.

Tock.

Click. The spell is broken as Sister Agatha sweeps quietly back into the room.

"It's time, Miss Evelyn."

"Okay."

"I'm sorry."

"Okay. It's okay." Evelyn nods, blinking rapidly against the tears, but there's no stopping them now.

She takes one last look at her daughter, feasting on the little face through her own swollen eyes, forcing down the panic. She catches herself glancing toward the window, but of course it's locked, and they're on the third floor. This prison is, as Maggie said, well designed, a series of snares and cages laid out inside a maze of confusion and lies. There's only one exit, and the prisoners can't leave until they make their final payment.

Evelyn's arms are shaking, she can't control it, and she worries for a moment she might drop her daughter. But Sister Agatha reaches out and takes the baby. The transaction is complete.

"Goodbye, baby girl," Evelyn whispers, her arms now empty in her lap. "I love you, sweetheart. Please forgive me. Please forgive me . . ."

All she can do is watch as Agatha carries her baby to the door and shuts it again behind her. She fights against the heat that's building in her chest. She doesn't want her daughter to hear this, to have any memory of her mother's pain, of her voice rising above anything but a gentle murmur. The door closes and she crumples to the floor. Maggie is crying, too, and Evelyn feels a surge of intense gratitude for her friend's sacrifice. Maggie kneels on the wooden floorboards and Evelyn lays her head in her friend's lap as Maggie strokes her hair back from her wet face.

Once she's sure Sister Agatha must be downstairs, Evelyn takes a shaky breath, then howls a scream of agony that's too big to be absorbed by the tiny Goodbye Room. It permeates the walls and ceiling, reverberates inside Evelyn's chest with nowhere else to go. It consumes her heart and lungs with fire as her face crumples against the burn.

"Shh shh shh, it's over now," Maggie whispers, wiping the tears from Evelyn's cheeks with a cold hand. "It'll be okay. One day, it'll all be okay. We have to believe that."

Downstairs in the tiny nursery near the Watchdog's office, Sister Agatha closes her eyes and holds her little hands over the baby's ears. The girls in the kitchen pause their work, suspended in tableau as they freeze at the sound. The imagined faces of their own babies flash into their minds. Their hands lower to their bellies until the scream dissipates, then they exhale with relief and try to push away thoughts of the inevitable.

But the barbed edges of those thoughts hook into their minds and latch on. They hear the *clip-clop* of the Watchdog's shoes ascending the stairs, and quickly return to their work. They go about their business as the commotion upstairs plays out in the background. Evelyn lets fly a different kind of scream now. Maggie is shouting her protest, trying to protect her friend. Evelyn keeps shrieking. And the girls in the kitchen dry the dishes and sweep the floors as the repeated snap of the Watchdog's whip drives them on.

· · · · · · · · · ·

Evelyn knows she should be dressed already.

It's a Wednesday morning, three weeks after her baby was taken from her. She's still lying in bed with the covers pulled right up over her head, her knees bent into the fetal position to make sure her feet stay covered under the inadequate blanket. The Watchdog's lashings left welts on her forearms that haven't fully disappeared, but her stitches have mostly healed, although the skin still sometimes aches with a dull longing at the memory of her daughter's birth.

Her milk has dried up now, and her body is beginning to feel a bit like her own again. The thought makes Evelyn want to weep. She would give anything to share her body with her baby once more. How did she not know how lucky she was to be pregnant? That the constant discomfort, exhaustion, and sleepless nights punctuated by her baby's kicks and rolls were a gift? She wished away the time as though the state of pregnancy were a curse to be thrown off in triumph, missing it for the blessing that it was. She wonders vaguely if her baby longs, in some unconscious way, for her own mother's breast, for the scent of her skin and the comfort of her arms.

What a foolish dream, Evelyn thinks. Her baby will never remember her.

The mornings have all been much like this, ever since she said goodbye. She hoped that over time she might start to feel a little more like her old self, but her old self is gone. Dead. And good riddance. That girl knew nothing of joy or love or loss. She understands now why their housemate Emma used to cry in the mornings, her sobs echoing down the hallway from the postpartum dormitory where Evelyn and Maggie now sleep. They felt badly for her, yes, but Evelyn had no idea it would feel like this. She remembers how Emma's eyes became like caverns after they took her baby. Evelyn saw her coming in the front door when she returned from the hospital, and she looked like a different person. She wandered like a lost spirit through these halls until she paid off her debt and was finally free to leave. Evelyn suspects she probably appears as departed and insubstantial now as Emma did. She wishes she had been kinder to her.

"Evelyn," Maggie says from their bedroom door. Evelyn squeezes her eyes shut tight. "It's nearly breakfast time. If you don't get downstairs soon the Watchdog'll be up. Come on, now."

Evelyn pulls the covers down a little to expose her face. Maggie is standing over her bed now with her hands on her thin hips.

"I'm not hungry," Evelyn says. "But you should eat. You're so skinny, Maggie."

Maggie sighs and sits on the edge of the bed. "You can't keep doing this. You have to get up."

"It's so hard."

"I know. I really do."

Evelyn clears the phlegm from her throat. "But you seem so strong, Maggie. Why can't I be more like you?"

"I'm not, really. Jane is still on my mind constantly . . ." She trails off, staring at her lap.

"Girls?" Sister Agatha appears in the doorway, her expression strained. "You're nearly late for breakfast."

"We're sorry, Sister Agatha," Maggie says. "We're coming now."

The nun frowns at Evelyn and hesitates before turning on her heel and disappearing down the hall.

"You named your baby?" Evelyn whispers.

"Yes."

"But we aren't supposed to."

"I know. I did anyway."

The moment feels like the time they revealed their last names to one another, a miniature rebellion that catches them both off guard.

"Sometimes I wish we had tried to get out, back when you first suggested it," Maggie says, picking at a little hole in the bedcover, avoiding Evelyn's eyes. "You were right, I think."

"No, *you* were right," Evelyn says. "We had nowhere to go."

"No," Maggie agrees. "But I guess I mean you were being strong then. You can be again. You have it in you. I've seen it." She looks down at Evelyn now. "We have to keep on pushing forward, Evelyn. Once we get out of here, maybe there will be a way to find our girls. But railing against the Watchdog while we're trapped inside these walls . . . it's only going to harm us in the short term, and it won't do any good in the long run. Like I told you before up in the Goodbye Room, we just have to believe it'll be okay one day. We'll never stop looking for them, Evelyn. We *will* find them. We just have to be patient." Her voice drops. "This isn't the end. I promise you."

Maggie stands up and pulls the bedcovers all the way back. Evelyn groans into her pillow but doesn't move. "It may as well be," she says.

. . . .

Two weeks later, Evelyn finally finds an opportunity to speak to Sister Agatha on her own. The damn house is so crowded, the girls and staff are practically tripping over one another. There's never any privacy to be had.

She spots the nun out in the garden during the afternoon outdoor time. It's a chilly, wet day and the drizzle has driven most of the girls indoors for the hour-long break, but Sister Agatha is in a corner of the small yard, trimming the hedge with a pair of rusted shears.

Evelyn approaches her from behind. "Sister Agatha?" she asks timidly.

Agatha turns. She's wearing an apron and rain jacket over her habit, and oversized Wellington boots on her small feet. She looks like a child playing dress-up. "Hello, Miss Evelyn."

Evelyn has practiced this speech in her head as she's gone about her chores over the past few days, imagined the conversation as she tosses and turns in bed at night, unable to sleep. But she decides to skip right to the point. She has a plan and she needs Agatha's help.

"Sister Agatha, I can't sleep. I can't eat. All I can think about is my baby, and where she is, whether she's happy, and, you know . . . loved." Her throat is so tight she's not sure she can get the words out. "I need to know where she is. I need to know who has her. I just don't think . . ." She shifts her weight to the other foot and her boot squelches into the soggy grass. "I can't see myself being able to move on if I don't know where she is. I need to know. I need your help."

The nun clutches the garden shears tightly in her gloved hand. "I think you just need to give it some more time, Miss Evelyn."

"I can't."

"But you must. It's early days, yet. This happens to most of the girls, right at first. It's very difficult. But given time, things usually start to look a little brighter. Especially after you go home."

Evelyn scoffs. "I need you to help me find out where she is."

"Oh, Miss Evelyn, I can't."

Evelyn watches the nun's eyes closely and starts to see a change in them. They droop somehow, weighed down. Her shoulders fall in defeat.

"Do you know something?" Evelyn's heart is racing now. "What is it?"

"I can't say," she says, glancing nervously back toward the house.

"Sister Agatha, *please*."

Agatha searches Evelyn's face, looking for something. Finally, she takes a deep, shuddering breath. "Your baby . . . your baby didn't make it, Miss Evelyn. She—she died."

The world stops moving, and all Evelyn can feel is the misty rain, blurring her vision. "She's . . . *dead*? But . . . *how*?"

Agatha takes a step toward Evelyn. "I'm sorry, I shouldn't have said." She looks agonized. "It's just one of those things. She was small, remember. But you can move on now, Miss Evelyn. There's nothing to chase or worry about. You can put all this behind you. You can . . . move on," she finishes weakly.

Evelyn starts to shake as the shock sets in. She can't process what she's just heard. She feels nothing and everything and all the things in between. She holds Sister Agatha's gaze in an iron stare as the young nun shrinks back, then turns on her slippery heel and staggers back toward the house.

CHAPTER 11

Angela

· · · · · · · · · ·

LATE JANUARY 2017

Since finding Frances Mitchell's letter and the note from the young girl named Margaret, Angela has been sending out messages to Nancy Mitchells everywhere in the Greater Toronto Area and beyond, but so far her search hasn't yielded any results. Despite Angela's niggling sense of shame at pursuing the unknown Nancy, she doesn't feel right sneaking around behind Tina's back, so she decides to tell her about "the Nancys," as she has collectively dubbed them in her head, on their way to the fertility clinic.

Tina nods in her usual sanguine way. "Okay. Thanks for telling me."

The rest of the car ride passes in a prickly silence that Angela acknowledges she may have imagined, but any lingering tension is instantly overshadowed once they enter the treatment room. They're in today for another expensive intrauterine insemination procedure— their ninth. Five of them didn't take at all. Two did, but both ended in miscarriages.

Almost a year ago, Angela had to go to an abortion clinic to treat one of the miscarriages that hadn't naturally completed. At the time, she had no idea that the abortion procedure was also used after some miscarriages. While she didn't have any real preconceptions of the women who access abortion services, she was reminded that these clinics aren't just filled with irresponsible teenagers. Even the most anti-abortion, right-wing woman might at some point need to have the procedure after a miscarriage to avoid a potential infection. After all is said and done, it's just like any other surgery or treatment. But the protesters outside the clinic didn't seem to have gotten that memo.

When she and Tina arrived at the clinic, they immediately noticed a crowd of people gathered on the south side of the street across from the entrance. They all wore the same black toque, and about half of them were carrying neon poster boards boasting a variety of ominous phrases in thick marker. Angela could see other signs with pink and red images on them, and more giant headlines propped up along the sidewalk. From a distance she couldn't tell what they were, but she could guess: gruesome photos of alleged fetuses juxtaposed with happy grannies holding fat white babies behind a soft blurry camera filter.

On the north side of the street, a few counterprotesters held up purple signs. Three police cars were parked in front of the clinic and the police were chatting with the counterprotesters. One officer was standing sentry near the front door of the building.

Tina took hold of Angela's gloved hand. The pro-choice counterprotesters waved them through, smiling at them both as they passed.

"Ignore them," one said to Angela, indicating the shouting mass across the street. "They know they've lost, and they're pissed off about it."

But they were, by design, difficult to ignore. Glancing sideways, Angela caught sight of some of their signs:

LIFE IS SACRED
ABORTION IS MURDER
YOUR ALL BABY KILERS

At least spell your fucking sign correctly, Angela thought wryly. There was even a small boy, just four or five years old, holding a placard that read MY MOTHER CHOSE LIFE. Her pulse had started to race then, and Angela couldn't stop herself.

"Do you think I actually want to be here?" she'd screamed at them. "Do you think I don't wish I were still pregnant? You ignorant fucks!"

"Ange!" Tina had grabbed her shoulders. "Ange, come on. Come on. It's not worth it. Leave it."

Their experiences at the fertility clinic are so bright and positive, despite the physical discomfort. The nurses and technicians offer well-wishes and support for their choice to become mothers. No one protests outside its doors, screaming at passing women and judging them for wanting to be pregnant. Yet aren't fertility clinics and abortion clinics just two sides of the same coin?

Angela was grateful that she hadn't needed to go back to that horrible place after the most recent miscarriage, which completed on its own.

But that was then, she reminds herself as they wait in the treatment room. Today is a day of positivity. Today they're at the point in the fertility roller coaster where their hopes are high for a successful insemination and implantation, and they try not to remember how crushingly disappointing it is if it doesn't take. Angela knows Tina is tired of the process, but she isn't ready to give up.

The next one will be it, she tells Tina every time, repeating the mantra to herself whenever she starts to doubt it. *The next one. The next one. We'll get a baby on the next one.*

Back before Christmas, when Angela got her period after the last failed treatment, she walked out of the bathroom sobbing, shaking with rage and resentment and a dozen other emotions. But mostly, she was full of hate. So full of it that she couldn't breathe.

She hated her friends who already had children.

She hated those stupid teenagers who got pregnant *by accident*, without even trying.

She hated how fucking hard this was on her body and her heart and her marriage. Her bank account.

She hated trying to get pregnant but hated the thought of not getting pregnant even more.

Tina came home from work to find Angela in her spot on the couch, a glass of real wine in her hand and Grizzly curled up in her lap as tears poured down her swollen face, and she knew immediately what had happened. They were both so intently tuned in to Angela's cycle, they knew that in the coming days they were approaching either the beginning or the end of something.

"Oh, Ange," Tina said, flopping down on the couch beside her wife and pulling her into a hug. Grizzly meowed between them, and to Angela it somehow sounded like an apology for everything they wanted and couldn't have. Angela sobbed even harder in Tina's arms, devastated by the loss of the possibility.

A couple of days later after Angela had calmed down enough, Tina broached the idea of adoption with her. They talked all evening, but Angela wouldn't budge. Having been adopted herself, there was a drive deep down in her being to have a biological baby of her own, a direct line where her child could connect the dots, without having to search for them like Angela had. Tina never wanted to be the one to carry, and Angela was determined.

Tina eventually agreed to keep trying, though Angela could tell she still worried about the impact their fertility efforts were having on them. People talked about it as a "journey," a trip down a winding road guided by a presumption that eventually they would reach their golden destination, but most of the time it just felt like a Sisyphean task. They never spoke about it directly, but Angela had the sense that there was a limit of some kind on the horizon—financial, emotional. She wasn't sure exactly what, but she could see it in the creases in Tina's forehead every time they came in for an IUI procedure. Every time one failed. Every time Angela started bleeding.

In the treatment room now, Angela looks up at her wife's face and sees those same creases of apprehension. But she squeezes Angela's hand as the nurse approaches the table with the syringe.

"All right, Angela, take a deep breath now and keep breathing. This'll only take a few minutes."

"Yeah," Angela says, letting her breath out in a long stream, staring at the institutional drop ceiling and thinking of all the other times she's lain on this table in a hospital gown, praying that this time will be the one. But she'll keep pushing that boulder up the hill as long as she can. "I know."

. . . .

Two weeks later, Angela unpacks a box of Valentine's Day decorations on the cash desk at the antiques shop. She dug out the dusty cardboard box from the bottom shelf of the tiny storeroom, and she's spent the past hour finding appropriate locations for the various shiny red baubles, glittery strings of beads, and pink plastic dollar-store hearts. It's a slow Monday morning at the shop, so she's getting the decorating finished before the foot traffic picks up later in the afternoon.

Angela puts her second pot of decaf on to brew, then carries some decorations, a pair of scissors, masking tape, and a step stool to the back of the store. She's just hung the first strand of hearts from the top of a bookshelf when the bells above the door jingle, welcoming her second customer of the day.

"Hello!" she calls, stepping down off the stool.

"Hi, there! Delivery for you," a male voice responds.

"Excellent, thank you."

Angela weaves her way to the front, brushing her hands on her jeans to rid them of the thick coat of dust and making a mental note to do a thorough spring-clean.

The delivery driver holds his mobile phone out to her, and she signs a sloppy signature with the tip of her index finger. She takes the first of several boxes from him without thinking. It's heavy, and she realizes that she'll have to ask him to bring the boxes around to the back of the cash desk next time. She shouldn't be lifting anything heavy at the moment.

The bells jingle as the driver leaves the shop, and a chorus of street sounds rushes inside before the door swings shut again.

After Angela finishes hanging the decorations, she pours herself a cup of coffee, then slits the tape on the first box and starts unpacking this month's shipment of used books.

It's a curious collection: contemporary and classic fiction—Angela swears they must already have fourteen copies of *The Complete Works of William Shakespeare*, and she's just unpacked another two—biographies and memoirs, outdated travel books that rarely sell, dog-eared and oil-splattered cookbooks, unread self-help guides, and a smattering of general nonfiction in a sweeping array of topics from war history to terrace gardening and horse breeding.

Angela sorts the books into piles by genre, entering each one into the computer system as she goes. She's nearly at the end of the fifth and final box when she pulls out a paperback bound in a slightly tattered black cover with a bold white title.

THE JANE NETWORK

The author is a Dr. Evelyn Taylor. There's no cover art or anything else to indicate what the book is about. Is it fiction or nonfiction? Both intrigued and a little irritated at the extra effort required to sort this book into the appropriate pile, Angela opens it to the copyright page, scanning for more detail. It's nonfiction, published in 1998. Under the subject heading, she reads: *Jane Network, The (abortion service) | Abortion services—Toronto—Ontario—CANADA | Abortion—Canada—History.*

"Wow." Angela's eyebrows pop up into her dark bangs. On the opposite page, she reads the dedication, which simply says: *For the Janes.* She flips two more pages and smooths down the table of contents.

1. *No Other Choice: A (Very) Brief History of Women's Reproductive Options to 1960*
2. *My Montreal Years: Training Under Dr. Morgentaler*
3. *A Right to Know: The Birth Control Handbook and Other Subversive Texts*
4. *The Revolution Begins: The Abortion Caravan of 1970*
5. *The Jane Network Is Born*
6. *"I'm Looking for Jane": Expanding the Service*
7. *Raids, Revival & Restructuring*
8. *R. v. Morgentaler (1988): The Trial & Decriminalization*
9. *"There Will Always Be a Need": Life After Jane*

"Huh." She sets the book aside near her computer monitor and quickly processes the remaining two books in the box. She glances at the clock; it's nearly time for lunch and she's starving. Angela heads into the storeroom and pulls her lunch out of the mini-fridge on the floor. She heats up her leftover soup in the microwave, tapping her finger impatiently on the white plastic door and ignoring the fact that she's now made the whole store smell like onions. Using her scarf as an oven mitt, she takes the steaming container back to the cash desk and settles down on the stool. Propping *The Jane Network* up against the computer monitor, she flips through its pages.

Angela wonders whether Tina has ever come across this organization in her academic life. Angela's never even heard of it. After blowing on her first spoonful of soup, she picks up her cell phone and dials her wife's number. Tina answers after two rings.

"Hey, T," Angela says. "Got a question for you. Have you ever heard of something called the Jane Network?"

PART II

CHAPTER 12

Evelyn

. . . .

OTTAWA | MAY 9, 1970

T he city is plastered with green and black posters. They've gone up
   everywhere: pinned to bulletin boards in steamy coffee shops with
mismatched chairs and chipped white mugs; pasted to store windows
along Sparks Street and in the ByWard Market boutiques; taped to the
backs of bathroom stall doors in the public libraries; stapled to telephone poles along all of Ottawa's busiest streets.

It's the first thing Evelyn notices when she emerges from the train
station on Saturday morning. She steps into the weak spring sunlight,
shifts her backpack to a more comfortable position on her shoulders,
and walks toward the nearest telephone pole.

THE WOMEN ARE COMING, the posters declare. Underneath, the
subtitle reads, *The Abortion Caravan*. Evelyn's stomach does a little back-
flip. She lets her breath out in an audible sigh, releasing some of the
tension in her chest. She can't recall having felt this excited, nervous,
and determined since the day she began medical school. It's a similar
feeling of exhilaration, another protest.

Nine years ago, Evelyn left St. Agnes's a different woman. After all the trauma, after the crippling sense of helplessness, and lack of control over her own life, she vowed she would never again be in a position where she would have to rely on anyone else or feel as powerless as she had. She wasn't interested in being a housewife, in starting over as if nothing had happened. She longed for a career that would ensure her independence. After convincing her family this was her only way forward, she applied and was accepted to medical school in Montreal.

She was one of only two women in the program, and things weren't easy for either her or Marie. But on her very first day, she also met Tom, who sat next to her in their Introduction to Human Anatomy class. He was different from the other men, who viewed Evelyn and Marie with either suspicion, disdain, or uninhibited sexual interest. Tom became not only her best friend, but her roommate, too, along with Marie and one of Tom's other friends. Despite a ripple of scandalized muttering from those who thought it inappropriate for unmarried women to be living with men, the arrangement worked well for Evelyn. Between having been deemed a "fallen" woman at such a young age and putting up with snide and cruel remarks from her male colleagues, she was past the point of caring much about other people's muttering, anyway.

But her life changed when Marie came to her room one night to ask her for a favor. She needed an abortion, and she wanted Evelyn to come with her.

"I can't give all this up," she told Evelyn, as she paced back and forth along the tattered secondhand bedroom rug. "Not now. I'm here because I want to do something more with my life than my mother did. I can't go back to being dependent on my parents. I can't even bear the thought. And I could never give a baby up for adoption. It would ruin me." She glanced at Evelyn through wet eyelashes. "I hope you don't think me awful for it."

Evelyn chewed her lip, then reached out, stopping Marie midstride. "I understand more than you can imagine, Marie."

After witnessing the procedure from her vantage point at the top of Dr. Henry Morgentaler's surgical table, where she held Marie's hand and spoke soothingly, Evelyn became possessed by an idea, which became a dare, and eventually a plan. She called Dr. Morgentaler's office to set up a meeting the following week, and told him exactly why she wanted to learn how to perform the abortion procedure. For the first time since she had left St. Agnes's, she spoke openly to a stranger about what had gone on there.

"I never had a say in what happened to me," she'd told the doctor. "I had no control. And watching you the other day, with Marie—if I had known the kind of pain I would feel, being forced to give up my child like that . . ." She shook her head. "I loved my daughter. I desperately wanted to keep her, and I wasn't allowed to. But if things had been different, if I had gotten pregnant today and didn't want to be, well, an abortion could save a woman from a life sentence of pain, couldn't it?"

As she spoke the truth that drove her to his office, Dr. Morgentaler watched her from behind the thick glasses perched on his nose. Evelyn looked down at her lap, traced her finger along the scar at her wrist, faded to white now after so many years.

"I lost everything. I wouldn't wish this on anyone. I don't want other women to have to feel what I feel. I *need* them to at least have a choice. And I saw that potential when I came in with Marie."

He was silent for a moment. Evelyn bit down hard on her fear and met his gaze, surprised by the kindness there.

"I understand, Miss Taylor," he said quietly.

Evelyn felt a prickle at the corners of her eyes. "Forgive me, Dr. Morgentaler. Women aren't permitted moments of weakness in the medical profession. I'm sorry."

"Don't be, please." Dr. Morgentaler unlinked his fingers and leaned forward in his chair. "And listen to me carefully, Miss Taylor, because this is very important. Do not mistake your humanity for weakness. It is, unfortunately, a common misconception."

Evelyn sniffed. "You could say I'm feeling quite human about the whole thing, then."

"The best physicians do, Miss Taylor. And your experience will allow you to offer a uniquely valuable level of compassion to your patients. Cultivate that. Cherish it. The terror you obviously experienced has brought you here to my office today, with this incredibly courageous request. You would not be here otherwise, now, would you?"

Evelyn couldn't argue. "So, will you teach me?"

"It would be my honor, Miss Taylor."

Evelyn's heart leaped in her chest. "Thank you, Dr. Morgentaler."

The doctor surveyed her for a moment. "Before you make this decision, let me ask you something. Do you have any loved ones close to you?"

"No. Not really," Evelyn replied, clearing the faces that floated into her mind. "Just my roommates, and a brother in Toronto. He's a doctor, too, his wife is a nurse. Why do you ask?"

"I ask because this window behind my head is made of bulletproof glass."

His words sucked the air from the room and a shivering silence descended. Evelyn's eyes were irresistibly drawn to the window. Leaves on the maple tree beyond it swayed innocently in the breeze.

When the doctor spoke again, his tone was carefully measured. "Providing abortions is, as you must know, illegal in this country, Miss Taylor, except under the strictest of circumstances. I assume you have familiarized yourself with them?"

Evelyn nodded. "Only if continuation of the pregnancy would endanger the life or health of the woman."

"Indeed. And the parameters of what constitutes 'health' are further determined by a biased and ludicrously broken system made up entirely of men. Thus, to fill the need, there are underground networks operating across Canada and the United States, and overseas as well. It is a *calling*, not a vocation, Miss Taylor. And it is a calling you can only answer at enormous personal risk. It is both morally and spiritually challenging. You must understand that the cost is high."

Evelyn took a long, deep breath. "Dr. Morgentaler, they can't take anything away from me that I haven't already lost. I assure you."

He paused, a sad smile on his face, then offered for her to come observe the three patients he had booked for that afternoon.

"I'm sorry, sir, did you say *three* procedures?" she asked him, incredulous.

"Yes."

"How . . . how many do you do in a week?"

"Ten to fifteen, usually."

Evelyn was stunned. "There's that much of a need?"

Dr. Morgentaler folded his hands together on his desk. His shoulders slumped imperceptibly.

"As long as the male sex continues to exist," he said, "there will always be a need, Miss Taylor."

Out on the sunny Ottawa street, Evelyn shakes her head to clear the weighty thoughts of the past. Today is about the future. She tears the Abortion Caravan poster off the telephone pole, folds it, and tucks it into the front pocket of her jeans, turning her feet in the direction of Parliament Hill.

She hails a taxi and throws herself into the back seat. "Confederation Park, please."

As the taxi crosses through a bustling intersection, Evelyn fishes the poster out of her pocket and lays it flat on her lap.

THE WOMEN ARE COMING, indeed. Several of them had set off from Vancouver several weeks ago, stopping in smaller towns and cities along the way to hold rallies, collect more troops, and stir up media coverage. Women's liberation is hot news, after all.

This protest is overdue and necessary. The radical feminists who started the abortion caravan in Vancouver say something needs to be done on a bigger scale. "A radical overhaul of the system," one woman shouted into the camera on last night's news. Her long blond hair flew around her face in the spring wind as she shouted, her eyes bright with anger and exhilaration. Evelyn thought she looked like a superhero. "The state needs to recognize women's rights to their own bodies," the woman said, "and make sure all women can exercise those rights regardless of their race or income."

Evelyn had watched the woman from her usual spot on the living room couch, felt her face flush with excitement in the glow of the television screen.

"You're going to go, aren't you?" Tom asked her in his melodious, English-accented voice from the other end of the couch. Evelyn glanced at him before returning her eyes to the screen. "Well, yes. I think I have to."

Tom was silent for a moment. "You could be risking your career, Eve. There will be arrests. This part might not be your fight, you know. You do enough."

The news anchor moved on to the next story and Evelyn had no excuse other than to turn to her best friend, whose eyes were filled with concern. She and Tom had moved into their own apartment, just the two of them, the previous year.

A couple of months into their friendship, Tom had been open with her about his sexuality to ensure she didn't get the wrong idea about his intentions. But for Evelyn, their relationship was a perfect scenario. She could talk to Tom on a level in a professional capacity, and he understood the demands of their work on her time and mental and emotional energy. They simply enjoyed each other's company. It was

straightforward and comfortable. Evelyn was looking for companionship, not romance. Someone to sit and read with when the snow is
falling outside, or talk to over coffee on lazy Sunday mornings while
she works on a crossword from the newspaper.

Tom knows what she does, but he's the only one. Since training with
Dr. Morgentaler five years ago, Evelyn has been secretly performing
abortions for university girls who find themselves in trouble. She has
appointments one night a week in addition to her shifts at a family
practice.

"I know, Tom. But don't you think it would be a bit hypocritical
of me to not support the women who are publicly fighting to make it
legal? They're risking just as much as I am."

"Are they? A fine for protesting and a prison sentence are two very
different outcomes."

They both fell silent as the tension settled between them on the
couch.

First thing this morning, Evelyn still headed to the train station,
leaving an envelope of cash and a note for Tom saying he should use it to
bail her out of jail, if necessary. But she really hopes it won't be necessary.

Evelyn reaches into her purse and pulls out the piece of paper she
scribbled the information down on last night. The organizers put the
word out to their networks that they would all meet on the lawn outside
the House of Commons on Saturday afternoon to protest and try to
speak to their elected officials, then plan their next move.

A few minutes later, the taxi pulls up along the south side of the
park. Evelyn pays the fare and hops out onto the sidewalk. She heads
up Elgin Street, past the brand-new National Arts Centre and the War
Memorial. The spectacular castle-like silhouette of the Château Laurier
looms large beside her, casting its shadow over the street as she makes
her way to the sprawling lawn outside Parliament Hill.

She hears the hum of noise emanating from the assembly before the crowd comes fully into view. There are hundreds of women, and some men. The slogan FREE ABORTION ON DEMAND! is scribbled in permanent marker on most of the placards she sees, along with some other, more militant demands like SMASH CAPITALISM!

Evelyn weaves her way through the crowd, the heat of all the excited bodies pressing in on her. But it's not oppressive; it's a good heat, like warm rain. She catches snippets of conversation, politically charged, angry voices raised, women laughing and smiling at one another. A chant rises up, starting from the center and working its way outward like ripples on a lake: "Every child a wanted child! Every mother a willing mother!" Evelyn is jostled as a woman knocks into her, apologizes, then shoves one of the placards into Evelyn's hands with a grin before returning to the chant.

Evelyn stops at a random spot, staking out her place in the scrum. The woman standing next to her smiles broadly and extends her right hand. Every single finger, including her thumb, is adorned with a chunky silver ring. "Welcome!" she shouts over the din. "I'm Paula."

"Evelyn."

They shake.

"Nice to meet you, Evelyn. Where you from?"

"Toronto originally. I'm in Montreal now, just finished medical school."

"Holy shit, wow! A doctor, eh?"

Evelyn smiles. "Yeah."

"What do you do? What kind of medicine?"

"Family medicine, and some gynecology."

"So is it like PAP tests and stuff, or, you know, *gyno*." Her eyebrows pop up and down suggestively.

Evelyn hesitates.

"It's safe here, you know," Paula says.

But Evelyn isn't sure she'll ever feel safe about this. She casts around for a change of subject. "So, what's the plan here?"

"We're waiting to see whether any of the fucking politicians are going to come out and talk to us, hear our demands," Paula says. "But it's seeming less and less likely. We've been here for hours now. I think they're afraid of us."

Evelyn continues to chat with Paula as the assembled protesters shout and chatter under the afternoon sun. When the breeze starts to cool and it's clear that no politicians are coming to speak with them, the crowd starts to thin out. Evelyn, thrilled but slightly disappointed, decides she better go find herself a hotel room for the night. She turns to say goodbye to Paula, but the woman grabs her arm.

"Hey, Evelyn, are you sticking around for a bit?"

"I hadn't planned on it. It kind of seems like things are over now. I think I got here too late. Everyone's leav—"

"Oh, things are *far* from over," Paula says. "They've only just begun."

Evelyn chuckles. "Now, why am I not surprised to hear you say that?"

Paula leans in toward Evelyn like a gossipy teenager. "My friend Cathy there is one of the organizers." She indicates a tall woman with a long brown ponytail that falls nearly to her waist. She's built like a marsh reed, but her face is fierce. "They brought a coffin in on the caravan, strapped to the roof of the car, you know, like a symbol for all our sisters who have died from *back-alley abortions*!" She tilts her head back and throws the words up into the sky.

They're a shocking bunch, these women. But then, that's really the whole point, isn't it? To shock the patriarchy into change.

"Yeah, I, uh, saw it on the news," Evelyn says.

"They used it to hold all their backpacks. Kind of clever, right? But now they want to deliver it right to Trudeau's front door. His abortion law is so restrictive, it might as well not even exist. A whole panel of men have to decide whether a woman *deserves* to be allowed to abort? I mean, fuck that, right? *Fuck that!*" She bellows into the heavens again.

There's a smattering of applause from the two dozen or so women remaining on the lawn.

"Yeah, you're right," Evelyn says. "There aren't exactly a lot of safe options."

She hitches her purse up onto her shoulder, readjusts her jacket. She hasn't had so much as an infection happen in the procedures she's performed so far, and she's damn proud of that fact. It's one of the reasons she does what she does, to help prevent deaths from botched abortions. Those stories are still in the news on a regular basis, but the laws refuse to catch up to the grim reality.

"That's an understatement, Eve," Paula says darkly. "And that's exactly why we want to go do this special little delivery. They say Trudeau isn't even in town today, and that's why he wouldn't meet with us. But fancy him coming home from wherever the hell he is to find a giant black coffin waiting for him on his stoop."

The image of the coffin stirs something deep inside Evelyn. "I want to come, too. I want to help."

Paula claps her on the shoulder. "I knew I liked you, Eve. Let's get this show on the road."

. . . .

The Prime Minister's house is only a five-minute drive from the Parliament buildings. Evelyn's grateful it isn't any longer, given that she's squished in the back seat of the car with three other women. Paula's hip bones dig into hers on one side, while the hard plastic of the car door presses uncomfortably on the other.

The women are all talking excitedly most of the way there, but a hush falls over the car in front of 24 Sussex Drive. Not surprisingly, a security gate with two guards blocks them from continuing up the gravel drive to the front doors.

"Figured we wouldn't be able to actually drop it on his doorstep, but we can leave it here, at least." Paula nudges Evelyn in the ribs. "Open the door."

Evelyn extracts herself from the car, Paula on her heel as the other women pile out of the vehicle, too.

"Thought we might be seeing you ladies!" one of the security guards calls. "We got a heads-up that you might try to pay the Prime Minster a visit, but I'm afraid he's not at home."

"But we have a gift for him!" Paula shouts, indicating the black coffin strapped to the roof of the car. "Let us up to the door to deliver it properly, would you?"

"Most certainly not, ma'am."

"Thought it was worth asking."

"M-hm. You can be on your way now."

"Not just yet, my friend."

Paula and two of the other women are already unstrapping the coffin from the car.

"I'd really rather you not do that," the guard calls to them.

"Too late!"

"Ma'am . . ."

Evelyn sees the other officer take out his radio. He's muttering into it, facing back toward the manor. Backup will be coming, and she'd really rather not be arrested if they can avoid it.

"Paula, we should go," Evelyn says.

But the women have the coffin in hand now, and Evelyn instinctively lunges forward to pick up the sagging foot of it as they carry it together, like pallbearers, their faces downcast, shouldering the weight of all the dead women's bodies it represents. They lay it down just feet from the guards, who swallow and stare at it with pinched mouths as though they've truly just been delivered a corpse.

The women stand for a long moment as the golden late afternoon sun warms their faces and a breeze rustles the leaves on the Prime Minister's lawn.

"This is for Mildred," the driver of their car, Cathy, finally says, a tear shimmering on her cheek. She turns and heads to the car, her long brown hair trailing behind her.

A pause.

"For my sister," another says, then follows her comrade. Each of the women steps forward in turn, naming their lost loved one.

"For *my* sister."

"Roberta."

"For my best friend."

Staring at the coffin, Evelyn sees all of their faces: her friends at St. Agnes's, her baby daughter, the two dozen women she's provided abortions for, the thousands more she'll provide between now and her eventual retirement. All the faces that led her to become Dr. Evelyn Taylor. She's in this now, and she will be forever.

"For all of them," she adds quietly, squinting into the sun. She walks back to the car with a heavy tread, barely registering the police sirens on the wind.

· · · · · · · · · ·

On Monday, Evelyn finds herself on the suited arm of a male ally of the cause, a man named Allan whom she met only ten minutes ago. They're waiting in a long line to get into Question Period.

Beards, Paula called the men. Decoys, so no one would notice all the single women entering the galleries in groups, or on their own. "Too many women that interested in Question Period on a single day will raise alarm bells, unfortunately," she said with a frown.

Paula approaches Evelyn and Allan now, sporting a blue shift dress and looking most unlike the version of Paula that Evelyn spent the weekend with, scouring secondhand shops for dresses and gloves to swap for their jeans and sweaters. They have to look the part of dignified ladies.

"The auto workers' union got the chains for us," she says. "Come here, Eve, hold out your bag. Allan, cover us."

Allan turns his back on the women, feigning interest in the stone carvings in the vaulted ceiling above his head. Paula lifts a length of chain out of her giant handbag and lowers it as slowly as she can into Evelyn's. The bustle and chatter of the people around them is noisy, but the clinking of the chains is still audible.

"How are we going to get them out of our bags once we're inside?" Evelyn asks in an undertone. "They're going to hear us, see us doing it."

Paula shrugs. "Just do your best. It's a protest. It won't be smooth and I'm sure it'll go sideways at some point. But it's the media coverage that counts, and if we can get Question Period shut down, so much the better. The point is, it's a bunch of men in there making decisions on our behalf, so we need to interrupt the decision-making. It's *our* turn to have a voice now, Eve. And remember, if you get hauled away by security, don't give them your name unless they absolutely force you to. We don't think they have the resources to actually arrest us all, and it would be a bad headline, anyway." Transfer of the chains complete, she adds, "Thanks, Allan!"

Evelyn's companion turns back around, winking at Paula. "Dinner tomorrow night, Paula, after I bail you out of jail? I think you still owe me dinner for the last time."

"I love and appreciate all the bailing you'll ever do for me, Allan."

Paula winks back at him, then disappears into the crowd to distribute more chains.

Within another half hour, Evelyn and Allan have settled themselves in their seats in the gallery. Evelyn's instructions are to wait for one of the leaders to stand up and start shouting her protest, at which point they assume several guards will haul her out of the gallery. During the commotion, the other women are supposed to whip out their chains and attach themselves to their chairs or the nearby railings. Then they'll each shout out in turn until—hopefully—the Speaker shuts down the proceedings.

Evelyn's heart starts to race as the doors are shut and locked by those very same security guards, each with crossed arms and generic stern faces.

"Bloody hell, this is fun," Allan mutters beside her with a chuckle.

Evelyn smiles, despite her nervousness. She glances down at the members of Parliament strolling in across the pea-green carpet below. Suits, bald heads, and shoes shinier than mirrors. The men who have never in their lives had to worry about getting pregnant, dying in childbirth, or trying to access an abortion within their own restrictive system. Paula's right, Evelyn thinks. It *is* time for their voices to be heard. To show these clueless men what it feels like to have your life disrupted by the actions of others. To feel helpless and afraid and angry and unable to stop what's happening to you.

Just a few minutes in, a woman on the west side of the gallery stands up and bellows down into the Chamber, shaking her fist. "Free abortion on demand! Women are dying because of your law, Trudeau! Shame on you, sir! Shame on all of you! Free abortion—"

The two guards at the gallery door immediately descend on her as the Prime Minister and all the representatives in the Chamber turn their heads up toward the commotion. The Prime Minister looks back down at his desk and purses his lips, ignoring the woman.

"Evelyn, the chain!" Allan says.

"Damn it!" She was so distracted by the shouting woman that she forgot her cue. "I'll wait for the next one," she whispers back, but already feels as though she's failed. Allan nods.

Almost instantly another woman yells out, this time in the east gallery. "We won't be silenced, Trudeau! Free abortion on demand! Free—"

The guards, anticipating the disturbance, apprehend the woman, but this time Evelyn is ready. She lifts the chain out of her purse and wraps it around and around the arm of her chair as quickly as she can with Allan's help. A woman behind her gasps.

"Order in the gallery!" the Speaker shouts upward, his booming voice carrying into the very back rows. "Order, I say! Control yourself, madam!"

The third protest comes from a woman several seats down on Evelyn's right. The fourth from the west side again. The fifth from Evelyn's own mouth, before she even has a chance to think about what she's saying. It's as if a stranger stood up in her body and shrieked the words over the excited, outraged chattering from the public gallery and the dark mutterings of deep male voices from the Chamber.

As the entire gallery erupts around her, Evelyn makes eye contact with the Prime Minister, who holds her gaze before strong male hands grasp each of her arms. She stiffens as one of the guards yanks on the chain, but when they nearly lift her rigid body into the air to carry her out, her self-defence training kicks in, and she goes limp. Both the guards pitch forward as her weight drags them all back down. Her head smacks against the back of the chair, and she winces as Allan shouts an admonishment to the guards. Everything is chaos. Evelyn stays as lifeless and heavy as a sack of onions. The guards end up half dragging her out of the gallery.

One of the guards gives her a kick in frustration. "Get *up*!" he bellows at her, his face beet-red and his doughy forehead beading with sweat. He's angry. He feels helpless. He's unable to stop what's happening. And that's all Evelyn needs.

"Make me, asshole!" She hardly recognizes herself, but she doesn't care. "Make me, then!"

He spits on her and reaches down, grasping her arm again in both his hands. He pulls —hard—and Evelyn feels something in her shoulder wrench out of place. She cries out as the other guard yells at his partner to stop.

Dizzy with the pain, all Evelyn registers is the utter pandemonium in the room, the shouting and screams and rattling chains, the Speaker bellowing commands that go unheeded. The sudden dampening of the sounds as she's hauled out of the gallery into the hallway. The relative quiet of the security office and the feel of the chair underneath her. The ache in her shoulder and head.

It isn't long before she's joined by a crowd of others, all the women who stood up to protest, and some of their male allies, too. She spots Paula among them. Everyone looks rather the worse for wear; collars are torn or sitting sideways, mascara is smeared, ties are crooked, hair has come down from carefully pinned coifs. Some of the women, like Evelyn, suffered injuries. Lips are bleeding and bare arms are blooming bruises.

The security guards shunt them all into the small office where Evelyn is still seated, and they bake in the heat for what feels like hours. Evelyn thinks her adrenaline should be wearing off by now, but the panic hasn't set in the way the pain in her shoulder has. She's still quaking with exhilaration at her own daring, and thinks wryly about what Tom's reaction will be when she calls to tell him that she has, in fact, been arrested and needs to be bailed out of an Ottawa jail.

There's much muttering and complaining in the holding room. "Our protest became a riot," Paula says proudly. "Well done, girls!"

"But when are we going to get out of here?"

"Where are the others?"

"Do you think they've shut it down?"

"Did we do it?"

"Are they going to arrest us, or what?"

"I don't think they have enough handcuffs .."

"They could borrow our chains!" Paula says.

There's a chorus of appreciative chuckling before the door finally opens and a tall, burly man with no neck strides into the room. All heads turn in his direction.

He glares at them, his lower lip downturned like an angry bulldog's. "I've never seen such madness in all my years here!" he barks. "You should be ashamed of yourselves. The Speaker's closed the Chamber."

Evelyn is proud to see all her fellow protesters meet his gaze with wide smiles. No one looks away. No one is backing down. It unnerves him, this huge presence of a man who takes pride in the fact that he can intimidate people. Evelyn can't remember the last time she felt so good. She could spit fire if she wanted to.

The man's Adam's apple slides up and down his thick, clean-shaven throat. "Well, we can't hold you all. Just get the hell out of this building within the next three minutes, or so help me God, you're all under arrest."

CHAPTER 13

Angela

. . . .

FEBRUARY 2017

When she leaves the store, Angela takes the copy of *The Jane Network* with her for Tina. They spoke briefly on the phone when Angela first discovered it, and Tina asked for a closer inspection.

After dinner, they're both delightfully full of fajitas and beer—Angela finally found a non-alcoholic one that she didn't hate—and Angela digs the book out of her tote bag and hands it to Tina.

"Here," Angela says to her wife, settling onto the couch with Grizzly. "I gave it a bit of a skim. I had no idea this piece of history existed."

"*The Jane Network*," Tina reads out. "Oh hey, this is Dr. Taylor's book!"

Angela stares back, nonplussed. "Sorry?"

"No, I mean I know her. I'm sure it must be the same Evelyn Taylor. She teaches at the university."

"Seriously?"

"Yeah, she gave my class a guest lecture, I don't know . . . three years ago? It's pretty well known among the faculty that she was part of an underground abortion group in the seventies and into the eighties, back before it was legalized." Tina flips to the table of contents, her eyes sliding down the page beneath her reading glasses. "She studied under Morgentaler, eh? Wow."

"I saw that. I've heard the name, but I don't really know who he is," Angela says.

"He's the one who went to the Supreme Court to challenge the constitutionality of the abortion law in the eighties. He even went to jail a couple of times. He's a pretty big deal." Tina shakes her head. "I had no idea she learned the procedure from him. She still teaches it. I brought her in for one of our closed-door lectures to tell the students about her experience. They loved it. I think it sparked a bunch of rebels."

Tina smiles and hands the book back to Angela, takes a sip of her beer. Candlelight from the coffee table glints off the brown glass.

"My book club was talking at our last meeting about how we should read some nonfiction this year," Angela says, studying the black-and-white cover. "I'm thinking of suggesting this."

"Do you think your book club girls would go for it?"

"Oh, for sure," Angela says, nodding. "They're a bunch of feminists; they'll find it interesting. Might be a good one to use to ease us all into nonfiction."

Tina's gaze drops. Grizzly hops from Angela's lap over to Tina's.

"You okay, hun?" Angela asks.

Tina tilts her head from side to side like a metronome. "Yeah. I guess I just wonder if you should read it, like, *right now.*"

Angela frowns. "What do you mean?"

Tina sighs. "To be blunt, I just mean do you really want to read a book about abortion while you're waiting to find out if you're pregnant? Now's probably not a great time to, you know . . ."

"Revisit that particular trauma?" Angela asks, meeting her wife's eyes.

"Yes."

Angela considers this for a moment. "Well, yeah. Maybe you're right. I'll hold off a bit. But on that note, I was actually thinking about doing a test. I know it's a bit early, but . . ."

With every fertility procedure, she's found it almost impossible to wait until after her expected period to take a pregnancy test. She knows she should wait, knows there likely isn't enough hormone in her system to register on the at-home tests, and that she might get a false negative that will send her spiraling. She had an early positive test once, too, but still got her period a few days later. After that, she swore she wouldn't test early, but her resolve hasn't held.

"You're just a couple of days off now, right?" Tina asks.

"Yeah."

"All right." She smiles. "Let's do it."

Fifteen minutes later, the two of them are squeezed into the tiny apartment bathroom with the pregnancy test resting on the counter. Angela lets her breath out in a guttural growl as Tina sets the timer on her phone for three minutes.

They wait in silence, Angela perched on the edge of the toilet, Tina leaning against the wall across from her. Both are fixated on the tile floor, trying to keep their eyes off the little window on the test that will determine what happens next.

Ten seconds to go.

"Remember, it's still early," Tina reminds her.

"I know."

"We'll test again in a few days."

"I know."

The buzzer goes off on Tina's phone and they both startle. Angela snatches the test from the countertop, heart hammering.

And there it is: if she turns it into the light *just* the right way . . . the faintest blue line. But it's there. It's *there.*

"T," Angela says, handing it to her wife with a shaky hand. "Look."

Tina has to squint a little, but her face breaks into a grin.

"You see it, too? I'm not dreaming?"

Tina wraps her arms around Angela, plants a kiss on her forehead. They hold each other under the harsh light of the old halogen light bulbs, the ones Angela usually hates because they highlight every little wrinkle and age spot, cast the most unappealing version of her face. But today those normally unkind lights dug deep to reveal that faint blue line. The bulbs glow over their heads—perhaps not so unkind after all—as tears slip down their cheeks. They'll cling to that little blue line of hope until they're forced to let go.

. . . .

A week later, Angela and Tina get off the subway and weave themselves in with the crush of other commuters climbing the slushy, slippery cement stairs up to the street level. They're meeting with their ob-gyn today for the results of the blood test Angela took three days ago, which will—hopefully—confirm the pregnancy. Angela took Tina's advice and held off on starting *The Jane Network* until they knew more.

They arrive at the clinic ten minutes early and check in with the receptionist in bubble-gum-pink scrubs at the front desk. "It's been six months since you updated your emergency contact," the receptionist says, eyes on her computer screen.

"Oh yeah, sure. It's still my wife, Tina."

"Same last name?" the receptionist asks.

"No, she's Hobbs and I'm Creighton."

"Okay, great, thank you. Just have a seat and the nurse will come get you in a moment."

Tina hangs their coats up on a spindly wooden rack and they sit down on the scratchy gray fabric chairs in the packed waiting room. They're called in twenty minutes later.

Their ob-gyn, Dr. Singh, breezes through the door of the exam room in her green scrubs.

"Hi, Angela, Tina." She smiles. "How are you both doing today?"

"We're a bit nervous," Angela says.

"Like always," Tina adds.

"Well, I'll get straight to the point: I have some very good news for you. You *are* pregnant."

Tina and Angela's faces crack into grins.

"We got a decent reading on the HCG in your system, Angela. We have good reason to be optimistic. Now, your iron was a bit low, so I'm going to put you on a supplement to get those levels back up where I'd like them to be, but beyond that, as always, just take it really easy over the next while. No strenuous activity."

Angela nods. "I know. Thanks."

"I know this has been a long road for you both," Dr. Singh says, looking at them each in turn. "It's not easy, but I'm confident we'll get there."

A lump forms in Angela's throat. "Thanks, Dr. Singh."

"Before you go, I'll just get you to give us a urine sample, Angela, and then you can head out. I'll see you again in a few weeks for your checkup."

They both nod and smile again as Dr. Singh hands Angela the plastic cup.

"And hey," she adds, turning back to face them on her way out the door. "Congratulations, you two."

. . . .

Tina has planned an elaborate celebratory meal for them back at home, but they call their parents to relay the news as soon as they set foot in the door. Their families have ridden this damn roller coaster right along with them, so they keep their tone cautiously optimistic, but it's a relief to be able to deliver some good news after their tragedy a couple of months ago.

As her parents' only child, Angela is the only one who might be able to deliver them grandchildren. Her parents have never pushed the matter, but she knows they're waiting on pins and needles just like she and Tina are. She called them first, and could hear the excitement in their voices, though they did their best to mirror Angela's reserved optimism.

She also phoned Sheila, whom she has kept in the loop since the start of their fertility process. Sheila was just a teenager when she gave Angela up for adoption. She isn't even sure who Angela's biological father is; it could be one of two men, but neither Sheila or Angela has ever pursued them. Sheila never wanted to be a mom, and certainly not so young. She's stayed single most of her adult life, preferring the flexibility afforded by fewer familial attachments. She was happy to reconnect with Angela, though, when Angela set out to find her. It was a little tricky to navigate at first, but they've developed a sisterly sort of relationship that works for them both without causing any tension between Angela and her mom. Angela hopes her birth mother will fill a role for her baby somewhere between an aunt and a grandma.

After they've made the calls, Tina good-naturedly orders Angela to lie down on the couch and rest while she cooks dinner.

"I certainly can't argue with that," Angela says, propping her feet up on the couch cushions and scooping Grizzly up into her lap. Tina kisses her for the twenty-seventh time that day. Once she drifts off into the kitchen, Angela pulls out her phone.

Same last name?

The receptionist's words are niggling at Angela, and she feels stupid for the oversight. The past few weeks she's been trying to find a woman named Nancy Mitchell, but it's entirely possible she has a different last name now, if she ever married. Angela's first thought is to search the classifieds in 1980s or '90s editions of the major Toronto newspapers and see if she can find any marriage announcements for Nancy Mitchells.

Angela sips her drink and lets the white noise of sizzling garlic drift along underneath the excited current of her thoughts. She uses Tina's credentials to log in to the university library's archive system, then navigates to the newspaper records. They have everything from 1980 onward in electronic format. It's unlikely Nancy was married before 1980, but it's possible. This is a start, at any rate. She isolates the classifieds from 1980 to 1999 and types in *Nancy* and *Mitchell*.

There are four hits. Two are unrelated news articles containing those names. One is a birth announcement from 1981, celebrating a baby girl born to a couple named Mitchell and Nancy Reynolds. The other is a marriage announcement from February 1986.

Mr. and Mrs. William and Frances Mitchell are pleased to announce the marriage of their daughter Nancy Eleanor to Mr. Michael James Birch.

"*Birch.* Nancy Birch . . . And Frances Mitchell. Got you." With a tingle of satisfaction, Angela immediately opens her Facebook app. She copies the same message she's been sending to the Nancy Mitchells, then enters the name Nancy Birch into the search box. It comes back with several hits. Once again, she sends the message to all the women who look to be about the right age, then sits back in the squishy couch cushion and pulls Grizzly close. He purrs into her neck, and Angela buries her face in his silky, glossy fur, feeling happier than she has in months.

CHAPTER 14

Evelyn

． ． ． ． ． ． ． ． ．

TORONTO | SPRING 1971

With a deep sigh, Evelyn closes her office for the day, locking the large wooden door with the satisfying *thunk* that signals the oncoming relief of the weekend. It's been a particularly hectic Friday afternoon and Evelyn's nurse, Alice, is busy straightening up the waiting room in the aftermath of a new patient: a four-year-old boy named Jeremy whom she has already nicknamed the Human Tornado.

"Evelyn," Alice says. "Do you have plans later tonight?"

Evelyn sits down in the chair next to the stack of children's books Alice just tidied and crosses one leg over the other, pressing a week's worth of exhaustion into the chair back.

"No, thank goodness. After our next appointment, I'm going home for a shamefully large glass of wine." She checks her watch. "She's coming in at six, right?"

Last summer, Evelyn told Tom that she wanted to relocate to Toronto and start her own practice, and he agreed to come with her. They bought this old house on Seaton Street and converted the main floor into a waiting room, reception space, and two exam rooms. Even with the rent from the apartment upstairs, Evelyn's still gone into more debt than she ever imagined possible. But despite the debt, she's proud; she has a full roster of patients.

Chester Braithwaite was her first. The octogenarian arrived on the porch of the clinic moments after she hung out her shingle, in an act that had instantly endeared him to her and dug a little divot into her heart.

"Hullo, Doctor," he said, actually tipping his gray wool cap in Evelyn's direction. "I live just down the street there and I've come to see if you're acceptin' new patients. My wife passed last year, ya see, and my daughter's been haranguing me to look after my health. Wondered if ya had room for an ol' fella like me. I'll tell ya right now, I've no intention of givin' up my nightly whiskey. I smoke a cigar once a week on Sunday evenings, and I don't eat vegetables. Not about to change my ways now. But my ticker's strong and I've a mind to live out at least another ten years, so ya'd be stuck with me for a while. Whaddya say, Doc?"

If pressed, she would never admit to harboring preferences, but Chester is her favorite. Aside from the delightfully frolicking cadence of his name, Evelyn is particularly fond of him for his paternal nature and unabashed honesty. During their exams, most of Evelyn's patients will overexaggerate the virtues of their diet and lifestyle while underreporting the prevalence of health-related vices. But not Mr. Braithwaite.

Chester referred several of his friends and neighbors to "that lovely young lady doctor down the street, ya know," which helped her practice flourish. And when she was able to hire a nurse, she plumbed her trusted networks for someone who would be supportive of her unique clinical offerings. Through a mutual friend who was also part of women's liberation, Paula connected her with Alice, and they hit it off after their first meeting over coffee.

Alice isn't much younger than Evelyn, somewhere in her mid-twenties. She's crusty on the outside with a soft center, like a well-made croissant, and even though they haven't known each other long, Evelyn

trusts her as much as she trusts Tom. She and Alice have been performing a couple of abortions after-hours each week for the past six months.

Now Alice sits in the chair across from Evelyn, leans forward with
her hands clasped tightly between her knees. "I want to run something
by you."

"Shoot."

Alice hesitates. "Remember when my sister Emily came in?"

"Of course." A smart girl. A failed condom.

"Well, a friend of hers was asking about it for a friend of *hers*, because
that girl's aunt had told her she could call around to doctors' offices
and ask for a woman named Jane."

"Jane?"

"Jane. Just Jane. It's a code word."

Evelyn shifts in her seat. "A code word for an abortion?"

"Kind of. A code name for this network that's connecting women
with doctors who will *provide* abortions. A whisper network, basically.
Apparently there's a big one in Chicago that's been using that code
name and it's caught on elsewhere. I guess it's generic enough to slide
under the radar."

Evelyn is quiet for a moment. "Someone I knew a long time ago
named her baby Jane," she mutters, running her index finger over a seam
in the thigh of her scrubs. "Interesting that they'd use a code."

"Very," Alice says. "It's a clever system."

Evelyn notices the spark of possibility in her eyes. "I see where you're
going with this, Alice, but—"

"Please just hear me out, Evelyn. Please."

Evelyn licks her dry lips, nods.

"So, there's a team of organizers for this network. They just call themselves Jane, or the Janes. It's basically a formalized version of what we do.
Right now women hear about us from their sister's friend's cousin, then
they call us, right? But it only allows a relatively small circle of women to

hear about the fact that we can offer safe abortions. Word isn't going to get out much further than a few degrees of removal from you and me."

"We do a couple of them a week, Alice. We're doing what we can."

"But not *all* we can, right?"

Evelyn chews the inside of her cheek. "What we're doing now is risky enough as it is."

"I know. But I want to do more. If we can." Alice lets out a long sigh. "The organizers are having a meeting tonight. I asked Emily to try to connect with one of them through her friend. She gave me the address. It's at eight o'clock. I'd like to go."

Evelyn surveys her nurse with a shrewd eye. "And you want me to come, too."

"Yes. Just come see what it's all about, and we can talk about it afterward. No commitment."

Alice smiles, her perfect teeth shining white in her dark face. She's a serious person and doesn't smile often, but when she does, it illuminates everything around her. It's so warm, perfect for calming the nerves of their after-hours patients.

Evelyn stands and paces the worn carpet a few times, stooping to pick up a rogue piece of yellow Lego before turning back to Alice. "I can imagine what it's about. It's a bunch of women risking everything by being brazen and too out in the open about what they're doing. It's easier the way we do it, Alice. The less people know about what we do here, the better. It keeps us safe, and that means we can continue to offer the service. We can't offer it if we're in prison. And neither can these Janes."

Alice meets Evelyn's eyes straight on. They're reflecting the soft light of the lamp on the reception desk.

"But what if we're *too* safe here? What if some desperate woman out there right now can't find us? What if she thinks there's no one who can help her?"

"We can't help everyone, Alice. I wish we could, but we can't."

"No, we can't help everyone, but we could be helping more."

The two women stare at one another for a long moment, each calculating the consequences of pushing too hard.

Evelyn exhales slowly, shrugs. "Let me think about it."

. . . .

Tom has already started on dinner when Evelyn arrives home. She can smell onions and what might be eggplant. They're both vegetarians, and Tom is one of the best cooks Evelyn has ever encountered. She hangs her purse and jacket up on a hook in the front hall and neatly sets her shoes on the boot tray before wandering down the long hallway to the kitchen, following the sound of classical music and sizzling veggies.

"Welcome home, dearest," Tom says. He plants a kiss on her cheek and hands her a large glass of red wine.

"Ah, cheers," Evelyn says with a sigh, settling herself down on a stool at the kitchen island.

"My wife seems taxed on this Friday evening," Tom says, his back to her as he tends to the frying pan. "Care to vent?"

Evelyn hadn't intended to get married, but Tom asked when she suggested they move to Toronto, and she'd agreed willingly. It was the most natural of seemingly unnatural choices, to marry a gay man. For both of them, it felt like an extension of their existing relationship.

But in the moment when Tom proposed, Evelyn had laughed aloud.

"I thought your intentions were entirely honorable, Mr. O'Reilly," she said with a smirk. "Or have you just been manipulating me all this time? Leading me into believing you're gay so you could sneak up on me with a surprise proposal?"

He dropped to one knee and held both of her hands in his own. "Marrying you would mean that I could enjoy a lifetime's supply of your lemon shortbread cookies, and that alone is worth the commitment."

She smiled wryly.

"But, Evelyn, you have truly made me happier than any other woman ever has at any point in my life."

The smile sank a couple of notches on Evelyn's face as she realized he was quite serious. His relationship with his mother was strained, to say the least. He had fled England to escape her snide remarks about his "nature" under the pretense of expanding his horizons with an overseas education.

"I know you have your reasons for never wanting to get married or have children," Tom continued. "You've trusted me with your biggest secrets, and I've trusted you with mine. But I think we could stay safe and be very happy sharing a life together."

Evelyn smiled, then, feigning outrage, cried, "You don't expect me to take your name, do you?"

"Of course not, my darling. I wouldn't dare suggest such a thing, for fear of grievous injury to my most delicate and valued organs."

Laughing, Evelyn nodded. "Okay."

"That's a yes?"

"That's a yes." And she let Tom slide a simple ring onto her finger.

Evelyn runs that same finger around the rim of her wineglass now, watching the diamond in her engagement ring catch the light from overhead as she considers how to broach the topic of the Jane network with Tom. They're rarely cagey with one another. Their shared bluntness is one of the things that's made their unique relationship work over the years. And how else *could* it work if they weren't brutally honest with one another? There's no space to play games with each other when your relationship is based on a mutual need to keep your true identity a secret.

"I know that look. Spit it out, love," Tom says, sitting down on the stool across from her.

Evelyn softens, takes a long sip of her drink. "Alice came to me with a proposal today."

"Mmm, bad timing. You're already married."

"Ha, ha, yes, I know. But seriously, she was asking me to join her at a meeting of an underground abortion network. It's called Jane."

"Jane?" Tom asks.

"Jane." Evelyn takes another large swig of wine.

"Huh. What are they doing that you aren't?"

"I'm not sure, really. Sticking their necks out unnecessarily. That's what I told Alice, anyway. Sounds like a whisper network of sorts, but I don't have much detail."

"Where's the harm in going to get that detail?"

"Mm?"

"Go to the meeting. There's nothing to lose, right?"

Evelyn considers for a moment, then shakes her head. "No. Not tonight, anyway. I need time to think." She pauses, then taps her finger on the side of her glass. "Can a girl get a top-up?"

Tom unfolds his long limbs and retrieves the bottle from the counter beside the stove, sets it down beside Evelyn before turning his attention back to meal preparation. Evelyn pours a little too much into her glass, then leans forward, settling her elbows onto the island.

"Alice is adamant that we can be doing more than we already are, but"—Evelyn shakes her head—"there's a lot to lose if we're found out."

Tom is quiet for a while, though Evelyn can tell he's thinking it over. "You remember the Parliament Hill protest?" he asks.

"Of course."

"Do you remember the conversation we had the night before you left?"

She can see where he's going with this. In medical school, his grades were always a couple of percentage points higher than hers. It was an ongoing joke at the time, but she's always felt like Tom benefits from a slight edge. He's often just one step ahead of her. It's a trait that makes him such an attentive husband, though. He anticipates her needs before she's fully aware of them herself.

"You thought I was worrying too much," he says. "And that you'd be a hypocrite for not going to the protest. You basically told me that if you're doing this, you're *doing this*, right?"

Evelyn holds his intense gaze with her own.

"Well," Tom says, "it would seem that other women are doing it, too. Maybe the need is coming out of the shadows a bit, and that's a good thing for everyone. It's illegal, full stop, so there will always be a risk, I grant you. But if more women are standing up to the illegality, fighting against it . . . why not join them? Maybe there is safety in numbers, in a way. You told me they couldn't arrest you all at the Hill protest. Not enough handcuffs, right?"

Evelyn takes another long draft from her glass, eyeing her irritatingly sensible husband. She nods again. "Not enough handcuffs."

. . . .

Evelyn and Alice wait for their after-hours appointment to arrive on a damp Tuesday evening. They got takeout from the Chinese food place two blocks away and sat on the floor of the waiting room, eating off the tiny coffee table.

"So," Alice begins, popping a chunk of broccoli into her mouth with the short wooden chopsticks. "Have you given any more consideration to the Janes?" She hasn't mentioned it at all since their first conversation a few weeks ago.

Evelyn keeps her eyes on her noodles. "A little bit, yes."

"And?"

"I spoke with Tom about it. But I'm still not sure."

Alice sighs. "Okay."

They sit in a sticky silence for another five minutes, each eating faster than they normally would. When they've finished, Evelyn stacks the take-out containers and walks them over to the reception desk garbage.

"Our patient'll be here in ten. Let's get prepped," she says.

Alice straightens, stretches her arms over her head. "What's her name?"

"Celeste."

Half an hour later, Celeste is on the surgery table with her socked feet in the stirrups. She's the youngest patient they've ever had. Only sixteen.

"How are you doing, there, Celeste?" Evelyn asks, fixing her surgical mask into place and pulling on her gloves. "Do you understand the procedure as Alice has explained it to you? You understand what we're about to do?"

Celeste nods, and the tears start to fall, as they often do right before Evelyn begins her work. Alice rushes over with some tissues and encourages Celeste to blow her nose.

"Sorry," Celeste says.

Evelyn can't count the number of times a patient has unnecessarily apologized to her in this room. "That's okay. Do you need a minute?"

"No, I'm okay. To be honest, I'm just grateful. I had a friend—" She swallows with difficulty. "I had a friend who died last year because she got pregnant. She comes from a really religious family and she panicked and thought she could get rid of it by drinking . . . drinking bleach. I thought I was really careful about not getting pregnant. And then when it happened, I just thought, *Oh my God, I'm going to die now.*"

Alice's wide eyes meet Evelyn's over the tops of their masks. The room is silent. A car passes by on the wet road outside the window.

Celeste takes a shaky breath. "I just figured, if I didn't want to be pregnant anymore, that I'd have to do one of those things you hear about, you know, like using a knitting needle. Or throwing myself down the fucking stairs. Sorry. My mom says I swear too much. But yeah, I called my doctor to just ask if there was anything I could do, and she wouldn't talk about it, but she gave me your number."

Evelyn's brow furrows. This isn't the first time they've gotten a referral from another physician's office. She's glad, in a way, that they know what she does and have the decency to refer their patients to her, but she resents the fact that they aren't willing to step the hell up themselves.

"Anyway, I really thought I was probably going to die," Celeste says again, her watery eyes reflecting the bright lights of the overhead halogens. "So, thank you. I just . . ." Her lip trembles. "I just wish I had known about you before Linda got pregnant. I can't—"

Alice steps forward with a cool cloth, brushes Celeste's hair back off her forehead.

At the end of the table, Evelyn is speechless. She tries to clear her head of the uncomfortable truths that she's beginning to fear may end up dictating her career.

"Okay, Celeste," she says gently to her patient. "Take some deep breaths and hold Alice's hand. This will all be over soon."

. . . .

"A church?" Evelyn asks Alice, stopping short on the sidewalk outside the ornate building. "Seems a bit . . . unlikely."

Immediately after they put Celeste in a cab on Tuesday night, Evelyn asked Alice to find out about the next meeting of the Janes. Alice engaged her grapevine and found out there was a meeting on Friday evening. They took the streetcar over together after veggie sandwiches and milkshakes at Fran's Diner.

Alice inspects the numbers on the red-brick exterior. "It's the right address. Besides, it's a United church. Can't be that bad, right? Let's go in and see."

Evelyn leads the way up the path, and they enter, letting the heavy wooden door close with a soft thud against the noise of the bustling street.

"Are you here for the Knitting Club meeting?"

Both Evelyn and Alice jump at the woman's voice, which echoes up into the cavernous ceiling. The speaker is standing in shadow to the left of the entryway. She's in her late twenties, Evelyn would guess, with large glasses and pin-straight dark brown hair that falls well past her shoulders.

"Um," Alice falters, but Evelyn catches on.

"We're here to see Jane," she says, her throat sticking.

"I don't think she's seen you before."

Evelyn and Alice exchange a look.

"My name's Alice and this is Evelyn," Alice begins, nodding at her boss. "We heard about you through my sister, who heard through a friend, et cetera. I followed up to get the information about when and where you'd be meeting."

"Okay. But you're not actually *looking* for Jane, though, are you?" the woman asks, frowning. "As in tonight? 'Cause that's not—"

"Oh, oh no," Alice interrupts. "I'm a nurse and Evelyn's a doctor and we're interested in—" Evelyn clears her throat loudly. "*Possibly* interested in helping out with, you know, the cause," Alice finishes, her cheeks flushing.

The woman's eyes pop like champagne corks and she extends a hand to Evelyn, who offers her own. The woman nearly crushes it with enthusiasm before grasping Alice's in turn. "That's excellent, *excellent* news, thank you both so much for coming. My name's Jeanette. We're in desperate need of willing doctors, that's the focus of the meeting tonight. Down the stairs to the right over there," she says with an enormous smile. "We'll be starting in a couple of minutes."

"Thank you," Evelyn and Alice say in unison, and head off in the direction of the staircase, which takes them down into the basement of the building. There's a single door with a paper sign that reads KNITTING CLUB MEETING scribbled in black marker. Alice raises an eyebrow at Evelyn and pulls the handle.

They emerge into a large community room. Orange plastic chairs are set up lecture-style facing a wooden pulpit with a brass cross inlaid onto the front of it. The air smells like a library, and it's full of the excited chatter of at least a dozen women. Evelyn gestures to a line of four empty seats at the back, and as they settle in, she scans the room with a keen eye. Her shoulders relax with relief that there's no one here she recognizes.

A few minutes later, a young woman who looks like she can't be more than twenty-five years old sidles up to the pulpit and grasps the sides of it in both hands. She leans forward, smiling at the assembly. Silence falls almost instantly, and Evelyn can feel an electricity in the room.

"Welcome everyone," the woman says with a voice like chocolate. "Thank you for coming to tonight's Knitting Club meeting." An appreciative chuckle from the crowd. "My name is Holly. I see we have a few new faces, so I'd like to ask our newcomers to hang back after the meeting so we can get to know each other a bit, and I can make sure you're not a spy."

She smiles, but a few of the women glance back at them with suspicion. Evelyn shifts in her seat.

"So, tonight's meeting is a bit of a check-in for the movement and the organization," Holly continues in a crisp tone, looking down at a sheet of paper in front of her. "I'm proud to say that since this movement began, we've been able to connect almost a thousand women with a few doctors who are willing to provide safe, effective abortions."

Applause erupts from the assembled women. One of them lets fly a *whoop!* of support.

"It's great, it really is, it's amazing," Holly says. "We've been able to save a lot of lives through the Jane Network and we couldn't have done that without all the time, energy, and sacrifice you've put into making it happen. So, thank you. But there are still a lot of women waiting. We've done our best to not turn anyone away. That was always one of our commitments, our goals. But one or two have fallen through the cracks. They came to us almost too late, needing a procedure immediately, and we didn't have a doctor available to perform it. And those cases weigh heavily on our collective conscience."

Evelyn catches herself holding her breath. The crowd is hushed. Holly may be young, but she certainly knows how to command a room.

"But we have a good news story here with us today," she goes on, smiling at a woman in the front row. "I'd like to hand the floor to Lillian, our guest speaker, who is going to share her experience with us. A little support for her, please!"

Holly initiates a round of applause and steps back from the pulpit as Lillian rises from her seat. Holly gives her a warm hug, then Lillian faces the Janes. She coughs into her fist, which is trembling slightly. She's a short girl with sandy blond hair and shoulders that turn inward, protective.

"Hi, there," she says.

A chorus of warm female voices call, "Hi, Lillian!"

"I, um, I don't have a whole lot to say, but I just wanted to come say thank you to every one of you who had a hand in helping me, you know, get an abortion." Her voice drops off on the last word. "I heard about Jane through a friend of a friend, like pretty much everyone does, I guess. I was really scared at first. I . . ." She falters, casts her eyes down. "I was really desperate. I—I got raped by my stepdad." Her voice goes up at the end, like it's a question she's still trying to answer. "After a lot of other abuse. For a long time. And obviously I couldn't . . ."

The unspoken words press down on the shoulders of every woman at the meeting. They all feel the magnitude of Lillian's experience, the crushing weight of it.

"It's a special kind of evil mother that allows that shit to happen under her own roof," Evelyn says bitterly.

Alice grasps Evelyn's cold hand in her own, squeezes it tight. "I know," she whispers.

"I didn't want to have a baby," Lillian continues. "I couldn't tell my mom. I'm in school. I want to be a teacher, so I would have had to drop out, and I didn't want to do that. I told my doctor, and he said he didn't think my situation would be enough for the abortion committee to approve. Can you believe that?" Lillian shakes her head in disbelief amid dark mutterings from the crowd. "He said even though it was rape, it might not be approved. He had another patient who was in the same situation, and they denied her an abortion because they didn't believe her. They thought she was just covering for a mistake." She pauses. "Anyway, all I mean to say is that access is really hard. I ended up just telling my doctor I had a miscarriage, but I don't think he believed me. There's a lot of girls like me who just have no other option, and getting help from you all has literally saved my life. I'm not sure I would have kept going otherwise. So, thank you."

She scurries back to her seat in the front row as applause erupts. Alice sniffs while Evelyn's finger gravitates, as it often does, toward the scar at her wrist.

She remembers with painful accuracy what it feels like to be pregnant and wish you weren't. To be in denial, then weeks later find yourself vomiting up your morning toast while the tears run down your face into the toilet. To feel the slight swell of your belly and the pain in your breasts and know that you won't be able to hide it much longer. To dream of ending it, any way at all. An accidental trip down a flight of stairs, or drinking *just* enough bleach to not quite kill yourself. Opening up your wrists in a bathtub.

Steam fogging up the bathroom mirror.
The feeling of falling, falling, the scent of roses on the warm air.
Her brother's voice calling her name.

Evelyn wrenches her mind out of that dark corner of her past, back into the bright lights of the church basement. She rolls her shoulders back, tries to focus.

Holly returns to the pulpit, her eyes shining with admiration and something deeper, a fiery determination that seems to glow. "Thank you,

Lillian," she says. "Thank you for your bravery in sharing your experience with us. It was our honor to help you exercise your right to determine what happens to your own body."

Evelyn's heart is racing as though she just ran up several flights of stairs. Holly reminds Evelyn a bit of Paula, her protest friend from the Abortion Caravan. She isn't as crass, but there's a fierceness to her entire presence that takes Evelyn back to those days in Ottawa. The steely yet pained expressions on her comrades' faces when they delivered the coffin to 24 Sussex Drive with the fire of the setting sun in their eyes. Paula screaming her outrage up into the sky because it was too big to be contained in her body. How the air in the House of Commons gallery was charged with the protesters' daring and resolve.

Evelyn feels that same energy hovering over the heads of the women gathered in this musty church basement tonight. The fight is still very much alive; it's simply changed its form.

"And that leads me into our big focus tonight," Holly says, shifting her weight. She's all business now. "Access. *Adequate,* on-demand access. As word has caught on about Jane, the demand has outstripped our resources. Lillian just demonstrated to us what we've known for a while now: that the abortion law is too restrictive. Women are coming to us instead of even trying to go the legal route because the powers that be want us subjugated. The truth is we desperately need more doctors. We need to be able to provide safe abortions to *every single woman* who calls Jane. It's our duty as resourceful, privileged women.

"So, if you have any friends who are sympathetic to the movement and have some time to spare—and are sensible enough to exercise discretion—please approach them. And if you know a doctor who might be willing to join our network, please, please, please"—she leans forward on the pulpit like a preacher—"ask them to reach out to us. It's a risk, yes, but these women need help."

"We can help." Evelyn is on her feet in the back row.

"Yes!" Alice gasps.

Every single face turns in their direction. It's unnerving, but Evelyn plows on. "My name is Evelyn Taylor. I'm a family physician and my nurse Alice and I"—she motions to Alice to stand—"have been performing abortions for the past several months at my practice, after-hours. I trained under Dr. Morgentaler in Montreal."

Suddenly Evelyn feels the intensity of all those eyes, the heat rising in her face. Alice gives Evelyn's hand another squeeze, but Evelyn keeps her eyes on Holly's. "We can help," she repeats.

A grin spreads across Holly's face. Everything in the room is lit up. She nods slowly. "All right, then, Dr. Taylor, Alice. Welcome to the Jane Network."

CHAPTER 15

Nancy

· · · · · · · · · ·

MARCH 1981

Nancy descends the creaky stairs of the old nursing home, heart fluttering in her chest as she recounts the days in her head. It's been two weeks. Turning right at the bottom of the staircase, she ducks into the public washroom near the reception desk. The young nun at the desk tosses her a smile, which Nancy returns with tight lips. She figures she may as well check one more time.

Despite the fact that her Grandmama passed several months ago, Nancy has been volunteering at her nursing home, offering much-needed companionship to those few poor souls with no family. Nancy sits by their bedside during those last days, once Death has announced his intent to visit and there is nothing anyone can do to stop his steady march.

And although Nancy spent her morning here, she should have been at home studying. She's behind on a couple of courses, and her grades are slipping, but part of the problem is that she doesn't care much about school right now. She's more interested in spending her time hearing about the ways other people managed to screw up their own lives—the secrets they kept, the painful buried truths. The lies they could never unravel.

Her grandmother's confessions in the haze of her last days and the resultant revelation have stuck with Nancy ever since, and she's found the same inclination among the other palliative residents she sits with. She's found that, more often than not, the presence of another person, even a stranger, sparks an urgency to relay anything left unsaid. To ensure someone will at least hear their story and carry it into the future for them in an existential relay. The prospect of death causes a person to shine a light into the darkest corners of their history, turning over the moss-covered rocks that have lain there for years. Undisturbed, perhaps, but certainly not forgotten. And Nancy likes to be there when the spotlight is flicked on for the Big Reveal. She watches the secrets begin to take shape, first with clouded edges, then sharpening with each word. The deepest thoughts these men and women dared not speak to their loved ones. The confessions and regrets, the things they did and the things they should have done.

The departing soul holds the words out to her. Nancy takes them gently in her hands, runs her fingers along the ragged edges, bumps, and sharp corners. She turns them over in her palm, viewing them from different angles, knowing that if she isn't careful, the cut could be deep.

But the danger is part of the appeal. They're all in Nancy's keeping now. She has become a collector of other people's secrets while her own just keep piling up.

In the washroom, Nancy locks the stall door and unzips her jeans. Nothing.

"Shit. *Fuck.*"

Her period is now officially two weeks late.

She hikes up her pants and slips out of the bathroom, making her way to the front doors of the nursing home. Her stomach churns as she walks; it could just be the nerves that are now setting in, or it could be more of the nausea she's been trying to ignore for the past few days. She threw up yesterday morning, but she'd chalked it up to the previous night of drinking with friends.

She's tried her best to put off the inevitable, but knows now that she'll have to bite the bullet and go get one of those new at-home pregnancy tests. And whatever the result is, she knows she won't be telling Len.

Len, she thinks darkly as she dodges her fellow bustling pedestrians out on the street, her head bowed down against the freezing spring drizzle. It's *Len* who got her into this damn mess in the first place. *Len* and his cheap candy-apple-red condoms. *Len Darlington,* with a name like a character from a drugstore romance novel. They've only been dating a few months, and on and off at that. Nothing serious. Nancy isn't even sure she would call it dating. They've slept together on a handful of occasions, and she thought they had been reasonably careful. Except for the past couple of times when she was too drunk to remember much. She's spent most of the past year drinking; too heavily, she knows. But it's an effective numbing agent.

She met Len back in the fall. He was a friend of a friend of Nancy's roommate Debbie, who introduced them at a cramped house party she threw on a Monday night without consulting Nancy or their other roommate, Susan. Debbie's immature antics are the only thing that ever causes Nancy to second-guess moving out of her parents' home, but it's better than having her overbearing mother breathing down her neck and asking her whether she's been seeing anyone lately. It seems to be Frances Mitchell's greatest wish that Nancy meet "some nice fellow" and settle down at the earliest opportunity. She has the Grandma Glint in her eye and doesn't hesitate to make this burning desire known to Nancy whenever possible. Nancy decided to bring Len home precisely because he was unlikely to pass Frances's strict standards for her daughter's suitors. Len served a purpose. That was all Nancy needed from him.

Despite the fact that her mother is clearly angling for grandchildren to dote upon, Nancy is pretty sure this isn't exactly what she had in mind. She rounds a corner and pulls open the door of the pharmacy.

She figures she'll give the home pregnancy test a try first; she can't bear to go to her family doctor. If she's going to get bad news, she wants to get it in the privacy of her own bathroom, where she won't have to temper her reaction. After a mortifying checkout encounter with a male cashier at least a decade older than her own father, Nancy sweeps from the shop with her head down.

She arrives back at her apartment to discover her roommates are, thankfully, both out. In the bathroom, Nancy pees into a plastic cup she took from the kitchen and then fusses with the finicky test tubes of the Predictor kit. She waits an agonizing two hours for the result, reading her novel without taking in a word of it, checking her watch every ten minutes. She prays to God for a negative, promising all manner of improved behavior in return, and crosses herself twice to seal the deal.

When an hour and fifty-eight minutes have passed, Nancy stumbles back to the bathroom. Fingers trembling, she picks up the test tube and sees a bright red ring around the base of it. A stone-cold, clear positive.

"Fuck." She slides down the bubbling wallpaper to the linoleum floor. "*Fuck!*"

She rakes a hand through her hair and looks at the test result half a dozen more times, willing it to spontaneously change as the blood drains from her face.

The front door clatters open, echoing down the hall.

"Heya!" Susan calls.

Nancy swallows with difficulty. "Hi—" Her voice cracks and she clears her throat. "Hi, Sue!"

Knowing there's nothing more to be gained from staring at the damned test, Nancy gathers the contents back into the paper pharmacy bag and wrenches open the bathroom door. She should go say hi to Susan, but she can't handle talking to anyone right now, so she darts across the hall into her bedroom and locks the door, flopping herself down on the edge of the bed. She's about to toss the paper bag with its incriminating contents into her wicker garbage bin when, glancing down, she spots a piece of bright red shiny plastic wedged between the nightstand and the wall. Nancy reaches to fish it out and, as she does so, recognizes it as a condom wrapper. Len must have missed the garbage when he tossed it. As she holds it between her fingers, it screams at her like an accusation.

She throws it into the garbage along with the pregnancy test, covering the evidence of her premarital transgressions. But covering it up isn't enough. She needs it erased. She needs it to be undone. She won't tell Len. She doesn't want to tell anyone. If she keeps it a secret, maybe she can pretend that it never happened at all.

Clara's words come unbidden to her mind from the day she called Nancy, asking her to come with her to the abortion. *No one ever needs to know . . .*

Nancy has just lain back on the pillows when the pink phone on her bedside table rings next to her ear. She ignores it, but after two rings, Susan's muffled voice drifts down the hall from the kitchen. A moment later, her roommate calls her name.

"Nance! It's your mom!"

Nancy groans. *Not now.* She opens her mouth to yell to Susan that she'll call her mother back when she remembers it's Saturday; they're having lunch together today. She glances at the clock on her bedside table. They're supposed to be meeting in one hour.

"Ugh, shit," she mutters. "Okay! Thanks!" She sits up and lets out a long breath before picking up the receiver. "Hey, Mum."

"Hello, dear." Her mother's sugary voice makes her want to weep right now. "How are you?"

"I'm, uh, I'm okay. Yeah. Just, you know, working on school stuff. How are you? How's Dad?"

"Well, that's actually why I'm calling. I'm feeling quite under the weather today and I'm afraid I must cancel our lunch."

A wave of relief washes over Nancy, but when it recedes, guilt rushes in to replace it. "I'm sorry to hear you're not feeling well."

"Oh, it's just my head, you know. The migraines."

She's suffered from them since Nancy was little. Nancy remembers twirling in a new Easter dress, her mother admiring the lace detailing even as she held a cold cloth to her forehead, insisting she was well enough to go with Nancy and her father to Easter mass. Without really registering what she's doing, Nancy places a hand on her stomach as her mind wanders toward Margaret, and what she might have dressed her in if things had turned out differently.

Once the shock of the Big Lie sank in last spring, she spent the next few weeks trying to decide what, if anything, to do with the information she now possessed. After some exhausting soul-searching and weighing the pros and cons, Nancy determined that it wasn't worth pursuing her birth mother. She had no idea how she would even begin trying to locate her. And she didn't plan on telling her parents what she had found. Oddly, she couldn't bear the thought of them feeling as though she had betrayed them, even though they were the ones who had been lying to her all along. Loyalty is a complicated thing.

"Nancy? Are you there, dear?"

"Yeah, Mum. Hi. Sorry. I spaced out for a second there."

"Are you okay?"

Nancy pinches her lips shut. She knew even before she took the pregnancy test that she didn't want a baby right now, but the confirmation has thrown a nasty wrench into her thoughts that weren't there yesterday, or even an hour ago. She thinks about what she knows from the secret box in her mother's dresser drawer. How much her parents wanted a child, the lengths they went to in order to adopt her. That there are people so desperate for children that they'll do almost anything to have one.

What if Nancy had this baby, and gave it up for adoption? It could be a dream come true for a loving couple like her parents. But what if she regretted it, like her birth mother did? She considers Margaret's note. What if Nancy spent the rest of her life grieving and trying to find her long-lost child?

And that's when it hits her like it never has before. She *gets it* now, what Margaret Roberts must have gone through, the terror she likely felt when she found out she was pregnant so young, and out of wedlock. Times were different then. Girls didn't have options.

No, Mum. I am very much not okay.

The tears have started now. She's on the verge of telling her mother everything. All of it. She's sick of carrying it around. It's too heavy and its sharp corners cut into her skin when she least expects it. But what if her mother wants her to keep the baby? What then?

And she's just so good at keeping secrets. What's one more?

"Yeah, I'm fine, Mum," Nancy answers, forcing down a sharp lump in her throat the exact size and shape of the lie she just told her mother.

"All right, dear. Well, again, I'm sorry to have to postpone. I just don't think I'd be up to it right now."

"It's okay. We can go another time when you're feeling better." She tries to redirect her own thoughts to something more mundane. "You've been having a lot of migraines lately, haven't you?"

There's a pause on the other end of the line.

"Mum?"

"Yes, yes, I have, actually. I've been to the doctor a couple of times now and they may run some tests, but he assures me everything is fine. Just fine."

"Tests?" Nancy asks, sitting up straighter on her bed.

"Just routine things, Nancy, dear. For heaven's sake, don't fret."

"Is that Beetle?" She hears her father in the background. "Tell her hello, then it's time for you to go back to bed."

"Can you put Dad on?" Nancy asks her mother.

"Oh, you can talk to him later, dear. I'm going to go try to sleep now. I'm sitting in the parlor in the dark and he keeps trying to shoo me back to bed."

"Mum?"

"Yes, dear?"

Nancy hesitates. "I just, uh, I just wanted to say I love you." She tilts her face up to the ceiling as the tears pool uncomfortably in her ears.

"I love you, too, poppet. You're my dream."

Nancy hangs up before the floodgates open, before she says something she won't be able to take back. She lies on her bed for two hours, staring up at the ceiling, processing an uncomfortable train of thought.

She's been reckless. It all boils down to that. The drinking and unsafe sex with Len—and others, she thinks, squirming a bit at the thought—had served a purpose when she was running from her past, but the consequence of that behavior is now threatening her future. Her grades have slipped, and now she's gone and gotten pregnant. But she's not about to let herself get tied to a loser like Len for the rest of her life, that's for sure.

Nancy pictures the dark, cold basement in the East End and a wave of nausea hits her. The smell of the man pouring rubbing alcohol on those flashing silver instruments blends into the scent of the hospital emergency room in her memory. But she can hear the kind doctor's voice, echoing back through the intervening years. Her words of a special secret:

Just tell them you're looking for Jane.

"Jane, eh?" Nancy mutters her birth name aloud to the empty room. "Well, isn't that just some sick twist of fate?"

The hot lump of regret and shame settles itself down in her gut as she wipes away more tears. She needs to get her act together. But first she needs someone who can fix this.

. . . .

After a half hour of meticulous searching and five ink-stained fingertips, Nancy has combed through the yellow pages and discovered that there are twenty-seven family physicians within reasonable walking distance of her apartment. Her plan is to begin with the few female names on her list, then work her way down to the male doctors.

She smooths the page of her notebook. Glancing up to make sure her bedroom door is closed, she clears her throat and picks up the receiver.

First: Dr. Linda Deactis.

Nancy dials the number, her insides constricting, curling in on themselves like a snake. It rings twice before a young woman with a voice like a bell answers the line.

"Dr. Deactis's office, hello."

Nancy pauses. "Hi. Um, I'm looking for Jane. Is there a Jane there?"

"This is the office of Dr. Linda Deactis, family physician."

"Right, right. Yeah, thank you. But I was told to ask for Jane?"

"I think you've got the wrong number. Sorry."

Nancy throws the phone back down onto its cradle, her heart racing. She can hear her roommates' muffled chatter through her bedroom wall. Debbie is home now, too. Their conversation is light with laughter.

Nancy consults her list. "Dr. Fields, you're next."

A butterfly beats its wings against the inside of her chest as she dials the next number.

"Good-afternoon-Doctor-Fields's-office-this-is-Nora," a woman blurts out in a rush on the other end of the line.

"Hi, there, I'm looking for Jane. Is Jane there?"

Silence, and then, "Not *here*, young lady. Not in *this* office!"

Click.

Nancy feels sick. Only eight words, and yet that woman's voice was dripping with hatred and disgust. She hugs her pillow to her stomach for comfort, then finds herself running her hand along it from side to side, up and down, testing out how it would feel to have a belly that big. The tears prick at her eyes again. She tosses the pillow aside, glaring at it. She *has* to do this.

Nancy dials the third number on the list. This time, a middle-aged woman answers the phone.

"Dr. Smithson's office, how can I help you?"

"Hi," Nancy says, a bit more confident this time. "I'm looking for Jane?"

"Did you say Jane?"

"Yes."

Click.

Nancy puts the phone down once again, takes a deep breath, then dials the next number.

"Dr. Sheen's office, this is Martha."

"Hi, Martha." Nancy braces for the verbal stabbing. "I'm looking for Jane. I was told to ask for Jane. Is she there?"

"Uh, no, we don't have a Jane here, but I think I may know who you're trying to reach. Do you have a pen?"

Nancy scrambles to grab the pen in her sweaty fingers. She cocks her head over her shoulder to hold the receiver against her ear. "Ready. Go ahead."

Martha gives her a number, which Nancy jots down, then repeats back.

"You got it," Martha says. "Good luck, honey."

Nancy's eyes sting again. "Thank you."

Martha hangs up, and Nancy follows suit. Steeling her resolve, she exhales quickly and dials the given number before she loses her nerve. The rotary dial on the old phone whirs back into place seven times, the zeros taking an eternity to complete their rotation. Nancy's foot jiggles as the phone rings through eight times. She's just started to panic about whether to leave a message on the answering machine or hang up when a woman picks up the line.

"Dr. Taylor's office."

"Um, hi, there. I'm looking for Jane. Someone told me I could speak with Jane here. She gave me your number."

"Please hold."

Some generic elevator music kicks in on the line, and Nancy waits, hardly daring to breathe. A minute or two later, a different woman comes on.

"Hi, there, I understand you're looking for Jane." She sounds older. Her voice is deeper and resonant, and it feels familiar and somehow calming to Nancy.

"Yes."

"Have you ever met Jane before?"

Silence. Nancy isn't sure how she's supposed to answer. Is this some kind of test, a second stage of the code she hadn't been told about? "No, I haven't. This is my first time."

"Okay. What's your name, miss?"

"Nancy. Nancy M—"

"No, no! No last names, Nancy."

"Oh. Sorry."

"Okay," the woman continues. "So, I understand you're running late. What time is it where you are? And by that, I mean, between one p.m. and nine p.m."

What?

The silence stretches the tension even tighter.

"Think about my question for a moment, Nancy."

She does, and starts to feel anxious again. And stupid. The butterfly has returned. She rakes her fingers through her hair, her ragged, chewed fingernails catching on the brown strands. And then two pieces snap into place in Nancy's mind.

"Oh! Yeah, I guess I'm—I'd guess it's about one o'clock or so."

"Very good, we can definitely accommodate that timeline. I'd like to have you over to visit Jane fairly soon. Are you free to come in to the office . . ." The voice trails off, and Nancy can hear the riffling of pages. "At seven-thirty next Saturday night?"

The butterfly is in her throat, flapping against her tonsils. "Saturday?"

Her major paper is due the following Monday and she hasn't even started it. But this can't wait, can it? No. She's certain in her decision. She just wants it done. She takes a deep breath.

"Yeah, I can do Saturday night. Seven-thirty, you said?"

"Yes."

"Okay. Do I need to bring anything, or . . . ?"

"No, just you. It's better that you come alone, actually. Do you have a pen?"

Nancy jots down the address the woman gives her. "All right. And how much is the fee?" Nancy braces for it. She'll just have to eat nothing but Kraft Dinner for the next few months.

"There is no fee. I do this for free for those who need it."

"Oh, wow. Okay, thank you. That's really helpful, honestly."

"I'm happy to help. But one last thing, Nancy: it's important that you knock seven times, loudly, when you arrive. Make sure you are here precisely at seven-thirty, okay? My nurse will come let you in. What do you look like?"

"Dark brown hair, brown eyes. I'm about five-six. I'll be wearing a red coat."

"Wear a black one."

Nancy shakes her head. "I'm sorry?"

"Wear a more discreet color, and knock seven times. We'll see you next Saturday night. Take care."

And with a sharp click, the line goes dead.

. . . .

Saturday has arrived. The Day.

A chill, damp March 21 smothered in steely gray cloud cover. It hasn't stopped raining all week, unless you count the hour of sleet and hail that lashed down on the city on Wednesday in the middle of afternoon rush hour. The pathetic remnants of winter are still evident along the street gutters: the ugly brown crust of dirt and salt and car exhaust that signals the end of winter's death grip and—finally—the beginning of spring.

Nancy hates winter. The end of it is usually a significant cause for celebration in her book. But not today. She can't ever remember feeling more unlike herself, and utterly unfocused on anything but the task at hand. And she's decided to think about this ordeal as exactly that: a task, a chore. She's packaged it up in her mind as something that she just needs to get through to move on to the Next Step, whatever that might be. If she's being honest with herself, she has no idea. She can't see much beyond the gray cloud of this evening.

Len tried calling her three times this week, looking for a "date." Susan loyally came up with various excuses for why Nancy couldn't come to the phone, but Nancy thinks she's starting to suspect she might be pregnant. Twice this week she asked how Nancy is feeling, and Nancy's sure she stopped outside the bathroom door on Wednesday morning, listening in as Nancy hurled her guts out into the toilet.

In a coat she borrowed from Susan, a heavy, scratchy gray wool mackintosh that falls past her knees, Nancy weaves her way through the crisscrossing paths and skeletal bare trees of Queen's Park. A couple of blocks later, she turns down Yonge Street, past the dazzling red, white, and yellow neon lights of Sam the Record Man that look as though they'd be more at home in Las Vegas than Toronto. She pulls back the sleeve of the coat to check her watch. It's only a quarter after seven. She slows her pace.

It's Saturday night, which means all the students and other carefree young people are out for dinner and drinks, dodging into basement bars for artsy poetry readings and billiards. The Leafs are playing Buffalo, and Susan invited Nancy to the game; her boyfriend's family has season tickets. Normally, Nancy would have jumped at the offer. But Susan had also hinted heavily that it was intended to be a double date with one of her boyfriend's fraternity brothers.

"You need to upgrade from that idiot Len, Nancy," Susan said, eyeing her friend shrewdly as she handed over her old gray coat.

"I know," Nancy replied. "That's what I'm heading out to do, actually."

"Mm. Special date?"

Nancy nodded, avoiding Susan's eyes. "Something like that, yeah."

She's swimming upstream now against a current of blue hockey jerseys and umbrellas all flooding toward the Gardens as she turns left onto Shuter Street and past Massey Hall. She passes underneath a streetlamp, the light reflecting in the damp pavement. Suddenly she's eighteen again, waiting for Clara underneath the lamp outside Ossington Station. A chill creeps up her neck at the thought.

This will be different, she reminds herself. *This is a real doctor who knows what she's doing.*

Nancy is so engrossed in the memories of that night as she winds her way toward Seaton Street that she overshoots the address. By the time she looks up, she's at number 103. Doubling back, she scans the line of houses for the right number until she arrives at the front gate.

This is it. There's nothing else for it. She checks her watch again.

7:29.

Nancy pauses on the sidewalk, hiking the collar of the coat with its unfamiliar smell farther up her neck. She stuffs her gloved hands deep into the pockets.

After a moment's consideration, Nancy nods in agreement with herself and reaches over the low iron gate to release the latch. She steps through, then guides it carefully shut behind her with a deafening creak.

Seaton is a quiet street, several blocks over now from the bustle of Yonge. She glances over her shoulder. The street is deserted. But when she turns back toward the house, Nancy sees movement on a porch several doors down. There's an older man outside, shoveling slush off his steps. He turns toward Nancy, leans on the shovel for support. She can't see his features in the dark, but the fact that she's about to—once again—do something illegal hits her more forcefully than she'd like.

But you have to do this, she tells herself. She's built this up in her mind as the keystone of her future. The abortion is the first step to setting herself back on track. After that, she hopes, everything else will fall into place. And surely there's no way this stranger would know why she's here. She could just be a friend visiting Dr. Taylor for drinks on a Saturday night.

Forcing herself to ignore the man, Nancy walks up the path and scales the three steps to the wooden porch. A small brass plaque at eye level beside the mailbox reads: DR. E. TAYLOR, MD—FAMILY PHYSICIAN.

Nancy removes the glove from her right hand and knocks loudly. There is no window, but a peephole instead. With a jolt in her stomach, she realizes she has, out of sheer habit, knocked her usual four quick raps.

Shit.

She hastily whips her fist up and knocks another three, loudly.

Shit shit shit.

She strains her ears toward the door. After only a beat, there's a rustling behind the wood. Nancy centers her face in the peephole so they can see her clearly. The speck of light visible inside is snuffed out. A moment later, the door opens by a few inches. A Black woman with a pleasant face pokes her head into the gap.

"Can I help you?"

"Hi, I'm Nancy. I have a seven-thirty appointment. Are you Dr. Taylor?"

"Hi, Nancy, we've been expecting you. I'm Alice," the woman says, stepping back to allow Nancy to pass over the threshold.

She's much shorter than Nancy, with curly brown hair and eyes that have seen enough to slightly dull the light behind them.

"There wasn't anyone out on the street, was there?" Alice asks. "No one saw you come in?"

"Actually, yes. An older man, a few doors down. He was shoveling his steps and he saw me."

Alice's brow knits. "A few doors down which way?"

Nancy indicates to her left.

"Ah, okay," Alice says, relaxing. "That's probably just Chester. He's a good neighbor, total sweetheart. He was Dr. Taylor's first ever patient, actually."

Nancy smiles tightly.

"Do you have to go to the washroom?" Alice asks. "If you do, you should go now. It's just off the hall through that door there."

"No, I'm okay. Thanks."

"All right, then. How are you feeling about this?"

Nancy hesitates.

"It's okay if you've changed your mind," Alice says. "It happens a lot. It's perfectly normal."

"No, no, honestly, I'm okay," Nancy tells her. "This is all just pretty weird. A bit surreal, you know? I feel like I'm in over my head. I didn't think this would ever happen to me."

Alice nods. "Most women don't."

"But this is—I mean, this is safe, right? It's just that I've actually seen this before, but not done by a doctor. And I'm a bit . . ."

"Ah. Okay. Come on with me, and we'll go meet Dr. Taylor. She'll explain the procedure, you can see the room, and hopefully that can help put your mind at ease. It's very common to be nervous."

Nancy follows the nurse toward another door at the end of the hallway. The floorboards creak: the hallway floor is covered with a worn rug that was probably deep red and green in days long past, but is now a faded pink and pale green. Glancing to her left, Nancy spots a waiting room in what probably used to be the dining room of the old house. It's dim in there, but she can see the institutional chairs that line the walls and a coffee table strewn with an untidy assortment of magazines. A water cooler stands sentry in one corner, the surface of the water glinting in the yellow light from the streetlamps outside. It's a warm and comfortable place, though. It smells like peppermint and old wood. Far more like a home than a doctor's office.

Alice opens the door at the end of the hall. It's much brighter in here, and Nancy's eyes squint as they struggle to adjust. Alice shuts the door behind them. Two locks slide into place, and Nancy recalls the many locks on the back-alley abortionist's door. Her heart begins to race, and she fights to push away the comparison.

She's facing a room that looks like a cross between a regular doctor's exam room and what Nancy figures a surgical room must look like, though she's never had so much as a broken bone in her entire life. The walls are painted plain white and unadorned with windows or decor, save for a fancy scrolled frame that displays Dr. Taylor's diploma with its official stamped red wax seal. A long exam table is situated in the center of the room. There are no black sheets this time, just the usual crunchy sterile paper running along the table's length, with metal stirrups propped up at the end. A pedestal tray stands beside one of the stirrups. It's covered in a blue fabric, like a paper napkin. Nancy can just make out a glint of silver poking out from underneath it. She swallows hard on a parched throat and turns her focus away from it.

A tall, thin woman with shoulder-length brown hair and sporting light blue scrubs strides toward Nancy and extends her hand. "Dr. Evelyn Taylor. You must be Nancy."

Nancy nods. "It's nice to meet you." They clasp hands. "Thank you for, you know . . ."

"Of course. You can set your coat and purse down over there, Nancy. Alice and I will give you a few minutes to get changed out of your clothes. I need you to undress from the waist down—you can keep your socks on if you like, sometimes it gets a bit chilly in here—and lie down on the table with this sheet over your bottom half."

"Okay."

"You've had a PAP test before, right?"

"Yeah."

"Well, parts of this procedure will be very similar to a PAP. You'll have your feet up in the stirrups, and I'll be using a speculum and inserting some instruments into your vagina, but this time I'll utilize others to open the cervix and remove the tissue from your uterus. We're going to give you some painkillers, and a local anesthetic. We try our very best to make this process as quick and painless as we possibly can."

A leather belt covered in teeth marks.

A subway seat soaked in blood.

"Okay."

"If you like, Alice will be here to hold your hand, give you a warm or cold cloth for your face, talk to you for a distraction, or whatever else you might need. We want you to feel as relaxed as you can, okay?"

"Okay."

Dr. Taylor nods again. She has a good manner for this, Nancy acknowledges through her nervousness. Calm and matter-of-fact, but compassionate. She understands what her patients are feeling and thinking. Nancy wonders if she's ever been on the table herself.

"We'll leave you to change. Take your time."

"Okay," Nancy says again, wondering why she keeps using the word when she knows for a fact that she has never felt less okay in her entire life.

. . . .

"We're about halfway through the procedure, Nancy. You're doing great."

Nancy nods to acknowledge Dr. Taylor's voice, but keeps her eyes closed. Alice squeezes her cold fingers and runs a hand through her hair.

I wonder if she's a mom, Nancy thinks. *She has mom hands.*

Then a series of loud bangs rattles the distant front door. Nancy's eyes snap open to the harsh light of the exam room. Dr. Taylor and Alice freeze mid-movement.

"That was ten—" Alice says.

"Alice! Evelyn!" Nancy hears a voice from down the hall. Another woman. "Code blue!"

"Jesus." Alice bolts to the door.

"Nancy, stay focused here," Dr. Taylor says from down between Nancy's feet. Above her mask, her eyes are trained on her task, but she continues talking. "That's just our neighbor from the apartment upstairs. She's another one of our Janes. Her sister Mary is a secretary at the police head-quarters. When she gets wind that there's going to be a raid on a clinic, Mary calls her sister and her sister gives all four of the clinics a heads-up. It's okay. This has happened before. And it might not even be our clinic today. That's why it's great that we have Mary now, to give us all a bit of notice. Just try to stay calm. We're almost done here, okay, sweetheart?"

But Nancy has already started to panic. "The *police* are coming?"

"Maybe. But we have a few minutes at least. Alice will try to stall them. We've done this before. The most important thing you can do for us both is to stay calm."

"It was that man, wasn't it!"

"What man?"

"I told Alice, when I was coming up the path there was a man a few doors down, watching me. She said his name was Charlie or something. A patient of yours. Did he call the cops on us?"

"Ah, Chester," Dr. Taylor says. "No, he's a sweet man, and I don't think he has any idea what goes on here. We're very careful. That's why I rent the upstairs apartment to a Jane, too."

Nancy is less convinced, but tries to focus on the stucco ceiling, a dark circle that might be water damage.

"Deep breaths, Nancy, okay? The more relaxed your muscles are, the quicker I can work."

Although she can't see what the doctor is doing, Nancy can hear the clicks and creaks of metal on metal. She wishes they'd given her earplugs.

A moment later, Alice slides back into the room. Her eyes are wide, and her face is stony. Nancy hears footfalls on a distant set of stairs as their informant slips back into her apartment.

"We don't have long, Evelyn," Alice says. "Minutes, maybe. It's us tonight."

"Okay," Dr. Taylor says. "Go into the hall and answer the front door when they come, Alice. If they press, tell them I'm doing a routine PAP exam, just like last time."

"They had a warrant last time."

"And they'll have one again this time, I'm sure. They're determined. I don't know why they're still bothering to waste their resources on us. This is kind of a moot point now," she mutters, more to herself than to anyone else. More clicking of metal. "I'm going to finish here, Alice, so we can get Nancy home as soon as possible for a good strong cup of tea and a warm bed. There won't be anything to arrest us on."

Alice disappears again.

"Hey, Nancy," Dr. Taylor says. "Look at me."

Nancy leans her head forward slightly and meets Dr. Taylor's eyes, her own brimming with the threat of tears.

"I can feel you shaking. I know this must be very scary for you, but for both our sakes, I need you to play along here and stick to the story."

Nancy's chest is tight and she's having trouble breathing. "Okay," she manages.

"Good. Now, you're here tonight for a routine PAP test. Your last one came back abnormal so you're getting a second opinion from another doctor that isn't your usual physician. Our schedules didn't line up this week during business hours, so you're here tonight instead. That's all. Okay?"

Nancy nods. "That's all?"

"That's all *you* need to remember. The less you say, the better. Just play along and don't act surprised by anything Alice or I say. Got it?"

"Yes."

"Nancy, this is critically important. I could go to prison."

Nancy nods again. She hates herself for asking it but blurts out the words anyway. "Can *I* go to prison for this? For having it done?"

Dr. Taylor doesn't answer. "I can tell you're a brave woman," she says instead. "We'll get through this together."

They hold each other's gaze tightly for a moment, a distant hug that calms Nancy a fraction as she tries to steady her breathing. Then Dr. Taylor speaks again.

"I'm truly very sorry to have to say this, but please wipe your eyes. There shouldn't be any reason for you to be crying. From *their* perspective, I mean."

Nancy turns to the ceiling, focusing once again on the dark stain that blights the otherwise perfect landscape of the pure white stucco. She wipes her eyes on the backs of her hands, then runs a finger along the rims to rub off the mascara that's probably smudged underneath her lower lashes. She sniffles her nose, clears her throat, and steels her resolve.

"That's my girl," Dr. Taylor says.

The doorbell rings, cracking into the smothering silence like a poorly timed joke. They're here.

Nancy can just hear the sound of a deeper male voice interspersed with Alice's when Dr. Taylor whispers, "That's it, Nancy. All done. It's over. Just stay still for now."

Nancy fights back the tears of mingled fear and relief that still threaten. She closes her eyes for a moment, listening as Dr. Taylor packs up her equipment. She opens her eyes again, blinking slowly. The tears are retreating for now, but she knows they'll be back later.

Dr. Taylor flies around the room, stashing things into locked cupboards. The ruffled snap of a garbage bag being tied. Voices out in the hallway. Nancy wants to go home more than she has ever wanted anything in her life. Dr. Taylor pulls out other items she didn't even use for the procedure, sets them out on the metal standing tray that's perched beside Nancy's ankle. The actors are taking their places, Nancy realizes, fixing their expressions into forced and gleaming smiles. Ready to fool their audience the moment the curtain rises on the scene.

Nancy is still taking deep, deliberate breaths in an effort not to vomit when Dr. Taylor resettles herself onto the small stool. She lets Nancy out of the stirrups and rubs her hands up and down the tops of her feet in reassurance.

"I can't let you get dressed just yet," she says through her mask. "I still need to check a couple of things. But I've set out everything I'd normally need for a PAP," she says, indicating the tray full of innocent tools. "That's all they'll see. As long as they don't catch us in the act, they can't charge us. We'll try to keep them away from you, but they won't want to come too close anyway. In my experience, men like these guys are thoroughly freaked out by anything to do with a vagina that isn't sex."

Despite the situation, Nancy feels the muscles of her face strain into a smile.

"Don't say anything unless they demand to speak with you. Then just stick to the story."

"Okay."

Dr. Taylor gives Nancy's left foot a small squeeze. The voices in the hall draw closer. Alice is demanding to see a warrant. Nancy can hear three or four men, their voices rising to an angry crescendo against Alice's protests.

A moment later, there's a soft knock on the door. It opens and Alice pokes her head through, eyes wide.

"Dr. Taylor?"

"Yes?"

"There are a few policemen here to speak with you. They have a warrant to search the premises." Alice's final word is still lingering in the stifling air of the bright room when the door is pushed open forcibly from over her shoulder. "Sir—"

"I understand you wish to speak with me, Officer." Dr. Taylor stands up now. She strides the few steps across the small room to the doorway. Nancy's breathing is shallow. She already misses the weight of Dr. Taylor's hand on her foot.

Dr. Taylor extends that hand instead to the policeman. The officer hesitates before shaking it.

"Pernith," he answers.

"Nice to meet you, Officer Pernith." She grips his hand before dropping it aggressively, as though she would rather throw it across the room. "I understand you and your fellows here have a search warrant for my practice?" She nods to the other three young officers who stand behind Pernith. Two of them, closest to the door, wear hard expressions, their jaws set tightly, eyes narrowed underneath their heavy brows. The other lurks much farther back down the hall, his eyes cast down at his shoes.

"Yes, we do, ma'am. We received information that you may be conducting illegal activity on these premises."

"Please, do tell. What illegal activity am I suspected of conducting?" Dr. Taylor steps forward through the doorway and tries to pull the door shut behind her, but Officer Pernith's well-practiced arm shoots out and holds the door open.

"I'm afraid I'm going to have to see inside this room, ma'am."

"My name is Dr. Taylor, not ma'am, if you please."

He chews his lip, but she holds her ground, though she's at least a head shorter than him. "I need to search the room, Doctor."

"I would like to see the warrant. If you are going to barge in on one of my patients during a perfectly routine exam of her vagina, I insist on seeing evidence that you have been granted such pointless authority."

Dr. Taylor's matter-of-fact pronouncement of the word "vagina" causes the heat to rise in his neck and stops him dead in his tracks. Officer Pernith clears his throat. Nancy sees the corner of Alice's mouth twitch.

"Stevenson." He beckons imperiously to one of his tight-jawed underlings, who thrusts a piece of paper into Dr. Taylor's outstretched hand. She examines it for a moment before her lips press into a thin line and she steps backward into the room. Nancy feels like her insides have melted.

"Lucy?" Dr. Taylor calls. Nancy turns toward the door, wondering who she's speaking to. Beside the policeman's shoulder, Dr. Taylor nods her head a fraction of an inch.

"Yes?" Nancy answers.

"These officers have a warrant to search my practice, which includes this exam room. They insist on coming in. Please stay where you are."

Officer Pernith strides into the room. He's a huge man with broad shoulders. All the cops look larger than normal men. His fellows and Alice follow them in. The room is now cramped with bodies, suffocating. Nancy catches a whiff of one of the policemen's cologne and her stomach falls through the floor. She would know the scent anywhere: Hugo Boss, the same one Len wears. She turns her head to face the wall and holds her breath as long as she can.

Alice scurries over to Nancy's side and takes her hand in both of her own. She grips it tightly. She's grounding, motherly, and Nancy half wishes her own mother could be here with her, but the thought of telling her about the pregnancy was unbearable. She closes her eyes, trying to block out the scene. But a moment later, Nancy hears the clip of shoes on the floor beside the exam table, senses a heavy presence beside her. The officer clears his throat.

"Miss?"

Oh for God's sake.

"Yes?" Her voice is croaky and quite unlike her own. But maybe that's a good thing.

The officer is clearly uncomfortable. "Can you tell me what you're doing here this evening?"

Nancy opens her eyes and looks up into the man's face. Beefy, square-jawed, with a healthy layer of stubble around his chin and neck. He's been on duty since this morning. He's probably tired and wants to go home to his wife. But instead, he's here, trying to prevent her from getting a safe abortion. From starting over. Nancy feels a burst of rage she's never experienced before. Hot and sharp, frightening yet tantalizing. A razor's edge.

Fuck this guy.

"I'm half naked and barely covered in a paper sheet on a doctor's exam table, and before you walked in, my feet were up in stirrups. What do you *think* I'm doing here? I got offered tickets to the Leafs game tonight. Trust me: I'd rather be at the Gardens stuffing my face with popcorn and shitty beer instead of getting myself cranked open with a car jack for a PAP test."

She can hardly believe the words came out of her mouth. She instantly regrets it and pinches her lips shut, her cheeks burning. Dr. Taylor. Prison. The script.

Officer Pernith fidgets with the notebook in his hands, and the eyes that meet Nancy's have more depth than she ever could have imagined.

"You know what, miss? I'd rather be at a hockey game, too. We'll be done here shortly. I apologize for the interruption. Just carrying out orders, you know. Good for you for getting this . . . test. My daughter needed one last year," he adds quietly. "I know it isn't pleasant, however necessary it might be."

Nancy's insides clench. Alice's hand flinches over hers.

"You ladies have a good night," Officer Pernith says.

Alice manages a weak thank-you.

Pernith waits by the door to the exam room while the other officers finish their halfhearted inspection. Finally, they take their leave and Dr. Taylor escorts them out. Nancy hears three locks slide into place at the front door, and a moment later Dr. Taylor reappears in the exam room.

She lets her breath out slowly, her mouth forming a small O. "Well, Nancy. You didn't exactly stick to the script."

"I'm so sorry, Dr. Taylor, I have no idea what—"

Dr. Taylor and Alice burst out laughing.

"It's okay, Nancy. It's more than okay," Dr. Taylor says, smiling. "We're frankly just impressed. That was some serious attitude."

"Amazing, Nancy," Alice adds, walking over to the sink. She reaches into her bra and produces a key like a magician. She unlocks the small bottom drawer of a filing cabinet and digs out a stack of papers. "They barely even checked the cupboards. I was worried they'd make me open it."

"I honestly don't know what came over me," Nancy says. "I just got so angry. Why do they care?"

"Because they would rather women die in alleyways, hemorrhaging with coat hangers sticking out from between their thighs," Alice says, her eyes flashing.

Dr. Taylor sighs, settles herself back down at Nancy's feet. "Let me just check on one more thing, okay, Nancy?"

A minute later, Dr. Taylor gives Nancy the okay to sit up.

"Everything looks good. Alice will give you some thick pads and instructions to prevent an infection. Make sure you take all the antibiotics until they're finished and follow all the instructions. If you do get an infection, call me right away. Do *not* go to the hospital, okay?"

"Okay."

"I don't want to scare you. Infections are very rare if the procedure is done properly and you take all the antibiotics. Avoid heavy exercise and sex for a while."

Nancy scoffs. "Yeah, that won't be a problem."

"But if something does happen," Dr. Taylor continues, "call me and Alice. The hospital will ask questions you won't be able to lie away, and then they'll call the police."

"I know they will," Nancy says. "I went with my cousin to some freak abortionist a couple of years ago. He nearly killed her. I had to drag her to the hospital afterward, she was bleeding so much."

"Jesus Christ." Dr. Taylor shakes her head. "This is why we do what we do."

"They asked me all kinds of questions at the hospital, and then one of the ER doctors told me if this ever happened again, I should call around to doctors' offices and ask for Jane. I had no idea what she meant, at the time. But I remembered it. That's how I found you."

"That's good for us to know, actually," Alice says. "Which hospital was that?"

"St. Joe's." Nancy sits up slowly, reaching out for Dr. Taylor's proffered hand. She winces. "It hurts."

"I know. It will for a couple of days; you can take over-the-counter painkillers. Drink plenty of water and try to get some sleep tonight. It can be difficult for a while. Emotionally, I mean. Your hormones will all be resetting once your body realizes it isn't pregnant anymore, and it can be a bit of a wild ride. Do you have a friend you can talk to about this?"

"Not really."

"A roommate at home? A sister?"

"My roommates, yeah. I'm pretty close with one of them. I think she might have suspected what was going on with me, anyway."

"Okay, that's good. Even if you don't tell them exactly what's happened, make sure someone's there with you for the next day or two, just in case. Write in a diary, talk to yourself, do what you need to do. But I must ask you again not to tell anyone my name, do you understand? That's part of the deal. The Janes can only continue to exist if we're not all in prison. If we can't exist, other girls can't get abortions."

Nancy nods. She likes Dr. Taylor.

Alice comes over with a sheet of paper, some pads, and a small white container of unlabeled pills, which she drops into a paper bag. "Take these, and follow the instructions. But please keep the instruction sheet safe from other eyes. At the bottom of your underwear drawer, or under a mattress is a popular spot, too. Burn them once you're done. Just in case."

"Okay. Yup. Thanks."

"We also like to give our patients a copy of *The Birth Control Handbook*, Nancy," Alice says. "Do you have a copy?"

"No. I've heard of it, though. Some girls on campus have it."

"There's a lot of misinformation out there, so we like to send our patients away with a reliable resource. Quite frankly, we don't want anyone to have to see us more than once."

"No, I know," Nancy says. "I need to be more careful."

"Don't beat yourself up," Alice says. "Just be sure to read the manual and take care of yourself. I'll go call you a taxi. Can you afford the fare, or do you need some money?"

"Oh no, I'll be okay. Thank you. You've both done enough already."

Nancy slides gingerly off the table as Alice leaves the room, and Dr. Taylor turns away to give her some privacy while she gets dressed. She gathers Susan's coat and her purse, pulls her boots back on. Dr. Taylor follows her out to the front door and slides back the locks.

Nancy turns to face her. "Thank you. I . . . I don't know what else to say."

"You're welcome, Nancy. I'm sorry again about the police. I think it'll stop eventually."

"It's okay. It's not your fault."

"It's not okay, but you're right, it's not my fault, or yours."

Both women stare at the floor, awaiting the honk of the taxi. For some reason, Nancy is having trouble saying goodbye. She feels safe here.

"If any of my friends ever need this, can I tell them to call you? Can I give them your name then?"

Dr. Taylor shakes her head. "No. But you can give them this number to call." She reaches into the pocket of her scrubs and pulls out a small white card, hands it to Nancy.

Nancy turns it over in her hand. There's nothing on it but a hand-written phone number. "Whose number is this?" she asks.

Three quick honks blare from outside, and Nancy nearly jumps out of her skin. Dr. Taylor reaches behind Nancy's back to turn the creaky brass handle, opening the door onto a blast of cold evening air.

"Just tell them to ask for Jane."

CHAPTER 16

Evelyn

. . . .

SUMMER 1983

I n her office at the back of the clinic, Evelyn reaches across the desk for her coffee mug and takes a swig. It went stone-cold hours ago, but with a busy practice, she's become quite used to cold coffee. She might even prefer it that way now.

She's been reviewing this week's patient charts in a bleary sort of way. She's tired enough that she should probably give up and go home. She has the house to herself tonight; Tom is out for dinner with a man named Reg, a lawyer he met through another gay friend at a party. This is their second date, and Evelyn's happy for him. She wishes he would get out and date more for his own sake, but she also enjoys the solitude of an empty house every once in a while to be alone with her thoughts.

Evelyn looks at her watch. She'll give it another ten minutes and then pack it in. Tomorrow she has a full day of regular patients and two abortions for the Janes in the evening.

Just as she's locking the charts away in the filing cabinet under her desk, the phone rings. Her receptionist went home an hour ago, and Evelyn hates leaving her patients hanging. Reliability is important.

With a sigh, she picks up the receiver. "Dr. Evelyn Taylor."

"Oh, Dr. Taylor? I'm so glad I caught you. I'm sorry to call so late in the day. It's Ilene Simpson."

Chester Braithwaite's daughter.

"Ilene! So nice to hear from you. How is everything?"

With a lurch in her gut, Evelyn braces for the worst. Despite Chester's initial assurances that he was in perfect health and only required the services of a doctor to appease his nagging daughter, he ran into some difficulties with his blood pressure and cholesterol. He came in for his flu shot and yearly checkups, but also for more minor concerns like a scab from a rope burn that didn't quite want to heal, or a stubbed baby toe he thought might be broken. His daughter and her family lived an hour's drive from the city center in the northern suburbs, and Evelyn often got the sense that Chester was simply lonely. His enthusiasm for Evelyn and her practice served as a welcome confidence boost in the absence of support from her own parents, so she didn't mind his frequent presence one bit.

Then there was a prostate cancer scare five years ago that precipitated tests which, to Evelyn's immense relief, came back negative, and his health was reasonably consistent until the whiskey finally caught up to his pancreas. Evelyn was in regular contact with Ilene as she struggled to provide care for him in her own home, and she made a dozen house calls before the family eventually decided to place Chester in nursing care a few months ago. Evelyn hadn't heard from Ilene since then.

"Well, he's . . . he's in his last weeks now," Ilene says. "Maybe days. They declared him palliative. There's nothing more to be done."

Evelyn sinks back down into her office chair. "Oh, Ilene. I'm so sorry." There's an unpleasant tightness in her chest. "He's really something special. It's been an honor, truly."

"Thank you, Dr. Taylor." Ilene takes a moment to compose herself. Evelyn waits. "He's been asking to see you. That's why I'm calling. To give you an update and, I guess, ask if you'd be willing to visit him. He was—*is*—so fond of you. I think he was always grateful you didn't make him give up the drinking."

Evelyn fights down a chuckle as she pictures Chester's round, bearded face. "Ah, well, it's one of those vices we weigh as doctors. Besides, I don't think I could have made him give it up if I'd tried. He made it clear to me from day one that I should not attempt to dissuade him."

Ilene actually laughs. "From his cold, dead hands, he used to say." A small gasp stutters through the phone line. "I'm sorry, that was a poor choice of words. His words, though, I suppose."

Evelyn smiles sadly.

"Oh hell, there was no stopping him." Ilene chuckles again, sniffles. "I'll be sorry to say goodbye."

Evelyn flips a pen cap through her fingertips and swallows the lump in her throat. "Me, too, Ilene."

Ilene heaves a sigh.

"So what nursing home is he at?" Evelyn asks. "I don't think I have that in my records."

"He's at St. Sebastian's, over on Riverdale Avenue."

A chill trickles down through Evelyn's body and she clenches the pen cap in her fist. The plastic tip cuts painfully into her palm.

"Do you know the one?" Ilene's words filter through the density of Evelyn's thoughts like static.

"Yes," she answers finally. "Yes, I know it."

"Do you think—would you be able to go visit him?"

Evelyn reaches up and massages her forehead. She can't refuse this. Not for Chester. "Yes. I think I can."

. . . .

The following day, Evelyn approaches the building warily. ST. SEBAS-TIAN'S HOME FOR THE AGED, the sign claims. There was no sign at all during its previous life as St. Agnes's Home for Unwed Mothers, just a rusted house number half-covered in ivy. She's avoided this entire block ever since she left. She never dreamed there would ever be a homecoming.

Her usually lithe legs stiffen as she nears the steps up to the front porch; the beautiful wooden wraparound, painted cream in the days she lived here, is now refinished in a more modern dark brown. The door is different, too, completely replaced and painted a truly glorious hunter green in a fancy high-gloss finish. It's remarkable what can be hidden underneath a pretty coat of paint.

Evelyn remembers the day she arrived here, her legs trembling with frayed nerves as she ascended the steps and hammered the brass knocker. It was autumn then, and the air had smelled like wood smoke and leaves. To anyone else, it might have smelled just like autumn ought to, like things transitioning from one state of being to another, both warm and cold at the same time. But to Evelyn, it was the scent of death. She couldn't smell the wood or the leaves, just the ash and rot they were becoming.

But it's summer now, a hot and sunny day nearly twenty-three years later, and the air is heavy with the lemony floral scent of roses and fresh-cut grass from the neighboring yards. Evelyn tries to focus on their perfume, but she knows that roses come with a price. She can't enjoy them without feeling the thorns pricking her skin.

Evelyn breathes deeply to calm her quickening heart rate, then hitches her purse onto her shoulder and marches up the porch stairs to face her past head-on. She tries to remember that she isn't the twitchy, grief-stricken mess she was when she arrived on this doorstep as a teenager. She's her own woman now, braver and stronger than before. She's here of her own volition this time, to say goodbye to Chester. She didn't have to come. She made the choice, and that's what matters. With a turn of the brass handle, Evelyn opens the door into her past.

The main floor of the home has changed since she was here. Walls have been taken down to make space for a large reception area and halls wide enough to maneuver wheelchairs. The creaky wooden floorboards have been replaced with quiet linoleum tile; the wallpaper stripped in favor of a pale peach paint. It would almost be nice, Evelyn thinks, if you didn't know the building's history. If you couldn't hear the long-forgotten cries of stolen babies and broken girls.

"Hi, there!" A young nun at the front desk smiles at Evelyn from beneath her habit. "Welcome to St. Sebastian's. Have you been here before?"

Evelyn's breath catches. *What a question.*

She recovers herself. "Yes. Yes, I have."

"All right, then, welcome back."

Evelyn finds she can't say thank you. "I, uh, I'm a doctor. Evelyn Taylor," she says softly, as though the walls might overhear and recognize her. "I'm here to see a patient of mine, Chester Braithwaite."

"Oh, certainly. I'll just need you to sign in here, please."

The nun slides a clipboard and pen over the desk and Evelyn signs with an awkward and shaky hand that doesn't even look like her writing.

The nun consults a chart taped to her desk. "He's up on the second floor, Dr. Taylor. Room 207."

The Watchdog's old room.

Her feet are rooted to the floor. She forces a wooden smile for the young nun. "Thank you."

"It's up the stairs here, and to the right."

Evelyn turns toward the staircase, trying in vain to settle the flutter in her stomach. Her feet drag as though she's just stepped in wet cement. The steps creak the same way they did all those years ago, and it sets her heart pounding in her ears. She turns right at the landing to head down the hall, passes two rooms, then a third. She freezes in her tracks at the doorway to her old dormitory. There's a young woman leaning over a bed, her curtain of long brown hair blocking her face as she speaks softly to a patient.

The woman in the bed turns her head. She looks vaguely familiar, but Evelyn can't place her. When she sees Evelyn through the doorway, she cries out as though burned. Evelyn jumps back, hastily walks away as a nurse darts past her into the room. The patient is whimpering faintly now, and Evelyn can hear the young woman and the nurse trying to soothe her.

Evelyn's nerves are on edge again, and she takes a moment outside the door of Room 207 to steady herself. She stretches her features into a forced smile, then passes through the open door.

Dim light emanates from a small bedside table lamp. Chester is tucked underneath the bedcovers, sleeping in plaid pyjamas. He's nearly bald now, with just a few wisps of white hair in a halo around his head. His grizzled beard cascades over a double chin.

A soft, rhythmic beeping issues from a monitor attached to an intravenous pole beside the bed. Dark brown curtains are pulled shut against the window, blocking the afternoon heat. The air is heavy with the fecal-chemical stench all hospitals share. It's a smell she's used to, of course. She can cope with it better than most. But the immediacy of Chester's impending death isn't something Evelyn has fully prepared herself for, and it catches her off guard. She sets her purse down on the floor, then reaches out and places her hand gently on the peak of Chester's foot. She's reluctant to wake him, but she knows how difficult it will be to convince herself to come back here a second time.

"Mr. Braithwaite?" she says loudly. "Mr. Braithwaite, it's Dr. Taylor."

She gives his foot a small squeeze, and his eyes flutter open. He blinks a few times, clearing the fog of sleep before a grin stretches across his face from ear to ear, like a cheerful hammock.

"Doc!" he wheezes. "Ah, love, thank ya for comin."

Evelyn smiles. "Of course, Chester."

"Do an old man a favor and open them damn curtains, eh? Can't see ya properly."

"There isn't any air conditioning. I think they're closed to keep you cool."

"Bah," Chester scoffs, waving his meaty hand through the air in dismissal. "I'll be stone-cold once I'm dead. Let me feel a bit o' heat for now."

Evelyn heeds his request, throwing wide the heavy curtains. The blaring light of the summer sun pours into the room.

"Ahh, 'at's better," Chester mutters.

It's as though a dam has burst, and Evelyn feels it, too. She glances down into the back garden, taking in the lush greenery of the hedges and lawn, the roses and peonies happily sunbathing in full bloom, flaunting the peak of their glory. A lawn mower sputters in a neighboring yard. Children laugh in the street. The twitter of birds fills the room. Evelyn wasn't at the home during the summer months. She had no idea its surroundings were this idyllic. The curtains were almost always drawn to protect the identities of the residents. Why couldn't there have been more light?

"Pull up the chair," he says, somewhat indignantly. "Stay awhile. Not planning on leaving right away, are ya?"

Evelyn tears her eyes away from the window. "No. I can stay for a bit."

"Good."

She pulls the guest chair over to his bedside and settles down into it. They look at each other for several long moments.

"I'm on my way out, Doc," Chester says.

Evelyn swallows a larger lump than she would have anticipated. "I know."

"I'm all right with it, ya know. Dyin'. That isn't botherin' me too much. Everyone has their time. My clock's just run out." He chuckles, and it turns into a violent cough that lasts a full minute. He sips some water and shakes his head.

"Have you had a whiskey since you've been here?" Evelyn asks.

"Pff. No. Bunch o' do-goodin' prohibitionists 'round here. Won't let me."

"What medications are you on, Chester?"

"No idea."

Evelyn consults the chart hanging at the end of the bed.

"Hey, now," Chester says, "don't bother yaself with all that nonsense. I wanted ya here for a visit, not a checkup. I got doctors in every bleedin' hour lookin' at that chart."

Satisfied, Evelyn sets it back on the hook and reaches for her purse. "I was looking at it to see what meds you're on, because . . ." She withdraws two minibar-sized bottles of whiskey and two rocks glasses from the depths of her bag. "I thought we might share a drink finally, after all these years."

The look on Chester's face makes Evelyn's heart swell to twice its normal size before it breaks. "God bless ya, Doc. Jesus H."

Evelyn sets the glasses down on Chester's bedside table, twists the caps off the tiny bottles, and pours them out. "I hope you don't mind neat. If you want rocks, I can go try to hunt down some ice chips."

"Nah, this is perfect."

Evelyn hands one of the glasses to her patient. She doesn't particularly like scotch, but she's dragged herself here for Chester, so she's determined to make the most of the sacrifice.

"A man shouldn't drink his last whiskey alone," Chester says, as though reading her thoughts. "Cheers, Doc."

"Cheers, Chester."

Their glasses clink. Usually it's the sound of celebration, not grief. But maybe this moment is both. Evelyn blinks several times and scratches her nose. Chester takes a sip.

"Don't go cryin', now, Doc."

"I'm not crying. The scotch is just smoky, that's all."

He smiles again, his dentures slipping a little. "Thanks for keepin' me alive all these years, eh. I know I was a grumpy old bugger."

Evelyn laughs through a sticky throat. "You're welcome, Chester. It's my job, but it was also my pleasure."

"I know it was. That's what sets ya apart."

Evelyn smiles, sips her own drink. Today she finds she's rather enjoying the taste. "You were my first patient, did you know that?"

"I figured. I was watchin' from down the road when ya moved in. The medical equipment and such. Didn't want to have to walk far for appointments, see."

"Well, I must say, I've nursed rather a soft spot for you, Chester. I'll—I've missed your visits." She can feel her nose starting to swell and takes another sip to disguise it.

"Ah, I'm too old for ya, Doc." He winks.

Evelyn sighs. They've both finished their drinks now, and a sense of finality settles over them like dust in an empty house. Evelyn reaches her hand out to clasp his. His grip is still strong.

"You're a kind soul, Doc," he says. "You make other folks' lives easier just by bein' you. You've got a reservation about ya, though. You were a hard nut for me to crack, kid. You . . . you risk a lot, doin' what ya do, and maybe it's made ya a bit tough."

Evelyn holds her breath, feels the rough skin of Chester's hand in hers, trembling slightly. He squeezes it.

"It's okay. I seen them all comin' and goin' over the years, waitin' out on your porch in the dark. You're a brave one. Ya did a good thing. Ya help people, that's what I'm sayin'. Just don't let it make ya too hard."

A quivering tear slips from the corner of Evelyn's eye.

"Oh, come, now," Chester says. "Give us a hug and be on your way."

Evelyn leans down and wraps her arms around the old man's thick frame. "Thank you, Chester," she whispers.

"You take care, now, Doc. I'll see ya on the other side."

She leaves one of the empty whiskey bottles for him. He'll twist the cap off and breathe in the smoky scent every night until he dies, six days from now on a warm Thursday evening. The window in his room will be opened wide like a gate, welcoming the tender soul that passes through it.

Evelyn doesn't look back as she closes the door of the room that used to be the Watchdog's. But it's Chester's now. She takes a minute to compose herself, looking around at the second-floor hallway and the many memories it conjures. From now on, she'll choose to think of Chester when she pictures Room 207, not the Watchdog. She'll hear his laugh instead of the echoes of so many girls' cries. She'll remember how the Goodbye Room was the only room in the home that glowed with natural light, a detail she'd been too distracted to notice at the time. She'll recall the sweet face of her friend as they sat knitting by a warm fireplace in the dead of winter. Evelyn understands now, for the first time, that she can choose what memories she takes with her from this place, and what to leave behind.

CHAPTER 17

Nancy

. . . .

SUMMER 1983

N ancy hikes her purse and canvas bag up onto her shoulder and strides across the nursing home lobby toward the big wooden staircase. She climbs the stairs, her steps creaking on the bare floorboards. The sound is magnified in the quiet of the afternoon. The house is nearly silent at this hour; most of the patients will be napping before dinner, sinking into the dense, foggy dreams of loved ones both present and past, the place where time becomes meaningless and they can be young and whole again.

Her assignment for this evening is Sister Mary Agatha. She isn't old, but was declared palliative the day before yesterday. Bone cancer that spread everywhere.

When she enters the nun's room, she sees it's dimly lit by a lace-covered lamp on the small bedside table. A narrow single bed juts out from the wall, where a crucifix hangs above the sleeping woman's head. Nancy creeps over to the small wooden guest chair. It's stifling in here. She unlatches the window and pushes the casement outward, locking it in place. A merciful summer breeze wafts in. This room looks out onto the back garden, which is much quieter than the street side. Nancy can smell the roses on the air, still fragrant from the afternoon heat.

It's her last day volunteering at St. Sebastian's. After some dedicated effort to get her grades back up where they needed to be, she was accepted to library school and was offered a position in the university archives. Between her studies and the job, her schedule won't allow for overnight visits to the nursing home, but Nancy is ready to move on, anyway—she has other emotional burdens to bear right now.

Her mother was diagnosed with brain cancer three months ago, though she didn't tell Nancy until last month. *Well, I didn't want to worry you, dear,* she said. It's unclear whether her history of migraines played any part in it, but regardless, Frances is undergoing chemotherapy, and sitting with palliative patients will do nothing to alleviate Nancy's dread.

One bright spot is Michael. She met him at the hospital the first time her mother allowed her to drive her there for treatment. He was slinging coffee in the cafeteria and he made her laugh. With how miserable Nancy was feeling at the time, that's all it took to get himself a date. They've only gone out twice, but she likes him.

Nancy turns her back to the window now and sits down, extricating a book from her satchel—*The Stone Angel.*

Sister Agatha's face is pale and thin, and much younger than most of Nancy's charges. Her hair falls in a neat braid down her shoulder, rests delicately on her sunken chest. Nancy suspects a nurse has kept Agatha's hair tidy. It's the little things that add up in these last few days, the seemingly minor details that help a person maintain their dignity and remember who they are. Or at least, who they once were.

Nancy lets out a sigh of sympathy and settles in to read, setting her bookmark down on the bedside table.

"What are you reading?"

Nancy's eyes flash up to meet Agatha's, whose lids are heavy with sleep.

"Oh, hello," Nancy says, closing her book. "I thought you were asleep. I'm so sorry. I'm Nancy."

"Hello, Nancy. I'm Sister Agatha."

"It's nice to meet you. How are you feeling?"

"Oh, you know. It's cancer. They tell me I haven't long. My priest has been here already for the rites. But I don't mind, my dear. God comes for all of us in his own time."

They're both quiet for a moment. The breeze flutters the curtains of the window. Nancy can smell fresh-cut grass in the heavy haze of summer air.

"What are you reading?" Sister Agatha asks again.

"Oh, it's, um . . ." *What a stupid choice.*

Sister Agatha waits, unblinking.

"It's *The Stone Angel* by Margaret Laurence. It's about, well . . ." Nancy can feel her face growing hot as she stumbles on the words. "A woman at the end of her life—"

"I know what it is, child."

Nancy slides the book back into her satchel.

"You needn't hide it. Don't be silly. I know I'm dying."

"How about we talk? Or I can just sit with you, if you want to go back to sleep, Sister. I'm here for whatever you need."

Sister Agatha considers Nancy for a moment. "Let us talk, then, my dear. Come sit closer to me. My eyes are not what they once were."

Nancy obeys, shifts the chair closer to Agatha's bedside.

"My goodness," Agatha says, her brow suddenly tight. "You are so young. What is your name, child?"

"Nancy."

"Nancy . . ." Agatha trails off, taking in Nancy's face. "You remind me of someone I used to know." She thinks for a moment. "She was young, too. They all were."

Nancy isn't sure what to say to this. "Is that so?"

"Mmm," Agatha says, nodding. "A long time ago, now."

A beat of silence as the intervening years fill up the empty space between them.

"Where did you meet her?" Nancy asks.

"Here," Agatha says, waving a papery hand at the walls. "It was full of girls for years. The home, you know."

"For wayward girls?"

"Yes. How did you know?"

"Sister Mary Anna told me once. The nun at the desk downstairs. She gets chatty."

Agatha grins, her dry lips pulling against the bones in her sunken face. "She does. Sweet girl."

"What did that mean back then, anyway? 'Wayward girls'? I figured they were petty criminals. Thieves or something."

Agatha holds Nancy's gaze. "Not criminals, no," she mutters. "Though they were treated like it sometimes. No older than you are now. I could tell you stories, my dear."

"Why were they treated so poorly?" Nancy feels a lick of foreboding swirl around in her chest. She's unearthed something.

"Oh, well—" Agatha begins before a coughing fit sets in. Nancy reaches for the plastic cup of water on the bedside table and waits for Agatha's cough to subside. The woman takes a few shaky sips.

Agatha rests her head back on the pale green pillowcase. "What was I saying? I get so confused." Her breathing begins to quicken, her chest rising and falling under the quilted coverlet. "What was her name? The one who died?"

"I don't—I don't know." Nancy takes Agatha's cold hand in hers and holds it between her own warm ones, young and strong, the fingers free of calluses and scars.

Agatha takes a moment to focus. Nancy can see the truth developing in Agatha's eyes, floating to the surface like photographs in a darkroom.

But this time she finds she doesn't want to hear it. She doesn't want to carry it with her.

"I can hear them crying. The girls and their babies," she mutters.

Nancy has to lean in closer to hear the older woman, and her long brown hair swings low over her shoulder, tickling her cheek.

"We stole their babies," Agatha whispers. "And she sold them. Even the ones who'd been raped. It wasn't their fault. And I lied to that poor girl. I told her that her baby had died. But it didn't. It didn't. I thought it was best. I thought it was a mercy, she was so terribly sad, but I was wrong. I was wrong. I thought it was best . . ."

Nancy's hand flinches in Agatha's cold grip. "You . . . you *sold* babies?"

Agatha doesn't seem to hear her. "Their faces are here sometimes. But the baby never died."

Agatha's glassy eyes stare at a spot behind Nancy and she whips her head around, but there's nothing there but fading wallpaper. Of course there isn't. She mentally shakes herself.

"Agatha." She leans in closer so she blocks out whatever Agatha thinks she's seeing behind Nancy. It works. The woman's eyes focus back on Nancy's face before flickering toward the open door.

She cries out, her lips pulling back against her teeth in fear. Nancy jumps and looks toward the door, but there's no one there. A heartbeat later, the nurse who greeted Nancy in the hall comes running into the room.

"What's happened?"

"I don't know," Nancy says, making room for the nurse. "She got really confused, she started talking about—she looked at the door and screamed. I don't—"

"I still see them sometimes," Agatha whimpers up at them both, her eyes swimming with tears now. "But I never know. I can never tell if it's all just in my head. I'm sorry. I'm so sorry. The baby never died. I need you to tell her. Someone needs to tell her, but the others don't listen."

"Shh shh shh," the nurse coos at Agatha. "Hush, now, Sister. It's all right. No one's going to harm you. It's okay. You're safe."

Agatha's face crumples, giving way to tears. Nancy reaches out to take her hand once again. Agatha starts as though surprised to be touched, but grips Nancy's fingers.

"Sister," the nurse says softly, "I'm going to give you something to make you more comfortable, okay?"

Agatha nods her understanding, her eyes closed.

The nurse turns to Nancy, her voice low. "I'm going to go get her something that'll put her to sleep. It's all we can really do for the panic and confusion. I wish we could do more, but it's in God's hands now." The nurse crosses herself.

"Of course," Nancy says.

"I'll be right back."

Nancy settles back down on the guest chair beside the bed, careful not to lose her grip on Agatha's cold fingers. Her body seems to soften, the tears subsiding. Sometimes we just need a hand to hold.

A moment later, Agatha opens her eyes again. They're foggy and a bit out of focus. "Please tell her," she whispers.

"I—I will," Nancy says, perplexed. She pats the woman's hand again.

To Nancy's relief, the nurse returns shortly with a syringe. She injects it into the IV beside Agatha's bed, frowning.

"She should be asleep in just a minute or two, Nancy," she says quietly. "You may as well go once she's asleep. We'll keep her out for the evening, I think. The confusion's just getting worse and worse by the hour, and we don't want her to feel afraid."

Nancy nods again. "Okay. That's fine."

Ten minutes later, once she's confident that Sister Agatha has succumbed fully to the sleeping medication, Nancy checks that her book is still in her bag and fastens the catch on her tote. She looks back at Agatha and reaches out for the peak she knows to be the dying woman's right foot. She holds it with a motherly tenderness—a soft touch that her hands shouldn't have learned yet—before she heads for the door.

She lingers outside the room, waits until the night nurse passes by again a minute later.

"Can I ask you something?" she says, hailing her.

"What is it, Nancy?"

Nancy hesitates, unsure how to phrase what she wants to ask without it sounding like an accusation. "What Sister Agatha just said—" She hikes the strap of her bag up onto her shoulder. "It was a bit disturbing. Before you came in, she told me that they used to steal babies and sell them here, when it was a home for wayward girls. What's she talking about?"

The nun's lips purse, and she glances over her shoulder. "There was something of a . . . controversy, back when this building served as the maternity home for the parish. It would seem some of the babies were sold to adoptive families. I think that's what she's referring to. I suspect Agatha holds a lot of guilt about her role in all that."

Nancy refrains from swearing with difficulty. "And she said something about a baby not dying?"

The nurse shakes her head. "I have no idea what that's about. You must understand that she's been very confused lately. Sometimes wires get crossed in the mind, you know, toward the end. Don't take any of it to heart," she adds. "That's all well in the past anyhow."

The nurse bustles off, leaving Nancy alone. She turns left down the hallway toward the staircase. A few steps down, she hears someone on the stairs behind her. When she reaches the front door, she instinctively holds it open.

"Thank you," the woman says, hurrying past Nancy out onto the porch.

Nancy catches a glimpse of the woman's profile and feels a twinge behind her navel. *Dr. Taylor?* At the end of the path, the woman turns left down the sidewalk into the evening sun.

"Dr. Taylor!" Nancy calls. "Dr. Taylor, wait!"

The woman hustles a few more feet before she slows, stops, turns. She's backlit in the sun, but Nancy is positive it's her.

"I'm sorry, do I know you?" Dr. Taylor asks.

Nancy falters. Dr. Taylor's eyes are bright, and her nose is pink, as though she's been crying. "You, um . . ." Nancy glances around, but they're alone on the street, save for a man washing his car several doors down. She closes the space between them. "You helped me out. You know, with a problem I had. A couple of years ago."

"Ahh, I see. Okay." Dr. Taylor surveys her for a moment, then nods slowly. "I remember your face now. The raid, right? March of '81?"

"That was me."

Nancy never would have expected to run into her, and feels a surprising sense of urgency. She needs to thank the doctor before she loses her chance. "What you did. You might have saved my life, in more ways than one. I know it sounds dramatic, but that's how it feels."

"I understand. I truly do." Dr. Taylor looks back at the nursing home, her face dark. "That's why I do what I do. And I'm so sorry, I see a lot of patients, and for the life of me I just can't recall your name."

"Nancy. Nancy Mitchell."

"Nancy. Hello again."

"What were you doing at St. Sebastian's?" Nancy asks, curious.

"I came to say goodbye to a patient of mine. My first patient, actually. And more of a friend than a patient, in the end."

"Oh." Nancy frowns. "I'm sorry."

"Thank you. And you?"

"I volunteer. I sit with the palliative patients. Or at least I used to. Today was my last day. I just got a job in my field."

Dr. Taylor smiles. "That's great news, congratulations. So, things have been good since I last saw you?"

"Yeah, pretty good. I just started dating a new guy. He's a lot different than the guy that— He seems like an adult, and he's sweet." Nancy blushes and casts around for a change of subject. "Are you still with Jane?"

A breeze flutters her hair and she pushes it back out of her face, squinting into the sun.

"Yes, very much so," Dr. Taylor says. "We're busier than ever, which is both a good thing and a bad thing. It means word is getting around and women are more comfortable calling us, and trusting us, but it's difficult to keep up with the demand. It's only a small team of us, right? Just a dozen or so volunteers, and a few doctors."

"Is Alice still with you?"

"Oh yes. Till the bitter end, I think. She's a firecracker."

"She was so kind," Nancy says. "Please tell her that from me. She made the whole thing a lot easier."

"I will."

Nancy licks her lips, the warm moment stretching out into awkwardness. She shared one of her most intimate, emotional experiences with Dr. Taylor, yet somehow she doesn't really know what else to say.

"I won't keep you, I'm sure you're busy. I just wanted to say thank you again. I don't think I really thanked you properly that night, because of the police and everything, and I was just so distracted and upset. And I didn't really appreciate it fully until later on. I thought about calling you to tell you that, afterward. I'm sorry now that I didn't. I want you to know I'm grateful."

"I know that."

"Well, I wanted you to hear it." Nancy smiles at her, wipes away a tear that has slipped down her face. "I don't know why I'm crying. It was the right thing. I've always known that. I knew it then and I know it now. I don't know what this is about." She indicates her face and splutters out an embarrassed laugh.

Dr. Taylor waits.

Nancy clears her throat. "Before I saw you, I had just found out something about my past. My family. And I think it kind of sent me off the deep end for a while. I wasn't careful. I dated a total loser and got pregnant. I'm ashamed of it, in hindsight. I didn't handle it well. But being able to get help from you and Alice, well . . ." She wipes her cheek and blinks. "It made all the difference, that's all. I was able to turn things around instead of getting stuck in the rut I was in with a terrible guy."

Dr. Taylor smiles, not showing her teeth. "I'm glad to hear that. Sometimes relief can be just as intense as regret. You must know that almost all the women I see shed tears at some point. And often it's a feeling of relief. Or regret, or shame, or all three all rolled into one messy ball. The point is, it's okay. To just feel it. To just cry."

Nancy sniffles. "I'm sorry."

"Stop apologizing."

"Just seeing you, I think it's bringing that back for me, you know?"

Dr. Taylor glances up at the house. "I know."

"Honestly, it feels like a relief to even be able to talk about it to you. I haven't told anyone. I've just been carrying it all here." She points to her chest. "And it gets heavy sometimes."

The two women stand across from each other on the sidewalk of the quiet side street, their private thoughts unknowingly overlapping across the sticky, shared memory of the night of Nancy's abortion. It's a perfect summer evening. A gentle breeze has picked up from the south, caressing the leaves of the lush maple trees. The sun is sinking in the sky, tiring out after a long day's work.

"I know what that's like," Dr. Taylor finally says. "It can be really difficult to trust anyone with something that huge. It took me a while to be comfortable telling my husband about some of my darkest spots. But in the future, you might feel differently."

Nancy watches the shadow flit across Dr. Taylor's face, wondering what those dark spots might be for her. Her eyes flicker toward the nursing home again, then back to Nancy, who remembers she's just come from saying goodbye to an old friend.

"Listen, I should get going," Nancy says. "I don't want to keep you."

Dr. Taylor extends a hand, which Nancy shakes. "You've got a good, strong handshake," she says. "I like that. Don't lose it. None of that wet-fish nonsense some women offer. You take care, now."

She lifts a hand in farewell and heads down the sidewalk into the sun. Nancy watches her go with a feeling of warmth that's woven with a prickly thread of loss.

"Wait!" she calls, and rushes forward again. "How, um, how can I help?"

"Help?"

"With the Janes," Nancy says. "You said you're strapped for volunteers?"

"We are, yes." She considers Nancy for a moment. "Do you think it would be doable for you? A lot of women find—afterward—that they just want to put it all behind them. But we do have a handful of Janes who started out as patients themselves. They often make the best counselors because they know what it's like."

"That makes sense to me," Nancy says. "It's just the experience I had with you and Alice, with the police raid, I mean, you saw how I reacted. I was so fed up. I shouldn't have had to track you down like I did, like abortion is some black-market luxury. But at least I felt safe. At least you knew what you were doing, and I didn't have to be afraid I was going to die. My cousin sure as hell didn't feel safe. She shouldn't have had to go through that. And it made me wonder how many other women are out there with no options. I feel like I was *lucky*, and that's not right, is it? With Jane, it's like you've taken it into your own hands somehow. It's women helping women, allowing us to be at the steering wheel of our own lives for once, right?"

"That's the idea, yes."

"I want to help other women feel that."

Dr. Taylor nods.

"This house," Nancy continues, gesturing back toward the old build-ing, "it used to be a home for wayward girls. They gave up their babies here. I can't imagine girls like me not having a choice. Of being forced into anything."

"A lot of them were even younger than you," Dr. Taylor says quietly. She holds Nancy's gaze for a long moment. "If you're really interested, you can come to the next volunteer recruitment meeting. We do them in batches, but I have to say, Nancy, a lot of the women who think they want to volunteer don't end up sticking around. We don't begrudge them for it. It's a pretty big risk. You have to accept going into it that what you're doing is criminal activity and you might get arrested. It can also bring up a lot of tough memories. It's pretty high stakes for a volunteer position."

The flare Nancy feels in her gut is excitement, not fear. "I'm sure. It's the least I can do. The Janes changed my life. I'd like to join."

CHAPTER 18

Angela

· · · · · · · · · ·

MARCH 2017

Angela hasn't received any positive responses yet from the Nancy Birches she sent Facebook messages to, so she's decided to shift tracks and instead try to locate Nancy's birth mother, Margaret Roberts. She's starting with St. Agnes's Home for Unwed Mothers, hoping they may have some kind of record that might help her track down its former resident.

She's spent the past two hours at the university library while Tina teaches an evening class. Nursing a decaf coffee, she started with a deep dive into Google, where she found brief references to the home in a couple of books and academic articles, but none of them listed what parish the home was connected to, which might have allowed her to track down the Roberts family. As of now, she can't even see the tip of a thread she might tug to unravel this mystery.

Reluctantly conceding that she isn't going to find the information she needs on the internet, Angela stands up from the uncomfortable chair she's been parked in all night and heads to the deserted microfilm room. At a computer, she navigates to the directory and enters the key-words: *Agnes Home Unwed Mothers Toronto*.

There's only one hit. She clicks on a scan of a news article from the *Toronto Star*, printed in August 1961.

SCANDAL-PLAGUED
ST. AGNES'S HOME TO CLOSE:
ABUSE, RESIDENT DEATH

St. Agnes's Home for Unwed Mothers in East Toronto will soon shutter its doors after a resident, who claimed she suffered abuse at the home, took her own life. In June, Toronto police received a letter from the woman in question containing allegations of systemic physical and mental abuse. Allegations were also made regarding the illegality of adoption contracts, stating mothers were forced to consent to adoptions under duress and by force, and that children were illegally sold to adoptive families. Investigations are currently underway. None of the allegations has been proven in court.

"Disgusting," Angela mutters, thinking over what she's just learned.

She glances at the date of the article. So the home shut down not long after Nancy Mitchell was born to Margaret Roberts; Nancy's adoptive mother had alluded to the closure in her letter. Angela wonders whether the poor girl might have been able to keep her baby if she had gotten pregnant just a few months later than she did. Although Margaret may then have simply gone to a different maternity home. Were they all this atrocious? And who was the resident who wrote a letter to the police in June 1961, then took her own life immediately afterward? She's the unnamed whistleblower at the center of this. Her death triggered the investigation and closure of the home.

Angela needs a break. She stretches her arms up over her head. There's no one else in the microfilm room, so she lunges across the worn carpet several times to stretch her stiff legs. She can already hear her doctor upbraiding her for neglecting her circulation.

It's nearly eight o'clock in the evening. The library will be closing at nine, and then she'll have to go meet Tina once her class gets out. She's hungry again and needs a fresh coffee. Temporarily abandoning her notebook and coat at the microfilm station, Angela grabs her purse and rides the elevator up to the main floor, where she can buy a stale decaf from the tiny kiosk that slings weak brew, browning bananas, and appallingly caloric cupcakes masquerading as muffins. It's student fuel, but it'll do. She's hungry enough right now to eat her own arm.

Coffee and muffin now in hand, Angela takes the stairs back down to the basement. She walks past two students, the only other people besides Angela in this section of the library. Both are bleary-eyed with teetering stacks of books piled beside their glowing laptop screens.

Back at her desk, she leans over the computer, isolates the article with the cursor, and hits print. She can hear the sleeping printer hum to life in the back corner of the room, a grumbling grandpa reluctantly waking from a nap. She wanders over and lifts the warm page off the printer output.

What next?

Angela swallows a bite of muffin and reconsiders her approach. She'll have to search for Margaret Roberts directly, though if she does find anything, without details from the home she doesn't have any information to cross-reference to confirm it's the woman she's looking for. Still, she types Margaret Roberts's name into the search box and begins sifting through the results. The better part of half an hour passes before she clicks on one that causes her finger to freeze, suspended over the mouse.

It's an obituary published in June 1961.

ROBERTS, Margaret Elizabeth of Toronto, Ont. Unexpectedly in her 20th yr. Survived by parents George and Esther Roberts, and brother John "Jack"

Roberts (Lorna). Remembered by several uncles, aunts, and cousins. Con-
dolences may be sent to the Roberts family directly. No funeral service to
be scheduled.

"Unexpectedly in her twentieth year..." Angela leans in toward the white glow of the screen.

Words like "suddenly at home" in an obituary often mean something like a heart attack. "Surrounded by family" translates to a slow death from cancer. "Tragically" denotes an accident of some kind, but "unexpectedly" is sometimes a euphemism for suicide, which could also explain the lack of funeral service. Angela shakes her head. Things were different in the sixties.

"*Shit*," she whispers. Tearing her eyes away from the screen, she picks up the printout of the news article about the closure of St. Agnes's, scanning it again. The timelines and details align.

Margaret Roberts is dead. She's the whistleblower whose daughter was taken away from her. She wrote to the police, then killed herself.

Angela heaves a deep sigh. She can't help Frances Mitchell fulfill her final wish that Nancy reunite with her birth mother. That door closed the day Margaret died.

She gulps her bitter coffee with a wince before giving up on it, rising from the computer chair, and tossing the cup in the garbage bin. She returns to the computer, arms crossed on her chest as though reluctant to sit back down and reread the obituary. If she doesn't read it again and doesn't hit print, maybe she can pretend she never saw it.

But Angela can't pretend. She feels a responsibility to Margaret now. A duty to put the pieces together and make sure that Margaret's last hope—for her baby girl to know she loved her and never wanted to give her up—is honored. It's the least she can do for the poor girl whose life was such a source of shame to her family that her death didn't even warrant a funeral.

She has to find Nancy Birch.

Angela pulls her scarf closer around her shoulders in a habitual gesture of self-protection before settling herself back down onto the rickety chair. She runs her hands over her midsection, thinking of the baby she'll hold in her arms this fall, imagining what it would be like to be separated from her child, to die alone without ever knowing what became of it.

She hits print.

. . . .

The few responses Angela has received from the Nancy Birches have been the same as the ones she got from the Nancy Mitchells: *Not me, sorry.* A part of her is grateful; now that she knows Margaret Roberts is dead, she's in no hurry to be the one to relay such news to the elusive Nancy. For the time being, she's stashed the obituary and news article printouts in a storage bin under her bed along with the letter and note.

Since Angela works Sundays on a regular basis, Saturday afternoons have become her favorite opportunity to read. She and Tina spent the morning doing their weekly grocery shop and other dull errands, then Tina headed to the gym while Angela tugged on her chunky knit reading socks and curled up on the couch with Grizzly and a steaming mug of tea.

Snow falls outside the living room window. There's something about a snowy weekend that feels like a freebie; like the earth is saying, *Slow down, enjoy yourself, there's nowhere to go anyway.* It's an invitation Angela warmly accepts as she sinks her teeth into her new book club pick.

The first chapter of *The Jane Network* is a sweeping survey of the history of women's reproductive options until 1960, a year before the first iteration of the birth control pill was introduced in America. After that, things changed a bit for women—mostly white—who had the means and legal opportunity to access the pill, a category that certainly did not include unmarried teenage girls.

Captivated, Angela reads about the various homes for unwed mothers, as they were then labeled, which took in pregnant girls and hid them for the duration of their pregnancies. The babies were almost always adopted, and, from what Dr. Taylor describes of her own experience at one of these homes, many of the adoptions occurred under duress, and some blatantly against the mother's will. Angela thinks of Margaret's note to her daughter Jane; the one she's read so many times now that she's committed it to memory. The haunting lyrics of a mournful goodbye.

I did not want to give you up.

Angela rolls her shoulders back, refocuses her eyes on the page in front of her. She's taken aback by the candidness of Dr. Taylor's memoir. Her experience sounds as horrific as she imagines Margaret Roberts's was, and the detail induces Angela to wrap one arm around her stomach. She can't imagine being forced to give up her baby like these girls were. She's about to set the book aside and give her emotions a break when she reads something that causes her breath to catch.

> *My best friend at the Home—I'll call her "Maggie"—took her own life after the trauma she experienced at that place. I lost both my best friend and my daughter to lack of choice, and I knew, after I left, that I would find a way to make sure other girls would always—*always—*have a choice.*

"Maggie?" Angela says aloud to Grizzly, who has curled up in a tight coil in the groove of her tented knees. "As in Margaret?"

Angela stares at the sentence, her thoughts whirring. In the introduction, Dr. Taylor said she would be changing the names of all the women she mentions in an effort to protect the true identities of anyone who might not want their criminal activity revealed, even all these years later. But Maggie? Margaret?

Angela chews her lip, then flips back a few pages, looking for where the author mentions the year she spent at the maternity home. She just says "the early 60s." Surely there were plenty of girls named Maggie at maternity homes at that time. Margaret was a fairly common name back then.

She hears the clicking of a key in the lock, the front door shutting.

"Woo! It's frickin' cold out there again!" Tina stomps the snow off her boots on the front hall mat. "Where the hell is spring? Taking it's sweet-ass time, apparently." A minute later, she's in the living room.

"Good workout?" Angela asks.

"Yeah, it was fine. Glad I went, anyway. Now I can have ice cream later and not feel guilty. That's how that works, right?"

Angela smiles in a vague way but isn't really listening. "Tina, would you be able to put me in touch with Evelyn Taylor?"

Tina's shiny brow furrows. "Sure, I guess. Why?"

PART III

CHAPTER 19

Nancy

. . . .

JULY 1984

O n a Thursday afternoon in the height of the summer heat, Nancy and her boyfriend Michael are sitting in a patch of welcome shade outside the café in Kensington Market where they had their first date. They happily sip fresh-squeezed lemonade and share a piece of truly exceptional almond coffee cake while people-watching out of the corner of their eye.

Nancy is on her summer holiday from work this week, and Michael planned his to coincide with hers. And at his suggestion, they whiled away the morning in the cool air-conditioned refuge of the art gallery, wandering its wide halls and dark exhibits. It was a welcome respite for Nancy, who has spent most of her vacation with her parents. Her mother is in remission from the cancer now. Her treatment went well, but she's a weaker, diminished version of her former self, somehow much more vulnerable than she used to be. Nancy worried that she should stay home with her, but when Frances heard that Michael was taking her out, she shooed her out the door.

Nancy had debated bringing Michael home to meet them last summer, but after a few dates, she'd realized quite quickly that he might be worth hanging on to, and decided to introduce him to her parents. The first time he leaned in to kiss her, on her front step after a date at the movies, he'd asked for her permission first. He supported her desire for a career of her own, worked hard, and didn't drink too much. And he turned out to be incredible with Frances. He connected with her in a way that Nancy had certainly never been able to, helping her off couches she was too weak to stand up from and telling jokes to distract her from the bouts of nausea she was still susceptible to. Nancy had never heard her mother laugh like she did with Michael, not before the cancer, and certainly not after. He even cooked the whole family dinner one night when Frances's blood pressure dropped so low that Nancy and her father had to rush her to the hospital. They came home to find Michael in the kitchen wearing her mother's floral apron with a pasta dinner ready on the table, complete with salad and wine.

"Hang on to this one, Beetle," Nancy's dad muttered under his breath as he helped her mother out of her jacket.

She worried then about what might happen if they broke up. Her mother would be devastated, and Nancy couldn't stand the thought of that. But nearly a year has passed since then, and she and Michael are still crazy about one another. It's the best Nancy has felt about her life in a long time, and for the most part she's comfortable being herself around him. She hasn't, however, shared with him that she's working with the Jane Network.

Not long after she ran into Dr. Taylor outside St. Sebastian's the previous summer, she went to the recruitment meeting. Her relationship with Michael was still so new, she told herself, and what she was doing was illegal. While her girlfriends are out doing normal things like shopping or going to the movies, she revels in the knowledge that she's helping other women gain power over their own lives. And although she trusts Michael, the less *anyone* knows about the network and its activity, the better, which is also why she's never told him about her own abortion.

"What next?" Nancy asks Michael now, as he insists she take the last bite of cake.

A family with three noisy children passes by their table on the sidewalk outside the café. The little girl points at Nancy's lemonade and starts shrieking that she wants one, too. Her rather harassed-looking, sweaty mother nods feebly and directs her family toward the doors to the café.

Michael smirks and shakes his head as though clearing his ears of the lingering squeal of the girl's high-pitched shriek.

"I was just thinking that myself," Michael says. "What's next."

Nancy stares back at him, brown eyes meeting blue over the tip of the straw from her glass. "I'm easy. Want to go down to the Queen's Quay? Or out to the island? Maybe rent some bikes?"

Michael rakes a hand through his sandy hair, then glances over his shoulder at the few other patrons who have braved the scorching heat of the patio on a day like this. He turns back to Nancy. "I was thinking a bit bigger than that."

Nancy sets down her empty glass. "Okay. What did you have in mind?"

Michael smiles and lets his breath out in one long, hot stream. Birds twitter in the small privet bush to Nancy's left.

"Well," Michael says, rising from his seat.

He reaches deep into the pocket of his shorts and pulls out a tiny black box. Nancy watches him kneel in front of her as though it's being played back to her in slow motion, like a dream. Her surroundings become blurred. All she can see is Michael's shining face looking up at her over the sparkling diamond ring in his hand.

"I was kind of thinking about forever. I think forever is next."

"Oh, Michael."

Nancy vaguely registers a gasp from one of the other patrons on the patio. "*Look! Look!*" the woman hisses at her husband.

"I wanted to bring you back to the place where I first fell in love with you. I knew as soon as I met you that you were the one for me. I was a goner. We sat at this table and you ordered me a double espresso that was so strong I nearly had a heart attack, but I didn't care. There was a glow about you that night just like there is now. Like a spotlight was shining down on you, leading me home."

Nancy presses her hand to her mouth and blinks back the tears.

"I love you, Nancy Mitchell. Will you marry me?"

Nancy throws her arms around Michael, burying her nose in his neck. She can feel him shaking.

"So, is that a yes?" Michael asks her, laughing.

She pulls back to see his face. "Yes! It's a yes. I love you."

Michael rises awkwardly to his feet, pulling Nancy with him as they kiss each other deeply. Only now does Nancy hear the applause issuing all around them. Even across the street, people are whooping and cheering for them.

When they pull apart, Nancy wipes her eyes with the back of her hand, then holds her left one out to Michael, who slides his ring onto her trembling finger. It fits perfectly. They kiss again, and Nancy feels like her feet might leave the ground. Or maybe she's already floating.

"I love you," she whispers, grinning.

"I love you, too."

"You're shaking. Are you okay?"

Michael nods. "Yeah. I mean, I was pretty sure I knew what the answer was going to be, but no one ever tells you how scary it is. My God, that was terrifying!"

. . . .

That night, Nancy and Michael change into fresh clothes at their respective apartments, then meet up to walk over to Nancy's parents' house to relay the happy news.

They already know, of course. Michael phoned them one night in June to invite himself over for an Important Conversation. He certainly didn't have to wrangle their blessing out of them.

"It was intimidating, to ask your dad," Michael tells her now as they stroll hand in hand the last few blocks toward the Mitchells' house.

Nancy smirks. "He's all bark. He loves you."

"I keep trying to figure out which of your parents you look more like. With most people you can usually see more of one than the other, but I can't really tell with your folks."

Nancy clears her throat and squeezes Michael's hand, her eyes on the sidewalk beneath her feet. She's thought about telling him the truth for a while, but has kept putting it off, telling herself that it's a conversation for another day. Now isn't the time. Not when their engagement is casting such a warm glow over everything. The truth might ruin all that, and what if Michael decided it was all too much for him? What if he got angry that she'd waited this long to tell him?

"Well," she says, deflecting the comment, "honestly, don't let anything my dad says bother you. He's just a giant teddy bear."

Michael chuckles. "And your mom is beyond thrilled. She started sobbing, said it gives her something to live for."

Nancy halts abruptly on the sidewalk. "That didn't . . ." She tries to stop herself from asking it but can't. "Her cancer doesn't have anything to do with you proposing, does it?"

Michael stops walking and turns to face her. His blue eyes squint into the sun as a lock of sandy hair falls across his forehead. "What?"

Nancy registers the unfamiliar sensation of her engagement ring between her fingers. "I just mean you're so close with her, and what you just said, about her saying it gives her something to live for . . ."

Michael drops her hand. "Jesus Christ, Nancy. You think I asked you to marry me because your mom was sick?"

"I—no, of course not."

"But that's exactly what you just asked me."

Nancy's breath is coming quicker. She regrets saying anything now. "I'm sorry, I shouldn't have said anything. It was just her comment, that's all. Why would she say that?"

Michael scoffs, shakes his head. "I don't think she was serious, really. Not in the literal sense. She was just excited, that's all. Jesus. What's your issue with her? You've done this before, gone out of your way to find issues with your mom. She's your *mom*. It's like you're ... suspicious of her or something. Or me," he adds.

"I'm not suspicious of you, Michael," Nancy says, reaching out for his hand again. He lets her link her fingers through. He must feel the ring, too, because his face softens. "I'm sorry I said anything. Just forget it. Please."

Michael takes a deep breath. "Okay. All right. Because I love you, you hear?" He brushes her cheek with his other hand and kisses her. "I'm not marrying your mom, I'm marrying *you*. She just finds me irresistible, that's all. And who can blame her?"

Nancy chuckles as Michael gives an exaggerated swagger, and they continue down the sidewalk, reaching her parents' house a moment later.

After the news is relayed and bone-crushing hugs are delivered, Nancy's father sneaks away to the kitchen.

"I've had a bottle of bubbly chilled ever since Mike came to chat with us," he calls from inside the refrigerator. "Glad he finally got around to asking! Thought I was going to have to drink this all myself."

"Oh, Bill!" Nancy's mother hisses. "It's his sense of humor, Michael," she adds.

"So I've heard," Michael says, winking at Nancy.

Nancy's dad returns to the living room with a frosty bottle of Brut and four champagne flutes. He sets them down neatly on the coffee table, then wiggles the cork out with the familiar pop that signals the start of something exciting. He pours champagne into the flutes with an expert hand; the foam reaches the very tops of the glasses, where it mushrooms threateningly but never overflows. They each take a glass.

Nancy's dad is still standing, as though about to make a speech, and affection bubbles in her chest as Nancy pictures him standing up just like this to give a toast at their wedding.

"To Nancy and Michael," he says now. "May the road rise to meet you."

He nods at them both as Frances once again gasps, "Oh, Bill!" this time with tears in her eyes.

"Thank you, Daddy," Nancy says, standing to kiss him on the cheek.

"So happy for you, Beetle," he mutters in her ear. His bristly moustache tickles her skin. "He's a good egg."

"I know, Dad."

They sit down again, and all four of them clink glasses over the coffee table. Nancy leans back on the couch, smiling at her mother across from her. Michael wraps his arm around her shoulders.

Frances reaches up and straightens her wig. Her hair has grown back since the chemo, but it's thin. Nancy suspects she might just wear wigs on a permanent basis now.

Frances claps her gloved hands together. "Well," she says. "I say we all go out for lunch tomorrow to celebrate. Somewhere smart. Us four, and your parents, too, Michael. We're so very excited to meet them."

Nancy winces guiltily. She has a shift with the Janes tomorrow, helping Dr. Taylor and Alice. They have three appointments lined up in the afternoon at a secret location off Spadina Avenue. Nancy is scheduled in for pre-op counseling.

"I actually can't tomorrow. I'm so sorry. How about Saturday?"

Frances's hand pauses midair, the champagne glass halfway to her red-stained lips. "Why not? What are you doing?"

. . . .

"Can that air conditioner blast any stronger than this?" Dr. Taylor asks.

Nancy mops her damp face with a piece of paper towel and glances toward the metal box in the apartment window. Its motor is grinding and humming as the paper ribbons tied to the grill flutter feebly. It's working, but barely.

She, Dr. Taylor, and Alice are clustered around a small wooden table in the kitchen of the apartment the Janes are currently using as their clinic, waiting for their next appointment. The unit is on the fourth floor of a cheap low-rise in Chinatown. They can hear the screech and dinging bells of the streetcars off in the distance, latchkey children shouting and playing skipping games in the street.

The Janes move around frequently to avoid detection and reduce the likelihood of police raids. Henry Morgentaler's clinic was nearly bombed the previous summer, and he was almost stabbed by a protester. The anti-choice movement is gaining momentum, and the Janes are determined to stay at least one step ahead.

In the past ten months, they have used space in the homes of three of their volunteer members—including an attic and a large backyard shed—as well as a dentist's office, thanks to Penny, one of the older Janes. This apartment in Chinatown belongs to the mother of one of the volunteers. She rents it out to university students from September through April, but it's been vacant since May. It has a kitchen, a living room that serves as their waiting area, and two bedrooms: one they use as their surgical room, the other as the recovery room. The apartment is discreet, centrally located, and the price is right, but the sweltering July heat and humidity have become almost unbearable. The rickety old air conditioning unit in the film-coated window isn't enough to stop Nancy from sweating through her shirt.

"It's not quite at full blast," Alice says with a frown, her own upper lip beading with sweat. "But Leslie says if we run it any harder, it's likely to kick the bucket. This is all we've got. We can try to bring some fans in from our houses, if anyone has extras they can spare. And I've still got Popsicles in the freezer, if you want one."

"Oh, yeah, excellent," Nancy says. Pushing her chair back with a screech, she strides to the refrigerator. The box of Popsicles is the only thing in the freezer besides some half-filled ice cube trays. Skipping over the grape Popsicles, she fishes three orange ones out of the bottom of the box and rips off the paper wrapping, stuffing them into the bin lined with a medical-grade garbage bag. She hands one to each of the other women.

"Has Kathleen been discharged yet?" she asks Alice.

"Just about to be. She's in the second bedroom on the recovery couch. Doris is in there with her." Alice drops her voice, and Dr. Taylor and Nancy lean in. "Poor thing had a really rough go. Three kids already and her husband is an unemployed drunk. I saw bruises on her arms, and she said he forces himself on her. Won't even let her use birth control. So we may see her again."

"Well, fuck that guy," Dr. Taylor says, biting the end off her Popsicle.

Nancy looks up at her. She's never heard her curse like that before.

"Yeah," Alice continues. "Doris said she's going to see if she's willing to go to a shelter. But they rarely are. I wish we could let them bring a close friend, or sister, but . . ."

"We can't. Not after Montreal—"

"I know," Alice says. "I just wish it were different."

The women exchange a dark look across the table. Dr. Taylor nods. "No kidding."

They used to allow their clients to bring their mother or sister, a friend, or even their boyfriend, if he was supportive of the decision. Until three months ago, when an underground clinic in Montreal got raided after a client's fickle friend reported the location to the local police. Charges are pending against the volunteers and doctor, a professional acquaintance of Dr. Taylor's from her medical school days. The network was destroyed. The Janes simply can't risk it. And if that weren't bad enough, their previous informant at the police headquarters, Mary, had to leave her job to stay home with her first baby. The Janes don't have anyone on the inside anymore to give them a heads-up about potential raids. Their advance warning system is gone.

They have two more procedures scheduled this afternoon. Normally they book their patients for Saturdays, when the volunteers are more available and the women can come see the Janes under the guise of running errands, but Alice is getting married tomorrow, and it's generally frowned upon for the bride to arrive at her wedding sweating buckets and covered in blood and amniotic fluid.

"Is everything all ready to go for tomorrow?" Nancy asks her now. Her own brand-new engagement ring glitters on her finger. She shared the news with Evelyn and Alice the moment she walked through the door this morning.

A smile creeps across Alice's usually stoic features. "Yes. It's a bit more splashy than I wanted, but you know Bob's mother. Everything is pink and peach." She rolls her eyes. "I never thought I would have a wedding at all, let alone some big ostentatious affair like this."

"You and Bob love each other," Dr. Taylor says. "That's all that matters. Just make sure you don't choke on peonies and lemon custard cake. I need you. Same goes for you, Nancy, when the time comes."

Alice and Nancy laugh as Dr. Taylor pops the rest of the Popsicle into her mouth. A buzzer sounds, and all three stiffen, alert.

"Just the two o'clock coming in," Nancy says, picking up her clipboard. She goes to answer the door. "Hello?"

"Hello," the crackly voice echoes back.

"What can I do for you?" Nancy asks.

"I'm, uh, I'm looking for Jane?" The voice sounds unsure.

"Is she expecting you?"

A pause. "Yes."

"What's your name?"

"Patricia."

"What number did Jane give you when you first called her?" Nancy asks.

"Hang on, it's in my purse. One sec."

The buzzer clicks off, and Nancy drums her fingers against the wall beside the door, waiting. The crackly voice returns.

"One-three-five-nine-two-two."

Nancy consults her clipboard to confirm the code is correct for their two o'clock appointment.

"Come on up," she says, and buzzes Patricia in.

Nancy will do a brief pre-screening counseling session in the operating room and explain the procedure to the patient before handing her off to Dr. Taylor. The Janes developed this two-step system to help spread out the responsibility so the doctors could focus solely on the medical side of things. Realizing she forgot to bring a pen for Patricia's intake, Nancy walks back to the kitchen, where Dr. Taylor and Alice are still in conversation.

"Will this always be necessary?" Alice asks.

"The code?" Dr. Taylor asks. "I think so. It's too—"

"No, not the security. I just mean abortions. Sometimes I think we've come so far, and with the pill and the movement and everything, the *Birth Control Handbook.* But we're still doing, what, four procedures a week? And that's just our clinic. I can't believe there's *still* that much of a need."

Nancy grabs a pen from the jar on the counter as Dr. Taylor looks down into Alice's kind face. The face she'll present to her husband tomorrow at her wedding, made-up and polished, full of love and commitment and hope for their future. The face that will calm the nerves of nearly ten thousand aborting women over the course of her forty-two-year career in obstetrics. Because it will never stop.

Dr. Taylor sighs heavily, but manages a weak smile nonetheless. "Yes, Alice. There will always be a need."

Nancy shakes her head sadly and returns to the front door. A minute or two later, her patient arrives.

"Patricia?" she asks, pen poised over her clipboard.

The woman standing in the doorway is exactly her age, according to the docket in Nancy's hands. She's wearing Bermuda shorts and a plaid shirt, dark hair pulled back in a loose ponytail. Nancy introduces herself and Patricia steps over the threshold. Her eyes flicker around the living room. Nancy knows how it looks: a cluster of old chairs, a coffee table, and some out-of-date magazines. It doesn't matter, though. Almost all the women who pick them up end up flipping through them without absorbing a single word, recipe, or beauty tip. Their eyes slide over the pages while their minds race; some balancing on the precipice of changing their decision, waffling back and forth between yes and no with every robotic turn of the crinkled, glossy pages. Others are far more sure, like Nancy was, and can't wait for it to be over.

Nancy leads Patricia into the master bedroom and gestures to one of the chairs beside the operating table. It's not a proper operating table, just a sturdy, fold-up portable table with a thin camping mattress on it, covered in plastic sheets. But it's the best they can do under these clandestine circumstances.

As Patricia sits down, her eyes flicker over to the tray next to the table, the silver instruments laid out on the blue paper. Her brows pinch together as she lowers her purse to the floor beside her.

"Would you like some water?" Nancy asks, trying to distract her from the sight of the surgical tools. It's always the first question she poses to her patients. A simple yes or no, non-threatening, and it puts them in control.

Patricia shakes her head no.

"And just to confirm, you're here of your own volition? We have to ask that of every woman who comes to see us. If you've been forced to come here by anyone, we can try to help you in other ways," Nancy says.

"Yeah. Yeah I'm here because I want to be."

"Okay, good. And have you ever had this procedure, Patricia?"

Patricia clears her throat and sits up straighter in the chair. "Um, no. No, I haven't."

"Okay, so the procedure itself is quite safe. We haven't yet had any issues or emergencies, and no one has ever gotten a post-op infection on our watch. Our doctor and nurse are highly trained professionals. They do about four of these a week. They're kind, compassionate women. You're in good hands here."

Patricia swallows and leans forward. "Could you tell me how it's done?"

"Of course, but you should tell me how much detail you want. Some women just want the general idea, and others are more comfortable if they know the specifics, so they can know exactly what to expect."

"I'd like to hear it step-by-step. If that's okay."

"Okay, if you're sure. So, the doctor will first examine your uterus using a speculum—the same kind they use for PAP tests. She'll then inject some medication into your cervix to numb the area, and stretch it out a bit," Nancy continues, eyeing Patricia closely. This is sometimes where she starts to lose a patient; some people have no idea what they're about to hear, and it's where even the most determined woman's resolve can start to splinter. "She'll insert a tube, and then—"

A piercing screech issues from somewhere on Patricia's body. Like the shrill tone of a poorly tuned violin, the sound hovers in the air, vibrates, then dissipates in a whistle.

The two women freeze in tableau.

"What . . . ?" Nancy trails off.

Patricia fumbles around with her shirt, lifting it to reveal a small black box with wires strapped to her midsection. "Shit," she whispers. There's a soft click as she flicks a switch.

Nancy opens her mouth to speak again, and at the same moment, Patricia reaches down to the floor and pulls a handgun out of her big black purse. Rising from her chair, she points it directly at Nancy.

"I'm going to need you to stand up slowly and put your hands behind your head."

CHAPTER 20

Evelyn

. . . .

JULY 1984

"What the hell was that?" Evelyn freezes, her pen suspended over the clipboard where she's reviewing that day's patient docket. She and Alice were just about to head into the procedure room.

She can hear muffled voices from inside the room. They layer themselves over the strange piercing screech that's still ringing in her ears.

"Evelyn?" Alice is immediately at her side. "What—?"

The door opens and Nancy emerges, her eyes wide and watering, hands clasped behind her head. Behind her is Evelyn's next patient, Patricia. Her shirt is pulled up at the beltline and tucked in behind a small black box at her waist. She's holding a gun in one hand and a walkie-talkie in the other, which she now speaks into.

"Suspects are neutralized. Move in." The static of the walkie-talkie clicks off and she slips it into the back pocket of her denim shorts.

"*Fuck*," Evelyn swears under her breath.

"Evelyn." Alice's voice is small, afraid.

"I'm so sorry," Nancy whimpers.

"Quiet!" Patricia snaps. She waves her gun at Evelyn and Alice. "Both of you, get your hands up, same as her."

Evelyn swallows the harsh reality of this inevitability. Alice's hands go up beside her, but Evelyn presses her thumb down on the metal clamp of the clipboard, removing the patient docket that lists the names of all the women who are scheduled to receive abortion procedures today. She folds it into quarters.

"I said get your fucking hands up!" Patricia shouts at her.

"I think I'm going to need to see some identification first, *Patricia*," Evelyn says, not taking her eyes off the officer's. Her stomach is sinking into her legs as she feigns boldness.

"Evelyn," Alice mutters beside her.

The police officer licks her lips. "Don't move." She reaches into the purse hanging off her shoulder, and in the fleeting seconds when she takes her eyes off her suspects to fish out her badge, Evelyn slides the paper into the waistband of her jeans.

Patricia holds out her badge and Evelyn nods curtly. She raises her hands up behind her head, heart hammering off the walls of her rib cage. "Well played, Officer."

"Be quiet."

The door bursts open and both Evelyn and Alice jump. Nancy yelps.

"Oh my God! Oh my God!" Nancy wails as a stream of three, four, five other officers force their way into the apartment. Suddenly it feels smaller and even more oppressive. Evelyn thinks of Doris, who left just before Patricia arrived to escort Kathleen into a taxi three blocks away. She's due back any minute.

"Who's in charge here?" one of the officers demands to the room at large.

"I am," Alice says immediately.

"Alice," Evelyn snaps, though she experiences a rush of affection for Alice's loyalty.

"No, she isn't. That's the doctor there." Patricia points to Evelyn, her gun still extended at Nancy, whose eyes close against a stream of tears. The brand-new diamond ring glints in the light from the window. *This girl has her whole life ahead of her*, Evelyn thinks. She can feel Alice shaking beside her. Alice, who's supposed to be getting married tomorrow . . .

"Is that gun really necessary at this point?" Evelyn shouts, her initial terror turning to anger. "Patricia, or whatever the hell your name actually is? You fucking traitor to women."

"That's enough, ma'am!" a burly male cop barks at her, his bristly moustache inches from her face.

"It's *Doctor*, not ma'am, Officer."

"It's *Sergeant*, not Officer, Doctor."

Evelyn physically bites down on her tongue to stop the retort she longs to throw at him. This had to happen eventually, she realizes. So why not today? It's as good a day as any. She stands up straighter, stares with all the hatred she can muster at the female police officer.

Do your worst, bitch.

"What's your name?" the large sergeant spits at her.

"*Doctor* Evelyn Taylor. Can we take our hands down now? You know we're unarmed."

"Yes, you can, actually. You can all put them behind your backs."

"Excellent," Evelyn mutters, as the female officer and two others each handcuff Evelyn, Alice, and Nancy. "And now I'm going to need you to tell me what we're under arrest for."

"I'm pretty sure you know what for," the female cop pipes up. "For inducing miscarriages out of an unregulated medical facility. Illegal abortions."

"Mmm," Evelyn says. "And what evidence do you have of that?"

While she fakes confidence, Evelyn's mind is racing. Alice disposed of the products of Kathleen's abortion while Nancy was doing pre-op prep with the so-called Patricia. There are medical instruments in the procedure room, but that doesn't prove anything. The only records they keep for a given day are currently folded neatly in her waistband; she can feel the crinkle of the paper against the backs of her thumbs.

"We have audio of this óne"—the female officer gestures to Nancy—"explaining the whole procedure to me."

Shit. The screech. We've been bugged.

"I never said anything about an abortion." Nancy's soft voice pipes up, her eyes still closed. The tears have stopped.

Silence in the room.

"Excuse me? Yes, you did."

"No, I didn't." Her eyes pop open and her posture straightens. "I asked you if you'd ever had this procedure before, and you said no. I never said anything about any abortion."

Evelyn's heart leaps and she feels a shiver of gratitude for her careful, quick-thinking volunteer.

The female officer's face pales, but she regains her composure almost instantly, addressing her boss, the sergeant. "I've got a tape, Barry."

He nods. "You're all coming down to the station."

Evelyn weighs their options and the possible outcomes. If Nancy is right, then the only evidence is the sheet in her waistband: the mention of pregnancy and the patients' names. Their third patient hasn't shown up yet. A painful stab of guilt pierces her heart at the thought of that woman not being able to get an abortion today. She'll show up and, what? Find the place cordoned off with police tape, and be scared off calling Jane again? Get no answer when she dials the buzzer number? There are another four women booked in for next week, and five the week after that. Hopefully the Janes can arrange for other doctors in their network to pick up the slack.

Evelyn turns her mind to the factors at hand, the ones she may still have some influence over. If the police could track down this morning's patient, Kathleen, with her first name and date of birth, there's a possibility she would confess and turn them in if the police offered her immunity from any charges. Evelyn knows it's not the individual patients the authorities want, it's the Janes and their ringleaders. The ones who provide options when no one else will. The women who dare to say *yes*.

"Come on," the large sergeant says to Evelyn, beckoning her forward. She swallows hard and complies. She's already cuffed; there's no point railing against them. Not yet, anyway. For now, it's best to just play along.

They make their way to the door, each of the Janes escorted by a police officer. Evelyn tries twice to make eye contact with the female officer, who is deliberately avoiding her gaze.

Good.

After a silent and painfully uncomfortable walk down to the main floor, the officers shove the Janes out the glass front doors of the apartment building and into the sweltering heat of the blinding afternoon sun. A paddy wagon is waiting for them at the curb, and the reality of their arrest hits Evelyn like a blow to the stomach. She glances left and right. A crowd has also formed, their heads pressed together, mouths moving excitedly. Evelyn wonders what they think has happened, why these three women are being escorted away in handcuffs.

A few paces from the back of the van, where another officer is now opening the doors, Evelyn catches a shock of orange out of the corner of her eye. Doris, her eyes wide underneath her mop of red curls. They lock eyes and Evelyn cocks her head back toward the building.

Clean up.

To her immense relief, Doris understands the gesture. She nods fervently, sinks back into the crowd, and disappears.

The doors to the back of the paddy wagon are open, like the mouth of a whale that's about to swallow the Janes whole, its insides dark and metallic. A hand shoves Evelyn's lower back.

"In."

"Do you seriously think I don't know that?" she says.

"Watch your mouth, sweetheart."

"Watch your sexism, asshole."

She pays for her attitude with a push to the back of the head this time, and falls into the van, smacking her knees on the metal floor and nearly breaking her front teeth as she pitches forward.

"Evelyn!" Alice cries, climbing into the van behind her.

"I'm fine. Just do what they say for now."

"That's the smartest thing you've said so far," the smart-mouthed sergeant tells her.

The last thing Evelyn sees is his smirking face as he slams the doors shut, and the lock slides home. Nancy is panting on the bench across from Evelyn. Alice is beside her, her face stricken. The engine rumbles to life and they each plant their feet as the vehicle lurches forward.

"I'm supposed to be getting married tomorrow!" Alice whimpers, appalled. "What do we do, Evelyn? What do we do?"

"We don't panic, first of all," Evelyn says. She tries to rally her team with the same forced bravado she's been faking since Patricia brought Nancy into the room at gunpoint. She drops her voice, and Nancy and Alice lean in, their three heads close together. The prisoner transport section of the van is completely separate from the cab, but right now Evelyn doesn't even trust the walls. "Nancy, you're serious about not using the word 'abortion'?"

"I'm positive," Nancy whispers. "I've found a lot of girls don't like to hear the word, so I stopped using it a while ago and just went with 'procedure.' I never said it, I'm sure of it."

"That's very, very good news."

"What are they going to do to us, Evelyn?" Alice is always so calm, it hurls Evelyn's own panic into overdrive to hear her second in command so unnerved.

"They need something to charge us with. And for that, they need evidence. Nancy says she never used the word 'abortion,' and you disposed of the products of Kathleen's while Nancy was in pre-op with this Patricia, right?"

Alice nods. "Of course, it's protocol."

"Okay, so . . ." Evelyn trails off, images in her mind whipping past at breakneck speed. They probably don't have far to go until they reach the station. "I saw Doris in the crowd and nodded to her to go clean up. She'll take out anything that shows we were even there, the instruments, magazines. There really isn't much. We keep it deliberately sparse." Evelyn pauses. "So, the only thing connecting us to what we were doing in that apartment is the patient sheet in my pants."

Nancy and Alice gasp.

"This is going to be a team effort," Evelyn says, attempting half a smile.

She kneels on the metal floor and turns her back to Alice and Nancy. She slides her thumb and index finger awkwardly into her waistband, straining against the handcuffs. Sweat trickles into her eye from the baking van, but her heart leaps as she grips and withdraws the folded piece of paper.

"Alice, take this."

Alice looks at the piece of paper for a moment, then leans in and bites down on the fold with her teeth.

Evelyn nearly laughs out loud. "That's it. Alice, you're brilliant."

Alice lets out a guttural sound through the paper that Evelyn takes as "*What?*"

Evelyn leans forward and Alice's eyes widen before Evelyn bites down on the paper, too. She twists her face quickly away from Alice's and most of the piece of paper comes with it. They both snort with laughter. Nancy shakes her head, shimmies toward Evelyn, and bites off her own piece of the sheet.

Evelyn lifts her eyebrows at them both and pulls the piece of paper farther into her mouth with her tongue. It's dry as all hell and the ink smells and tastes like chemicals. Alice follows suit, and after a groan, so does Nancy. The three of them sit there, moistening the paper with their saliva until it's soft enough to try to chew it. It's harsh on Evelyn's teeth and a few seconds into the process, Nancy gags hers up and has to start all over again.

By the time the van slows to a final stop, all three of them have swallowed their pieces of paper. The last bit of evidence is destroyed. Tears are pouring down Nancy's face now, but she's also laughing. Alice and Evelyn join in, and when the burly cop rattles the doors open, ready to intimidate and haul them into the station, he's met with three sweaty arrestees, their hair plastered to their necks, laughing their heads off like a pack of hyenas.

"I'm not sure what's so funny here, ladies," he says, scowling like a Scottish terrier.

"Ohhh, we happen to think it's pretty funny, Officer. You've got nothing to hold us on." Evelyn flashes a smile at him, but her stomach churns all the same.

"Yeah, we'll see about that." His fellow officers pop their heads around the doors of the van; the female cop is nowhere to be seen. "Get them out," he barks.

They yank the women roughly out of the back of the van and frog-march them into the station. They pass through a hallway that's lit with harsh halogen strip lighting and smells like rubber, sweat, and cigarette smoke.

"We want to speak to legal counsel immediately," Evelyn says loudly. "Let me call—"

"She's already here," the sergeant snaps at her, wrenching her by the elbow and directing her toward an interrogation room.

"Evelyn!" Alice shouts from behind her. Evelyn cranes her neck over her shoulder; Alice and Nancy are being guided toward a set of hard green plastic chairs set against a painted brick wall. One of the officers shoves Alice hard in the back and she stumbles and falls, barely avoiding landing face-first in the lineup of chairs. He hurls a racial slur at her, and Nancy tells him to fuck off.

"Leave it, Nancy!" Alice snaps, struggling to her feet, hands still cuffed behind her back.

"Why aren't they coming with me?" Evelyn fires at the sergeant.

"You think we don't know who's running the show here, *Doctor?* Come on."

"Hold the fuck on—" Evelyn says, doing her best to plant her feet on the slippery tile floor. She wheels to face him. They're eye to eye.

"What did you just say to me?"

Evelyn takes a deep breath. "Are we under arrest or not? You can't hold us if we're not under arrest."

"Do you *want* me to arrest you? Because keep talking to me like that, and that's exactly what you'll get. Now move."

He shoves her toward the door and nods to the guard beside it, some rookie kid with no identifying features who unlocks the door. He swings it open and Evelyn is pushed into the harshly lit room.

There's a woman standing beside the metal table, tall and broad-shouldered and also wearing heels, so she positively towers over Evelyn and Sergeant Moustache. The mop of brown curls piled on top of her head adds several inches to her height. She's dressed in a smart navy skirt and suit jacket; the crisp white lapels of her shirt collar are ironed to perfection. She's an intimidating presence, and Evelyn isn't surprised to feel the sergeant loosen his grip on her arm.

"Selena Donovan," the woman says. Her voice is booming yet efficient in its delivery. "I'll shake your hand once these kind officers remove your handcuffs."

A thrill of relief washes over Evelyn. Donovan. This must be a relative of Doris's.

"Thank you for coming, Ms. Donovan."

"Happy to help," she says, turning now to the policeman. "Could you remove the handcuffs from my client please, Officer?"

He blinks at her twice before recovering himself. "No."

"Why not?"

"Because she's in custody. And it's Sergeant."

"I didn't think she was actually under arrest, unless the situation has changed since I was first contacted."

The sergeant shifts his feet. "We haven't formally arrested them, no."

"Then she poses no threat. This is purely an exploratory conversation and she is free to go whenever she wishes. You will remove her cuffs, please."

He hesitates for a moment, then lets out a frustrated sigh as he unlocks the cuffs from Evelyn's wrists and tosses them on the metal table. Evelyn jumps at the sound, which was of course his intention. Selena extends her hand and grips Evelyn's firmly, a proper handshake that Evelyn returns with interest.

"Be my guest, Miss Donovan," he says.

"Counselor, please."

"Excuse me?"

"You may call me Counselor Donovan."

"But *she* called you Miss Donovan." He gestures at Evelyn's back as she takes a seat at the table, massaging her bad shoulder.

"She actually called me *Miz* Donovan. But regardless—*you* may call me Counselor."

Sergeant Moustache presses his tongue into the inside of his cheek. "Whatever."

Selena sits down across from Evelyn. She pulls a voice recorder out of her purse, sets it on the table, and presses the red button with a click. "Have you done anything wrong, Dr. Taylor?" she asks, a smirk playing around her lips.

"Wrong?" Evelyn asks, considering. "Not wrong, no." *Illegal, maybe.*

"Under what pretense were Dr. Taylor and her associates taken from the apartment off Spadina this afternoon, Officer?"

"*Sergeant*," he spits at her. "And we had received intelligence that Dr. Taylor and her associates were running an abortion operation at that address, which is against the law."

"Yes, Sergeant, as a criminal defense lawyer, I am intimately familiar with the Criminal Code and what is *against the law*."

His eyes narrow under his thick brow line.

"How was this alleged intelligence gathered?" Selena presses.

"Via a woman officer whose close friend reported that an acquaintance of hers had received an abortion from someone at that address. She provided a phone number to call, and our undercover officer made an appointment. Our officer proceeded to the address this afternoon at the appointed time, wearing an audio recording device. A tactical unit, including me, was waiting across the street, ready to move in once our officer had retrieved the desired evidence and given us the go-ahead."

"And what evidence is this?" Selena asks.

"Audio of one of these women describing an abortion."

"Could we hear that audio recording, please?"

"Yeah, we've got it. Officer Heinz is waiting outside. Don't move, I'll be back."

"Yes, please do go retrieve your *woman officer*, Sergeant. We'll wait."

His shoes whisper on the tile floor. The door shuts behind him and they hear him calling imperiously for Officer Heinz. Selena presses the stop button on the recording device and her head snaps up. Evelyn suddenly has the sense she's in a giant spotlight under the intensity of this woman's eyes.

"My cousin Doris called me," Selena says.

"I figured, by your name. Thank you for coming."

"I'm happy to help. Listen: What's this about an audio recording? What am I walking into here?"

"My nurse and I were out in the kitchen, and our volunteer was in the procedure room with a woman we thought was called Patricia. She was our two o'clock. Protocol is one of our volunteers debriefs the patient on the procedure beforehand."

"Shit. What did the volunteer say?"

"That's the thing; she swears she never said the word 'abortion.' That everything she said could potentially be open to interpretation, inconclusive."

Selena nods curtly. "Okay. I guess we'll see when he comes back with it. Is there any other evidence anywhere that might be a problem?"

Evelyn smiles. "Not anywhere they'll be able to find, that's for sure."

"You're sure about that?"

"Quite sure."

"Okay, then. Let's see what happens."

Evelyn swallows, and they wait another minute or so before Sergeant Moustache bursts back into the room, followed closely by Evelyn's would-be patient, Officer Heinz.

The officer is still in her civilian wear. She's young and pretty, just doing her job, but in this moment Evelyn wants to rip her limb from limb. She settles for biting sarcasm. She's learned it's a powerful tool; you can't prove sarcasm.

"Nice to see you again, Patricia," she says.

This earns her a kick under the table from Selena, who hits the record button on the machine again.

Officer Heinz sets another black device down on the table beside Selena's voice recorder. This one is clearly a set of speakers for the tape she had strapped to her waist during her pre-op with Nancy. Evelyn can feel her shoulders rising to meet her ears like high tide.

The machine crackles with a sound like static, then Evelyn hears the officer's soft voice mumble, "Testing. Testing. Testing." She clears her throat. Some rustling, likely the microphone being adjusted on the inside of her blouse. A few minutes pass with no sound at all, then there's the distant screech of the streetcar and quiet children's laughter, barely audible. The waiting room.

Evelyn, Selena, Sergeant Moustache, and Officer Heinz all breathe quietly together, staring at the box. Four actors waiting for their cue to start the scripted argument at center stage.

The click and creak of a door being opened.

"Patricia?" Nancy's voice pops into being. A rustling of papers, and a long pause. A high-pitched screech fills the room, shrill and piercing.

"Jesus," Sergeant Moustache mumbles. Evelyn's ears are ringing from it.

"Feedback," Heinz replies, shrugging.

"Shh." Selena hushes them as the recording plays out. Evelyn tries not to smile at her lawyer. *What a badass. Definitely a Jane.*

Nancy's voice comes through again. "Have you ever had this procedure?"

A small cough. "Um, no. No, I haven't."

They all lean forward as they listen in on the conversation. Evelyn holds her breath.

". . . I'd like to hear it step-by-step. If that's okay," Officer Heinz says.

What a scam, Evelyn thinks. She can feel the heat starting to rise up her neck, but this time it's rage, not fear.

Suddenly the sound begins to waver, a low hum blocking out most of the conversation. ". . . medic . . . stretch . . . into your . . . then . . ." The piercing screech causes all four of them to wince.

"What . . . ?" Nancy's voice on the tape is crackly but recognizable, confused.

"Shit . . ."

Click.

Evelyn looks up from the black box. Selena is grinning in the most accurate impression of the Cheshire Cat she's ever seen.

"Well, then!" Selena says brightly, pushing her chair away from the table and standing up. "If that's all you've got, Sergeant, my clients and I will be on our way."

"What the fuck was that, Heinz?" the sergeant shouts at his officer.

"Barry, I don't know, it happened in that room, there was so much feedback, I—"

"We can go, Evelyn," Selena says under her breath, cocking her head toward the exit.

"Where do you think you're going, Counselor?"

Selena pulls her shoulders back and leans over the sergeant. He shrinks back an inch. "Are you quite serious? You have no evidence whatsoever to hold these women, place them under arrest, or charge them with anything. Have a nice night, Sergeant, Officer."

She sweeps open the door for Evelyn, who wanders out in a daze, and Selena closes the door against the stunned faces of Evelyn's interrogators.

"That's it?"

"Just keep walking; waaaaaalk walk walk walk walk walk." Selena presses her hand into Evelyn's bad shoulder, moving her forward.

"Evelyn!" Alice and Nancy jump up from the chairs they've been slumped in across the hall from the interrogation room. They've been uncuffed. No doubt someone finally had the sense to acknowledge that they didn't pose a threat.

"Come, come!" Selena calls to them, eyeing Alice in particular. "Quickly, now. Quickly quickly."

They scurry along in her wake, trying to keep up with her long strides. Once out on the street, they all blink, their eyes watering in the bright summer sunlight.

"All right, then," Selena says, ushering them down the busy sidewalk to nowhere in particular. "You understand you now have to abandon that location, correct?"

They all nod.

"All right. Now we need to think beyond today. Is there anything else anywhere? Any files? Patient records? Where do you keep those?"

"We don't," Evelyn says. "We only have one patient docket per day, just for that day's use, then it gets shredded."

"Where's the one for today?"

There's a single beat before Evelyn answers. "We ate it."

Selena halts in her tracks, turns to face the other three women with her hand in the air like a stop sign. Both Nancy and Alice nearly plow into her. "Excuse me?"

"We ate it. In the van."

"Ate the what?"

"The record."

"The *paper* record?"

"Yes."

Selena's eyebrows pop up. "Huh. Well . . . it sounds like you could all use a cold beer to wash it down, then. My treat. Let's go find a patio."

CHAPTER 21

Nancy

EARLY FALL, 1985

Nancy is folded up in a comfortable armchair in the living room of one of the Janes, a thirty-something legal secretary named Wendy. She's responsible for the administration of the network: locating new doctors who are willing to help, booking patients, and scheduling check-in meetings like this one.

Since the raid last summer, the Janes have had to be even more careful and creative with their meeting locations. Now, more than ever, they're painfully aware of the razor's edge on which the network exists. The anti-abortion factions have become more vocal, and the police have ramped up their efforts to locate the network. Paradoxically, "Jane" is better known than ever before, but they're also more determined to keep themselves hidden. They're so busy now, Nancy's work with the Janes has taken up all the free time she's able to squeeze in around her job, parents, Michael, and planning their upcoming wedding.

Tonight, Wendy has gathered ten of the Jane volunteers in her own living room. Her husband knows about and supports what she does, so the women can have more comfortable meetings here than they can masquerading as a knitting club in a church basement downtown. Some of the Janes—Alice and Dr. Taylor among them—have told their husbands or partners what they do, but most have kept it a secret, including Nancy. She absently fingers her ring as she focuses on Dr. Taylor, who has taken a seat by the fireplace—the naturally established pulpit of the room—and the reason for this evening's meeting.

Things have changed for the Janes and the women who come to them for help. Up until now, the abortion procedure was limited to the standard dilation and curettage—or "D and C"—method, the more invasive version that Nancy underwent just four years ago. But there's a new procedure now that will allow them to expand their services even further.

"This new method we're hearing about out of Chicago," Dr. Taylor says, "involves inserting a paste into the cervix, which dilates it and effectively causes a miscarriage. This means that, first of all, the procedure doesn't have to be as invasive a process for women as the D and C, which can help reduce the potential for physical trauma. It'll play out pretty much the way a natural miscarriage would. Also, it allows us to perform later-term abortions: women and girls who come to us between twelve and eighteen weeks can still receive a safe abortion when other methods are no longer available to them."

There's a chorus of murmuring at this news.

"How does this work for the network, then?" Wendy asks.

"I'm thinking we can line up appointments for insertion of the paste," Dr. Taylor says, "which our doctors can do as quickly as a PAP test, then have our counselors monitor the women over the day or two it takes for the paste to take effect. They would watch for any signs of medical distress and support the women emotionally through the miscarriage."

An impressed silence hangs over the room, blending with the haze of cigarette smoke.

"Wow," says one of the Janes, a doctor named Phyllis sitting to Nancy's left. "That's incredible."

Dr. Taylor nods. "I know. It really opens things up for us."

Wendy leans forward in her chair. "From a planning perspective, what are the logistics of this? Where would the miscarriages happen? At the woman's house, or . . . ?"

"I was initially thinking the homes of the women *if* they either live alone or are among supportive family," Dr. Taylor says. "But for those keeping it a secret—which is the vast majority—I think we would need to consider our own homes." She hesitates before continuing. "As we all know, Morgentaler was attacked and his clinic was almost bombed, just blocks from here. I think, generally speaking, we ought to consider using alternative locations as much as possible, going forward. Personally, I find the prospect of risking my clinic and the well-being of my regular Monday through Friday patients deeply concerning."

Another silence follows this. Phyllis nods in agreement. Some of the Janes chew their lips in skepticism. Others frown.

"We don't have the budget to rent an apartment specifically for this purpose," Wendy says after a moment. "I think the only option is for the women to tell their families they're going to visit a friend for the weekend, then come to one of our homes."

Dr. Taylor nods. "I think that could work."

Wendy turns to face the room. "Could I get a show of hands? Those who might be willing or able to use their own homes for this purpose?"

Nancy considers, and slowly raises her hand, along with two other women.

"I could," she says. "At least until the winter. After that, well, I'll be married and moving in with my husband, so it might be more difficult then. But for now, I can do it."

"Excellent, thank you, Nancy," Wendy says. She turns her attention to one of the other women who volunteered, and the conversation moves on to an in-depth discussion of the new method and the logistics for the home-based miscarriages.

Nancy glances down at her hand, spins the diamond ring around and around her finger as though she's tightening a bolt. An uncomfortable knot has twisted in her stomach as her thoughts drift toward Michael. He's never given her a reason to doubt him, but still she isn't sure she'll ever tell him the hidden truths that have shaped her. She knows this natural instinct for secrecy can't be a great sign in terms of trust in their relationship, something she's ignored until now. She loves him, but what restrictions will she have to put on herself and her interests once she's married? Just how much of her life does she plan on hiding from her husband?

. . . .

The question haunts Nancy as she heads to the rare book library the next morning. It's just after seven. She's always been an early riser, and she likes getting into the office when it's still nice and quiet. She arrives not long after the overnight janitors have finished cleaning, settles herself down in the small communal office the archivists share with a cup of tea, and sorts out her tasks for the day into neat checklists. Nancy loves her job; it's like a combination of librarian, detective, and museum curator. It fits her like a glove and she's proud to say that she's damn good at it, too.

She goes about her work for nearly an hour before the mail arrives. She hears the squeak and click of the mail slot beside the front door of the office, followed by a soft *splat* as that day's deliveries cascade into a messy heap in the plastic bin underneath.

"Good timing," Nancy mutters to herself. She needs a stretch anyway.

She walks down the short, carpeted hallway to the office door and scoops up the mail. She tosses most of it into the in-tray at the front counter, but takes the newspaper back to her desk.

She spreads the paper out and leans forward, breathing in the smell of fresh ink. She peruses the day's news in a cursory way before she flips to the back section and folds the paper over to isolate the classifieds.

Nancy usually never looks through the classifieds, but she and Michael have been on the lookout for a secondhand dining set for when they move into their new shared apartment after the wedding, so she's been scoping out the ads regularly for the past couple of weeks, but to no avail. Her eyes scan the appeals for nannies and handymen, the used vehicle offerings. She finally spots an ad claiming to have an oak table and chairs for sale in Mississauga for a price just slightly over their budget. Hoping Michael might be able to leverage his charm to haggle it down, she circles the ad with a highlighter. It feels like everything is coming together.

Nancy reaches out for the telephone on her desk, finger poised to dial the number, when her eyes slide sideways to the ad beside the one for the table.

SEEKING LOST CHILD. Looking for my daughter who was adopted from St. Agnes's Home in 1961. Trying to contact her if she is still in Toronto area.

A phone number is listed below the ad, but no name.

Nancy's heart leaps up into her throat, hammering hard. The moment stretches out until the silence is shattered by an aggressive beeping issuing from the phone receiver in her hand. She's waited too long to dial. The automated voice tells her to hang up and try again.

She lays the receiver back down on its cradle, breathes in deeply, then lets it all out in a long stream.

There's nothing to say this classified ad was placed by a Margaret Roberts. There's no name attached to it, and there must have been lots of babies born in those homes in the sixties.

But in 1961 specifically?

What are the chances? How many girls would have given up babies in a single year? Possibly quite a few. And why is this ad so vague? Why isn't there a name attached, or a precise birth date? There's nothing to confirm for Nancy whether she should even attempt to call the number.

And what if it's not her birth mother? Odds are it isn't. What if she calls and a woman answers and thinks her long-lost daughter has finally made contact, only to discover that it's the wrong girl? She doesn't want to cause anyone that kind of pain. Besides, she's wondered before whether perhaps Margaret felt differently about the adoption years later. If that note was written right when Nancy was adopted, hardly a week after Margaret gave birth, of course the girl was distraught; of course, in the rawness of her pain, she would write a note swearing such undying love and determination to find her baby. But what if Margaret changed her mind later on, once she had some distance on the decision and moved on with her life?

Nancy's changed her mind about wanting children, too. It wasn't until she was in the right life circumstances, found the right partner in Michael, that the idea of motherhood became appealing in a way it certainly hadn't been when she had the abortion years ago. People change. Margaret probably did, too.

Nancy made a deliberate decision not to look for her; a responsible, adult decision that helped offset her guilt at the childish act of sneaking around her parents' bedroom searching for clues. She'd like to think she's grown since then, become less impulsive. More mature. In a few months she'll be a married woman, and Michael is keen to start a family. She might even have children of her own soon. Recklessness is a youthful indulgence. She has to be responsible and sensible now.

The truth is, it was easier not to look for Margaret because she had no leads to work from. But now this one has dropped into her lap. What if this ad *was* placed by Margaret Roberts?

She has to try.

Nancy reaches for the phone again, and in that moment, she's back in the upstairs hallway of her parents' house, turning the door handle. She dials the number and starts to shiver.

It's ringing. She waits.

"Hello?" a man's voice asks.

Nancy's mouth has gone dry.

"Hello?"

"I'm sorry," Nancy croaks. "I've got the wrong number. I was looking for someone else."

"Who—" The man begins, but Nancy slams the phone back down with a crash.

Not three seconds later, the phone rings again, blaring like a fire alarm. She glances up at the clock on the wall above her door. It's opening time. This could be a patron. She reaches out and picks up the receiver.

"This is the rare book library. Miss Mitchell speaking."

Michael's voice sings through the line. "Hello, soon-to-be Mrs. Birch! I've been testing it out, what do you think? Can't believe I tricked you into marrying me."

"Ha!" Nancy grips the phone with a sweaty palm. "Hey, Mike. How are you doing? Didn't we just see each other?" Her voice cracks, and she curses herself.

Michael pauses. "Nance? You okay? You sound a little funny."

Nancy can't breathe. She should tell him. Everything. Now's the time. But she hesitates, and the tension stretches tighter and tighter before finally—inevitably—it snaps.

"Mike, I'm sorry. I'm fine, but I have to go. I can't talk right now. I'm sorry. I love you."

Nancy hangs up on her fiancé before she reveals something she can't take back.

She hurries down the hallway to the single-stall bathroom, pulls the light chain overhead, and slams the door shut behind her. She sinks down onto the linoleum with her back against the door. With her knees to her chest, she buries her head and releases the renewed grief that's holding her lungs hostage.

After a minute or two, she hears the front door of the office open, feels it rattle the bathroom doorframe as it shuts.

"Morning!" It's her coworker Lisa.

Nancy struggles upright, smooths the skirt of her dress, and fixes her mascara in the mirror over the sink. She runs the cold water, cups it in her hands, and gulps it, feeling the chill trickle down through her body. She squares her shoulders in the mirror.

"Let it go," she tells herself. Her voice echoes off the bare walls as her reflection nods its agreement.

She clears her throat, fluffs her bangs, and pulls open the bathroom door.

. . . .

Three days later, Nancy is standing up on a carpeted dais inside a bridal store in the West End, wearing a gown she wouldn't be caught dead in. Predictably, her mother is already in love with it.

"It's just like what Princess Diana had!" Frances coos from the cushy pink chair she's perched on the edge of.

The ivory satin dress has billowing, puffy sleeves that make Nancy feel like a football player, and a train that she knows for a fact is going to trip her on her way up the aisle.

"I don't know, Mum," Nancy says, surveying herself again in the mirror and doing her best not to wince. "It doesn't really feel very *me*."

"Oh, pish," Frances says, waving her hands. "It's just such high fashion, dear. Of course you feel strange in it. It's the most formal thing you've ever put on in your entire life. Especially since you refuse to wear anything but those tatty jeans of yours. You're supposed to feel a bit odd in your wedding dress."

"Am I, though?" Nancy says weakly.

Her mother ignores her, as does the saleswoman, a stout fifty-something with crunchy blond curls and heavily lined eyes under a thick layer of makeup that highlights rather than masks her age.

"It's very on trend, as you say, ma'am, because of the princess's exquisite taste," she says, honing in on the potential sale like a taffeta-clad sniper. "Your daughter would be showcasing the most modern style wearing this dress. She's a beautiful girl already," she adds, turning back to Nancy and batting her false lashes, "and the dress highlights her thin waist and brings out the very best in her fine features."

Nancy passes off her grimace for a modest smile as the woman addresses her mother once again.

"You look so alike, you two," she says, looking past their mismatched hair and eye color, Nancy's thin chin and Frances's square jaw, the several inches' difference in their height. Nancy's stomach flips underneath the layers of satin and lace.

"Oh my, well, yes," Frances says, blushing like any proud mother would.

Nancy watches her mother's features for a crack in the facade. She isn't sure whether to feel relieved or disappointed when she sees none.

"We should get you into a mother-of-the-bride ensemble that will set your daughter's dress off perfectly," the saleswoman plows on, pushing another sale. "We have an extensive mother-of-the-bride section at the back of the shop. Right this way, ma'am."

She's walking toward the back of the store before Frances has even had a chance to respond to the summons.

"Oh yes, of course," Frances says, rising from the chair and patting the curls on her wig. "Nancy, dear, you just spend a few more minutes in that dress and see if you can get it to grow on you. I really do think it's the one!"

"Do you need a hand, Mum?" Nancy asks.

"Goodness, no, I'm fine, I'm fine."

Part of the tumor is still in her brain; they weren't ever able to remove it all without further damage. It's weakened her. She walks slower than she ever used to. Her gait could be supported by a cane, but her stubborn dignity prohibits its employment.

She pads down the hallway to the back of the store on unsteady feet, leaving Nancy to stare at her reflection in the oversized gilded mirrors.

After the engagement last summer, Frances was beside herself with excitement over the prospect of wedding preparations. Seeing how eager she was, Nancy let her mother indulge herself in all the trappings of the process. Michael insisted they hold their ground on the dinner menu and guest list, but they've agreed on a traditional ceremony at their parish church, and Frances has gone completely overboard with every other aspect of the production. Nancy doesn't mind too much, though. The wedding is just a day. Most of all, she's looking forward to being married to Michael and starting their life together.

"And apparently we'll be starting our life together with me dressed like a cupcake," she says to the woman in the mirror dressed like a cupcake. She turns from side to side, swishes the layers of crinoline and skirt, and catches a glimpse of the hundred buttons dotting their way up the back of the dress. She can already tell Michael's going to hate it. *And hate trying to get me out of it at the end of the night*, she thinks with a grin.

It's a winter wedding, and she wonders whether her mother's wedding cape might serve to hide some of the ostentatiousness of the style, or if the addition of yet another layer of fabric might further overwhelm it. But at the thought of the wedding cape, she recalls her grandmama's words that day at the nursing home.

That was right around the time they got you.

Nancy's finding it hard to breathe through the cinched corset of the dress, and her calves are starting to protest in the expensive mile-high heels the saleswoman shoved onto her feet before parading her out of the changing room and up onto the dais. With difficulty, she hikes up the layers of fabric, piling it in her arms. She kicks off the shoes and digs her toes gratefully into the scratchy carpet before flopping down, none too gracefully, onto her bum. The dress pools around her and she wonders how long her mother will be with the saleswoman.

A set of bells tinkles over the shop door and Nancy watches in the mirror as a mother and daughter enter. Sounds from the street rush in with them, and Nancy aches to get the hell out of this dress and go home. She watches for a while as they paw through the racks of dresses, blond heads together, smiling and critiquing the styles in low voices. The women look up from the racks. But for the lines in the older woman's face, they could be sisters.

Nancy's mind wanders to Margaret Roberts. Ever since she saw the ad, she can't stop thinking about her. Now she wonders what kind of taste she had. In some alternate reality, would they have sorted through the racks together in this same bridal store?

"Good Lord, Nancy!" Nancy's eyes snap from the mother-daughter pair over to Frances, who has emerged from the back room, cheeks flushed with embarrassment. "Get up off the floor! What are you doing?"

"I'm sorry!" Nancy says, scrambling to her feet as best she can and nearly tripping over the fabric as she descends the stairs from the dais in her bare feet. "I could hardly breathe in it, I needed to sit down." She lets the dress fall again and it swishes out to the sides and back.

"You are not supposed to sit down in a gown such as this," the saleswoman tells her. She's carrying a burgundy taffeta mother-of-the-bride ensemble. "The dress should wear *you*, not vice versa."

"Am I supposed to eat my dinner standing up, then?"

"Well, what do you think?" Frances interjects. "Is this the one?"

"It's beautiful!" the blond girl calls from the racks.

"You should do it!" her mother adds.

"See?" Frances says, and Nancy spots a smug smirk on the saleswoman's face as she relieves Frances of the taffeta dress and clip-clops over to the cash desk.

Nancy looks at her mother. Her eyes are sparkling with love—for both her daughter and the designer dress—and Nancy feels the futility of the situation settle on her puffed-up shoulders. She pastes a smile on her face.

Frances turns to the saleswoman. "We'll take it."

CHAPTER 22

Angela

· · · · · · · · · ·

MARCH 2017

T hree days after Angela requested that Tina put her in touch with Dr. Evelyn Taylor, Angela finds herself standing outside the doctor's apartment door with a box of bakery brownies in hand.

After Angela explained her theory about "Maggie" to her initially skeptical, then increasingly intrigued wife, Tina emailed Dr. Taylor to ask if she might be willing to speak to Angela about her experience at the maternity home. Angela feels a squirm of guilt that they didn't warn Dr. Taylor about precisely why Angela was so eager to meet with her. Tina just told her Angela had been reading *The Jane Network* and was keen to talk about it. Which is true, but if there's the slightest chance Dr. Taylor *was* best friends with Margaret Roberts, Nancy's birth mother, she might know something Angela doesn't. It's worth a conversation and some overpriced brownies to find out.

Dr. Taylor's apartment is only a few blocks away from Thompson's Antiques at the end of a quiet side street that will be gloriously full of lush leaves and flowering trees in a few weeks. Angela knocks on the street-level door, and a minute later hears steps on the stairwell. The door opens, and Dr. Evelyn Taylor appears. She's tall and wearing jeans and a black sweater over a striped collared shirt.

"You must be Angela," she says, extending her hand.

Angela shifts the box of brownies and grasps the doctor's hand. "Hi! Thank you so much for taking the time to meet with me, Dr. Taylor."

"Evelyn, please. And it's my pleasure. I'm a big fan of your wife, plus you brought baked goods, so we're going to get on just fine. Come on in."

She steps sideways and Angela crosses the threshold, climbs the creaky stairs to the second floor.

"Head straight on in," Evelyn says from behind her.

Angela turns the knob and enters the apartment, which she instantly falls in love with. The trim around the doors, windows, and baseboard is all in the old craftsman style, painted matte white. Old-fashioned, but considered chic now that it's back in vogue. The ceiling is surprisingly high for a second-floor apartment, the plaster design a repeating swirl pattern reminiscent of ocean waves. The walls are painted a pale sage green, fresh and relaxing. The windows facing out onto the street run nearly floor to ceiling, allowing the soft winter light to filter in between the floaty, sheer curtains.

"Coffee?" Evelyn asks with a smile.

Her gray hair is cropped in a short, smooth bob that flatters her fine features, and it's that even, soft shade of gray, like a November sky. Angela hopes her own hair will gray that beautifully thirty years from now.

"I hate to be a bother, but would you happen to have decaf? I'm off caffeine for a while, as much as it pains me to say so."

"I do! I keep some on hand for those late-night cravings."

"That's great, thanks so much."

"Cream or sugar?"

"Just black, thank you, Evelyn."

"Psychopath."

Angela freezes, brownie box in hand. "Excuse me?"

The corner of Evelyn's mouth curls up. "A dubiously scientific study says that if you drink your coffee black, you might be a psychopath."

Angela isn't sure what to say to this pronouncement, so she chuckles awkwardly.

"It's more correlation than causation, I'm sure. Something about a preference for bitter tastes." She winks. "Can I take the brownies?"

"Oh yes, thank you."

"Go ahead and hang your coat up on the wall there. Make yourself at home."

She disappears into the kitchen and comes back a minute later with two plates. She hands one to Angela, then sets her own down on the coffee table. "Defend my brownie from Darwin, will you?" she says, drifting off into the kitchen again.

As if on cue, a giant orange tabby cat slinks his way around the side of the love seat, amber eyes trained on the brownie. Angela snatches the plate up.

"He likes brownies?" Angela calls.

"He's really more like a dog, to be honest," Evelyn replies, her voice slightly muffled by the wall between them. Angela jiggles her foot and takes in the decor for a few minutes before Evelyn returns with a French press of coffee and two mismatched mugs. She sits down on the couch across from Angela and scoops the cat into her lap. "People think you can't train cats, but you can. And this chubby gent here loves to play fetch and has a distinct sweet tooth."

Angela hands Evelyn's plate to her and digs into her own brownie before Darwin can try to claim it. They are both quiet for a few moments, munching and sipping. Angela isn't sure how to open the conversation, but Evelyn beats her to it.

"So! You've been reading my book, Tina says."

"Yes, I—" She swallows her last bite of brownie, then sets her empty plate down on the coffee table. Darwin immediately pounces on it, licking the crumbs and smears of icing. "Oh, shoot, sorry! Should I—"

"Oh no, let him have it," Evelyn says with a vague wave of her hand. "He'll have diabetes any day now, either way. Death by brownie certainly isn't the worst way to go."

Angela nearly spits out her coffee. This woman obviously doesn't pull any punches. Maybe she should try the same tack.

"I'm interested in your time at the maternity home, actually. It's a long story, but I was wondering about your friend who . . . took her own life. Maggie, was it?"

Evelyn nods, and Angela's fingers start to tingle.

"So, Maggie wasn't a false name you gave someone else?"

Evelyn looks up. Their eyes lock. "Excuse me?"

"You said in the introduction that you had given false names to the women you mention, to protect their identities. But your friend's name really was Maggie?"

Evelyn hesitates. "Why do you want to know that?"

"I'm so sorry," Angela says, her face growing hot. "I should have explained more to begin with, but by any chance, was your friend Maggie's full name Margaret Roberts?"

Evelyn's mouth falls open ever so slightly. "Why do you ask? How do you know this?"

Angela takes a deep breath. Both their coffees sit forgotten on the table.

"Because I think I'm close to finding her daughter. Or at least, I hope I am."

The room is silent. Even Darwin has stopped purring in Evelyn's lap, as though he, too, is holding his breath, waiting.

"How?" Evelyn finally asks.

"I found a letter in the store I work at. Thompson's Antiques, just a few blocks from here. It's a letter from the adoptive mother confessing to the adoption, which had been kept a secret until her death. There's an apartment above the shop, where Margaret's daughter lived, and I suspect it was just delivered to the wrong mailbox. A simple mistake."

Evelyn sits forward in her seat. "When did this happen? What was the date on the letter?"

"Twenty-ten. I didn't find it until a few months ago, though. I've been trying to track down the daughter, but I haven't had any luck yet, so I shifted gears and tried to find Margaret instead." She hesitates again. "I found an obituary for a Margaret Roberts, who died when she was nineteen in 1961, and I put the pieces together with an article I found about one of the maternity homes. It was St. Agnes's, the home you and Margaret were at together. Wasn't it?"

"Ye—" Evelyn's voice catches. "Yes. I'm sorry, this is a bit . . ."

"I know. I apologize."

Evelyn nods but doesn't make eye contact.

"Tina and I should have been more up-front about why I wanted to speak with you." Angela takes another deep breath. She's half regretting reaching out to Evelyn at all. Maybe Tina was right, and this search for Nancy Mitchell is going to get too messy. "If Margaret Roberts is dead, I wondered whether *you* might be willing to meet her daughter, you know, as sort of the next best thing. Since I found the adoptive mother's letter, I've felt a bit of a responsibility to connect these dots. If I can locate Margaret's daughter, would you maybe be interested in meeting her? Telling her a bit about her mother, if she wants to know?"

Angela watches Evelyn's features morph as a wave of emotions color the canvas of her face.

"Yes," she says, her eyes shining. "I'd like that very much."

. . . .

A few days after Angela's tense meeting with Dr. Taylor, she and Tina are back at their ob-gyn's office for the results of Angela's early ultrasound. Tina perches on the edge of a chair in the corner of the cool, brightly lit room while Angela settles herself down on the crunchy white paper of the exam table. The nurse today is a squat, curvy twenty-something woman with black hair pulled up in a puffy topknot. Her scrubs have Simpsons characters on them, and Angela likes her immediately.

"Is this your first pregnancy ultrasound?" she asks Angela with a toothy smile.

Angela hesitates. "You mean for *this* pregnancy?"

The nurse's smile falters. "Yes."

Angela nods.

"Okay, excellent. And you're at, what"—she consults her computer screen—"about seven weeks?"

"Yup." Angela's stomach is fluttering with nerves now. But the good kind. Like a first kiss.

"Okay, good. Good. And how have you been feeling?"

"Nervous."

The nurse nods sympathetically and types several words into the system while Angela waits. Tina catches her eye and winks. "All right, then! Dr. Singh will be with you shortly. Hang tight."

She slips out the door and leaves Tina and Angela alone again. They can hear a child wailing from another room down the hall. A phone rings.

"Always lots of waiting, eh?" Tina says. Her hands are fidgeting in her lap.

"Ha! Yeah. The anticipation is kind of killing me, T."

"Oh my God, I know."

"Right?"

"Fuck."

They both laugh. Angela shakes her head and lets her eyes wander across the walls, vaguely registering the crayon children's drawings and public service announcements for the flu shot. A few minutes later, the door finally opens again.

"Hi, Angela, Tina," Dr. Singh says, nodding at them both. "Nice to see you again."

"You, too," they mutter in unison.

"Well," Dr. Singh says. "I have some more very good news for you both. Based on what we could see in the imaging, you have at least one viable sac in the uterus."

"Did you say at *least* one?" Tina pipes up.

Dr. Singh is smiling. "Yes. There's a shadow behind the first sac and they couldn't quite get a clear angle on it during the ultrasound. There's a chance you may be pregnant with twins, but we can confirm that today with a fetal Doppler."

Tina is on her feet now, striding over to Angela. She puts her arm around her wife's shoulders. "So you mean we can . . ."

"Listen to the heartbeat. Or possibly heart*beats*, yes."

"Ha!" Tina exclaims.

Angela can't stop smiling. "We're really pregnant, T!"

Tina plants a kiss on her forehead. They're beaming like newlyweds.

"I'll just get the monitor set up for you," Dr. Singh mutters, busying herself with a small white machine Angela doesn't take much notice of. "Just lie back, Angela, and lift your shirt. This will be just like an ultrasound."

Dr. Singh squeezes the cold blue gel onto Angela's midsection. She turns up the volume on the system and all three of them freeze, their breath caught. She glides the wand over Angela's belly as the Doppler crackles. It reminds Angela of trying to tune an old radio.

A moment later, the doctor stops the wand and holds it steady.

Thump-thump-thump-thump-thump-thump goes the machine, but there's another strand of beats weaving in with the first. The most beautiful sound Angela has ever heard. A perfect harmony.

"That's two heartbeats, ladies," Dr. Singh confirms, and both Angela and Tina burst into tears at the same moment. Tina nearly crushes Angela's hand as she squeezes it.

"I love you," she says.

"I love you, too."

The moment suspends itself in time, drawn out and shimmering with a pale golden light. A precious and rare moment of pure, unadulterated joy.

"Congratulations," Dr. Singh says. "You're having twins."

CHAPTER 23

Nancy

. . . .

SPRING 1987

Nancy has spent the half-hour streetcar ride to Dr. Taylor's house thinking about how much she's been lying to her husband.

Nearing the intersection closest to Dr. Taylor's street, Nancy tugs the cord for her stop and pulls herself to her feet, cradling her pregnant belly with one hand and bracing herself against the nearest seat back with the other. A woman in a seat across from the back door smiles at her, and she feels her baby squirm along with her guilt.

Nancy realized she was pregnant right before their first Christmas as a married couple. She had missed her period, her boobs were sore, and the dreaded morning sickness was back. She'd welcomed the symptoms, knowing what they meant, though she didn't tell Michael she knew the signs from past experience. It had been difficult to pretend, but once she got past the first month, the experience became new again, unfamiliar, and it belonged to both of them.

They went to the doctor and got the results confirmed, and Michael picked her up and swung her around in celebration on the sidewalk outside the clinic. It was a moment of true happiness. Possibly the first of Nancy's adult life. And she couldn't believe how stark the difference was between learning about this pregnancy versus her first one. She hadn't been too concerned about her fertility, but discovered, with no small measure of surprise, that there was a razor's edge in her life where she went from being terrified of getting pregnant to terrified of *not* getting pregnant. You could hardly fit a toothpick in the space between.

She's at six months now, with a beautiful rounded belly and breasts firmer and bigger than she'd ever dreamed possible. Aside from the usual tiredness, swelling, and difficulty bending over, her pregnancy is going smoothly, and her relationship with Michael is strong—except for the fact that she continues to lie to him about where she disappears to on evenings and weekends when she goes to work for the Janes.

She isn't sure how much longer she can keep finding excuses. When Michael asked her this afternoon where she was heading off to, she told him she would be out shopping for baby things for the next few hours and would be home in time for dinner. But that didn't seem to cut it this time. As her pregnancy has progressed, Michael has become more and more protective of her, and less inclined to let her run errands or overtax herself.

"Whatever it is, I can do it, just give me a list," he'd said, tossing a dishcloth into the sink and frowning at her. "You don't have to do all of this yourself, Nancy. Let me help."

Nancy muttered something noncommittal and left for the streetcar without looking back. She knows she's running from something dangerous here. It's been weighing on her mind at three in the morning when her pinched bladder drives her from her bed and the pregnancy insomnia takes hold. She lies awake for hours at a time, considering whether it's still even going to be viable for her to volunteer her time with the Janes once the baby arrives. She hasn't told Evelyn or Alice about the possibility of quitting yet, and she would hate to have to give it up. But there's a part of her that might welcome it. The risk of arrest has stressed her out more since she became pregnant, and it would be a relief to stop lying to Michael about this particular secret. The baby will bring them closer together, she figures, and if she bows out of the Janes at the same time, well, maybe this is the fresh start she needs. She's wondered before how the other Janes manage to navigate this with their husbands. Does the secrecy weigh on them like it does on her?

Shaking off the discomfort that's settled on her shoulders, Nancy walks the final few steps to the path up to Dr. Taylor's home. They're meeting a patient here today for the procedure. In an effort to reduce the number of abortions they perform at the medical clinics of the Jane doctors, they've moved as many as they can to their private homes, many of which are unlisted anyway, for security reasons. And this patient has opted for the D and C. They give their patients the option now, but a lot of them still don't want to miscarry at home. A few of them have told Nancy during their intake counseling that they didn't want their homes to be haunted by memories of the abortion. They prefer unfamiliar territory they won't have to return to. Physically, anyway. As Nancy knows, it's hard to escape it in your mind, even when you know it was the right choice. It's always there. Every day. Every time a friend gets pregnant. Every time you pass a baby on the street. Through all your subsequent pregnancies. You wonder what might have been. You're always returning to it.

Nancy knocks, and a few moments later a tall, attractive man with a graying beard and temples answers the door.

"Hello, love. You must be Nancy, then. I'm Tom, Evelyn's better half. Come on in."

He steps aside and ushers her over the threshold, and Nancy registers her relief at the coolness of the air. She doesn't mind making the trek out to Dr. Taylor's house, but she's worked up a sweat in the spring warmth, and needs to rest her puffy feet.

She extends her hand and introduces herself. Dr. Taylor's husband is a warm and cheery fellow. His voice sounds familiar; his English accent is similar to her mother's.

Dr. Taylor and Alice emerge from a door to the right off the foyer.

"Well, I'll leave you to it." Tom floats back down the hall toward the kitchen.

"You have a beautiful home," Nancy tells Dr. Taylor, looking around at the gleaming wooden staircase and ornate chandelier. *Two doctors' incomes, I guess.*

"Thank you, Nancy," Dr. Taylor says. "Come on in. You could probably do with a chair and a cold drink, I imagine?"

"Yes, please, thanks, Dr. Taylor."

They settle Nancy down in a squishy armchair in the sitting room at the front of the house, facing the street, and she fishes her intake forms, clipboard, and a pen out of her bag.

"How are you doing, Nancy?" Alice asks, smiling. "I haven't seen you in a few weeks. Everything still going well?"

"Yeah. Seems to be. I find myself tiring out more quickly now. My mum's having a shower for me in a couple of weeks," she says, rolling her eyes. "Not exactly my idea of a good time, but it's a big help. Getting all the baby things together is really starting to make it feel real."

"But your blood pressure has been good?" Dr. Taylor asks, her brow knitting. "No cramping or bleeding? Have your iron levels been checked? Is the baby kicking and moving regularly?"

Alice elbows Dr. Taylor in the ribs. "You just can't help yourself, can you?"

Dr. Taylor flushes. "Just checking in, that's all. Pardon me for caring about her well-being."

"I'm sure Nancy has a good OB who's monitoring all that."

"Yes, I'm sure she does."

Nancy takes a sip of her lemonade and smiles at the bickering pair. Her heart sinks a little at the thought of not seeing them anymore if she does quit the Janes.

"I'm definitely being well cared for, Dr. Taylor, but thank you," she says.

Dr. Taylor nods in an embarrassed sort of way, then shifts tracks to the business of the day. "Our patient's name is Brenda. She's thirty-eight years old and ten weeks pregnant. It shouldn't be more than a few minutes before she gets here. Once you're done, Nancy, if there are no red flags, bring her down the hall to the door on the right. It's an office I've converted to a surgery space for the time being."

"Okay. Sounds good."

Alice and Dr. Taylor head back to the surgery room, and Nancy only waits a few minutes before seven knocks sound on the front door. She shuffles into the foyer and opens the door for her patient.

"Hi," the woman says loudly. "I'm Brenda. I have an appointment."

"Hi, Brenda, I'm Nancy. Come on in." She shuts and locks the door and leads Brenda into the sitting room.

"Go ahead and take your coat off, make yourself comfortable," Nancy says, smiling at the woman to help ease any anxiety. Brenda's eyes flash down to Nancy's belly as she settles herself on the chair across from her.

"You're pregnant?" Brenda asks bluntly.

"Yes." She's gotten used to this over the past couple of months since she started to show.

"But you work for an abortion network?"

"I volunteer."

"How long have you been doing this?"

"A few years now." Nancy is starting to feel like she's the one being interviewed instead of the other way around.

"Huh. I kind of just figured . . . I don't know. I thought you guys were all about abortion."

Nancy shakes her head. "We're all about choice." She can already see the question forming in Brenda's eyes, so she answers it. "And yes, I'm currently pregnant, but I've had an abortion in the past. I know firsthand what you're about to go through."

Brenda jiggles her foot on the carpet. "Okay."

Nancy tilts her head to the side, considering her patient. Her permed and bleached blond hair is pulled up in a messy ponytail tied with a neon scrunchie. A thick layer of concealer doesn't quite manage to hide the dark circles under her eyes.

"Women's lives change quickly," she says. "I think you make the best decision you can for yourself at the time you need to make it. I made a choice six years ago that I wouldn't make today because my life has changed drastically since then. I'm making a choice to stay pregnant, just like you're making the choice not to."

Brenda chews on her cheek.

"So, just to confirm, then," Nancy continues, "you're making this choice of your own volition, correct?"

"Yeah. For sure. But, uh, there's something I need to mention first." Nancy waits as the woman teeters on the precipice of something. "I'm a cop."

The blood drains from Nancy's face. "Excuse me?"

"I'm a cop, but listen, that's not why I'm here. I'm here because I need an abortion. I know about the undercover operation that raided you guys in '84. I'm not in the same precinct, but word sure got around, I'll tell you that. But that's why I wanted to come clean right off the bat. I'm not here to make trouble."

"Just . . ." Nancy holds up a hand to stop Brenda from saying any more. "Just stay right there."

She heaves herself out of the squishy chair, scurries down the hall, and knocks on the door on the right. When Dr. Taylor opens it, Nancy throws herself inside, slamming the door behind her harder than she intended to.

"Nancy, what—?"

"She's a cop."

Both Dr. Taylor and Alice gape at her. "What?" they demand in unison.

"I was doing the intake and she said, 'There's something I need you to know.' Said she wanted us to know beforehand that she's not here to rat us out. She said she heard about the raid on Spadina."

Alice and Dr. Taylor exchange a meaningful look. "Shit," Dr. Taylor breathes.

"Why the hell would she come here?" Alice says, incredulous.

Dr. Taylor turns from Alice's grave face to Nancy.

"I don't know," Nancy answers. "We didn't get that far. She said she was a cop and I told her to wait."

There's silence for several long moments while all three women consider their next move. Memories of the raid hang over their heads like dense fog. The kind where you can't see the dangers in front of you until you're right on top of them.

"Is it . . ." Alice begins. "Is it worth just talking to her, Evelyn? I mean, we haven't heard her leave yet, so she must really need to be here. Why would she tell us if she was actually a threat?"

"She doesn't know whose home this is. That's why we have the volunteers answer the door on home visits," Dr. Taylor says, more to herself than to Alice or Nancy.

Nancy holds her belly and waits. The tension in this tiny room is palpable, and for a moment the three of them are right back in that tin can of a paddy wagon, sweating in fear and the blazing summer heat.

"Okay," Dr. Taylor says after a long pause, composing herself with a shivery shrug. "I'm going to go talk to her. Follow me, ladies."

Dr. Taylor strides confidently into the hallway. Alice follows, with Nancy on her heels. They find Brenda right where Nancy left her in the sitting room. Her foot is jiggling even faster now. She leaps to her feet when Dr. Taylor walks into the room, like a military grunt saluting her drill sergeant.

"So, Nancy here says you're a cop," Dr. Taylor snaps. "Tell us about that."

Brenda clears her throat and extends a hand, which Dr. Taylor shakes, grasping it vigorously.

"Yes, I'm a police officer. I'm, uh, I'm here because I'm thirty-eight and never wanted kids, and I was denied an abortion through the government's Therapeutic Abortion Committee. I tried to go the legal route but now I have no other option. As I told Nancy"—she makes eye contact with her—"I wanted to be honest about what I do because I want you to know that I'm not here as a police officer. Today I'm just Brenda. I just—I don't know. I thought it was best to be up-front about it. I'm an up-front kind of girl."

Alice stands stock-still beside Nancy, whose eyes are now flicking back and forth between Brenda and Dr. Taylor.

"Why did the committee deny you?" Dr. Taylor asks.

"They said it wasn't medically necessary for either my physical or mental well-being. I have no history of depression or other conditions that wouldn't tolerate a pregnancy, so, essentially . . . just not wanting to support a child for the rest of my damn life isn't a good enough reason. And I'm a tough broad, but quite frankly I know I couldn't ever give a child up for adoption. I don't know how those women do it, but they sure as hell must be made of tougher shit than I am."

Dr. Taylor clears her throat. Nancy blinks rapidly, her eyes on the carpet. Alice sighs and her eyes flicker to Dr. Taylor.

"I thought it would be easier to get an approval," Brenda says, "so I didn't think to lie through my teeth. Lying doesn't come naturally to me. But I see now that's what I should have done, if I were smart."

Dr. Taylor licks her lips. A car drives by on the street outside the front window. A dog barks in a neighboring yard.

"Okay. We'll help you. But as I'm sure you'll understand, we're going to have a few restrictions."

Brenda nods.

"You'll leave your coat, shoes, and purse here in the sitting room. Normally I ask my patients to undress from the waist down, but since the undercover who paid us a visit had a wire on under her clothes, I'll need you to get completely naked and use a hospital gown. Can we compromise on that?"

"Of course."

"Okay, then. Why don't you go on down the hall with Alice to the procedure room? I'll be with you in a minute."

"Thank you," Brenda says, trying out a small smile.

Dr. Taylor returns it tightly. "See you soon."

Alice leads Brenda down the hall and the surgery door shuts with a snap.

Dr. Taylor throws herself down on the couch in an uncharacteristic display of frustration. She lets out something between a sigh and a growl. The afternoon light pours in through the big bay window behind her, the stained glass casting rainbow shadows on the carpet. "Thank you for your help today, Nancy. I'm sorry you came all the way here for this."

"It's okay, really."

"Before you go, could I ask you to check her shoes and purse for bugs?"

"Sure."

Dr. Taylor studies her shrewdly from the couch. "You certainly keep getting all the dramatic experiences, don't you?"

Nancy chuckles. "Never a dull moment, that's for sure."

Dr. Taylor rakes a hand through her hair. Nancy has noticed she's cut it shorter and shorter each year, and it's flecked with gray now.

"I hate having to do this," Dr. Taylor says. "I was probably too harsh with her. But I sure as hell never want another gun pointed at my face. I bet you of all people can appreciate that."

"No shit."

Dr. Taylor's gaze slips into the middle distance, examining the memory of that long-ago day. "I'm willing to compromise one woman's dignity if it means we can continue helping all the other women out there who aren't trying to bring the network down."

Nancy shrugs. "I really don't think Brenda is trying to bring us down. She told me she just needs an abortion. That's the only reason she's here. If the committee denied her . . ."

"I know." Dr. Taylor heaves a long sigh. Nancy can see the exhaustion etched in the creases around her eyelids. There's something else there, too. She's seen it before. A shadow that Nancy hasn't been able to identify. Dr. Taylor is usually so professional, one might even call her closed-off. She doesn't share much.

"We're getting closer to legalization, but we aren't there yet. And it can't come soon enough, for Christ's sake." Her mouth tenses and she seems to grapple with what she's about to say. "The truth is, this has been a long haul, and I'm getting tired, Nancy. I'm frustrated. I know this is all worth it. But sometimes . . ." She meets Nancy's eyes. "Just barely."

· · · · · · · · · · ·

Six weeks later, Nancy is reclined in the depths of one of the pink velvet wing chairs in her parents' living room, surrounded by a large group of chattering women and piles of gifts in pink, white, and blue wrapping paper.

Nancy hated her own wedding shower; being thrust into the spotlight and trotted out on display for her mother's church friends made her intensely uncomfortable. But Frances is so excited about becoming a grandmother for the first time, and quite frankly, Nancy didn't have the energy to push back about the baby shower. She hardly has the energy to put on her own shoes these days, let alone get into an argument with her mother.

Nancy's dad has slunk off to hide in the den at the back of the house, parked in front of a football game with a plate of deviled eggs and sliced ham from the ladies' potluck buffet, leaving Nancy alone among the twittering mass of women.

"Traitor," Nancy accused him when they met at the punch bowl an hour before. "Thanks for throwing me to the she-wolves."

"You don't seriously expect me to stick around with this lot, do you?" he asked. "If I don't bail out, your mother will pop a doily on top of my head and use my body for a side table to hold the dessert tray. Good luck, Beetle."

And so, out of options for a reasonable escape, Nancy has spent the past hour opening gifts to a chorus of feminine gasping. As the pile finally dwindles, she reaches out to take the last gift from her aunt Lois. Nancy opens the box to find a truly gorgeous crocheted ivory baby blanket.

"Oh, Aunt Lois, thank you," Nancy says, and she means it. "It's beautiful. Did you make it?" She drapes it across her belly and runs her fingers over the intricate pattern.

"I did!" Lois says, grinning a little soppily at the group as the *ooohs* and *ahhhs* echo around the room. "Sometimes you just can't beat handmade, especially for something like this. I made one for Clara when she had her baby last year, too."

Nancy meets Clara's eyes over the blanket, but her cousin looks away quickly. They still have never talked about That Night, and it put a wedge between them. They aren't nearly as close as they used to be.

"Well," Nancy's mother chimes in from where she's been hovering near the buffet table, refilling the punch bowl. "There was no need to go to such trouble, Lois."

Nancy's mother and aunt have a relationship that always seems to be locked on the Combat setting. The fact that Clara got married and had her first baby before Nancy did was a sore point, and Aunt Lois loved to remind her sister of this victory at every opportunity.

"Oh, it was no trouble at all, none at all," Lois trills, lifting a cup of tea to her lips.

Frances sets down the pitcher of punch and glances at Nancy. "It just so happens that I have a little something of my own to give you. Be back in a flash."

She bustles from the room and Nancy can hear her climbing the stairs. She still moves a bit slowly, but she's too stubborn to ask Nancy's father to go fetch whatever it is. Chatter breaks out among the assembled women and several get up to refill their plates of hors d'oeuvres. Nancy sinks back in her chair, grateful the event is nearly over. Her mind starts to wander to the rest of her day. She and Michael have planned to have a nice dinner together and watch the hockey game, since opportunities for that will be thin on the ground a few weeks from now.

When her mother returns a few minutes later, she's clutching a small box tied with a yellow ribbon.

"Here you are, Nancy, dear," her mother says, perching herself on the arm of the couch across from Nancy. One of the guests shifts her ample bottom over to make room for Frances, but is ignored. Frances only has eyes for Nancy. "Open it."

Her mother has already bought countless outfits for the baby, and her parents have helped fund the nursery furniture. Nancy wasn't expecting another gift. "Mum," she says, "you didn't have to do this."

Balancing the present on her large belly, she gives the ribbon a tug and opens the box.

All the air gets sucked out of the room. It happens instantly, like the door blowing off an airplane at ten thousand feet. Nancy sits there, stunned, staring down at her mother's gift.

"What is it?" Aunt Lois demands. Her shrill voice cuts through the buzzing in Nancy's head.

Nancy swallows hard and lifts out the pair of yellow baby booties. Margaret's booties. She doesn't even hear the cooing from her mother's friends.

"They were handmade with a lot of love," Frances says, her eyes bright.

"Oh, are you knitting now, Frances?" Lois asks pointedly.

"Not me, no."

Nancy can hardly stand to ask it, but she does anyway. She has to. "Where did you get these, Mum?"

"At, uh, a craft fair down at the Exhibition," she says. "A local woman makes them."

"I've wondered about setting up a booth at one of those fairs, you know," Lois chimes in, nodding into her cup of tea. "Lots of ladies willing to spend good money for quality items like that."

Several women begin talking at once about the craft fair, and the conversation moves on.

Frances walks over to her daughter. Reaching out, she takes Nancy's cheeks in her hands and stares into her eyes, blue into brown. As always, Nancy can't read them. Frances plants a kiss on top of her head and lingers for a moment. Electricity passes between them, and then her mother lets go, and shuffles away again to attend to her guests.

Nancy can't breathe. Clutching the booties, she mumbles something about having to pee and heaves herself up from the chair. She waddles out of the stifling living room, loud once again with chatter, into the cool air of the hallway. She stumbles into the powder room near the kitchen and shuts the door behind her, sits down on the carpeted toilet seat cover.

Is this a message from her mother? A confession? *Is this finally happening?* Nancy wonders. She wriggles her fingers down into each of the booties in turn, searching for Margaret's note.

She checks three times, actually turning the booties inside out to make sure she hasn't missed it, but it isn't there.

It isn't there.

The fresh betrayal slashes open the half-healed wound on Nancy's heart. She throws the booties onto the floor at her feet and crumples over her swollen belly, clutching at it with shaking hands. Laughter drifts into the hallway from the living room as Nancy begins to sob.

·　·　·　·　·　·　·　·　·　·

She arrives back home in the passenger seat of her dad's car. The back seat and trunk are full to the brim with blankets, toys, teething rings, stuffed animals, and baby clothes. Michael comes out of the house when they pull up, grinning at her through the windshield. She smiles back in an automatic sort of way and gets out of the car.

"Did the guest of honor enjoy herself?" he asks, planting a kiss on her cheek. When she doesn't respond, he peers at her face. "Hey, are you okay?"

"Of course, yeah, I'm just tired. Overstimulated, you know."

Michael pats her gently on the back. "Well, we've got a nice quiet evening planned anyway, eh?"

He helps her dad unload the haul of gifts while Nancy watches, one hand on her belly and the other clutching her purse. The booties are stuffed into an inside pocket, hidden once again.

When the last of the gifts have been brought into the front hall of their town house, her father turns to her. "Looks like you came out unscathed. Thank you for doing that, Beetle. I can tell your mother had a great time."

He pulls Nancy into a hug that she returns without passion. When they break apart, she looks up into his face. "Dad . . ."

He waits. "Yeah?"

Nancy doesn't know what to say. Should she ask him? Confront him right here on the sidewalk? Did he even know Frances was going to give Margaret's booties to Nancy? Would he have agreed? Would he have included the note if it had been up to him?

She shakes her head, and the realization that there will never be a right time and place for this conversation comes crashing down on her. "Nothing. Thanks for the ride home. We'll see you guys later."

"Oh. Okay," her dad says, nonplussed. "See you later."

Nancy walks toward the front door. Michael says goodbye to her dad and follows.

Later that night, Michael comes to find her in the nursery. The noise of the hockey game was getting on her nerves, so she left him alone on the couch to come sort baby clothes. She's passed an hour arranging and rearranging items in the chest of drawers. Her mind is racing and she can't seem to settle.

"Are you sure you're okay, Nance?" Michael asks again. He's standing in the doorway, watching her fuss with a sleeper. "You've seemed really off since you got home. Did your mom say something to get to you?"

Nancy takes in her husband's sandy hair and blue eyes, reflected in the soft light from the bedside table lamp she picked out at Eaton's a few weeks ago. He's so handsome, and thoughtful, and she knows she's lucky to have him. If they have a boy, she hopes he turns out just like his dad.

She looks down at the striped green sleeper in her hands, marvels at how tiny the little feet are. She can hardly believe that in a few weeks she'll be holding something so small and vulnerable in her arms. Something that she and Michael created together in love.

"Nancy?"

Michael is in the room now, walking toward her with his brow knitted. She steps over to the rocking chair, avoiding him, and settles herself down into it with the usual grunting sigh that now accompanies any kind of exertion.

"What's wrong? What is it? Is the baby okay?" he asks, kneeling on the rug at her feet.

Nancy is hit with a pang of guilt. "Oh God, yes, the baby is fine. Kicking and moving a lot. It's not that, Mike. I don't know. I'm fine. I just got overwhelmed at the shower today, that's all."

"Is it? You've been quiet and avoiding me all night. I think I know you better than that, Nance."

Oh, Michael. Do you? Nancy rubs her belly in circles to give her hands something to do.

He rocks back on his feet. "I guess . . ." he begins, picking at a spot on the carpet before looking up into her eyes. "I guess I've just felt for a while like there's something you're not telling me. I know you well enough to know there's something I *don't* know, if that makes sense. But I can't tell if things are just weird because of the pregnancy—I know you don't feel great—or if there's something else. Are you having second thoughts about this, or me?"

"No, Mike, of course not." Nancy reaches for his hand, but his grip is loose in hers.

A shadow crosses his face. "Then why do I feel like I'm on the outside of our relationship looking in?"

Nancy swallows on a tight throat.

"Whatever it is, you can trust me," he says. "Just tell me what's going on with you. Let me in."

Nancy stares down at her husband, considering. She can feel her toes teetering on the edge of truth, but she's afraid to jump. If she tells him about the adoption, that opens a whole world of questions that she herself can't yet answer. Michael is practical, straightforward. And he's close with her parents. She knows he'll insist she confront them, that the two of them can't keep this under wraps from her parents for the rest of their lives. And yet, that's exactly what Nancy's plan has been. There's too much on the line. It's easier for her to keep it to herself. Easier to deny it when she needs to, with no one there to remind her of the truth when she'd rather ignore it.

But she has to give him something.

She can't tell him about the Janes, and that leaves her with one option. The least threatening one. It's not *the* truth that he's digging for, but it's still a way to let him in, and hopefully stop any further questioning.

Her mouth has gone dry, but she meets his eyes and says the words anyway. "I had an abortion, Mike. Before I met you."

He stares back at her. The room is silent.

"You . . . what?"

"I got pregnant, and I had an abortion. A couple of years before I met you."

She watches him process the information, emotions sliding across his features one after another. He rises to his feet and starts to pace.

"How did you— Why would you tell me this now? Why didn't you tell me before?"

"Does it change anything?"

"Well . . . I don't know, Nancy! We've been together how long? We're married, we're having a baby, and the whole time you've been keeping something this huge from me?"

"It's not—" she begins, faltering. "It *is* huge, but it's also not, Mike. It doesn't change anything for you and me."

"But you didn't trust me enough before to tell me about this part of your life?"

Nancy hesitates a moment too long.

"Jesus Christ, Nancy! I'm your husband. Do you not trust me?"

"I do, I do! That's not it—"

"Explain to me how this isn't a trust issue. Seriously. Explain."

His features are dark now. Nancy wants to get up and turn on the overhead light. Everything seems more dramatic in the dimness. But she's frozen in the rocking chair under Michael's accusatory stare.

"I never told *anyone*, Mike. Not my parents, my friends, no one."

"So, it's not just me you don't trust. You don't trust anyone at all, is that right? That's fucked-up, Nancy."

"Excuse me?"

An uncharacteristic grimace pinches his mouth. "That's fucked-up. And let me get this straight: You've been pregnant before. You felt sick before, got a positive test before, went through all that before, and you, what, pretended that this was the first time for you?"

"I wasn't pretending, Mike. It was so different this time. I *wanted* to be pregnant this time! I can't even tell you how different it is."

"Well, I thought this was the first time for both of us, but it turns out you were lying about that. That feels great, Nancy. Really great." Michael halts in his tracks again, hands on his hips. "What the fuck else have you been lying about?"

The words smack her across the face. She feels a hot flush creep up her neck. There's no reply she can give him that won't be another lie.

"I need to . . ." Michael trails off, runs a hand through his hair. "I need to get out of here. I'll see you later."

He turns on his heel and leaves. Nancy listens to his footsteps disappear down the hall. A moment later the front door slams and locks.

Nancy isn't sure how much time passes while she rocks back and forth in the chair, massaging her belly as the tears run down her cheeks. Their trust was an illusion to begin with, but now even that's broken. Michael doesn't trust her, and she sees now that she can't trust him, either. How would he have reacted if she'd told him about one of her other secrets?

What a stupid move, she thinks. *Keep yourself to yourself.* Nancy understands now why her parents haven't told her about the adoption. You can control the internal damage caused by keeping secrets far easier than the external damage. The consequences, as Michael has just shown Nancy, are unpredictable. Lethal.

Because once a secret is out there, there's no reeling it back in.

PART IV

CHAPTER 24

Evelyn

· · · · · · · · · ·

JANUARY 28, 1988

Snow is falling, as is often the case on a January day in Toronto. It's cold, and a bit damp, and there might only be two hours of sunlight today. Or maybe none at all.

People go about their business, bustling to and from stuffy administrative offices, pharmacies, and retail stores. The mundanities of life carry on. Everything is just the same as always, except on this day, everything has changed. On this day, the Supreme Court of Canada granted women the rights to their own bodies in a groundbreaking court case against Henry Morgentaler.

Abortion is now legal.

Evelyn and Alice were glued to the radio all day while they saw to their patients. When the decision came down, Evelyn was in the treatment room with a patient, but she heard Alice's shriek from her office down the hall. It was all she could do to keep her hands from trembling as she made notes on her patient's file and tried to maintain her composure. When the patient left, Evelyn burst through the door of the office to find Alice in a state of ecstatic agitation, tears streaming down her smiling face.

"Struck down?" she demanded.

"Struck down!" Alice shouted, pulling Evelyn into a tight hug.

The two women sobbed and cheered for ten minutes until they were forced to return to work. Fortunately, they had a light patient load today, so Evelyn was able to close the practice early and send Alice home with a promise that she would meet up with her later to celebrate. A rally has been planned outside Morgentaler's clinic on Harbord Street later in the evening. Tom told her he'll be joining with Reg, once they both finish work.

Evelyn has been sitting in a coffee shop around the corner from Morgentaler's clinic since she left the office two hours ago, sipping a rare hot coffee and staring out the foggy window of the café. She's been perusing the newspaper and reflecting on her career, the Janes, and the fight to get where they are today.

She has two appointments lined up tomorrow, and it will be the first time she can perform them without the fear of going to prison. She can't even imagine what it will feel like to have that weight lifted from her shoulders, but she'll find out tomorrow.

As the snow falls outside, Evelyn considers where Paula and the other women of the Abortion Caravan will be tonight. Celebrating similarly, she's sure, at a pub somewhere near the Supreme Court building. Evelyn grins thinking about them all, a twinge of jealousy mixed in with the jubilation at how lucky they are to be in Ottawa tonight, right down in the thick of things near the seat of power that's determined she's no longer a criminal. But she decided to stay in Toronto, to be here with the Janes as they all rally around Morgentaler's clinic.

She flips a page of the newspaper as she sips her coffee and notices a new ad in the classifieds today from a maternity home survivor seeking her child. She's seen these ads regularly over the years. It's both soothing and devastating to know that she isn't alone in this lifelong struggle to reconcile what happened to her, that other women suffered the same way she did and have spent their lives wishing for an alternate ending to their story. She wonders, not for the first time, if any of the women behind these ads have ever found their children and reunited. The fact that they continue to appear in the classifieds underscores the scope of this tragedy, the number of lives that were impacted.

Shaking off these dark thoughts, Evelyn instead focuses on the prospect of drinking her coffee over *tomorrow's* newspaper, with its bold headline that will confirm this groundbreaking victory for women. Evelyn plans to frame the front page and hang it up in her office as a daily reminder that she doesn't need to be afraid anymore.

But her throat tightens as she thinks of her own lost daughter. Because the abortion rights activists didn't win this fight just for themselves. This fight and this victory was for their daughters, and their daughters' daughters. To make sure a horrible cycle was broken, and the next generation would be better off than their own. To leave these women a world where no one can tell them that they don't own their own bodies. Where they don't need to hang themselves or try to slit their wrists in a bathtub just to know what it feels like to have control. It all comes down to having the right to make the choice.

Every child a wanted child, every mother a willing mother. That's the possibility they've achieved today. That's what they can leave their daughters.

"Need a warm-up?"

Evelyn is pulled from her thoughts by the arrival of the waitress, a twenty-something with a round face and long blond hair. She's holding out a steaming coffeepot. Evelyn clears her throat to free her voice.

"Yes, please, thank you."

"Need any cream? Dessert?"

"Yes, to the cream. No dessert. I'm going to head over to Harbord's for a brownie after this."

"Don't blame you one bit. Their brownies are the best."

But Evelyn realizes she should eat something before the rally. People will start getting off work around four-thirty and heading down here to the clinic, and then it'll be a long night.

"Actually, can I get a BLT and some fries, too?"

"For sure. I'll be back in a few."

"Thank you."

When the waitress returns with Evelyn's sandwich a short while later, the skin between her brows is pinched with concentration.

"You look kind of familiar to me, you know," she says.

This isn't the first time this has happened to Evelyn. She smiles and looks the girl squarely in the face. "I have a medical practice over on Seaton Street."

It only takes a moment.

"Ohhhhh!"

Evelyn can see the red patches creeping up the waitress's neck over the collar of her yellow uniform.

Jane? she mouths.

Evelyn nods. She expects the young woman to scurry away, but she glances over her shoulder, then sits down in the chair across from Evelyn, setting the coffeepot between them on the sticky table.

She exhales, shakes her head. "Thank you."

"You're welcome."

"I honestly don't know how you do it."

Evelyn considers the comment. "Do you mean it was unclear to you how the procedure was done, or do you mean you don't know how I do it from a moral perspective?"

The girl shrugs. "Neither. I just mean it's such an awful thing. No one should have to go through it, but because, you know—*things happen*—it's amazing that you and, uh, Jane were there to help. I imagine it can't be easy for you."

Evelyn stuffs two fries into her mouth. "It's not about me, it's about my patients."

"Jesus, can't you take a compliment?" The girl smirks.

Evelyn laughs out loud. It feels good. "Point taken. I guess my answer is: I do it because few people can. I'm in a privileged position, and I'm able to provide something that women need. It's something that would have changed my own life a long time ago, but it wasn't an option for me. So, I do it. Is it easy? No. Does it keep me up at night?" She shakes her head. "Honestly, it doesn't."

The young woman listens with an impassive face, then nods. "Well, I should get back to it," she says, getting to her feet and lifting the coffeepot. "But thanks again. I can't believe I ran into you, today of all days."

"You pay attention to the news, then, eh?"

"Yeah. It's on the TV back at the bar. It's been hard to ignore. Not that I wanted to," she rushes to clarify. "But it's everywhere. It's a big day."

"That it is."

"So, what are you going to do now that it's legal?"

Evelyn eats another fry. "The same thing I've been doing for years."

"Really?"

"Well, yes. Just because it's legal now doesn't mean no one needs it anymore, right? I'll do it as long as they need me."

The girl cocks her head to the side. "I guess you're right. But do you think they'll always need you?"

Evelyn's coffee mug is halfway to her mouth when she pauses. She sets it back down on the table. She takes in the waitress's youthfulness. She doesn't remember whether this girl ever told her why she came in for an abortion. She never inquires, of course. Their services are on-demand, no questions asked. But many of the women willingly tell her why, either to remind themselves for the twelfth time that day that this is the right decision, or to alleviate a persistent sense of guilt. All the stories her patients have ever told her run through her mind like a film reel. Their reasons are numerous and varied and hardly any two are exactly the same.

Suddenly she feels tired. "Yes. There will always be a need."

CHAPTER 25

Nancy

. . . .

WINTER 2010

Nancy opens the front door of her parents' house and enters a space that still smells like the mother she'll never see again. She surveys her surroundings.

The house is silent except for the *tick tock tick tock* of the antique grandfather clock in the hallway. He forges on, resolutely counting down the seconds for no one in particular. Nancy feels an odd stab of pity for him, at his lack of awareness that his mistress doesn't need him anymore. His usefulness has ended, and he doesn't even know it.

No one told Nancy how difficult this part was going to be. That when your last parent dies, everyone around you is focused on helping you cope with the grief of their passing and plan all the details of the funeral. They send casseroles for the nights when you're too exhausted and heartbroken to even shower, let alone cook for yourself. Flowers for something bright and pretty to look at before they wither into brown, crispy, rotted stems, leaving you with one more reminder that death is inevitable. As if you didn't already know.

And no one told her what it would be like after the funeral was over, how it would feel to paw through her mother's personal effects and clear out her home. A decade older than Frances, Nancy's dad died years ago, but there wasn't a lot for Nancy to do then, since her mother refused to move out of the house. Nancy had helped plan the funeral, of course, and gave the eulogy, but Frances's stubbornness and need to maintain normalcy meant that she didn't want a fuss and didn't want help. She planned to trek on as though nothing had changed.

Nancy gave herself a full three days after Frances's funeral before she bit the bullet, grabbed the keys to her mother's house, and drove over here with a stack of moving boxes to deal with the inevitable. She knew Michael wouldn't be any help with this. Since their divorce, things between them have been chilly but civil. He attended the funeral, at their daughter Katherine's insistence, but he made it clear he was there to support their daughter's grief, not Nancy's.

Michael had an affair two years ago, which ended their marriage in a formal way, though things had been going downhill for years. When Nancy confronted him about his infidelity, he threw her accusations of lies and secrets right back in her face. She could hardly blame him, really. The hypocrisy was stark. Michael had wanted to do couples' therapy after the revelation of his affair, convinced that his infidelity was a symptom of everything else that was failing in their marriage, that they could work things out. But Nancy had refused, fearing she would be forced to reveal more of herself than she wanted to. She stopped working with the Janes when they disbanded after abortion became legal, but she was still keeping plenty from Michael. And a part of her was relieved for it to be over, anyway. It had been an exhausting twenty-five-year marriage, with neither of them ever fully trusting the other after Nancy's confession in the nursery. They only ever ended up having the one child, though that, too, was a bone of contention between them. Michael always wanted more, but Nancy just couldn't do it.

Katherine offered to help clear out Frances's house, which was sweet, but Nancy knew this was something she had to do by herself. Although she has the booties, she assumes the hidden box and Margaret's note will still be inside the special drawer, and she wants to be alone in the room with that secret.

She climbs the staircase. The stairs and her knees both creak a little with age. As she drags her feet one step at a time, she thinks about the night she discovered the secret of her birth. The night from which there was no turning back. She set out alone and dug too deep for her buried treasure, breathless with anticipation and the promise of possibility. But she couldn't find her way back out, and there was no one waiting up at the surface to throw her a rope.

She turns the corner at the top of the stairs, running her hand along the banister as she walks down the short hallway toward her parents' bedroom. It looks the same as it always has. A deep red patterned runner muffles her footfalls across the creaky pine floorboards of the hallway. A weak, icy gray winter light filters through the lace curtains on the window facing the street.

As she reaches for the doorknob, she can see her younger self layered in a translucent mist underneath, like a ghost; the smooth skin of her hand grasping the door handle, recklessly determined to uncover a dangerous truth. Her older hand, with its protruding veins and thinning skin, turns the knob more slowly, aware that all kinds of things can irreparably break if they aren't handled with care.

Nancy steps into the quiet darkness of her parents' room and in that moment, as the smells and sights hit her senses, she experiences the crushing realization that she's now an orphan. Alone.

She drops the flattened moving boxes and garbage bags she's been carrying and flicks on the light. It all looks exactly as it did before her mother went into the hospital. The bed is made, but Nancy finds a half-drunk cup of tea resting on the bedside table, the milk now curdled, a brown ring stained into the inside rim. It sits on top of a book her mother will never finish; a delicate crocheted bookmark is tucked in between pages 364 and 365, just nearing the end. The sight of that makes Nancy's heart ache even more. The thought that her mother would have left anything undone is just so uncharacteristic, but once the brain tumor had regrown, reading became much more of a challenge.

Nancy picks up the novel, walks it back over to the pile of boxes and bags. She supposes she has to start somewhere, so she wrestles the moving box into its proper four-walled placement—earning herself a deep paper cut for her efforts—and sets the book down in it. She'll keep it and finish it for her mother. She needs to know how it ends.

Nancy works her way through her mother's closet now. She wants to bury herself in the dresses and sweaters, breathe in Frances's smell in a sobbing heap on the floor of the bedroom. Or maybe just stay here forever and pretend she's still a child playing dress-up in her mother's old high heels, because the thought of being motherless is simply too horrifying to bear. But instead, she pulls the items out one by one and weighs their sentimental value against the limited storage space in her basement, tossing most of them into the garbage bags bound for a secondhand store. Nancy does her best to remember that it isn't her own mother she's discarding. They're just clothes.

And now there's the personal items to sort through: the trinkets and memory box contents. The *things* that made up the trappings of her mother's life, that had meaning to her and marked her most important memories. Some Nancy recognizes, but others remain a mystery in Frances's death, and Nancy is left with a box of unfamiliar knickknacks and a gut-wrenching assortment of questions that will go forever unanswered.

There is nothing like clearing out your dead mother's house to make you wonder whether you ever knew her at all.

By the time she reaches the chest of drawers, it's late afternoon and the fickle winter sun has set. She's left The Drawer until the end, unsure whether she would have been able to finish the task of packing up the room if she started with this piece of furniture. She knows what's in there now, yet she's more afraid to open it than she was all those years ago. Because it's more threatening now than it ever was before.

When her mother was still alive, Nancy had the luxury of choice; she could choose to reveal her knowledge if she ever wanted to, and somehow that lingering option alleviated some of the weight of the secret. But Frances's death has eliminated that possibility, and now the finality of Nancy's decision threatens to choke her. Right up until the end of her mother's life, Nancy remained about eighty percent sure she made the right decision, but now that twenty percent festers like a sliver in her brain, and for the rest of her life, it will never quite work its way out.

She takes an unsteady breath as she walks over to the chest of drawers with false confidence. Her mother's jasmine perfume bottle sits among a litter of other products, hand lotions and joint creams. Nancy lifts it carefully—it might be the last bottle—and slides off the gold-plated lid. She spritzes it onto her own wrists, turns them inward and inhales the floral springtime scent. She can feel her nose start to swell.

"Oh, Mum," Nancy mutters. "God, I miss you already."

She caps the perfume and places it in the "to keep" box, nestling it into the folds of the Burberry scarf her dad got her mum for Christmas the winter before he died.

Nancy smiles at the bittersweet sting of the memory. After depositing Frances at the nail salon, she had taken her dad out for lunch and some Christmas shopping. They'd made their way downtown on the crowded, steamy streetcar, getting off on Queen Street and stopping outside the Bay. The windows were decorated with several four-foot-tall fake trees, which were spray-painted with a white sparkly substance that made them glitter like real snow. They were surrounded by an array of presents wrapped in multicolored metallic wrapping paper, each topped with a glittery silver bow.

"What do they call this?" her dad asked.

"A window display, Dad." Nancy looped her arm underneath his. His balance wasn't good in those days, and the sidewalk was icy.

"Yes, I know it's a *window display*, Beetle. I'm not senile, you know." Nancy chuckled. "What did you mean, then?"

"I mean this is all a bunch of hooey." He squinted through his glasses at the store sign high on the wall and frowned. "When Eaton's was here, now, *they* knew how to do a Christmas display."

Nancy refrained with difficulty from rolling her eyes. Her dad often waxed nostalgic about how the closure of Eaton's department store had signaled the death knell of civil society.

"I used to come down here as a kid, you know. My parents would bring us, me and your uncle, to see the new toys that were in the catalogue, so we could pick out something that we wanted for Christmas."

Nancy guided her father closer to the window as a large group of rowdy teens unloaded from a bus behind them and swarmed like ants onto the sidewalk.

"There were mechanical toys back then. Elves that walked up and down staircases. Wheels that spun. Little train sets chugging along with their whistles." He paused, smiling. "There was something *real* about it, the carved and painted wood, the train tracks laid just so. It was . . ." He trailed off.

Nancy watched her dad as the years fell away, the wrinkles at the corners of his eyes faded to youthful smoothness, the hair turned from gray to brown. She could see him as a child, face pressed against this window beside his older brother, their breath fogging up the glass, deciding which toy they wanted most of all.

"These are just empty boxes, you know." He waved a gloved hand at the piles of shiny purple and teal presents. "There's nothing to them. They're wrapped up all pretty like they're hiding a nice secret. They want us to imagine what's inside."

A chill ran down Nancy's spine as her father turned away from the window to face her.

"But it's like most secrets, Nancy. It's better for us to be left wondering if there's something inside the box, or if it's just air. It's better for us not to know."

The snow started up again, flecking her dad's glasses with droplets. The sound from the street became a faint hum as she met her father's eyes. Nancy was sure he was trying to tell her something, but neither of them was willing or able to name the chasm between them.

"I love you, Dad," Nancy said instead, pulling him in tightly for a hug.

He wrapped his arms around her. "I love you, too, Beetle."

Nancy wipes away the tears at the corners of her eyes now, snatching a Kleenex from the dresser and blowing her nose hard.

"Well, let's do this, then," she says aloud to the empty room.

She pulls open the top drawer of her mother's dresser and peers inside. It looks the same as it did all those years ago. Last time she had to keep careful track of where each item was placed as she removed it from The Drawer, but this time she doesn't need to, and the knowledge pulls at her insides. She lifts out the envelopes full of deeds, her parents' wills, and other documents she ignored before but knows she's going to need now.

She opens the box containing her mother's sapphire engagement ring and slides it onto her right hand. It fits perfectly, and she won't take it off from this moment onward. She picks up the pearls. Perhaps she'll give them to Katherine for her thirtieth birthday. Finally she reaches the back corner with the thin leather case.

The memory of this discovery all those years ago comes rushing back to her in a tsunami of grief. Nancy swallows hard and spins the dials, entering her birth date in the English order. She presses down on the snaps and the case pops open. Her breath snags on the sight.

It's empty.

Nancy stands at the dresser, her mind racing. Her mother must have disposed of Margaret's note, knowing Nancy would be going through her parents' home once Frances passed. She supposes she shouldn't feel shocked, and she doesn't. Not really. After Frances gave Nancy the booties at her baby shower, Nancy accepted that her parents were never planning on telling her. She closed that door in her heart and moved on, but she had hoped she might be able to keep Margaret's note.

A decade ago, Nancy finally decided to put her name down at one of the agencies that helps birth parents and children locate one another. A fresh resentment settles over her, but she shakes it off. After all, she's never heard anything from Margaret Roberts. Both her mothers have betrayed her in different ways.

Nancy leaves the box and wanders over to her mother's bed, then lowers herself onto the floor and leans back against the bed frame. Not for the first time, she wonders how different things might have been if Frances had been honest with her, or if she had confronted her parents about it. If she hadn't kept it from Michael.

She's tried to be a better mother to Katherine than her own mothers were to her. She hasn't kept secrets from her daughter, at least none other than the Big One. She's always tried to instill a policy of transparency and truth, to break the toxic cycle. And she's succeeded, for the most part. She and Katherine are close. Her daughter is an honest woman who wears her heart on her sleeve—much more like her father than like Nancy.

Nancy picks idly at a loose thread on the seam of her jeans as these thoughts roll over one another in her mind, ironing themselves out. After a while, she realizes there's nothing left to consider. She has a job to do here, and that's to clean out her mother's house so that it can be sold. That's a plain truth, something black and white and industrious.

She gets up, shakes open a garbage bag, and begins to discard the past.

CHAPTER 26

Angela

. . . .

SPRING 2017

It's a damp early spring afternoon at Thompson's Antiques & Used Books when Angela receives a response on Facebook from another Nancy Birch. She'd had so many misses and non-answers that she'd nearly given up trying, guiltily accepting that, after inserting herself into Evelyn Taylor's life and dangling the prospect of a meeting with Margaret Roberts's daughter in front of her face, she would have to retract it and admit failure. Every time she saw the red dot appear on the app, signaling she had a new message, her adrenaline would spike at the possibility that this could be the one, but she was always disappointed.

Then, just before five in the afternoon when Angela was getting ready to pack up and hand the store over to the evening clerk, a very different message came through.

Hi there—I think I might be the person you're looking for. I used to live in the apartment above Thompson's—we got each other's mail all the time.

"Oh my God!" Angela yelps into the empty store. "Oh my God!"

She nearly drops her phone in her haste to respond, but holds off when she sees three gray dots. Nancy Birch is typing another message.

Sorry I didn't respond until now. I hardly use social media anymore.

Angela waits until the gray dots disappear before responding.

Totally understandable! I'm so glad to hear from you. There's actually more to the letter . . . I know this is forward, but would you mind giving me a call to discuss?

She includes her cell number and hits send, then bites down on her lip, half wishing Nancy will say no, that she doesn't want to talk.

Sure thing. Are you free right now?

"Ohhh my God. Okay. Yeah," Angela says aloud.

Yup, she texts, then exits the app. She waits. A moment later, her phone rings. The caller ID lists a local number, but no name.

"Hello?" Angela's heart is thumping.

"Hi, Angela? It's Nancy Mitchell. Nancy Birch," she adds.

"Nancy, hi! Hi."

"Hi."

"So." Angela gathers her thoughts. "I found this letter in an old chest of drawers at Thompson's, and I think you'll want to see it. That's why I've been trying so hard to track you down."

"Oh, okay. What's in it?"

"It's, um, it's actually a letter from Frances, your mother."

Five heartbeats pass before Nancy speaks again. Her voice is slightly raspy. "Okay. Thanks. Did you open it?"

Angela's insides squirm. Tina was right. Maybe she never should have dug into this mess. "I kind of had to, to get information on how to find you. I'm sorry. It was half-open anyway, the glue ..." She cuts off the lie before it can swell any bigger.

"What does it say?"

"It's very personal. It's about your parents."

Nancy sighs. "Does it say I'm adopted?"

Angela's jaw falls open. "Y-yes it does," she stammers. "How did you—"

"I really appreciate you going to the trouble to find me, but I actually already knew this."

Angela's heart falls. *All that effort.* She tries to keep her tone light. "Hey, no worries. It just seemed like pretty big news, and I obviously wanted to make sure you received it."

"I appreciate that."

Angela runs her thumb absently along the edge of the keyboard. "So, there was something else in the envelope along with Frances's letter. There's also a note from your birth mother."

Another sigh. "Oh, wow. Okay. That's good. I never knew what happened to it."

Angela pauses. "I'm sorry?"

"I found that note in a drawer in my mother's room, back in the eighties. That's how I knew I was adopted. But I cleaned out her room when she died, and it was missing from the drawer. I always assumed she had destroyed it, to be honest. I guess she sent it before she went into the hospital."

"Yes, that's explained in the letter. I'm sorry. I didn't realize you knew."

"Yeah. I went looking for information I shouldn't have when I was young and stupid. You know how it is."

"For sure." Angela isn't quite sure how to broach what she wants to say next. "So, do you mind if I ask ... have you ever tried to find your birth mother?"

Silence on the line. Angela knows she's overstepped.

"I'm sorry, I realize that's a really personal question, but—sorry, I'm trying to gather my thoughts here. When I first found the letter, I figured I would try to find Margaret, your birth mother. And . . ." Angela takes a deep breath. Her stomach flutters with a wave of nausea. "I'm really sorry to have to be the one to tell you this, but she passed not long after you were born." She waits another beat, then plows on. "I found an obituary with her name, and that, combined with a news story about the maternity home . . . Well, I kind of put the pieces together, and an old friend of hers confirmed it for me. Again, I'm so sorry."

There's a long pause where neither of the women seems to breathe. Then a deep sigh whispers through the receiver, followed by a nose being blown. Angela immediately regrets relaying the information, but what should she have done? Left Nancy Birch to go do the same digging she herself did, only to have it end in certain heartache?

"Okay. Thanks. Thanks for telling me," Nancy says. "Would you be able to send me my mother's letter, and Margaret's note? And maybe the obit and article, too? I just need to see them for myself, I think."

"For sure. No problem."

Angela is relieved Nancy isn't screaming at her, and she's fulfilled what she set out to do: Margaret's daughter will read her note and know that she never wanted to give her baby up.

Her hand rests, as it often does these days, on her belly button. She hardly dares to say anything more to Nancy. And yet, she does.

"Nancy, there's another reason why I wanted to speak on the phone instead of texting. It's a long story, but I've come across a woman who was a good friend of your mother's—I'm sorry," she curses herself for the slip, "of Margaret's. They were at the maternity home together. She's the one who confirmed Margaret's death. I've met with her, and if you're interested, she'd like to speak with you."

A long silence follows Angela's words. She bites her lip again, waiting.

"Nancy . . . ?"

"Thank you, but I don't think so." She sniffles. "I really appreciate you tracking me down for the letter. I'll be glad to have the note back, but I don't think I can meet with this woman. I'm just—I've been trying to move on from it and I've done pretty well, to be honest. I don't want to pick at that scab again, if you know what I mean."

Angela nods to the empty store around her. "Yeah. Yeah, I get it. Totally."

"So, I'll send you my address. If you can mail everything over, that would be great. Thanks again for your help."

And before Angela can respond, the line goes dead.

CHAPTER 27

Nancy

. . . .

SPRING 2017

The package has collected a fine layer of dust.

Nancy's been avoiding opening it since Angela Creighton sent it over a few weeks ago. It's been moved from the sideboard in the front hall to the kitchen counter, to the desk in her office, to the top of the dresser in her bedroom. Every time she moves it during a weekly tidy-up blitz, she halfheartedly considers opening it and just getting the whole damn thing over with. She figured she knew what was in Frances's letter, but had no desire to willfully rip open a wound that she had carefully stitched together over the past thirty-seven years. That scar is fine and faded now; sometimes she can hardly even tell it's there. Unless she inspects it too closely, which is exactly what this package is calling her to do.

On a warm Saturday afternoon, Nancy finally gets up the courage to open it. She fetches a pair of scissors from the overflowing junk drawer in the kitchen and climbs the stairs back up to her room. She sits down on the bed and with a sigh, snips open the white bubble mailer, emptying the contents onto her lap.

Nancy picks up Margaret's note. She notices that the edges are singed on one side of the note, burn marks that weren't there when she first discovered it all those years ago. She pictures her mother, striking a match over the sink and holding the flame to the note before having a change of heart. Nancy knows that the prevailing wisdom at the time was to not tell children they were adopted, but her mother obviously had some reservations about that, even though she never acted on them. She wonders if Frances had kept the note and booties as some kind of shrine to Margaret, the girl who had given her the child she and her husband so desperately wanted.

She unfolds the photocopy of the obituary Angela Creighton found, sees Margaret Roberts's name in black and white. She reaches over to her bedside table and opens the drawer, digs in the back, and withdraws the small drawstring pouch she's kept Margaret's booties in since her mother gifted them to her at her baby shower.

She lifts the booties and Margaret's note up to her heart and holds them there for a long time, as though trying to absorb some of their long-forgotten energy. At least now she knows why no Margaret Roberts ever contacted her, tried to find her. She's carried that resentment around for decades, but she can release it now.

Next, Nancy reads the news article about the closure of the maternity home, considers the horrors Margaret and the other girls might have experienced there. Her heart fills with a new kind of compassion for the poor girl. She remembers the confessions of that nun she sat with at St. Sebastian's, that the girls at that home were lied to, their babies sold. A new wave of horrendous realization hits her at the thought that she may have been *purchased* by her parents. Was the home she was born at anything like the one that existed in the St. Sebastian's building? She bookmarks that for now. It deserves a deeper dive if she can handle the research. And she should try to learn more about Margaret, if there is any more to learn.

Wiping away a tear, she picks up the final item in the package: her mother's letter. She deliberately left it for last. It's written on the same heavyweight paper Frances always used, purchased from an expensive British stationer in Rosedale. As soon as she sees her mother's handwriting, the tears start to fall in earnest. When she's finished reading, she curls up on the bed, bringing her head to her hands as she sobs into them.

Please forgive me, my dear.

She would give everything she owns for the opportunity to tell her mother that she does forgive her. That as a mother now herself, she understands the overwhelming power of a parent's desire to protect their child from harm and heartache.

She thinks back to 2010, trying to recall everything about that year and pinpoint how the letter went astray.

She was living in the apartment above Thompson's then. After the affair, she'd been the one to move out of their family home. Katherine was angry with them both but didn't want her dad to leave, and a big part of Nancy was happy for the solitude. She wanted to go back to the city, to walk the streets she'd walked as a young woman, before she met Len, or Michael, or had the responsibilities of a career and children. When she was a purer version of herself and hadn't made so many concessions yet. Hadn't told so many lies. She needed to find herself again.

The apartment was meant to be a stopgap until her divorce from Michael was finalized and their assets were split, but she'd ended up staying longer than expected when Frances's health rapidly declined. She didn't have the energy to look for a new place until after the funeral. That's when she bought this house in Oakville, with an extra room for Katherine, who divided her time between Nancy and Michael.

Frances died in February 2010, so it's likely the letter was posted by her lawyer sometime that month. Nancy thinks back on all the times she reached into that mailbox and pulled out the flyers and bills that were addressed to the antiques store. She would pop into the shop right away, if it was open, and hand the rogue mail over to the bleached, tucked, and highly polished woman who owned the store. Nancy wonders which day it was that she reached her hand into her own mailbox, never knowing that the most important letter of her life was waiting for her just inches away, inside the box for Thompson's.

Nancy sits up, crosses her legs underneath her on the cream-colored duvet, and reads her mother's letter through again. She wanted Nancy to go find Margaret, but Nancy failed. Margaret Roberts is dead, and Nancy can never fulfill her mother's final wish. She adds it to the long list of things she should have done in her life and didn't.

The tears are still pouring down Nancy's face when Katherine appears at her open bedroom door.

"Mom? What's wrong?"

"Oh, Jesus. I'm sorry, Katherine," Nancy mutters, swiping ineffectively at her eyes. She should have locked her door. Damnit. "I—"

"What is it? What happened?" Her daughter steps into the room and sits down beside Nancy. Katherine is thirty now, but still living at home while she finishes a seemingly never-ending Ph.D. program. "Mom? You're scaring me."

"Oh, sweetheart, I'm sorry," Nancy says, pulling her into a tight hug. "Everything's fine, it's fine. No one's sick or anything. It's just . . ."

She releases Katherine, tucks a strand of sandy hair behind her daughter's ear, casting around for some excuse to give, a white lie to tell.

"Mom, whatever it is, you have to just let it out."

Nancy lets her daughter's words sink in, so similar to what Michael said that night in the nursery when he begged her to be honest with him. Nancy hadn't expected to be taking advice from her own kid just yet. But Katherine is introverted and wise, and Nancy promised herself to always be as truthful as possible with her daughter.

As she looks into Katherine's wide blue eyes, identical to Michael's, the exhaustion finally bears down on Nancy's shoulders. She's so tired of running from this, of collecting secrets and keeping them sealed up in the impenetrable vault inside her heart. It's time to set them free. She sees her mother's words, and decides—for once—to take her advice. Heed her warning.

If I have learned anything from this, it is not to keep secrets. They fester like wounds, and take even longer to heal once the damage sets in. It's permanent, and crippling, and I want more for you than that.

She takes Katherine's hands in her own and tells her daughter the thing she has never revealed to a single living soul.

"I was adopted."

Nancy spends the next fifteen minutes relaying her story to Katherine. She tells her about Margaret being dead, and that her birth name was Jane. That Katherine's grandmother kept the secret from Nancy until she died, never knowing that Nancy already knew. Katherine holds her mother's hands and passes a tissue when she needs it. She's a good listener, and helps Nancy release the demon that's been lodged in her chest for decades.

"I'm so sorry, Mom. So, you never told *anyone* about this?" Katherine asks. "You never even told Dad?"

"No. No, I didn't. To be honest with you, I didn't tell him a lot of things. When you find your person, Katherine, don't make the same mistake I did. Please."

Katherine purses her lips and seems to waffle on the edge of saying something.

"What is it?" Nancy asks.

Katherine shakes her head, her curtain of hair swinging back and forth. "I just think you guys need to talk to each other," she says. "He's still really sad, Mom. He has been since you separated. I know that's not related to this." She indicates the pile of evidence on the bed beside Nancy. "But regardless, I think you should tell him this *and* talk to him about how he's feeling. And I know you miss him, too, I mean come on."

Nancy notices a warm flare in her gut. "He didn't put you up to this, did he?"

"Of course not. I shouldn't have even said anything, but you seem so sad, and Dad's sad, and I think you might be sad for the same reasons. Just call him."

Nancy nods, though unsure. "Okay. Maybe I will. Sorry about this." She waves a hand at her blotchy, damp face.

"It's okay. I love you, Mom." Katherine plants a kiss on Nancy's cheek and makes her way to the door.

"Katherine."

She turns, and Nancy sees it more clearly this time: her daughter is indeed wise beyond her years. "Yeah?"

"Thank you for being here for me."

"S'okay. I love you."

"I love you, too," Nancy says.

"I'm gonna go run you a bath, okay?"

Nancy nods. "Thank you, dear. That sounds great."

Nancy tries to compose herself, listens to the bathroom door opening, Katherine turning on the faucet, the thunderous gush of the bathtub filling up.

After Katherine wanders back across the hall to her own bedroom, Nancy reads through Margaret's note and her mother's letter one more time, then stumbles downstairs to the kitchen and pours herself a large glass of red wine.

A minute later, she turns off the faucet, plucks her lavender oil from the medicine cabinet, and shakes a few drops into the tub. Nancy watches the ripple effect, considers the chain of events in her own life that began small, then grew so big that she couldn't have stopped them from expanding even if she'd tried.

But she never really tried.

She sets her wineglass down with a *clink* on the ceramic ledge, places her phone on the floor beside it, then lets her clothes fall to the tile floor of the bathroom and slides into the tub, relaxing into the heat with puffy eyes.

The house is silent again, and her thoughts are loud in her mind.

Half an hour later, the water has cooled and Nancy's eyes have dried. She reaches over the tub ledge, dripping water all over the tiles, and picks up her phone. She sends a message to Angela Creighton.

I'm sorry I was short with you before. It was a lot to take in. I've changed my mind about speaking with Margaret's friend—could you please set up the meeting?

· · · · · · · · · · ·

When Nancy calls Michael to see if he would be willing to speak with her, she fully expects him to say no. She didn't want to hope that what Katherine said was true; that he *had* been lonely and unhappy since they divorced. It's only once she actually dials Michael's number that it occurs to her this may be some misplaced *Parent Trap* effort on Katherine's part, but much to Nancy's surprise, it isn't. Michael agrees to meet with her for coffee, and they arrange a date and time and hang up the phone.

After that, Nancy wears her carpet bare pacing back and forth, wondering what she will say. She isn't entirely sure what she's hoping for, but she knows this is a step she must take. If Michael is still as miserable as she is after all these years of separation, it's at least worth a shot to try to make amends, explain to him her theory of why she thinks their marriage failed. Because despite his affair, she takes responsibility. She married him without ever telling him the secret of her birth, of her clandestine operations as part of the Jane Network, or even that she'd had an abortion before they met. She kept under wraps most of the things that defined her. It hadn't been fair of her to expect Michael to understand her or trust her.

Nancy arrives at the café in advance, hoping that sitting down with a cup of herbal tea for a while might calm her nerves somewhat. When she sees Michael approaching the door through the front window of the café, her stomach leaps and she notices how gray his temples and beard are now. But the thing that catches her breath is the thought of how crushed she'll feel if he isn't willing to give their marriage another chance. It catches her off guard, and she's therefore unprepared when Michael, after a moment of hesitation, moves in for a hug.

"Good to see you, Nancy," he says in a rather formal way, as though they're old work colleagues and nothing more. In a way, they are. Between monitoring finances, scheduling extracurricular activities, and the never-ending stream of logistical planning required for both the present and future, a good percentage of marriage is just business management.

"You, too, Mike." Nancy sits back down and clears her throat. "I ordered you a coffee. It should be here in a sec. You still take it two creams, right?"

Michael smiles without showing his teeth. "Yup. Thanks."

The coffee arrives a moment later and the barista shuffles off.

Nancy forces herself to make eye contact with her ex-husband. They haven't been alone together in a long time.

"So, thanks for coming to meet me," she begins. "Katherine told me that I should maybe contact you. That you had said some things to her that made her think we should . . . talk."

Michael shifts in his seat and his eyes dart toward the door of the café. She hopes he isn't thinking of leaving.

"Yeah. I probably shouldn't have said anything. It was over Christmas, and you know, *Christmas*. It's packed full of nostalgia. My mom had just died, and on her way out she got me thinking about the past. Reviewing things, you know."

Nancy nods, thinking of her own grandmama.

The Past, my dear.

He runs his hand over the table, flicks a crumb off the surface, and Nancy resists the urge to reach out for his hand. "Having Katherine there with me, but without you, it just, it felt like something was missing. Katherine asked if I was okay. She's pretty intuitive."

Nancy smiles. "Yes, she is."

"And I guess I told her—" He fidgets with the mug handle, then looks at Nancy. "I told her I had been thinking about you, and, I don't know, maybe wishing things could be more like they were before."

Nancy takes a sip of her tea, considering. "Hmm. She's not very good at keeping secrets, is she? Good girl," she adds in an undertone.

Michael exhales a small chuckle. "No."

"Not like her mother," Nancy says. She didn't intend to blurt it out like that. But then, she supposes that's why she asked Michael to meet with her, so maybe it's best to just spit it out. "The thing is, Mike, I don't think you ever really knew me at all," Nancy says through a thick throat. "And that's my fault. I own that."

Michael sighs heavily, eyes falling to his hands clasped around the glass mug. The memories of other sighs, of love and pleasure and mutual adoration of their child, echo back at her across the table.

"Mike—"

"I've really missed you, Nance."

They hold their breath and absorb what he's just admitted. What it might mean for them both. The spring wind whispers through the leaves of the trees in the park next to the café. The trees that, in a few short months, will turn red and gold in one last spectacular curtain call before the bitter winter strips them bare.

All of this is fleeting, it says. *There's no more time to waste . . .*

Nancy's having a reckless week, agreeing to meet with her birth mother's friend and maybe get some closure there, and now stumbling through a desperate reconciliation with her ex-husband. She might as well tell him how she's truly feeing. Nancy licks her lips and glances up at Michael, then sees Katherine in the clear blue of his eyes. The child that binds them together, no matter what.

"Oh, Mike. I miss you, too. So much."

She reaches across the table and squeezes the tops of his hands with her own. She remembers holding his hands like this all those years ago when they slid golden rings onto each other's fingers and vowed to always be honest and true.

Nancy wasn't.

She holds his gaze and forces herself to not let go.

"I need to tell you about Jane."

CHAPTER 28

Angela

. . . .

SPRING 2017

"Brownies, from Harbord's!"

Angela presents the neat white box to Evelyn as soon as the older woman opens the door. Evelyn cradles it in her hands. "Oh, you wonderful woman! Walnuts?"

"Of course not. I'm insulted you would even suggest such sacrilege. What self-respecting brownie allows its fudgy splendor to be ruined by nuts?" Angela cocks one sarcastic eyebrow.

"I knew I liked you." Evelyn beckons Angela across the threshold and shoulders the stiff door shut on the street.

The smell of the bakery nearly made Angela vomit, but she persevered, determined to make up for what in retrospect she feels was a somewhat disastrous first meeting a few weeks ago.

They climb the creaky stairs to the second-floor apartment and Evelyn closes the door behind them. "I'll put the kettle on for coffee." She smiles at Angela. "Have a seat."

Angela settles herself down on the squishy cream-colored couch near the window. Evelyn has the curtains open today to tempt in the fresh spring air. The scent from a clutch of deep purple lilacs in a vase on the windowsill wafts into the room, as though to underline the fact that winter is finally passed and the blooms will have their time in the spotlight now.

"How did you get the lilacs?" Angela asks. "I didn't see any trees around here. Thank you!" she adds, as Evelyn hands her a plate. She'll get through what she can of the brownie, though sweets make her stomach churn these days.

Evelyn sits down beside Angela on the couch, delicately crossing one ankle over the other, like a lady. "I stole them."

"Ha! What?"

"Technically, I guess. The campus is full of flowering trees. Yesterday I clipped some. They were only out on a few branches, but I couldn't resist."

"Do you keep gardening shears in your purse?"

Evelyn raises a forkful of brownie with a look of reverence and pops it in her mouth. "Mmm. These are perfect, Angela." She swallows. "I have a Swiss Army knife my brother gave me one Christmas. Do you have one? They come in handy from time to time. Especially the corkscrew."

Angela chuckles, nearly choking on a bite of brownie. The kettle screams its impatience at them, and Evelyn jumps up, displaying the reflexes of a much younger woman. She returns with the coffee a moment later.

"So! What's this update you have for me?" Darwin eyes the coffee in her hands and mewls with impatience, wanting a brownie.

Angela sets her coffee down on the table to cool. "Well, I definitely found Margaret's daughter."

"My goodness . . ."

"I was looking for the wrong name at first. She's divorced now, but still using her married name. Ironically, I think it's to make it easier for people to find her on social media, since she was known by that name for so long. I just told her who I was and that I had a letter that was supposed to be delivered to her old apartment but somehow ended up in a drawer in our shop."

Angela looks up from her brownie to glance at Evelyn, whose face is so pale it's blending into the cream fabric of the couch behind her.

"Oh my God, Evelyn, are you okay?" Angela reaches out for Evelyn's hand, which is as cold as ice. Angela can feel it trembling. "Evelyn?"

Evelyn squeezes her hand, which reassures Angela slightly. All of a sudden she's acutely aware of Evelyn's age and the fact that she herself has no first aid training.

"What's wrong? Should I call someone?"

Evelyn's face flushes, red blotches patchy among the white. And then she starts to cry. Confused and frightened, Angela wraps her arms around Evelyn, unsure what else to do. She's thin and feels frail under Angela's hands, as though any more pressure might shatter her entirely. *What the hell is going on?* Angela's mind races but she can't catch up. After a minute or two, Evelyn's breathing slows, and her sobs fade to hiccups. She sits up straighter as Darwin slinks his way underneath their elbows, settling himself down in his mistress's lap, trying his best to keep her grounded with his warm, soft weight.

It works. Evelyn leans back to rest her head on the couch cushion as her hand strokes Darwin's back. Angela spots a box of tissues on the side table. She snatches three out of the floral cardboard box and taps Evelyn's shoulder. "Here you go."

"Thank you, dear," Evelyn mutters, her voice hardly above a whisper. She mops her face and blows her nose hard. "I was at St. Agnes's, too, Angela."

Angela nods. "I know."

Evelyn turns to face her. The tears pour fast down her heart-shaped face. It's only now that Angela really notices the wrinkles around Evelyn's eyes and mouth, the leathery texture of her aging skin, the eyes that are no longer bright and clear. They're tired and sore and the light is starting to fade from them.

"I gave birth to a baby girl there. She was stolen from me after just a few days in my arms."

Something cold licks at Angela's insides before Evelyn speaks again. She watches Evelyn run her hands along each opposite arm now, as though cradling the baby she once held. Her right hand moves from her left forearm down to the wrist. She traces her middle finger across a long, faded scar.

"My name was Maggie then. And my baby's name was Jane."

CHAPTER 29

Maggie

. . . .

MAY 1961

M aggie wakes to the sound of breaking glass.

Or at least, she thinks she does. As she starts to come to, the room sliding into focus in the dim bluish light of dawn, she isn't sure anymore. Maybe it was just a dream after all. She's had such strange dreams since coming to the home, and now that she's in the postpartum wing of the building, she's woken up twice in a hazy confusion, as if someone had carried her out of her normal bed in the middle of the night and set her down somewhere odd and unusual.

Maggie rubs her eyes and rolls over onto her side. As she does so, she hears and feels a crinkle beneath her arm.

She sits up, blinks at the two white envelopes resting on her pillow. Glancing over, she sees that Evelyn's bed is empty, and stripped bare of its sheets. She picks up the envelopes as a strange tingling sensation creeps downward from the top of her head.

Maggie, the first envelope says. The second is labeled *Mother & Father*.

Maggie's heart is racing as she tears open the envelope with her name on it. There are two letters inside. One for her, and one addressed to the

Toronto Police Department. The letter for Maggie is on top. She begins to read, heart hammering in her throat.

> *Dear Maggie,*
>
> *It pains me to write these words because it will somehow confirm their truth. But I found out yesterday from Agatha that my baby has died. I went to Agatha to ask for help, thinking she might be willing to find a name or an address. Something. Anything to help me find her. And this is the news she brings me. My baby was sold, and then she died.*
>
> *It is dreadful enough that I was separated from her, but now I cannot even find comfort in the knowledge that she would be the deeply loved child of some barren woman. She is dead, and this is the end for me, too.*
>
> *To be honest with you, it feels empowering. We are all here because we were never given any choices. We were never in control. And this is something I can do to be in control. I can choose how and when I die. I have no fear for the fate of my soul. I only know that it will be free and at peace, reunited with my poor Leo and our beautiful baby girl.*
>
> *If the only way I can be with them is in death, then so be it.*
>
> *Now, I must ask a favor of you before I go.*
>
> *I have left two other letters with you—one pre-addressed for my parents, and one for the police, enclosed with yours. Keep them hidden and safe beneath your mattress or anywhere else you can hide them, and take them with you when you leave. Please post them as soon as you can. I have said my final goodbye to my parents and brother, and in my account to the police I have explained in detail the atrocities of this place, of the Watchdog's assaults and the sale of the children. I hope it may be enough to ruin the home, at the very least. It would be too much to ask that the Watchdog get her comeuppance, but perhaps I will be able to haunt her. Because who knows, my dear, what awaits us on the other side?*
>
> *This may sound incredibly odd, but for the first time in a long while, I have hope.*

And I love you, Maggie. You have been like a sister to me since we arrived at this horrible place, and your presence has been a balm for my heart. I am so terribly sorry to leave you, but I know you will leave here yourself, very soon, and go on to do great things. I implore you to live your life fully, for the both of us. And never, never stop looking for Jane. I know you will find her.

With love, I will remain,

Evelyn Taylor

Maggie's hands are shaking.

Thud.

She jumps at the sound from downstairs, disoriented and afraid. She throws her legs over the side of the bed, clutches the letters in her hand, and pads quietly toward the bedroom door. She glances down the length of the hall, but no one else is stirring. The blue glow of dawn tints the walls and wooden floorboards. The house is silent.

She turns and heads toward the stairs and the sound that has her insides locked in an iron grip, pinching off the air in her lungs.

Creeping down the stairs, Maggie is careful to avoid the creaky step at the midpoint, and lands at the bottom of the staircase. She turns to face the parlor and nearly collapses at the sight.

Evelyn is hanging from the beam above the doorway, her head in a makeshift noose of bedsheets tied end-to-end. Her legs hang limply below the hem of her gray nightgown. Her eyes are mercifully closed, but her lips stand out in a face the color of cement. Her blond hair falls loosely over her shoulders. Beneath her dangling feet, a dining chair is resting on its side.

Maggie doesn't notice her body sink to the floor, but she finds herself there a moment later. She clutches the letters in her hand and tries to catch a staggering breath. She wants to look anywhere else but can't. She can't ever un-see this. She'll see it every time she closes her eyes.

After a minute that might be an hour, Maggie manages to stand up with help from the banister. She hauls herself to her feet and stumbles over to Evelyn, her lip trembling beneath beads of cold sweat and tears, then feels a sharp pain in her foot.

She gasps and winces at the shard of glass poking out of the skin. Looking down, she sees the floor is dusted with a shimmering coat of the stained glass that once graced the transom above the doorway. Evelyn must have broken it to throw the sheets over the beam. Maggie plucks the shard from her foot, then hops over to the front door and pulls on a pair of the communal Wellington boots. The glass crunches like gravel under her as she steps back over to the body.

"Oh, *Evelyn*," she whispers, reaching out for her friend's hand. She grasps it briefly, and finds it isn't even cold yet. Evelyn's soul has only just flitted away. She's only minutes too late. The thought cuts into her like barbed wire. She runs her hand gently along Evelyn's arm. But it's not Evelyn, she tells herself. Evelyn is gone.

She lets go.

Maggie stares up at her friend for several long moments, thinking over the contents of the letter that's still clutched in her hand, remembering Evelyn's smile close to her face while they whispered late at night and kept each other warm in the early mornings. Maggie commits this scene to memory, absorbing every detail of Evelyn's broken body, how it came to be at St. Agnes's in the first place, and all the reasons why it ended up hanging from the parlor transom in the cold light of dawn on this May morning.

Because the anger has started now. No, not the anger. The *rage*. A white-hot, savage rage is coursing through Maggie's veins like poison.

Evelyn is dead. Maggie's own baby, Jane, is long gone. She thinks about her father's friend Joe. She thinks about the Watchdog, about the parents and priests of the girls who've been sent away, urging them to "do the right thing." Maggie has a far different sense of what's right and wrong than she did before she came to St. Agnes's. And she needs to make this right.

As the first red-breasted robins start to twitter their sweetness to each other in the hedge outside the parlor window, Maggie comes to a decision.

"Goodbye, sweet friend," she whispers, gliding her fingers along the sleeve of Evelyn's nightgown one last time.

It's time to go.

She folds the letters in half and slides them down into her boot. With confident steps, she strides down the hall toward the kitchen. A mouse scurries along the countertop and out of sight, fleeing the disturbance. Maggie heads straight to the knife drawer. She slides it open and selects her favorite, a paring knife she always prefers. Medium length, with excellent control and a broad handle.

She stomps back across the foyer and with one last glance at Evelyn's body, she creeps back up the staircase, almost stepping on the squeaky stair halfway up. But she won't need to keep quiet much longer. She turns right at the top. She knows the locations of all the creaks in the floor; she sees them like a map in her mind as she picks her way down the hallway, carefully avoiding the floorboards that could betray her.

Gripping the knife so tightly her knuckles stand out white against the black handle, Maggie reaches for the doorknob of the Watchdog's bedroom. An excited flare sparks in her gut at the thought of the justice she's about to deliver. She knows her Bible. It's been drilled into her brain since birth and aggressively reinforced over the course of her time at St. Agnes's.

Assuredly, the evil man will not go unpunished.

She redoubles her grip on the knife and closes her eyes for a moment, preparing. She can feel the crinkle of paper in her boot and the hard steel of the knife handle as she sees Evelyn's handwriting dance across her mind's eye.

We were never in control. And this is something I can do to be in control.

She can still smell her own attacker's breath on the back of her neck late at night. She can feel the strength of Joe's hands holding her down.

She lets the rage flow freely again, lets it fill up her heart and mind and permeate every cell in her body as she pushes the door open into the dark silence of the Watchdog's room. The heavy curtains are drawn over the large window and it takes Maggie's eyes a moment to adjust to the dim light. She blinks several times, then sees the outline of the ornate chest of drawers, the bedposts, the lumpy blankets. She moves into the room. The Watchdog is lying on her back, fast asleep, arms curled up over her head like a serene child.

Maggie wonders, briefly, what she's dreaming of. Then the corners of her own mouth curl up at the knowledge that she's about to interrupt whatever sweetness the Watchdog is experiencing right now. That she's in complete control, about to change this woman's life forever, just like she's changed theirs.

Tonight, the Watchdog is everyone Maggie needs her to be.

The mantel clock above the small fireplace ticks away the seconds, counting down for Maggie as she hesitates to act. The Watchdog moves, twitching one arm, then her head. Slowly she wakes, her eyes heavy with sleep. They focus on Maggie, whose heart skips a beat in her throat. It's now or never.

She tightens her hold on the knife at her side and lunges forward, plunging the blade into the Watchdog with every ounce of her remaining strength.

The blood blooms onto the white linen sheets as the nun's agonized scream fills the room. Maggie raises the knife and lowers it again as the nun's arm whips out at her in panic and fury.

The Watchdog lets out another piercing scream, scrambling to press the sheet against the wounds in her leg and hip. She slides off the bed with a gasp, landing roughly on her knees.

Maggie flies from the room, leaving the Watchdog kneeling in a pool of blood, and nearly collides with Sister Agatha at the top of the stairs. She's still in her dressing gown and cap, wide-eyed and fearful. Doors are opening all along the hallway. Maggie vaguely registers the sounds of other girls' voices, calling questions to one another.

"What's happening?"

"Good Lord, Maggie," Sister Agatha gasps, taking in the blood smears on Maggie's hands. She looks over Maggie's shoulder toward the Watchdog's door as the warden lets out an anguished cry for help.

"Come with me," she mutters. "Quickly."

She runs back down the hallway faster than Maggie has ever seen her move. Maggie is hard on Agatha's heels as the young nun clambers down the old servants' stairs at the back of the house and out into the kitchen. She lunges for the garden door, which is always dead-bolted and requires a key.

Agatha snatches the key ring from her pocket and fumbles with the lock, her hands shaking. Maggie can hear girls' screams from upstairs now. Then Maggie's blood runs cold at the voice of Father Leclerc, who has finally emerged from his room, shouting at the girls to be quiet, demanding answers.

"Your hands!" Agatha gasps.

Maggie dashes to the sink and turns the tap, runs her hands under the water, watching the blood disappear as her heart pounds in her throat.

The screaming from upstairs grows louder. Sister Agatha turns the door handle and opens it onto the back garden.

"Go, Maggie, go!" she says, breathless. "Just run and keep running. Go!"

They meet eyes for only a second, but Maggie sees everything that's transpired over the past few months reflected in Agatha's wide eyes.

The snap of the Watchdog's whip.

Christmas candles and the smell of Pine-Sol.

Agatha with baby Jane in her arms, walking out the door of the Goodbye Room.

Evelyn's body hanging from the doorway. The glittering glass beneath it.

Blood on her hands, a knife, and cold water.

"Thank you, Agatha," she whispers.

"Go!" the young nun urges, shoving her in the back, and Maggie bursts out of the garden gate just as a girl's scream from the front hall pierces the quiet dawn.

. . . .

Maggie pushes open the iron gate to her brother Jack's house, vaguely registering the familiar creak of the hinges, then stumbles her way up the gravel path. He never responded to any of her letters and eventually she gave up sending them, but Jack is her only option. If he won't take her in, she doesn't know what she'll do.

She knocks on the front door, then reaches a weak arm out to steady herself against the brown brick. She can already feel her body sinking into itself. For a moment she worries that her brother and his wife aren't home, and wonders if she'll have to huddle against the porch railing and wait for them to return. But then Maggie hears her sister-in-law's high-pitched voice call from inside the house. There's movement rippling in the glass before a lock slides back and the door opens.

"Maggie! Good Lord!"

"I need a bath," Maggie says stupidly, leaning more of her weight onto her wobbling arm, her thin skin pressing into the rough surface of the brick.

"Jack! Come quickly!" Lorna screams over her shoulder as Maggie collapses to the ground.

. . . .

Maggie closes the bathroom door behind her. Her sister-in-law has draped an assortment of fussy lace doilies over the back of the toilet tank. Several pots of face and hand creams are clustered together on the counter beside the sink. Rolls of fluffy pink hand towels are folded with unnatural neatness on a shelf above the toilet.

Maggie turns the brass key in the lock and hears it slide into place with a satisfying click. She doesn't want to be disturbed. For months now, she has not had a moment alone. She craves peace and quiet and solitude and an end to the chaos. Her brother told her to go take a bath, then have a nap, and that they would talk once she had rested awhile.

She grips her hands on the edge of the counter now, bracing her weak body as she observes herself in the mirror. The girls were not allowed a mirror at the home, but it's only now that Maggie truly wonders why they were denied one; she can barely stand to look at her reflection, meet her own eyes, heavy with an indescribable exhaustion she fears she won't ever recover from. Her complexion is pallid, her features sunken and waxy. Her cheekbones are sharper than she's ever seen them.

Maggie glances down at the stack of *Chatelaine* magazines in the rack beside the toilet. A fresh young brunette graces the cover with penciled brows, red lips, and full, rouged cheeks. Pretty and clean and new. She'll teach you how to make the perfect Bundt cake for Sunday tea and settle a fussy child. How to clean your husband's shirts to pure white perfection, starched and ironed and ready for him each morning. Maggie wonders if the smiling cover girl can also offer lessons on how to scrub away the sweat and blood of the past, the incriminating stains of transgressions and bad fortune. Lipstick from your husband's collar in a shade you don't own.

Maggie leans over the bathtub and turns on the hot water at full blast, barely tempering it with cold. She spent months feeling cold both inside and out, and now she wants her skin to burn. When the tub is full, she begins to take off her clothes, muscles aching as she unties her nightgown and pulls off her underwear. She steps into the water, wincing. The spot where she pulled the glass out of her foot stings in the heat. She settles herself down and lets her body float, her mind drifting along in its wake.

The house is silent, and situated on a quiet side street, but she can hear a muffled hum of traffic down on the main road a block away. A bar of her sister-in-law's pink flowery soap rests in a seashell-shaped dish on the tub ledge. Maggie brings it to her nose and inhales deeply; the lemony rose perfume reminds her of her mother's rosebushes, her pride and joy. Every summer her mother would pick fresh pink and white blooms from her garden and prop them in ceramic vases in every room of the house. She closes her eyes and imagines the windows open to welcome in the breeze, and the scratchiness of her Sunday church dress in the heat. Her mother in white gloves and a sun hat. Fresh lemonade and the smell of cut grass.

Maggie senses the tear tracks running down to her jawbone. How had it all gone so wrong? One night, that's all it took. One event that separated her life into Before and After. One moment that will now define her life completely.

Her parents have disowned her. Her brother is allowing her to stay with him for the time being. But what happens when she wears out her welcome? How long can they keep her presence a secret from their parents? Will the police be coming after her?

Maggie blinks. Her eyes are so tired and scratchy they can hardly focus. She closes them again, but this time, all she can see is black. A black future with nothing in it, no landmark or point of reference to guide her. Just a never-ending expanse of darkness. She feels more exhausted than she has ever felt in her life. There is no way back. And no way forward.

Maggie runs the bar of soap up and down her arms, slowly. She has so little energy to spare. Her gaze slides into the middle distance and lands on the counter next to the sink. Her eyes focus now on the box of razor blades. Maggie stares at it for a while. Her mind is strangely blank. She isn't even sure what exactly she's considering. But she feels a pull toward the box.

They have already titled her a Fallen woman. How much farther can she fall? She can use one sin to erase all the others. And then she won't have to care anymore. Her heart won't feel like lead in her chest. Her skeletal body won't need to recover. Her mind can finally be blank. That's what she wants now. Darkness and silence.

Maggie raises herself out of the tub and shivers slightly in the cold air. She flips open the little box with a wet finger, leaving moist spots on the yellow cardboard. She picks out a razor, holding it gingerly in the pruned palm of her hand. There is a stillness in the air now, the heavy mist of the hot water has clouded the windowpane and condensed on the glass jars and bottles beside the sink. She hears a car horn from far away, but it is well beyond this dream.

Maggie swallows the lick of fear that has climbed up her throat and settles herself back down into the tub. She looks at her wrists. Her skin is soft from the bath, and she has no fat on her body anymore. That will make it easier.

It.

The thought hovers like a hummingbird in the air above Maggie's head as she runs her thumb over the flat edge of the blade. This might even be easy. Likely painless. And then it will be nothing. She needn't worry about anything beyond that. The thought settles itself down deep in Maggie's core, warm and reassuring.

She doesn't know what she's doing, but it seems intuitive. Maggie lets out one last breath, then runs the blade along her wrist, pressing down as hard as she can, grimacing against the welcome sting. She doesn't stop, even when her stomach feels as though it's flipping over. Even when the blood pours into the bathwater, unfurling like red smoke beneath the surface. Even when every instinct in her body is screaming at her to stop.

Stop! she hears.

Soon.

Maggie!

It's done now anyway.

Maggie lets the blade fall from her slippery fingers as the bathwater turns redder with each passing moment. She leans back against the hard ceramic.

Now she's floating. She's a child again, and all she can smell is roses. She can taste lemonade and hear the rustling of the maple trees. Her brother calling out her name across the garden. She plucks one of the roses. A thorn pricks her finger, and she sees a red pearl bloom on her skin. A woman's voice, probably her mother's, asking her what she's doing. Grabbing her by the hand, demanding an answer, as always.

Maggie, you promised.

I am dying, Mother. And you cannot stop me.

Maggie smiles and slips out of her grasp as she fades into the fog of the past.

The bathtub is filling with blood as the curls of dark crimson waft from her wrist. The razor blade drops and sinks down into the dark water. She closes her eyes and her head swivels to the side, knocking the soap dish off the edge of the tub. It falls to the tile floor and shatters.

"Maggie?" Jack's voice calls from downstairs.

Silence.

Moments later, a key jiggles in the lock. Jack is on the other side of the door, shouting to someone.

The door opens, and a gasp shoots through the misty air of the bathroom.

In a single lunge, Jack is at the edge of the bathtub.

"Lorna! Lorna, get my kit!" he screams over his shoulder.

Jack holds Maggie's wrist tightly in one hand, his thumb pressing the wound. He reaches down into the tub and there's an unmistakable *plunk* of the plug being pulled, the deep grumble and sucking sounds of the water swirling down into the drain.

"Maggie!" Jack gasps. "Maggie. Oh my God. Maggie, please don't . . ."

Lorna bursts into the room, a large black case in her arms. "I'm sorry, I couldn't find it right away! It wasn't in the closet and I had to look." She gasps. "Oh my God, Jack. Is she . . . ?"

"There's a pulse but it's weak. Quickly, Lorna. I need to transfuse her."

She rummages around in the bag and begins pulling out instruments: a long tube, needles, and other implements. "I'm going to call an ambulance."

"No!"

Lorna looks down at him, stunned. "Are you *serious*, Jack? She's dying! She might be dead!"

"She's *not* dead, Lorna, and I need you. Sanitize the needles with alcohol, then come here and suture her wrist. I can't do it with the needle in my arm and I need to transfuse her."

Lorna hesitates. "Will this work?"

Her husband sniffs and wipes his nose on the back of his hand. "I don't know. But we have to try."

. . . .

Maggie's eyes flutter open slowly, the sleep sticking her eyelids together. She rubs the inside corners with her knuckles, flicking away the crust. Her dry eyes itch as they strain to focus on the wall across from the bed. A painting of a pair of white kittens, cuddling on a puffy chair.

Where am I?

It takes her a moment. Her brother's voice is faint in the distance, echoing up the stairs from the floor below. The same voice that had sternly instructed her to hold his hand when they were children, crossing the street on their way to school. The voice that had helped her to say aloud the secret she was carrying in her heart and belly, encouraging her to tell their parents, who would of course understand. The voice that drifted in and out, said her name over and over, pleading with her—*Stay with me, Maggie, stay with me*—as he filled her veins with his own blood.

He says her name again, this time from outside the door. "Maggie?"

She buries her face in a pillow that smells like dust and lavender. She's in Jack and Lorna's guest room at the end of the upstairs hallway, decorated sparsely with an odd collection of outdated furniture, lamps, and art prints.

"Maggie? Are you awake?" A soft knock on the door.

"Yes," Maggie answers, and immediately regrets it.

The door handle turns with a small creak, and her brother's nose appears in the crack. "Are you decent?"

"Are you trying to be funny?"

Jack pushes the door open with the corner of the tray he's carrying, laden with a full English breakfast of eggs and sausage, toast with Lorna's own black-currant jam, fried tomatoes, and tea. Maggie pushes herself up into a sitting position, leans against the hard wooden headboard, and looks skeptically at the breakfast tray.

"You slept straight through two meals. You need to eat." Her brother lowers the tray onto Maggie's lap, then perches himself at the bottom corner of the bed. He's facing the door, as though planning a quick escape. Maggie's throat tightens when she sees the dark circles under his eyes, the slump of his shoulders.

"Jack—"

"Why, Maggie? Why would you do such a thing?"

Maggie's gaze falls from her brother's anguished face. She can hear birds outside the window, and it dawns on her how desperate she is for fresh air.

"Maggie." Jack presses for an answer. "Look at me."

She meets her brother's eyes under wet lashes.

"Why?" He waits, hands folded neatly in his lap.

Maggie picks up the tea, takes a slow sip. The clink of plates and glasses drifts into the room from downstairs in the kitchen where Lorna is doing the washing up. She knows she owes them the truth.

"You never got any of my letters?"

"No, we didn't. How many did you send?"

"Once a month, pretty much. More often at first. Ten or twelve?" As if it even matters at this point. "The Watchdog must have destroyed them. Our letters were all posted for us. Or at least we thought they were."

"Who is the Watchdog?" asks Jack.

"Basically the matron of the home. The head nun. She's . . ." Maggie trails off.

Jack clears his throat. "That's okay. It doesn't matter now." A long pause, then, quietly, "Where is the baby, Maggie?"

Maggie fights it briefly, but her eyes pinch shut, and she feels an unpleasant swoop cut through her gut.

"They took her away, Jack," Maggie manages, her voice sticking in her throat like clay. "She was adopted."

She picks up the cloth napkin from the breakfast tray and mops her face. She has never cried this much in front of anyone before. She's never cried this much, full stop. She hates feeling so weak.

Jack is silent for a moment. He nods to himself before speaking, as though confirming a thought. "But you were going to give it—*her*—up for adoption anyway, right? Wasn't that the plan, Meg?"

"Yes. It was, at first. But after I'd had her, held her, then I wasn't so sure. After I saw her face. She looked like you." She chokes on a sob.

Jack takes the tray from her lap, placing it on the dresser while Maggie composes herself, but brings her back the tea, which she sips gratefully.

"In one of the letters . . ." She pauses. "I asked you whether . . . whether you and Lorna might want to adopt her. Because, well . . ."

"Ah." Jack heaves a silent sigh. "I see. That might have made sense. I understand. Lorna brought it up one night, but I think she was afraid to really suggest it. I never told her what happened to you, Maggie, but frankly I thought, given how the baby came to be—I thought you'd want nothing to do with that child. I thought you were content enough with giving it up."

Jack was the first person she told. He sat with her and held her hand while she relayed the news to her parents. They believed her about the pregnancy, but refused to accept how it had happened.

"I thought I was, too," she says. "But things changed once I felt like she was mine. And if you and Lorna had taken her—she told me about her miscarriages last year—I just thought it might have been a decent solution that we all could have benefited from."

"But Maggie, I—"

"I know. I *know*, Jack."

She realizes he is truly the only person she has now in this world.

"What . . ." Jack begins, faltering. "What happened there? How did it all lead you to opening up your wrist in my bathtub, Maggie? I need to understand."

Maggie takes a deep breath in, then bravely replays the nightmare, recounting every detail to her brother: the workhouse labour, the conditions, Father Leclerc, the Watchdog, and Evelyn's death. Jack shifts in his seat, but she doesn't stop.

"And they sold the babies. *Sold them*, Jack."

Jack's brow is furrowed under the swoop of his sandy hairline. "But how did they give it away without your say-so?"

"They made me sign before they would give me the painkillers," she says.

Jack's mouth falls open. "But Maggie, they can't make you sign a contract under those conditions. It's not binding, it's invalid. We could fight this!"

A dense silence follows Jack's words. They meet eyes across the bed, brown mirroring brown. Deep in her chest, Maggie feels the unfamiliar sensation of hope struggling to its feet.

"But who's going to believe me, Jack? A lot of the girls that go through that place willingly give their babies up. They convince you to, coerce you into agreeing. They tell you your baby will have a better life with an adopted family, that you can't afford it, you'll end up shamed and prostituting on the street. They terrify those girls into signing off on the adoptions. It's the Church, Jack. Who's going to believe us? Even if they do believe me, they would probably still agree that the baby is better off with an adopted family. Forced or not. We wouldn't stand a chance."

Jack chews his lip the same way Maggie does. "I assume you didn't see the name on the adoption papers? Of the parents?"

Maggie shakes her head. "I hardly remember signing."

She knows her brother means well, but there's no point discussing the *what-ifs*. It's not possible now. There's nothing to be done. It's over. Jane is gone. "There is something else, though," she says.

Jack waits.

"I, um, I attacked Sister Teresa. The warden."

Jack springs off the bed. "What?"

"Jack, she had it coming, I promise you."

"What? What do you mean, 'had it coming'?"

Maggie can feel the burn of shame creeping up her neck. "She beat us. She *sold* our babies. She's evil, Jack."

Jack opens and closes his mouth, then throws himself back down on the bed. "What did you do?"

"I stabbed her."

"God, Maggie." Jack buries his head in his hands for a moment, then rakes them through his sleek hair. "But they'll be coming to find you. The police could be arriving here at any moment! Why didn't you say something when you first got here?"

Maggie tenses at his raised voice, curling her shoulders inward. Jack notices, immediately apologetic.

"I'm sorry, Maggie. Where did you stab her?" he asks, wincing. "Is there a chance she's dead?"

Maggie shakes her head. "Probably not."

"Probably not?"

"I can't say for sure. I don't know. It was right after I found my friend Evelyn dead. I'd just had enough. Something snapped. I had Joe's face in my mind. And I stabbed her and ran. Sister Agatha unlocked the door for me and told me to run. I didn't know where else to go, so I came here. I thought they would be after me right away, like you said." Maggie picks at her cuticles. "Your razors were right there. I thought I could just drift off, and . . . I woke up here this morning, and I'm alive because of you." She reaches out and strokes his arm, trying to avoid looking at the gauze wrapped around her wrist. "The police haven't shown up, so I'm sure the Watchdog isn't dead. Have you heard from Mother?"

Jack shakes his head.

"So, they're not coming for me, I'm sure of it," she says. "Listen, I have a letter from Evelyn, addressed to the police. She asked me to post it for her, as her final wish. I'm hoping, when they read it, they might actually come after the Watchdog. It shouldn't be me they want. And the home has to deal with the body of a—a dead girl, and a stabbed warden. The house will be in chaos right now. They won't come after me. And the letter is my insurance policy."

Jack collects his thoughts, then reaches out and pulls Maggie into a hug that crushes her starved frame. He lets out a breath into her shoulder.

He's warm and solid and smells like the cedar aftershave Maggie gave him for his birthday the previous year. She smiles through her tears.

"I'm so sorry, Maggie," he whispers into her ear. "I should have gotten you out of there. I'm so sorry."

"You didn't know, Jack."

"I love you, Maggie."

"I love you, too."

The room is silent. Maggie can hear the rhythmic ticking of the clock on the bedside table. Twenty-one ticks, she counts. She and her brother hold each other for twenty-one seconds until her breathing slows and matches his. Twenty-one seconds that heal the temporary divide and bind them together again. Twenty-one seconds until they break apart and Jack asks the impossible question:

"So. What happens now?"

CHAPTER 30

Evelyn

. . . .

SPRING 2017

Evelyn looks up from her own hand, which has been steadily stroking Darwin for the past hour as she told Angela her story. She has rarely in her life experienced such an enormous relief. She released some of the pain when she told Tom her secret, but this time with Angela feels different, as if she can see the way forward now. After decades of hoping, she might finally—almost—find Jane.

Tissues lay crumpled and scattered over the surface of the white coffee table. Angela stares at them through filmy eyes. Evelyn can tell she isn't quite sure what to say next. She's still reeling from Evelyn's revelation and the exposition of the maternity home's horrors, from start to finish, all the way up to the morning after Evelyn's escape and attempted suicide.

"So . . ." she begins. "So, what happened once you moved back to Toronto? Do you see Jack? Did you ever marry or have any other children? I'm sorry, I just have so many questions."

"Yes, I still see Jack. We're very close." A smile slowly creeps across Evelyn's face, as though unsure whether or not it's allowed to be there. "And I was married for a long time, actually. To a man."

Angela raises her eyebrows. "Do tell."

"Until a little over ten years ago. His name is Tom O'Reilly. He's my best friend. We divorced so he could marry his longtime lover, Reg. Once it was finally legal."

"Why did you marry a gay man?"

Evelyn shoots Angela a pitying look. "So that we could both hide, my dear."

Angela tips her head to the side, inviting Evelyn to continue.

"Tom was a doctor, too. We met while we were studying in Montreal and became fast friends. He needed an intelligent wife as an accessory for fancy surgeons' dinner parties, and him being a bachelor for too long would have raised eyebrows. As much as a female doctor was a relatively unusual thing anyway, being an *unmarried* female doctor wouldn't have been good for business, either. So, we married and continued to just live together as best friends. We wore wedding rings and trotted each other out in public when the occasion called for it, but other than that, we lived our own lives. I see Tom and Reg often. We spend holidays together still. And I've lived here ever since the divorce. I like being in the city, in the thick of it. When things get too quiet, my mind starts to wander. I think too much. About . . ."

She rests her forehead in the hand that isn't stroking Darwin, and Angela hands her another tissue.

"Good Lord. I hate being such a mess," Evelyn says, rolling her eyes. "I didn't get this far by blubbering away at every sad memory."

"I think given the circumstances you can cut yourself some slack."

Evelyn lets out a sound somewhere between and scoff and a chuckle. "You're right. Young people are often wiser than we old sods give you credit for."

Angela smiles grimly, then asks the question that's been niggling at her. "Did the Watchdog die?"

Evelyn shakes her head. "No. Well, eventually, but not at my hand. Jack and I scoured the newspaper after my escape, but we never saw a thing about the home until they announced the closure later that summer, after I sent the real Evelyn's letter to the police. But back in the late nineties, Jack told me he'd heard through someone at his church that she had passed. Thank God."

Angela sighs. "And do you mind if I ask? Did you ever make amends with your parents? Did they ever apologize for not stopping the abuse from your dad's friend, or . . . ?"

Evelyn stares into the empty mug in her hands. "They made it clear to Jack that they didn't want anything to do with me if I continued to insist that their friend had raped me. They refused to believe it. Or at least, they pretended to refuse to believe it. The power of denial can be incredibly strong. But I couldn't forgive them for any of it. They thought I was dead, and my brother and I maintained that deception until their deaths."

"Oh."

"Jack split the inheritance with me, though, when my mother died. She passed a few years after my father; I went to the funeral and sat in the back. I used the money to set up the Evelyn Taylor Medical Scholarship." She smiles. "It's a modest scholarship for single mothers attending medical school."

"When I was initially researching trying to find Margaret Roberts to see if she—*you*—were still alive, I found an obituary in some microfilms of the *Star* from the sixties," Angela says.

"My brother placed that obit as part of the ruse. I have a copy somewhere, too."

"But how do you just place an obituary without an actual death?"

"It was easy back then," Evelyn says with a shrug. "There weren't the detailed records and government red tape we have now. Especially for women. Evelyn and I were young; neither of us had even voted yet, we weren't enrolled in school anymore. We didn't have a driver's license or any other identification. Government health coverage didn't exist, so no health card, no credit cards. It used to be far easier to disappear or change your name. I told Jack we needed a plan for me to start over completely. We talked and talked, and finally we decided that he needed to report me missing. And then I suggested the obituary: paper-and-ink evidence that Margaret Roberts was dead. It was the cleanest solution."

Evelyn continues to stroke Darwin, who arcs his back into her palm. "So, Jack told my parents I had escaped the home, and a couple of weeks later I wrote a suicide letter to him in my own hand, saying I was in hiding somewhere in the city and was planning on killing myself, when really I was still tucked away in his guest room. He showed that to my parents, and he placed the obit. The shame that I had committed suicide meant there was no funeral. No one followed up. Why would they? I was a 'fallen' girl. Honestly, it was easy. For me, anyway," she adds, running her thumb slowly around the rim of her mug. "But Jack sacrificed a great deal to help me start over. He loved me so much. Loves me still."

She takes a deep breath. "Anyway, I had wanted to go to university, and after Evelyn's letter, well, I suggested medical school to Jack. Since he and Lorna didn't have any children—despite their best efforts, poor things—he had the money to loan me for tuition. I'd always had stellar marks in school. We applied to McGill under the name Evelyn Taylor, and I was accepted."

"Why did you pick Evelyn Taylor?"

She considers the question for a moment, remembers lying in bed with her friend on that cold winter morning, discussing Evelyn's hopes for her future, a future that would be snuffed out just months later. The words drift back to her, an echo across the surface of a deep lake.

"Dr. Evelyn Taylor just has a nice ring to it, don't you think?"

Angela shifts into a more comfortable position. "So, you just assumed the real Evelyn's identity once you started medical school in Montreal?"

Evelyn frowns. "I didn't assume her identity. We didn't look much alike. It's more like I assumed her dreams, her future. I embodied it for the both of us, since she couldn't fulfill it anymore. She asked me in her goodbye letter to go live for both of us, and I've spent every day since then trying to live up to her last wish." She pauses. "There wasn't much left to my own identity at that point anyway. I was just the remainder of some previous sum. It started with one lie, and I guess I just kept lying." Her eyes gloss over again. "The longer you keep a secret, Angela, the bigger it gets. The more power it has over you."

Each of the women is lost in her own thoughts. Angela comes back first.

"Seems a bit macabre for you to still have the obituary," she says.

"I have the real Evelyn's, too."

"Wow."

"I suppose a part of me was mourning the loss of Maggie Roberts, too. I had to become Evelyn Taylor so quickly, I never really had a chance to say goodbye to Maggie." Evelyn gives Angela a watery smile. "It's all a complicated soup of emotions."

"I can't even begin to imagine."

Evelyn reaches out and runs a thumb down the younger woman's cheek. "I'm so glad you don't have to, my dear."

Angela sighs. "We have more options now, that's for sure. Thank you for that."

"Ha! Well, you're welcome. We did it for our daughters, our grand-daughters, and their granddaughters. We did it for all of us. All of you."

The sun is glowing orange outside the window. It's late afternoon now.

Angela runs a finger around the rim of her coffee mug. "Did you ever look for Jane? Your note—I'm sorry, I read it. It feels like an invasion of your privacy now, but I had to. And it said you would never stop searching for her."

Evelyn nods. "Yes. I searched as best I could. It was difficult; they didn't have the networks back then like they do now. Or the internet. Some search agencies started to pop up in the eighties, but both the parent and child had to register for the matching system to work. I placed ads in the classifieds for years and years, but I couldn't use my real name, you see. And that's the only name Jane would have known, if she ever read my note, which, frankly, I assumed she hadn't. I figured the adoptive parents would have thrown it away. Tom says he got a call once from a young woman who hesitated on the phone, then said she had the wrong number and hung up. That was decades ago now. I tried to hope, but it was probably just the wrong number."

She closes her eyes, crosses her arms over her chest and leans into them. "I can still *feel* her. I didn't want her at first, because of how she came to be. But it was when I felt her move. Everything changed right from that moment. She became mine."

Angela swallows hard and strokes Evelyn's shoulder.

"What's her adopted name?" Evelyn asks Angela.

"Nancy Mitchell. But she goes by Birch online. That's why I—"

"Nancy *Mitchell?*"

"Yes, I've spoken with her, Evelyn." She sits forward in her seat, as though she's been itching to say this. "She's very eager for me to set up a meeting. Would you like to meet your daughter?"

Evelyn repeats the name. "Nancy Mitchell?"

Angela nods. "Yes."

The memories rush forward, tripping over one another in Evelyn's mind.

Nancy Mitchell, on her exam table.

Nancy Mitchell, holding the door for her on her way out of St. Agnes's after she said goodbye to Chester Braithwaite, hugging her on the street in the setting sun.

Nancy Mitchell, who joined the Janes and became part of the movement alongside Evelyn.

Nancy Mitchell, whose bravery sparked like lightning when a traitor pointed a gun at the back of her head.

Nancy.

Jane.

Her daughter.

"Would you like to meet her?" Angela asks again.

"Angela," Evelyn begins, overcome by the reality of what she's about to say. "I think I already have."

CHAPTER 31

Evelyn

. . . .

SPRING 2017

1 2:35 p.m.

It's nearly time.

Evelyn is in a state of high agitation, and she's been doing her best to keep herself busy this morning. She's washed and folded three loads of laundry since she woke up at four o'clock after an almost sleepless night. The third load was a set of towels she'd put through the laundry two days ago and didn't need washing again. She made herself one cup of strong coffee around five, and has since switched to decaf; she doesn't need addictive stimulants putting her any more on edge than she already is today.

Nancy is arriving at one o'clock. With Angela acting as her proxy, Evelyn invited Nancy to meet for tea at her apartment, and in the intervening two days since Nancy accepted her offer, Evelyn has thought a great deal about the ridiculousness of the invitation. One "meets for tea" with an old friend to catch up after a few months apart, discuss the politics of a wedding guest list, or plan a weekend getaway in the country. You don't "meet for tea" to reunite with your long-lost daughter.

But in a situation this absurd and remarkable, how else are you supposed to officially reunite? What are the expectations? There is no normal way to do this. No handbook. What could Evelyn have offered Nancy, except to meet for tea?

Angela spoke with Nancy and confirmed that she was indeed the Nancy Mitchell who worked with the Jane Network, then she explained who Evelyn really was. Angela says it took Nancy a while to absorb it, believe it. They talked for over an hour. But now she knows, and she still wants to meet with Evelyn.

After changing her outfit four times, Evelyn finally decided on a pair of neat jeans and a blouse in the same shade of yellow as the booties she knitted for Jane all those years ago. She wonders whether Nancy ever saw them. She makes a mental note to ask.

She's smoothed her gray hair and even put on a little bit of lipstick, which she rarely does. She scrubbed her entire house from top to bottom yesterday and refilled the vase on the windowsill with fresh lilacs. The smell fills the room now as she opens the window a crack to let in a whiff of the cool spring breeze. The smell of the city in springtime—mud and exhaust and flowering trees—fills her nostrils and the familiarity calms her nerves, if only a little.

Evelyn glances at the clock again.

12:40.

She breathes her nervousness out through pinched lips just like she does in her yoga classes, and heads for the door. The sound of the traffic and chatter rises as she steps out onto the sidewalk. The sunlight hits her, and she winces, but smiles. Springtime and the return of the sun is such a relief at the best of times, and today it cracks a grin into Evelyn's usually serious features.

She doesn't bother locking the door; she'll only be a minute fetching Angela from Thompson's. It's Saturday afternoon, so there's another person working in the shop today who's agreed to cover Angela's break while, at Evelyn's request, she acts as a buffer for the reunion. Angela offered to come directly to her apartment, but Evelyn told her she wants to see the mailboxes. She needs to see the mistake that cheated her out of so much time with Nancy.

Outside Thompson's, Evelyn stops in front of the two boxes screwed into the brick wall beside the door. The chatter of pedestrians on the sidewalk behind her, the car horns, and the screech of the streetcar all fade into the background. She pictures Nancy reaching her hand under the creaking, rusted metal flap to retrieve the unwanted junk mail and hydro bills, never knowing there was supposed to be another letter for her. It hurts Evelyn's heart just to look at it.

While Evelyn is in quite good health for her age, she's in the home stretch now, and there isn't enough time left to make mistakes. And, even more critically, to fix those mistakes.

When you're young, you get to look at time through the reduction end of the telescope. The wrong end, the generous end that makes everything appear so far away, that gives the impression that there are light-years of space between you and those magically distant objects. And then, without warning, time turns it around on you, and suddenly you're looking through the correct end, the end you were always supposed to be looking through, if you were paying attention. The end where everything is magnified and perilously close. The end that zooms in without mercy and forces you to see the detail you should have been focusing on all along.

While Evelyn and Nancy were so close to one another for years, they never knew each other's true identity. Evelyn has tried to think back on those memories and count them as time spent with her daughter, but it's not the same.

She returns her gaze to the mailboxes, considering the turn of events. Even if Frances Mitchell's letter had been delivered properly, it might have taken Nancy the same number of years to locate Evelyn, or she might never have been able to find her at all, given Evelyn's name change. In a way, perhaps Frances's letter being delivered to the wrong mailbox made sure that the two women were reunited. If not for Angela finding it and making the connection, maybe Evelyn wouldn't be meeting with Nancy today at all. Maybe she would have gone to her grave never knowing that Nancy Mitchell is her daughter Jane.

Evelyn hasn't believed in any kind of god for decades now, and she doesn't subscribe to the concept of fate. Life is simply too cruel for those things to exist. But, like many people, she does wonder every now and then about the strange and serendipitous ways in which things sometimes seem to just work themselves out.

The sound from the street roars back into focus as Evelyn turns the doorknob and enters the shop with a jingling of bells overhead. Angela is perched on a stool behind the antique cash desk. She's tapping a pen at breakneck speed and her eyes are bright underneath her dark bangs. She looks up at Evelyn, then at the clock on the wall. Evelyn's eyes follow.

12:48.

"It's time?"

"It's time," Evelyn replies.

Angela comes around the desk to Evelyn and pulls her into a hug. Evelyn is surprised at the affection she's developed for the young woman.

"How you doing, Eve?"

Evelyn's throat is stuck, but she nods and leads Angela back out the jingling door of the shop. They walk a few minutes in silence back to Evelyn's apartment. Once she's shut the inner door behind Angela, she lets her breath out.

"I'm really nervous, Angela. I don't know what to do with myself."

"That's completely understandable. Just remember that Nancy wants to see you. And you aren't meeting each other for the first time today, as weird and wonderful as that fact is. She knows you. Her adoptive mother *encouraged* her to find you. This is all going to be okay. It really,

really is. This is just one huge hurdle that you have to get over. Waiting for today was probably the worst part. Once she's here . . . I think it'll feel different."

Evelyn tries to take Angela's words to heart, but her mind is racing. "Before I knew Nancy was Jane, I dreamed about meeting her, what that would be like. But this is far worse than I imagined. It's so real now. I mean, what if she doesn't— When do I tell her about— What do we even talk about? I feel like I'm going to vomit. Or maybe have a heart attack." She's panicking now.

Angela takes a step toward her, eyes shining. "I'm adopted, Evelyn." Her words distract Evelyn just enough that she's able to listen.

"You are?"

"Yes. And when I met my birth mother, we were both nervous, too. I remember that anxiety so vividly. But I *needed* to meet her, and my mom was supportive of that." Face flushed, she rests one hand on her midsection, and Evelyn notices a curve that wasn't there a few weeks ago. Her own stomach gives a little jolt, remembering how that felt, a lifetime ago. "I know my situation isn't the same as Nancy's," Angela continues, "and my birth mother's wasn't the same as yours, but I can tell you I'm sure this is going to go a lot better than you're imagining. This is a good thing, I promise. Now let's sit down. I'll get you some water."

Angela disappears into the kitchen and comes back with a cold glass. They settle down together on Evelyn's puffy couch and Angela reaches out for Evelyn's hand. They intertwine their fingers on the seat between them.

"Thank you, Angela," she mutters, taking a sip. "For everything."

"You're welcome." Angela smiles, squeezes her fingers.

They sit there, side by side, for a few minutes, each staring out the window ahead of them as the clock on the wall ticks away the seconds until Nancy's arrival. It's a breathtaking wait.

And then the doorbell rings.

A little gasp escapes Evelyn's mouth.

"I'll get it," Angela says, releasing Evelyn's hand.

Evelyn knows she should answer the door herself, but she's rooted to the spot. "Thank you," she whispers.

Angela pulls herself up off the couch and walks toward the door. A moment later, Evelyn hears the street level door unlocking, sounds from the city floating in.

Her daughter's voice.

Jane's voice.

"Hi! You must be Angela!"

"Yeah! Hi, Nancy. It's nice to finally be able to put a face to your name. Come on in. Evelyn's just upstairs."

Nancy's voice echoes in the stairwell.

"Thank you so much for making the effort to find me, honestly," Nancy says. "This is the best shock I could possibly imagine. I know I was a bit speechless when you called."

They're right outside the door.

"You're welcome. I just, well . . . I *had* to."

Evelyn rises from her chair with difficulty. Her legs feel like they're made of glue. She stands still in the middle of the living room. Angela is turning the handle. She's back inside the apartment. Nancy follows closely behind her, and the room becomes cloudy and silent to Evelyn, as though she's about to faint. Now all she can see is Nancy's face. Her daughter's face.

Jane's face.

She's aged since Evelyn saw her last, on the cold January night when the Janes celebrated legalization together, raised a glass to the fact that their underground operation was no longer needed. Nancy's brown temples are graying, her face is a little more angled, with crow's-feet around her eyes and laugh lines in her cheeks. She's in her mid-fifties now. Evelyn notes how thrilled she is that her daughter spent her life smiling so much that she now has such generous wrinkles. They are the precious souvenirs of a life well lived.

Angela retreats and closes the apartment door quietly, leaving Evelyn and Nancy alone.

Nancy clears her throat, and sets her purse down. Her hands twitch at her sides as she steps forward toward Evelyn.

Toward Maggie.

Toward her mother.

"Nancy . . ." Maggie begins.

"I can't believe it's you," Nancy says, her voice breaking.

"I know." Maggie nods. "I know. I was worried you wouldn't."

Nancy shakes her head, and Maggie can see the tears welling in her daughter's eyes now. "I have so many questions," she says. "How did you— *How?*"

A knot the size of a golf ball is fighting its way up Maggie's throat. "Nancy, I—"

"You can . . . you can call me Jane, if you want."

The tears start to slip from the corners of her daughter's eyes now, but Maggie continues to fight her own, worried that once she starts, she won't be able to stop. She needs to control it.

And then, in an instant, she understands that there's no need for control anymore. This moment will only happen once, and it's perhaps the most important moment of her entire life. There are no do-overs on this. She can't stifle the tidal wave of feelings raging in her heart right now, and if she tries, she'll certainly regret it later. And there's been too much regret already.

So she lets the moment flow through her, lets the tears fall, and in a few hurried steps Jane is in Maggie's arms again, the arms that have been aching to hold her since the day Maggie handed her to Agatha and felt her heart tear into two pieces. Two pieces, she thought, that could never be put back together again.

But she was wrong.

"Jane," she whispers into her daughter's hair, rubbing her hand in soothing circles on Jane's back as they press their grief into one another, holding each other up against the gravity of all those years of lost time. Maggie remembers her daughter's tiny body, swaddled tightly in the crook of her arm in the Goodbye Room as she tucked the yellow booties and note deep into the folds of Jane's blanket. Holding her grown daughter in this moment, she can still feel her baby.

"Jane," she says again, and her daughter pulls her head back from her mother's shoulder, her face shining with tears and joy. Maggie looks deep into her daughter's eyes and finds herself there in the streaks of brown and gold.

"I've been looking for you."

Author's Note

. . . .

Dear Reader,

When people ask me, "So what's your book about?," my first inclination is always to say "Abortion." But it isn't. *Looking for Jane* is about motherhood. About wanting to be a mother and not wanting to be a mother, and all the gray areas in between. It's about the lengths to which women will go to end a pregnancy, and to become pregnant. And, as Nancy says, that razor-thin edge where many people find themselves hovering at some point in their lives, right between the terror of getting pregnant by accident and the terror of not getting pregnant when you want to. But most importantly, it's about women supporting one another through their individual choices and the outcomes of those choices.

I wrote the first draft of *Looking for Jane* before my husband and I had even begun trying to start our family. I was pregnant throughout the editing process, and was the mother of a young baby when the book was released in Canada and the U.K. I undertook a lot of research and conducted interviews about individual experiences with pregnancy and childbirth to ensure this story rings true, but the fact that I became pregnant during the editing process ended up being quite a gift, because it gave me a more nuanced perspective on abortion. I recall thinking, during the first trimester, that this was the time frame in which most abortions take place. I knew rationally that the being growing in my uterus was a cluster of cells, a fetus, but I called it my baby. My husband and I even gave it a nickname. Its organs were forming. It had fingers and toes and an upper lip. A heartbeat that I got to hear for the first time at six weeks' gestation. Now that I've experienced a pregnancy, I understand more than ever why abortion is a deeply emotional issue that causes severe, irreconcilable sociopolitical divisions. Why some will view the fetus as a life unto itself. But although my baby had a heartbeat and fingers and toes and an upper lip, it still resided inside my body.

My. Body.

Like many people, I had a really rough time with my pregnancy, and I expressed to loved ones on a number of occasions that sometimes I didn't feel like I was in control of my own body anymore. That was a bit unnerving, even though my pregnancy was a wonderful thing for my husband and me, and my baby was so very, very wanted. So I couldn't imagine being pregnant against my will; not having legal control over my own body with the right to end that pregnancy if I wanted to. The prospect was horrifying. And equally horrifying was the idea of being told—like the girls at the postwar maternity homes were—that I was not allowed to keep my child; that my parents, the state, and the Church were together going to make the decision for me that I must relinquish a baby that I want to keep, regardless of my own desires.

And that's why my pregnancy gave me a deeper understanding of the power and critical importance of bodily autonomy, and perhaps why I feel more strongly about reproductive choice and abortion access than ever. Because I can now put myself in the shoes of the pregnant person who doesn't want to be pregnant. I can imagine how terrifying that could feel for them. Now that I'm a mother, this book and its messages are more real to me than ever before.

So with that said, let me tell you a little bit about how *Looking for Jane* and its story came to be.

THE MATERNITY HOME SYSTEM

St. Agnes's Home for Unwed Mothers is itself a product of my imagination. (St. Agnes is the patron saint of virgins, girls, and chastity, so it seemed fitting in a tongue-in-cheek sort of way.) But it's intended to serve as a composite, representing the countless maternity homes that existed in various countries—including Canada and the United States—in the postwar years. In Canada, they were funded by the government and mainly run by churches and the Salvation Army. A handful were nondenominational. In the U.S., they were primarily operated by the Florence Crittenton Association of America, the Salvation Army, and Catholic charities. In the years after World War II, there was a strong societal push for the expansion of the nuclear family. For those who were unable to have biological families of their own, adoption was an attractive option, and spurred a robust demand for white babies during these years. Mothers of color were not often sent to these maternity homes, as babies of color were considered less desirable or even unadoptable.

During my research on these institutions in Canada and the United States, I discovered some truly shocking facts from firsthand accounts of those who attended them as teenagers or young women. Few women reported having had any kind of positive experience at the homes (perhaps aside from the occasional forbidden friendships they forged within), and most described their time at these institutions on a spectrum from moderately unpleasant to horrendously abusive, including systemic physical, psychological, emotional, and sexual abuse.

I regret to inform you that use of the term "inmates" by the administration, girls being coerced into signing adoption papers before they were allowed to hold their baby after birth (or before painkillers would be administered), and being told their babies had died were not exaggerations on my part. They are appalling truths drawn from real eyewitness accounts I uncovered during my research. Girls were also often kept in the dark about the facts of their pregnancy or what to expect during the labor and delivery process, and many were left alone in hospital or dormitory beds to labor, unsupported, for hours at a time. Women described having bags put over their heads so they wouldn't see the baby emerge, and nurses refusing to allow them to hold their babies at all before they were taken away. The system was humiliating, punitive, and violent. I assure you I made a very deliberate decision not to exaggerate or sugar-coat what girls might have thought, felt, and experienced at a place like St. Agnes's in the 1960s.

These women's descriptions of their feelings about the adoption, how it impacted their mental health at the time and for decades afterward—including crippling depression, post-traumatic stress disorder, inability to form meaningful relationships, fear of having more children or having those children taken away from them, and suicide attempts—and their desperation to locate their lost children in later years were some of the most powerful accounts I have ever read as a student of history. I tried to weave many of them into Maggie/Evelyn's thoughts and emotions about being forcibly separated from Jane/Nancy.

I extend sincere gratitude (along with my deepest condolences) to the women who have, over time, shared their heartbreaking experiences with interested researchers. I could not have brought this story to life without your bravery and willingness to relive your trauma.

But now, dear reader, I will ask you to hold my beer as I climb up onto my soap box. Because these women deserve more than my thanks.

They deserve justice.

According to Statistics Canada, between 1945 and 1971, almost 600,000 babies were born to unmarried mothers, their births recorded as "illegitimate." Researcher Valerie Andrews has estimated that over 300,000 mothers in Canada alone were forced or coerced into giving their babies up for adoption within the postwar era maternity home system (in the United States, that number is likely significantly higher). These programs were funded by the federal government.

In late 2017, Canada's Standing Senate Committee on Social Affairs, Science and Technology undertook a study of the postwar maternity home program. The committee heard from witnesses who gave testimony regarding the irreparable psychological and emotional damage they suffered as a result of this system. Of the several religious organizations (including Catholic, Anglican, United, and Presbyterian churches, and the Salvation Army) that delivered these programs on behalf of the government, only the United Church agreed to participate in the Senate's study and admit any responsibility whatsoever.

Based on the results of the study, in July 2018 the committee put forth a recommendation to the Government of Canada that it should publicly acknowledge that this practice took place, and issue a formal apology to the women and children who were deeply traumatized and whose lives were forever changed by the maternity home system. The Australian federal government extended an unconditional apology to survivors of its maternity homes in 2013, as did the government of Ireland in 2021.

As of the time of writing, no such apology or reparation proposal has been offered by the Government of Canada. This is a government that has (as it should) issued formal apologies to various groups that have suffered appalling treatment at the hands of—or by willful blindness of—the Canadian government throughout its severely blemished history. Yet it has inexplicably ignored the very straightforward recommendations from its own Senate committee to issue a similar apology to those impacted by the maternity home system. This is beyond shameful.

THE JANE NETWORK

Like St. Agnes's, the Jane Network in this novel is also a composite of the many underground abortion networks that existed in major cities around the world prior to the legalization or decriminalization of abortion in their respective jurisdictions. Without a doubt, many of these types of networks still exist today in jurisdictions where abortion remains illegal or inaccessible.

When I set out to undertake preliminary research for a novel about an underground abortion network and the history of reproductive rights access in my home country of Canada, I found some interesting things. Among them was a reference to an organization called the Abortion Counseling Service of Women's Liberation that had the unofficial nickname of "Jane." It operated in Chicago in the late 1960s and early 1970s, prior to *Roe v. Wade* (HBO released a documentary on the Janes in June 2022, and public awareness of their history has grown enormously in recent years). The Canadian abortion networks didn't have a particular name, records almost certainly weren't kept for security reasons, and thus the details were more difficult for me to research. But as I wrote the early draft of this novel, the name "Jane" became very much representative of the anonymous, everywoman nature of all these networks, and seemed the most fitting for a story that attempts to capture the breadth and depth of these remarkable, life-saving organizations. While I certainly paid deliberate homage to the "Chicago Janes" through the fictionalization of a real life event (their volunteers actually did eat patient records in the back of a paddy wagon to hide the women's identities from police—cue applause), the rest is borne of creative license based on facts I gathered about illegal and underground abortion initiatives through various research and interviews.

In the Canadian context, the legalization that came in 1988 with the groundbreaking *R. v. Morgentaler* Supreme Court decision arrived only after years of provincial court battles on Dr. Henry Morgentaler's part, and I believe legalization would not have occurred as quickly without his courageous determination and the efforts of those who worked closely with him. I will thank her again in my acknowledgments, but I must extend particular thanks to (in)famous feminist activist and fellow author Judy Rebick for taking the time to meet with me for an interview. Her recollections of Henry Morgentaler and her involvement in the Canadian abortion rights movement throughout the 1970s and 1980s helped mold my foundational ideas for the Janes' storyline. With that said, the scene where Evelyn interacts with Dr. Morgentaler in his Montreal office is entirely fictional.

However, the Abortion Caravan was indeed a real series of events that occurred in 1970. After a large protest on the lawn at Parliament Hill in Ottawa, these women delivered a symbolic coffin to Prime Minister Trudeau (senior)'s house, and chained themselves to the railings in the House of Commons to disrupt the proceedings and attract media attention to the issue of abortion access. The details of these events as depicted in the novel are my own creative products, though I drew inspiration for them from Judy Rebick's *Ten Thousand Roses: The Making of a Feminist Revolution.*

To all the "Janes," near and far, past and present, who made and continue to make incredible sacrifices, risking arrest and bodily harm to help people access safe abortions, I thank you from the bottom of my bleeding feminist heart. The illegality of these organizations has meant that the vast majority of the participants' true identities remain unknown, but I hope through this novel I have helped to give them a voice and honor them for their outstanding contribution to women's and human rights history.

THE FALL OF *ROE*

I write this section of the Author's Note from a place of cautious comfort, as a Canadian living in a country where—given the differences in our governmental and legal framework—access to abortion services covered by public health insurance would appear to be, for the time being, reasonably secure. With that said, inequitable access and government funding are still issues we contend with here, and I think Canadians should remain hyper-vigilant in the defense of abortion rights. But the threat we might feel tugging occasionally at our shirt collars is nothing compared to the literal war currently being waged in America against women and pregnant people.

When news of the leaked Supreme Court decision to overturn *Roe v. Wade* hit my social media feed late in the evening back in May 2022, my initial reaction was to burst into tears of despair. But that feeling quickly turned into a searing rage I've rarely experienced. It was toxic, and overwhelming. I didn't know where to put it. It took me a long time to get to sleep that night. Over the following days, I heard from countless readers in Canada who told me "I saw the news from the U.S., and I can't stop thinking about your book." Neither could I. *Looking for Jane* is, purportedly, historical fiction, at least for those of us in my home country of Canada. However, I know that for people in many countries around the world (including Brazil, where *Jane* has also been published), the fight for reproductive rights and the systematic stripping away of safe reproductive health care is a present reality.

Reproductive rights and abortion access have been the subjects of perpetual so-called "controversy" (I don't actually consider them controversial, because they are *essential*) for decades, and the politicization of pregnant bodies will seemingly never stop. But when I wrote the first draft of *Looking for Jane* in 2019, I could not have predicted it would be this horrifyingly relevant in 2023. And its increasing relevance continues to enrage me. I never dreamed that most of the U.S. would end up right back where women like Evelyn, Alice, and Nancy started decades ago, working underground (or sideways, or in the shadows), and fighting for the fundamental right to determine what happens to their own bodies.

I'm writing this on the hot and sunny afternoon of June 25, 2022, the day after women and pregnant people in America were reduced to something less than human. Despicably, you were also reduced to something less than assault rifles. There are few words adequate enough to describe the dehumanization that has occurred for at least half of the American population.

It is my belief that people inherently own the rights to their own bodies. Period. Full stop. I believe anyone should be able to access safe medical care to terminate a pregnancy at any time, for any reason at all. No conditions, no questions asked. Because when abortion access comes with conditions and is limited to specific—and often horrific—circumstances like rape or incest, it suggests that a woman does not inherently own the rights to her own body, as men do, but that something horrific must happen *to her* in order for her to gain access to those rights.

In the aftermath of *Roe* being overturned, I've thought a lot about the women who were so instrumental in the fight for reproductive justice in the years prior to 1973. In every country where underground abortion networks exist(ed), I can only imagine how it must feel to see your years of hard work and dedication, your passion, blood, sweat, and tears disappear in the blink of an eye because a select few in power hold radical religious beliefs that (*allegedly*) dictate forced birth at all costs.

My grief and rage run deeper than I can express, and my heart bleeds for you all. But I believe the only course of action going forward is to keep fighting like hell at the political level, and for women and pregnant people to support one another in every way possible. For those who can afford to, please donate generously to organizations that help patients access safe reproductive medical care, particularly so that those who are forced to travel far from home can afford to do so without debilitating financial strain. Keep spreading the word about resources and organizations offering safe and financially viable birth control and abortion options. And whatever you do, do not give up this fight. I know you won't, but I still need to say it.

People around the world stand with you in solidarity. I hope that between the time I write this note and the time the book is published, that things have already started to look brighter for America. Reason and humanity and compassion might eventually choke out the hate and extremism, but in the meantime: Stay optimistic, stay angry, and stay safe.

Acknowledgments

· · · · · · · · · · ·

This is probably the part of the publication process I was looking forward to the most, where I get to gush about all the wonderful human beings who helped bring *Jane* to life.

First, thank you to my phenomenally talented and dedicated powerhouse of an agent, Hayley Steed. You truly deserve your own page in my acknowledgments; I am so very lucky to have you. Thanks also to the entire team at the Madeleine Milburn Agency for believing in me right from the start and recognizing *Jane*'s potential. The team at the MM Agency has without a doubt changed my life forever and made my dream come true. I can never thank you all enough.

Thank you to my original editors Sarah St. Pierre (Simon & Schuster Canada) and Sara Nisha Adams (Hodder Studio UK) for helping me hone the manuscript into everything I wanted it to be, and to my editor Natalie Hallak at Atria Books for championing *Jane* for American readers. I'm so grateful for your instant and absolute support for this story and everything it represents. Thanks to everyone on Team Jane at Atria, including Lindsay Sagnette, Libby McGuire, Dana Trocker, Ariele Fredman, Lisa Sciambra, and Katelyn Phillips for all your hard work on this project. And thanks also to James Iacobelli for the phenomenal cover design, and for incorporating the rotary dial that I loved so much from the Canadian edition!

Thanks to my beloved first readers Denise, Kim, Marilyn, Angela, Laurie, Jenn, Mallory, Cara Beth, Sarah, Lauren D., Lauren F., Katie, Lindsay, Yoda, and Alli, who provided invaluable feedback on the first draft of this novel. You got to read *Jane* in her first iteration (of many!), and you hold a special place in my heart for doing so.

To my legal and medical "consultants" and badass friends Sarah Donohue and Dr. Cara Beth Lee, who graciously answered my questions about the ins and outs of 1970s criminal law and the abortion procedure, respectively. Thanks also to Jen and Andrea Dunn for sharing the details and realities of your IUI journey with me; you helped bring Angela and Tina's story to life. Please send big hugs to C and C, your two little heartbeats.

To the incomparable Judy Rebick, for your time, the beer, and your recollections on the Canadian abortion rights movement. You breathed life into all the women and allies who took astonishing risks and made incredible sacrifices to help secure reproductive rights for my and future generations of Canadians. We are forever in your debt.

Thank you to the women of all ages who courageously confronted their past trauma to speak to me about their individual experiences with abortion, as well as those who shared their thoughts on all the dark corners, sunny patches, and gray areas of childbirth and motherhood.

To my workshop colleagues and the faculty at the Humber School for Writers in Toronto, who saw a glimmer of something in the sample I sent in for their consideration long before the first draft was even complete. To Reed, Julia, and Stephanie, who always encouraged me to write and write and write some more and not shy away from wrestling down the Big Scary Topics. And thanks to Margaret, for telling me to not be afraid.

At my wedding, I couldn't thank my parents without Uncontrollable Ugly Crying, so fortunately I'm writing this where no one can see me sob. My parents raised me to be a feminist from birth, and they have been my biggest cheerleaders and champions throughout my life. Mum and Dad, you are truly the most reliable and supportive parents anyone could ask for (you're the best grandparents of all time), and I am grateful every single day that you're mine. Thanks also to my brother for the de-stressing giggly chats, and for being so excited for me when I set out on this crazy adventure. You had hands-down *the* best reaction when I called to tell you about my first book deal.

And last—but most certainly not least—thank you to my husband for your love, your faith in me, and your ongoing support for my writing. You've bribed me with chocolate to hit my daily word targets, delivered me cups upon cups of tea and coffee, acted as my sounding board for great (and not-so-great) ideas, and made sure I'm fed and watered when I'm on a roll and can't stop writing or the world might end. You've also given me the most beautiful baby boy I could have dreamed of. You are the greatest thing to ever happen to me. I would be lost without you.

LOOKING
FOR
JANE

HEATHER MARSHALL

This reading group guide for LOOKING FOR JANE *includes an introduction, discussion questions, ideas for enhancing your book club, and a Q&A with author Heather Marshall. The suggested questions are intended to help your reading group find new and interesting angles and topics for your discussion. We hope that these ideas will enrich your conversation and increase your enjoyment of the book.*

2017 When Angela Creighton discovers a mysterious letter containing a life-shattering confession, she is determined to find the intended recipient. Her search takes her back to the 1970s when a group of daring women operated an illegal underground abortion network in Toronto known only by its whispered code name: *Jane.*

1971 As a teenager, Dr. Evelyn Taylor was sent to a home for "fallen" women where she was forced to give up her baby for adoption—a trauma she has never recovered from. Despite harrowing police raids and the constant threat of arrest, she joins the Jane Network as an abortion provider, determined to give other women the choice she never had.

1980 After discovering a shocking secret about her family, twenty-year-old Nancy Mitchell begins to question everything she has ever known. When she unexpectedly becomes pregnant, she feels like she has no one to turn to for help. Grappling with her decision, she locates "Jane" and finds a place of her own alongside Dr. Taylor within the network's ranks, but she can never escape the lies that haunt her.

TOPICS & QUESTIONS FOR DISCUSSION

1 What do Angela's, Nancy's, and Evelyn's individual and shared experiences offer us in our understanding of the legalization of abortion in their given time periods? How does Marshall's narrative contribute to the larger conversation of abortion laws in the United States today?

2 Due to an unfortunate mistake, the letter addressed to Nancy doesn't arrive to her in 2010. How do you think her life might have been different if she received it then?

3 What are some of the societal expectations of women we see throughout the novel? How do those expectations differ in each time period, and how do the women in the novel fulfill or circumvent these expectations?

4 Evelyn's narrative offers two different experiences (i.e., hers and Maggie's) from their time at St. Agnes's Home for Unwed Mothers. How do Evelyn's and Maggie's experiences differ, and what do we glean from their accounts about the events that occurred during their time there?

5 What are the different factors that inspired Evelyn to become a doctor? What do you think she could offer to her patients that others couldn't?

6 Dr. Morgentaler warns Evelyn that the costs of illegally providing abortions are high. What risks do Evelyn—and others fighting for women's rights—face? What sacrifices do these women take in order to contribute to this cause?

7 Multiple groups of women contributed in some way to the advancement of women's rights throughout the narrative. Offer examples of these groups and what the results of their actions entailed? How does this speak to the history of women who contributed to this cause?

8 How does Angela's storyline illustrate the evolution of women's rights? In what way do they still need to advance?

9 Some scenes throughout the novel highlight instances of extreme joy or, conversely, extreme sorrow. Consider examples of these extreme emotions and how they might further our understanding of the different experiences women have during their pregnancy.

10 Contrast the experience Nancy has at Clara's abortion against her own. What do their accounts offer to our understanding of the freedom of choice and the importance of accessibility?

11 How did Angela, Evelyn, and Nancy each come to know about Jane? What were their individual contributions to the cause and how did they each help the women who came looking for her?

12 Consider the encounter between Brenda and Nancy on p. 285. What does this exchange tell us about the importance of the phrase, "the right to choose"?

13 The novel explores mother-daughter relationships, particularly through Nancy, but also Angela. How are these women shaped by their mothers' decisions, and how do those choices affect their own attitudes toward pregnancy and motherhood?

14 Consider the difference between Angela's pregnancy and that of the women who look for Jane. How do these experiences contrast throughout the novel and how does it contribute to our understanding of bodily autonomy?

15 What is the significance of the title *Looking for Jane*?

1 Research "the Jane Collective" and discuss their contributions to women's rights. Consider your research in comparison to their representation in the novel.

2 Discuss the *Roe v. Wade* court case and its impact on women's rights in 1973. Consider how abortion laws have evolved throughout history and what those laws entail today.

3 Watch *Call Jane* (2022). Consider the representation of the Jane Collective in the movie compared to the novel and your own research.

A CONVERSATION WITH HEATHER MARSHALL

Q: Every woman in your novel contributes in some way to the furtherment of women's rights. Besides the Jane Collective, can you share other women or groups of women that came up in your research who also made significant contributions to the women's rights movement?

A: In Canada, one of the biggest political pushes came in the form of the Abortion Caravan, which is depicted in the novel. This group of women and allies traveled across the country stirring up media coverage to shine a light on the issue of abortion rights and reproductive justice. The abortion law was only vaguely relaxed in 1969 to be allowed under very restricted circumstances, and that happened because the recorded death toll from "back-alley" abortions got so high that the government was forced to address it in some manner. But the women of the Abortion Caravan pushed the issue further for abortion on demand.

Q: Why was it important for you to include all three of Angela's, Evelyn's, and Nancy's narratives and their given time periods? What did you hope readers would take away from each of their accounts?

A: I didn't want to give just a snapshot of how reproductive rights affected women in a single era, like the 1960s or 1980s. I really wanted to showcase the evolution of reproductive rights in Canada over the course of several decades, from the 1960s when the birth control pill wasn't even widely available yet and social mores put enormous restrictions on women's bodily autonomy, options, and choices, all the way through to essentially the present day where abortion is legalized and people have access to procedures like IVF and IUI to aid in conception and pregnancy. I wanted to show how far we have come over the past several decades, but also how far we still have to go, in many ways. Reproductive injustices still exist in Canada and in other jurisdictions that have legalized abortion. Women of color, trans women, and women living in rural areas where maternal healthcare is more difficult to access are just a few examples of groups that face barriers to reproductive justice and equitable access. In terms of the characters themselves, I wanted to provide three narratives that were in many ways different from one another, but in many ways the same, in that all three of these women were seeking control over their own lives. And each of them was, in one way or another, looking for Jane.

Q: You mentioned in your author's note that you were pregnant while editing this novel. Can you speak to that experience and how being pregnant contributed to the narrative, and vice versa?

A: It's interesting, but I'm so glad I wrote this book before I became pregnant and had my first child, because I don't think I could have handled the research otherwise. It was some of the most distressing research I've ever done. I interviewed a lot of women about their personal experiences with pregnancy, childbirth, and motherhood to ensure accuracy (keeping in mind of course that no two peoples' experiences with these things are ever exactly the same), but because I was pregnant while editing it, it did give me a chance to include bits of my own experience, which gave me an even deeper connection to the story as the writer. It was difficult, though. I ended up editing the scene in the Goodbye Room when my own baby was only a few weeks old, and that hit me hard. The topics in the story became far more personally relatable to me once I had my own child.

Q: Your author's note speaks to the recent news of *Roe v. Wade* being overturned. How might your novel contribute to the larger conversation of abortion laws and what do you hope readers will learn from each of your characters' experiences?

A: Since *Looking for Jane* was released in Canada and other countries, I've heard from so many readers that the book has spurred conversations about so many of the issues covered in the book, particularly all the gray areas of abortion (people exploring different angles of it that they hadn't considered before, on both sides), and the dark aspects of motherhood that are often only whispered about and also carry a lot of stigma and shame, like infertility and miscarriage. I would certainly hope that the book helps galvanize readers into political action to ensure abortion rights are retained. But part of the reason I wrote the book, and also chose to have multiple points of view in different time periods, was to help put some faces on an issue that has become so politicized and disconnected from the real people who are impacted by laws surrounding reproductive justice. I wanted readers to connect with each of the characters to understand where they're coming from, to walk in their shoes, to understand why they would make the choices they did, and perhaps to have a bit more compassion for others' choices in the real world. Regardless of how you might feel about abortion, I hope we can come to a place that isn't quite so polarized and politicized; where even if you would choose differently than the person standing beside you, that you can simply respect their right to choose and leave it at that.

Q: Which point of view (i.e., Angela's, Evelyn's, and Nancy's) did you find the hardest to distill? Which was the easiest?

A: That's a great question. I think because Evelyn's experience was so deeply traumatic, and that it echoed and stayed with her across the decades, influencing and even dictating her life choices in the aftermath of the trauma, it may have been the hardest to distill. I also really wanted to be able to explore Angela's infertility struggle in more depth, but unfortunately I did have a word limit to stick to. There was just so much incredible, heartbreaking, and thought-provoking content in the research about the maternity homes and those women's experiences, the history of the fight for abortion access, and my interviewees' fertility struggles that a lot ended up hitting the cutting room floor. In some ways I only scratched the surface, but I hope we'll see more books that explore these issues in an open and candid way.

Q: Can you speak to Evelyn's narrative and your decision to include Maggie's experience via her perspective? Why did you decide to resolve their narrative in the way you did?

A: This was a creative decision with a couple of reasons behind it. First, the novel explores the concept of identity a lot, and their relationship with identity, particularly through both Evelyn/Maggie and Nancy's perspectives, but also with Angela as an adoptee who knew her birth mother. I knew from the outset that the "real" Evelyn's character was going to take her own life as a result of her trauma. As I played with the plot development, I thought it might be interesting and kind of powerful to have Maggie live for both of them into the future, and that her actions going forward after her time at the maternity home would be based in part on a need to deliver justice to Evelyn. Given the circumstances of how Maggie came to be pregnant, her parents' rejection of her, the loss of her child, and the assault on Sister Teresa, it seemed likely to me that Maggie would have been seriously struggling with her own identity, the idea of taking on someone else's might have seemed quite appealing, or even necessary. Also, as a writer it's just fun to write a big plot twist. In terms of the resolution, again, from the very first thoughts I had about this book, I knew I wanted Maggie and Jane to have a reunion, and that that would be the final scene in the book, with the final line of "I've been looking for you." That's how the title came to be too. I knew as soon as I started writing it that it would be called *Looking for Jane*, carrying a few different meanings.

Q: What inspired you to write a novel based on the Jane Collective?

A: The seeds for this novel were planted at two different times. Years ago when I was doing my history master's, I wrote a paper on Dr. Morgentaler's provincial court battles in Ontario and Quebec in the years leading up to the 1988 Supreme Court decision that legalized abortion in Canada, and at the time I thought "Wow, this would make a great novel." It was such a naturally compelling and dramatic story, and I knew that as a consumer of historical fiction, that was something I personally would love to read about, and I didn't think anyone had done it before. Years later, I stumbled across an article on the maternity home scandal and was shocked by what I was reading. I was a feminist history student and had never come across a reference to these homes or the 300,000+ girls and women who had their babies taken from them by force or coercion. So it made me wonder how few people knew that they existed and the trauma they inflicted on so many people. Three hundred thousand is a staggering number. At that point I was taking my writing a lot more seriously, and I was looking for a topic for a novel. I knew I wanted to tell the maternity home story. So I had these two different ideas for novels and couldn't really get them to work on their own, and then one day it finally clicked for me that they were two threads of the same story: of women's fight for control over their bodies and their lives. Once that clicked, the novel just poured out of me. During my research on underground abortion networks in various jurisdictions, I came across a reference to the Jane Collective in Chicago. Similar networks existed in Canada but didn't have a particular name, so I called them Jane, too, because they were all facing the same battle and fighting for the same rights. In that sense, "Jane" still exists all over the world.